"*Crossing the Line* has an engaging storyline with richly developed characters. The author communicates how that in the most important ways, foreign peoples and places are not so different from our own. In traveling with Roberto and Luis from Guatemala toward supposed prosperity, readers share their joys and pains, as plans change along with those who make them. You will see through new eyes how responses to adversity make or break individuals, as colorful characters uncover secrets, discover integrity's rewards, experience dishonesty's consequences, and count the cost of Christian discipleship."
—Cole Thomas Westwood, Ph.D.
Lead Pastor, Covenant Community Chu~

"The title *Crossing the Line* is well cho~ ~ many lines one crosses in life be they internatio~ ~s, legal lines, social respect lines, or ethical lines. The st~ ~sses the role of one's cultural background and how one can draw strength from it during challenging times. The story includes many accurate foodservice facts and even refers to the recent trend of 'farm to table.' It also contains details on the struggles parents have as their children grow and create their own lives and what a big impact one's early upbringing has years later. The strong role religion can play in daily lives is included, and how intercultural understanding is facilitated by strong religious beliefs."
—Dr. Polly Buchanan, Associate Professor Emeritus, Eastern Michigan University

"The story is absorbing, impelling the reader to go on with curiosity, sympathy, and eagerness to learn the travails of the migrants from Latino countries. The style is smooth with interesting cultural mix as the author—the observer—narrates the adventure of those of a different culture. The author has done well to depict the innocence of the young, the caution and sentimentality of the 'foreigners' still glancing at home left behind, yet looking forward at the prospect of a better life in the land of their dreams."
—Dr. John Reynolds

"This was a great book to read. I can't wait for the sequel. The ending was interesting and unexpected." —Alex Franco, student in Hospitality/Culinary Program, Down River Career and Technical Consortium, Michigan

"This story shows the struggles, ongoing push of stamina, and bits of fun found among both the management and diverse individuals in the restaurant business. The author offers the reader a view of what restaurants often deal with on a daily basis. So, read the book and walk onto the cook's line."
—Blake Harte, Chef Owner/Café West/Trenton, Mi

"Through Stolt's carefully crafted tale, I was privy to a world about which I knew little. At the same time, Roberto's journey felt familiar, as so many of the families in the US were immigrants at one time, including my own: crossing the ocean, crossing the line." —Maris Miller, Teacher, Riverview Community Schools, MI

"Much of America has been lately consumed with the culinary world, from chefs teaching recipes, kitchen competitions, and even restaurant makeovers televised. This author gives an interesting look into the nuts and bolts of the restaurant business that may provide insight for the novice to the commercial kitchen and a small smile to those who live the moments." —Matt Hurst, Culinarian/Chef, Grosse Isle, MI

"This story helps us understand the hardships that cause illegal immigrants to risk life and limb to find a job in the US. It also reminds us of the need to show the love of Christ to strangers in our communities."
—Dr. Frank Severn, General Director Emeritus, Send International.

"This book provides a unique view of an immigrant's journey to America. Mr. Stolt has done a remarkable job in developing characters you can relate to and want to see succeed in their journey. The book follows their lives through so many trials and challenges. It also takes into account their religious background and the strong impact it has on these characters."
—Maxine Yetter, Retired School Teacher and Administrator

"As an immigration attorney and former Justice Department worker, I can say that Mr. Stolt has uniquely captured the modern American immigration experience. Mr. Stolt's book weaves endearing tales of those who risk everything to simply arrive in America." —Randal L. Schmidt, PLC, Plymouth, MI

"The author does a fine job infusing the story with the sport of soccer. Detailed sequences lead the reader to actually visualize the interaction of players on an actual soccer field." —Micheal Hatfield, Soccer Coach

Crossing the Line

Wayne Stolt

AXIOM PRESS

Mobile, Alabama

Axiom Press
P.O. Box 191540 • Mobile, AL 36619
800-367-8203

For the Hispanic immigrant,

many of whom seek a taste of the American dream.

Also for Renee, my wife and best friend.

Acknowledgments

Thanks to Joe Ciluffo for extensive consultation on the manuscript. The story represents much of the ministry he and his wife Jeanie Ciluffo do as they serve with Cam International to the local Hispanic population in Pontiac and Auburn Hills, Michigan.

Thanks to Porfirio and Chabelo for their stories of friends and family in Central America and North America.

Many thanks to Alicia Pearce, a colleague in teaching for help in checking the manuscript.

Thanks to Steve Baker and Ron Baker, as they were instrumental in defining the locale for the major accident scene in Guatemala.

Thanks to Tom Rebant, as he reviewed the scenes regarding the assault investigation.

I would also like to thank Benjamin Zolynsky, an instructor and soccer coach at Riverview Community Schools, for his input on the soccer scenes.

Thanks to my wife, Irene, who has supported and encouraged this endeavor in its entirety.

"No one understands and appreciates the American Dream of hard work leading to material rewards better than a non-American."
— *Anthony Bourdain (Kitchen Confidential: Adventures in the Culinary Underbelly)*

"I score many lucky goals in my football life because I am always there, trying to shoot. For me the best goals are the ones like this when the ball just crosses the line."
— *Mateja Kezman*

At dawn he appeared again in the temple courts, where all the people gathered around him, and he sat down to teach them. The teachers of the law and the Pharisees brought in a woman caught in adultery. They made her stand before the group and said to Jesus, "Teacher, this woman was caught in the act of adultery. In the Law Moses commanded us to stone such women. Now what do you say?" They were using this question as a trap, in order to have a basis for accusing him.

But Jesus bent down and started to write on the ground with his finger. When they kept on questioning him, he straightened up and said to them, "If any one of you is without sin, let him be the first to throw a stone at her." Again he stooped down and wrote on the ground.

At this, those who heard began to go away one at a time, the older ones first, until Jesus was left, with the woman still standing there. Jesus straightened up and asked her, "Woman, where are they? Has no one condemned you?" "No one, sir," she said.

"Then neither do I condemn you," Jesus declared. "Go now and leave your life of sin."

—John 8:2-11 (NIV)

PROLOGUE

JANUARY 1999
MEXICAN AND TEXAN BORDER CROSSING

The coffee truck made its way across the Ysleta Bridge, also known as the "Zaragoza Bridge." The coffee truck transported imported coffee across the border from a Maquiladora plant, or "twin plant," where manufacturing parent companies house facilities on the Mexican side, and product was dispensed from a warehouse on the American side. Although the coffee truck completed the preliminary checks on the American side, a produce truck with a flatbed trailer was holding up the second checkpoint. Three well-hidden Hispanics in the coffee truck began to question how much more in their journey they would be asked to suffer. Salvador, their coyote (one who helps others cross the border illegally for a hefty sum), winked at the other two and patted their shoulders reassuringly.

All three listened intently while the produce driver protested the delay. The driver mumbled while unlocking the back of the truck, but a guard knocked vehemently on the door and pointed to the flatbed.

"Not the truck, amigo! Usually your food sits lower in the trailer." The guard moved to begin lifting a tarp in the trailer. "What's the change today?"

"Pull this truck and trailer all the way over to the right and park it," the second guard yelled sternly while pulling back the tarp completely. A family of four, with two children's shoulders barely visible among the rows of twined plantains, lay prone in the back of the trailer. "We see you every week, amigo. Why start this now?"

The driver protested his ignorance with a smattering blend of English and Spanish expletives while the family stretched cramped limbs and climbed down from the trailer. The produce driver's protests got louder and a bit shrill as the family was escorted to the building for deportees.

The coffee truck cargo area was silent and still until the truck moves forward.

Both of the Guatemalans glared at Salvador with real fear and asked desperately, "If they caught a produce regular, how would this coffee truck be any better?"

The American border guards inspected not only the exterior body of their truck but also insisted on seeing some of the coffee product. The search revealed nothing more than the fragrant aromas of fresh-bagged coffee boxed, stacked, and tiered in four layers.

The truck traveled on and was waved through and turned right away from the bridge onto the 375 loop. It traveled only for about fifteen minutes in El Paso and stopped at a receiving warehouse where the coffee crates would be shipped by semi across America.

Once the large warehouse doors were shut, the coffee driver hopped down and banged roughly on the outside wall of the truck. He strode to the back and opened the back latches with a deep sigh.

"All right, boys!" the driver yelled into the truck, "Squeeze out from behind the coffee crates. We're in the US now!"

The men slowly squirmed out from between the coffee boxes. They each tip toed among the length of imported coffee rows and then jumped down to the ground. There were immediate hugs between the two younger men and heavy pats on the back for the older man.

"Salvador, this is amazing! We thought for sure it was us returning on the train back home. After they inspected and caught that family on the produce wagon, it seemed like it would have to be us too! We would have spilt all over the bridge road among fresh coffee beans if either of those Customs agents had looked a little harder," the younger Guatemalan exclaimed, as he stretched his shoulders and nudged his long, dark unkempt hair out of his eyes.

Salvador had kindly provided newer clothes for both of them, but little time was left for a fresh haircut.

"You said it and I wish I could sing it loud," the other young man sighed as he set the guitar he had been cradling against a six foot wooden table resting in front of the truck. "The god of travel must have had his eye on us."

"Roberto and Luis, sit down at the table here as real people should and don't be smothered in a corner like smuggled teenagers." Salvador, the seasoned coyote in his late twenties pulled out two wooden folding chairs on the far side away from the guitar. "Our driver is bringing bottled cold water with some Better Made chips. You know they're made in your new home."

"Salvador, many local natives in Guatemala told Luis and I about the perils of traveling across the border into Mexico." Roberto slid the paperback Western from his back pocket, smoothed the cover out, and sat with a deep sigh.

"Other than those Custom guards scaring the breath out of us when they knocked around the coffee crates, this crossing seemed far less harsh than we encountered coming into Mexico."

"Roberto thought he was going to nearly drown in the Rio Grande, and it was just sweat pouring down the back of his stringy hair." Luis smiled broadly.

While pulling his chair out, he tugged on Roberto's hair hanging behind his ears. He glanced down the table at his gift, the newer guitar, with its shiny six strings and starburst sound board. "Roberto is right, I'm glad we didn't have to chance ruining my new baby."

"Well, up until a few years ago, that's what we did most of the time at this crossing. Why it could have been any number of choices for you boys." Salvador smiled and winked their way. "Chances are I would have had you two on a small boat, a wooden raft, or even in round inner tubes."

"I'm not sure I would have liked floating across the Rio in a rubber tube." Roberto frowned as he sealed his second button. "Our lives were almost lost coming into Mexico in a much smaller river."

"Ah, the trouble you saw! Bolivia spoke of it to me, and it happens once or twice in a lifetime. You would have been fine in the Rio today." Shaking his head with a slight smile he continued, "But Roberto, the Border Guard's presence has increased dramatically in the last few years. So I charge more for the choice and risk you travelers want to make. Some pay more for the risk of traveling across just outside of El Paso. Others I send to my cousin, who takes them across further down at the Arizona border. That route is tough, as my cousin may put them in a van or sometimes they have to walk through hot portions of the desert or across some of the mountainside to meet our contacts."

"But we were brought over in the coffee truck?" Luis interrupted with a mouthful of chips, "How did you work that out?"

"It worked for two reasons. First, I have a cousin who works for the coffee maquiladora plant, that has a solid system in bringing coffee from the Mexican warehouse to the American warehouse. He has worked out the weight that is expected in crossing and keeps a low profile for the reputation of the coffee plant. He and I don't smuggle people often; but when we do, we watch which guards and supervisors are working what shifts. So we charge even more for the planning and potential danger of my cousin losing his job. But Roberto has a friend in his family who has some history with our family, and it all worked out for you two."

Luis slapped Roberto's back and Roberto smiled wanly.

1988—SAN MIGUEL ACATÁN— (ST. MICHAEL THE ARCHANGEL)—GUATEMALA

The city was bigger than some but not nearly as big as Antigua or the capital, Guatemala City. To boys of eight years of age, however, it seemed as if their home went on endlessly, and they would happily explore street upon street. Roberto and Luis had been friends for a year, since Luis' father moved his family into the city just a few houses away from Roberto's home. Roberto had already by this age become fully engaged in reading. He read anything and everything he could put his hands on, from loosely thumbed comics to short stories from his teacher and to copies of the local newspaper. Roberto's father instilled in him an ethic for working hard, while his mother influenced him heavily with an avid interest in reading. Although neither parent passed much in stature onto him, he sometimes wondered if he would ever get as tall as other boys. Short, thin, and thoughtful as a boy, he listened more than spoke. Often he heard snippets of conversations between his parents about which side of the tracks they came from. His father's family was of a lower economic status and left him little opportunity to finish school. In fact, Roberto's father left school as a teenager and began working with his own father. His mother's family, on the other hand, came from a bit higher economic status. Not only was she able to finish high school but enjoyed the time she spent there. She was able to afford some of the nicer amenities in life, including having her nails done often and a different hair-do every season.

Luis' parents were childhood sweethearts and always showed this love to their two sons. Luis and his younger brother, Eduardo, were three years apart but still a strong bond held between them. Eduardo showed much of his mother's temperament, a mild personality that tried to please everyone but struggled with it. His mood slipped from a solemn one to bouts of laughter, and he was fairly introverted. Luis showed more of his father's sense of adventure and willingness to take chances. Luis was already more of an extrovert as a child. He chose the fun side of life even as a young child, pushing himself in attempts at jokes, even at the expense of his brother and friend. He was already taller with longer legs and arms for his age. As a bigger boy, he excelled in sports at school or in the neighborhood and loved it.

Thus Roberto and Luis were quite a pair, who somehow complimented each other as friends. They walked to school together and then explored the neighborhood together after school. The streets offered a whole range of oddities for young boys to find, especially when one of them was new to the area with a fresh set of eyes in this small world of theirs. Luis's family came from a rural area, where they worked the land with many others in their extended family. Adventure for him often led him to find the closest farm to the one in which they were currently working. Sometimes it would take an hour or more to find new property as he bravely explored while his parents were taking a siesta. When Luis pushed Roberto to run with him and explore the area around their homes, something that brought Luis joy with each moment. The streets, though small relative to a city, posed new routes to run around. The outskirts of the town turned to high fields and then sloped down to the low flowing river. It was quite different than working farms that seemed endlessly the same.

Although Luis and Roberto had barely been exposed to the concept of Spanish explorers such as Cortez or American ones like Lewis and Clark, already both had inklings of the exploration bug akin to the restless innate push many trappers, hunters, and explorers had centuries ago. Their teacher, Ms. Hernandez, just last week had told them of months of travel by great Spaniards who came and explored various parts of Central America. The glory in seeing with new eyes the land and its different peoples for the first time, enraptured the boys' attention in class. The class did not dwell on the civilizing of the Mayan peoples that day, but instead concentrated on the initial introduction of the Spaniards to the native peoples. When they left the building that was somehow called a school in their part of the city, they walked with a piece of history and the wanderlust to which Ms. Hernandez had introduced them. Years later, Roberto would think back and wonder about Ms. Hernandez, and her heritage. Was she more Spanish, or did she have more of native Guatemaltecos lineage in her?

It had been a tough week in the lives of the boys. In school they had a test in two subjects on Friday—math and history. The history test wasn't too hard, since much of the material centered around great explorers, gold hunters, and others whom they began to idolize. In addition, their favorite football team, or American soccer, had lost its game last night. Their team played hard, with Roberto's brother in for half the game, but they lost in extra time. Today was a welcome break for them as they walked with their sticks guiding their steps, as if they were woodsmen of old. The difference for these explorers was there were fewer trees to create a woodsy feel as they wandered the city, and of course the ball they kicked to and fro' broke the historic scene. After an hour of walking they came to the outskirts of the city, where the river ran along the main highway out of town. The other side of the river was a great rolling field, with a scattering of tall trees that gradually inclined up the side of a mountainous volcano outside of the city. Sometimes, it even smoked a bit and they wondered if it would ever spout while they lived here.

As they were watching the volcano puff a bit, clouds began to roll

6

overhead and seemingly out of nowhere it started to sprinkle. Luis sug-gested they keep walking because a bit of rain never hurt anyone. Roberto disagreed and said that he had to get back home for lunch with his family. Luis came up and tapped Roberto on the shoulder with the walking stick he had been using. He laughed and wondered if the explorers turned back in the rain. Roberto shoved Luis hard over a puddle and Luis caught himself with his stick. Roberto laughed and turned around with the ball. Luis turned also and waited. Roberto threw the ball overhead and started to walk faster. They worked to pass the ball between each other, Luis dribbling with his explorer stick. By then the rain pushed down more in heavy sheets, and there was not a bright spot left in sky.

The boys started dribbling, running in a skip-type motion. Roberto ran along the bank of the river and passed the ball lightly to Luis, who reacted with a swift pass back. The ball tumbled and rolled to the shore along the river. Roberto ran to the edge of the embankment and scur-ried on his behind to the bank of the river. As he scrambled down, Roberto looked back up the side of the riverbank. He reached the water's edge and saw the ball. But the water seemed to grow in waves like the ocean they had seen in the textbook. He had never seen it like this before. It rose even higher and started to pull the ball into its grasp. Roberto hurriedly reached for the ball as it started to get pulled into the current. The ball bobbed in and out of the water like a child-hood toy. Just as he had the ball in his palms, his worn out shoes slipped in the mud, and he fell forward into the crazy current.

Luis reached the shore and watched unbelievingly as Roberto tried to unsuccessfully keep his head above the water. Luis raced ahead and reached out the walking stick with one arm and held onto a tree with the other. Roberto missed the stick and went under. Luis ran ahead and tried the stick again, this time stepping out into the water while holding a branch over his head. Roberto caught the stick and began kicking to-ward Luis. Luis pulled more and more until Roberto reached the shore and fell onto the sand with a final heave. The walking stick swung up-ward, while Luis fell backward, and the walking stick hit his face, stop-ping at his ear. They caught their breath, and then hugged as only friends can who find moments of truth in trauma. Roberto knew even as a boy what it meant to be indebted to a friend, a friend willing to sacrifice. Both boys kept the memories with small scars. Roberto had one in the palm of his hand from the strain on the stick, while Luis found his below his ear from the deep scraping of the walking stick. The scars reminded them each of the sacrifice that day.

BOOK I

~ 1 ~

SAN MIGUEL ACATÁN, GUATEMALA
1996—ROBERTO, AGE 16

"Papa, kick the ball over to me. I am so close to the net. Ball, ball, Luis is coming strong." The ball quickly spurted into the air, bounding just a few feet over my head. Jumping with both legs to tap the ball, I tried to turn the direction of the ball, but missed by a margin as I hadn't grown as tall as many in my family had. I turned and found the ball, hurling the heel of my foot into the twirling ball just as it bounced to the ground. The effort I exerted into the ball ended in some shameful pain as Jesús threw his body into the ball and my shoulder.

I sputtered around while regaining my foothold on the ground, and my brother heartily laughed. He easily maneuvered a series of graceful dribbles around our father and then a fierce pass into the net just ten feet beyond. Jesús ran up to Luis and slapped him on the back, and then snagged a handful of my long hair as he raced forward. Papa kicked the ball out again, and off we went running full tilt after the ball. Jesús abruptly stopped the ball with his left instep and passed it over to Luis. Luis began to dribble it until Papa stole it out from under him and dribbled from left to right and back again all the way to our opposing net and scores.

"Gooooalllll!!" Papa screamed, and we both jumped up with the joy of winning that a son and a father feel, though I wasn't much help. But still, he ran up and hugged me with glee, leaving Luis to wait on our moment. Jesús bantered something about age not showing too much on our father's play. Although, I know, as Papa's chest heaves, he needed more than just a hug, he needed a breather. Oh, what shots we made that day, though with just the four of us we seemed to have run

9

more than when I had practiced with my friends from school.

We had such fun, when my father and Jesús came home for a two-day break. We got my friend Luis and played just down the block behind the chapel. Jesús would get his professional ball from the league he played on for a short time, and I'd lace up my shoes extra tight to give me more speed. Papa would put on his shorts that he only wore for football and send me to find Luis. Luis would always be home plunking on that old guitar his uncle gave him.

"Roberto, why will you not eat the chicken? I did not go to the market and pick out just the right one and then spend more time cooking dinner for the three of us just to have it get cold as you daydream again."

Mama woke me from my dream of fun from years ago. Man, do I miss my years as a boy. I wished it could be like that again.

"And why do we not talk anymore? You used to come home from school and tell me about your day, and now I all hear is Christina's complaining about the boys who pick at her and the girls who do not talk to her."

"Yes, Mama. I was only thinking of a football game," I replied while I worked some beans from around my plate onto a wedge of tortilla and shoveled it into my mouth. Mama's tortillas are the best, but the beans get messy. I wipe my sleeve over my mouth, as some beans drip on the corner of my mouth.

Mama glared at my dripping but just continued on. "What are you thinking of now? You're still sixteen years old. You ought to be loving life, but I think you're wondering about one of those television football games you and Cesar are always betting on. I wish to God that your José never told you of the money he won from those games. José says he is like a father for you, but I'm not sure of these things he is teaching you. Our Father in heaven knows we can't afford for you to get mixed up in that horrible habit."

"Please Mama; it was just a game from years ago when Papa and Jesús played with us. It was so good to have them both home with us, away from driving people place to place, and able to take time to play with Luis and me."

Mama stared at me for a second that seemed like a lifetime. Finally she set her fork down. "I know you miss them both, as we all do. But you should get out there more and find joy in football again like you used to. You don't play but once in a while. Instead you read, read, and read more. Who needs to reads so many books and newspapers?"

I pulled my hair back out of my eyes and scratched the scar on my hand. "You wanted me to be more educated. More than Papa's family. I have found real life in reading about the lives of so many others in the world and the history they've made. Now you complain to me as I've grown to love the words of many.'"

Mama shrugged her shoulders. "Roberto, I want a better life than what your father's side was used to, and even more than what my family provided. But I so want you to love life itself, too. The *moments* you must live, and not just others you read of. Play more. And *live!*"

"Roberto, I'll play football with you. I can kick and dribble with the best of my friends in my class," Christina interrupted as she looked up with shining eyes.

"No, my little Tina, it is not you I wish to play with. Although, later tonight I promise to practice with you. You must practice more. I'm not the potential pro that Jesús may have been, but I can still practice with you."

"Tell me, Roberto, wasn't Jesús a great player for our city? And why did he stop playing? How many games did Jesús help win? What of the final championship game, and the picture hanging on the wall in the market? I stare it so much and wonder about our older brother in it," she exclaimed with a deep sigh.

"Oh, that picture again, Christina. Some man caught a great moment from our brother's time on the field. He was such a fun player to watch. He could spark up the whole team and, at times, even all those watching, with his quick movements, easy smile, and intense play. Those eyes of his could stab any soul."

"Tell me the story again, Roberto. Please, please."

"Okay, my little hermanita." I laughed loudly at her eagerness to

11

hear the story again and began reminiscing about my eldest brother. "Jesús knew well how to handle the ball, and that made him so successful on the Huehuetenango city championship team. In fact, this team had done so well locally that they moved up the ranks and ended up in the final game in the capital. Father, Mama, Luis, and I were lucky to get tickets from a friend of Dona for whom Papa had provided free fare to visit an ailing grandfather in another city. The seats were just two rows above the field, and centered at mid-field. Oh, what a beautiful and glorious day it was! The sun shone so bright and the breeze blew the flags and ruffled the bright blue shirt Mama had bought for me at the market."

"Come now, enough of flags and weather, what of the game?" My little sister, who was soon to become a teenager hadn't learned any patience yet. I took a deep breath and sat silent for a few extra seconds just for fun and effect. From the corner of my eye I caught Mama peaking a look at us from the kitchen area.

"Christina, you can't rush a good story, especially one that has little of me in it." I smiled a little, having more fun at her waiting. "I have to get me in there somehow." She couldn't know how I valued any time I got with my brother Jesús. He was a hero in my mind. I had always missed him terribly when he was away playing or working with father. And now I miss him even more, 'cause I know I will never again see the glint in his eye as he runs by me.

"Roberto, just the story of the picture . . . please, hmmm?"

"All right then, the story it is. It was the second half, and both teams were already very tired because they had been playing tough and physical. There was much tackling, pushing, and grabbing, and even more falls, fouls, and headers."

"Were they like the circus acrobats, flying into each other's arms?" Tina waved her arms up and about, somersaulting her hands together.

"At times it did seem so with the players sliding around and getting their legs tangled and going after the spinning ball. But especially at the goal, it got really crazy with a lot of hard tackles and grabbing, and many injuries and fouls. But it got real physical with arm bars, pushing and pulling amongst the goalkeeper, defenders, and attacking players.

What the referee didn't see wouldn't hurt much. The emotion really grew as the ball drew nearer the net, and the goalkeeper dove on the ball just before a mob of the opposing players pounced upon him. I was lost in the whole game. It was like a dream as Jesús led our local club up and down the pitch."

"Finally a day when Christina stops with that endless chatter and sits quietly as a child should," Mama stated with a grin as she walked in to clear the remaining food away from the table. "I just wish I could hear more of that chatter in this house, especially since there are fewer bodies in it. We need more chatter about . . . I know!" she suddenly exclaimed. "I think a party would befit this house. Um, um . . . whom should I call?" She paused to think. Christiana and I looked at her silently. Then she began again. "What 'bout my Rosa, best friend from years ago, and your father's two brothers, with their children? Oh, no, I just don't know about José coming with Rosa. I wonder if he's still crazy or has settled down."

On and on she muttered and mumbled as a plan formulated in her quick mind. She was never at ease unless some project was boiling away in that pot of hers, stirring it constantly as she would create a plan for the household, the extended family, or the local parish. Her mind swirled around like a stew she insists cooking on higher heat as she turns the brown cracked spoon in figure eights. I could often tell when her mind wasn't on the food at hand. In fact, often it was far away with others on her mind, and I'm sure it was her heart softly grieving again. I often know it's not me she's thinking of when the faraway look forms in her eyes, and then again tough stew meat on my plate doesn't help much either. Thank God, it was chicken today, 'cause I don't know if could have been dealt another blow from beef stew as a holiday special that's not really all that special. If only I was older, and it could have been me instead of Jesús. Perhaps she would be happier today with him at her table.

"Roberto, you start the story and then you let Mama stop it." Christina pounded her fist lightly on the table, staring at me.

"Yes, my little one. Let's see, the game was close to being over, and the teams were tied one to one. The mood of our crowd changed as our team handled the ball, and our side sang with our hearts full in voice and song. The opposing team's goalie had the ball and kicked it high so that it reached almost half field. We leapt up and began screaming. Jesús stopped the ball by jumping high in the air where he trapped it in his chest and then deadened it down to the ground in one quick motion. He kicked it with his heel toward a teammate to the right and then turned left to avoid an oncoming tackle. Jesús started to stumble slightly away from the pursuing player. Another player had already shot past the net, and there was a clump of players crowded in the right back corner of the net.

"Finally, somehow the ball was put back in play. Uncle José, Luis, and father were all screaming around me, and we had our arms waving about, as if somehow we could help in the play. I could hardly think of anything but reaching the goal. I knew I did not have the skills, but how I wished to part be of the game so badly! Then, the ball was kicked laterally across to the left as the goalie was moving to and fro like a cat hunting for a mouse. You know the look our kitty gets, Tina, when he is chasing a mouse in the corner of kitchen? Well, the goalie, his eyes and body movements were much the same as our little Diablo who purrs like he is King of the Jungle.

"Jesús sprinted while he was trailing the play. He dribbled forward and kicked the ball over both his head and the oncoming opponents. Jesús stepped over the ball to freeze the last defender, and then did the three-sixty move known as the maredona. The crowd cried in amazement as we all could see he wasn't to be slowed down with any tackling attempts. The amazing move made it seem like he was in slow motion. The goalie jumped to his right when he heard Jesús contact with the ball. Jesús shot the ball like a rocket with precise aim and force, and it slid in the upper ninety, or right hand goal, just out of the goalie's reach. It seemed to fly just inches between his hands on one side and the post on the other and into the net.

"Jesús ran to the right corner flag, ripped his shirt and held it over his face in joy. The rest of the team slid knees first right into him, knocking him over with their joy. We all had our hands high up in the air and we were screaming, "Hey Sus!" He looked up at us and pointed at us with real fun in his eyes. As we were screaming, I blinked from a quick blinding light and realized the man above us had gotten the picture just in time. It was a miracle, and I said a quick prayer of thanksgiving. All of us on the bench had a group hug, and father had a tear or two.

"I asked, 'Papa, are you sad right now?' and he laughed that hearty laugh of his and just shook his head. Soon after the game was over we all rushed the field like children at a local festival. Laughing and singing, we searched for Jesús and cheered when we saw his teammates were carrying him like a great warrior around the field. What a day that was!"

~ 2 ~

TÍA ROSA'S HOME

Mama took Tina and I with her to see Tiá Rosa. Rosa and José were married and had been family friends for many years. Rosa seemed like family to us since she and Mama had grown up together. Rosa and José had two sons, Cesar and Carlos, who played football with me. Mama's family had moved away for better business ventures, and she did not like for us to see much of Papa's side of the family.

Rosa's family became our family, but in the previous few years we hadn't seen them much. Mama, she has loved and cared for us alone. My soul ached for family to share with and though Mama would never admit to it, I know she dearly missed the family sense we shared with Rosa and José.

"Rosa, thank you so much for accepting my request to come over this afternoon. I just needed to sit down and plan the party with our family," Mama smiled, as she sat down at table with us and set down her coffee. I sat on the other side, doodling with Tina.

"Maria, I can always make time to sit with you over coffee. But I don't see the need to call a big party for the family to get together when we can just have dinner any Saturday night. Years ago we got together almost weekly, and dinner as a family was lots of fun with gossiping about the town, eating everyone's specialty dish, and just laughing and singing along to the strumming of our boys' guitar playing. Where did those times go?"

Tiá Rosa looked at Mama and pushed some long hair away from Mama's face. Mama shook back her head and said nothing. I turned to get more water from the pitcher between Tina and me, thinking about the fun times we had missed lately.

"Just because we lost two of our loved ones, doesn't mean we must give up our family core. We lost your boys, and then we, as a family, lost the rest of you as part of our family. You never returned our calls or invitations for dinner. It seems as if you blocked the rest of us out as a way of dealing with the loss."

Tiá Rosa wasn't holding it back today, and I felt glad Tina had gone outside to play in the back after she emptied her water. I could see her running, trying to dribble the ball to Cesar's side of the field.

"Rosa, you were never afraid to touch the sore spots. I remember even as girls and I fell in the dirt when we were playing ball, you were quick to bandage my painful sores. Now, here you are trying put a quick band-aid on my heart, when all I wish is to keep it in the past," Mama spoke slowly. Her voice seemed to get colder, like when she used to firmly discipline me after I was out late.

"Yes, I know you want to keep those memories in the past, but you're failing miserably at it. I can see it in your eyes and in the movements around the house when I stop to check in on you, in the low whispers among your children and the hushed tones as your Tina plays with her doll."

"Oh, Rosa, I get so afraid of opening up to anyone, even longtime friends like you. For when I open the well of emotions, out pours the rest of my feelings and my broken heart. Stupid man, that Paco. Dios mio, I wish the stuff had never been invented. Liquor was his answer for any of life's problems. He turned to a shot of that cheap booze with even the smallest and simplest problem. I tried to rid the house of it, but somehow I'd find another stash of bottles in a new place."

I turned around, and wondered if they had forgotten I was still sipping my ice water behind. I stood quietly and walked just inside the kitchen, thinking I might hear some new things about Mama and Papa. I think I'm ready.

"I'm so bitter about him: his addiction to alcohol, his lack of love for me and little Christina, and worst of all his carelessness in allowing Jesús to be killed. The accident, Mother of God, why on earth couldn't he have stopped the senseless death of my little Jesús, my oldest son, whom we all loved? This whole town each day mourns the loss with me. All loved him so, and yet he's gone."

As Mama took a deep breath, she started to sob some. I pushed all my hair back over my head and rubbed my eyes with my right hand. The ice started to wiggle as my left hand started to shake, and I quietly set my glass down on the kitchen counter so as not draw attention to myself. Perhaps I'm not ready to hear this much after all?

"Maria, you need to start to heal," Tiá Rosa responds. "Paco loved you so deep and wide, and he loved your daughter also. I'm sure of it. When I rode with him to the other city, he spoke of longing to be with you. In fact, I spent an entire afternoon walking with him through all of Huehue's central market in search of the perfect gift for you. He was never quite satisfied with any of my ideas, from the color of clothes to the jewelry; we just kept looking for you." Mama's face lit up some as she heard a new story of her Paco.

"My whole day trip was spent with him as he kept looking; he spoke of special moments with you. The day trips you two would take, and the trips to the local market where you two would walk arm in arm laughing till you both began to cry about some small comment one of your children said so seriously. Paco, he loved his whole family, but he had a hard time showing it to his wife and daughter sometimes. It was easier to play football with boys and wrestle with them until you called them for dinner." She laughed at that final thought. In the kitchen I smiled at the memory.

"Fine, fine," Mama stammered. "Perhaps he did love me and Tina. But what about his weakness that brought down the family and worst of all, the toll on the life of my most precious one? The one I named in honor of our Lord, one who was still working on modeling the love and character of our God's Son? He deserved more time on this land of ours, and still, he is gone like the last drop of coffee in my cup. All I have is the memory of the taste of our time with him. With bitterness sitting on the edge of my tongue, I taste his memory every day and blame no one but Paco and sometimes . . . Dios mio."

"Maria, you cannot blame God, and you need to let go of Paco. He is gone, and yet your children are still here and they need you. God in heaven loves you, even with all of the trash you carry with you. Take it to the Virgin today, so she can plead to God for you. Your house is always so very clean, and still inside you remain heart heavy."

Mama looked up toward Tiá Rosa's kitchen silently. I saw her head come up and quickly stepped out of her line of vision. I heard her pull the chain back and forth from around her neck, the crucifix sliding the front length, as it often does. "I prayed to God for safety for my whole family. He let me down. He let the whole town down with our loss. Years ago I had gone to the market and purchased a statue of Michael, the Archangel to protect us. Paco and I, we placed Michael among the dry annual flowers, just a few steps to the right of our walkway to the front porch. But even after the payment and the daily prayers I sent to heaven, the worst happened. Jesús, and then later Paco—they are both gone."

Tiá Rosa sat silently and looked at the clock and then the front door. She stood up and hugged her. "Maria, I'm sorry not only for your loss, but also so sad that you haven't come to me till now. We have made such progress today, and it has been so good to see you and the children. I have missed you so much. Promise me we will have more time together. I have the mornings to spare for us, and it is most important that we start to heal. Right now I need to get ready to go to the market. I promised José his favorite meal, and I must haggle with the little money left to me in order to make it."

"Rosa, I am so thankful that you agreed to meet me today. Of course we will have coffee again, for we have yet to plan the party. So many things to do and only us who truly understand all that goes into a great dinner party for the family—a memorable one, where cousins will wish they had come instead of watching senseless television." She called for me to find Christiana and meet her out front. This will be great fun. It will be like years ago. I think often about the huge parties we used to have. Neighbors and friends were closer than family.

~ 3 ~

TIÁ ROSA AND TIÓ JOSÉ'S HOME

Several days later I took leftovers to Tiá Rosa's house. Their home was at least a half hour's walk away, and that was if I didn't stop and speak to people along the way. Many people around the area knew of me because of my father, who was well traveled with his route, and my brother, with his great football skills. The walk still seemed long, but I was happy as the sun shimmered between the houses and made my eyes narrow from the sparkling rays and dust bunnies scooped up with my scruffy shoes.

I was as happy, I guess, as any lost teen boy could be. For lost is how I often feel with my older brother, and then my father, dead. They both were my stars and I looked up to them. They were stable and stood tall in the skies that I looked to. Both, in their own way, gave me direction with a slight hand gesture, a quick word spoken at the right moment, or even an intense smile flashed my way.

Empanadas is my favorite meal that Mama baked for Tina and me; there was enough left for Tió José and his boys, Cesar and Carlos. They eat twice as much as me, and I'm older than they are. Mama says it's because they are teenagers still growing and feel they must eat Aunt Rosa's pantry empty.

It's just after dinnertime, and I'm almost there. I can see movement in the window as they help to put the food away and the dishes near the sink. Through the window I even see the picture hanging there, the one where Jesús scored the goal that everyone talks about. What a great day that was, but I wonder where Tió José got the photo from. What noise there'll be when I knock on the door! The whole family loves Mama's famous empanadas. Her recipe is spoken of all throughout the

20

extended family, and any who eat it claim it's a piece of heaven on earth.

"Roberto, is that you knocking at our door?" Tió José yelled through the door. "Stop that tat-a-tatting and get in here." When I entered he continued, "We just finished eating and we're about to watch the game on TV. What's this in your hand? Oh….oh….Rosa! Look at what our long-haired, scruffy nephew dragged in. Oh, don't tell me it's Maria's empanadas. Cesar, shut the door; and Carlos, you take the plate from Roberto so he can take those shoes off and sit down."

"My, my, Roberto. It's good to see you." Tiá Rosa lightly walked in and hugged me right after I handed the plate to Carlos. She had great hugs. "I just spoke to your mother the other morning, and here you are bearing gifts from her heart. What moved her to think of us when she could have these delights for days or even sold them at the market?"

"Well, you know, Tiá Rosa, she spoke of you with such a smile. I think she really made these for your family, not as a treat for us kids like she let on. Who really knows the mind of my mother, other than God, of course?"

"'Berto, you want the corner seat or the middle, since I need to watch this game?" Cesar asked.

"I don't much care, Cesar. I can't stay and visit too long. I've got a few chores to do when I get back home, and I've got to be up early for the last days of school. This school year is almost done, and then there's just one more year! The writing class I took really pushed me, and I have to finish writing one last paper for it. Then another year in school before I'll be off to university, just as Mama wants."

"I can't believe you're almost done with school, and we've still got so much more to go. I keep telling Papa we don't need to finish since we can go right to working for him in the shop."

"Cesar we're not talking about that right now," Tió José pointed to an empty chair, "and Roberto, go ahead now and sit."

"Yes, yes, Roberto, go ahead and sit so you can tell us all about your sister, your mama and why don't you have a girlfriend?" Tiá Rosa stood smiling from the kitchen and waited for me to sit.

"Rosa, the boy doesn't want to talk about any of that stuff. C'mon

Roberto, let's go sit down out back on the porch. We'll get scores from the boys, 'cause your Tiá Rosa will never let you get much of a word in."

As Tió José and I sat on the porch enjoying the evening, he started to speak. "Roberto, just look at the sun as she thinks about setting. I love my view over the hilltop this side of the valley. The colors, some dry and dull and others sharp and shining from the flowering weeds, they're mixing right in with the slant of the sun as it starts to curve down."

"Tió José, I never much thought of you as a poet. A car and bus mechanic who actually sees the beauty behind his back door—will wonders really never cease as I grow?" I turned to look at him, teasing.

"You think 'cause your finishing most of school that you are the only one who appreciates beauty? Why, that's how I first met your Tiá Rosa. I saw the beauty in her face as she tipped her head ever so when she walked right by my papa's shop. He was always making me work on oil changing, and I near banged my head trying to catch that smile as she turned back. But back then she was coy and wanted no part in looking my way. God knows there was some dress on sale next door. I thank the saints that the women's shop is now closed and turned into a produce market."

"I never heard that story. What a great one to tell your grandkids one day!"

"Yes, I guess so. If those boys ever rightly find love, outside of loving the feel of the ball kicked between them and the net. You'd think they'd realize life has more than football to it. I know you, Paco, and Jesús had some real times on the grass. Not the view I have but great for kicking the ball around."

I thought about this for a moment. "Tió José, I really miss them both. Mama refuses to talk about them much, and I know she dwells on them in her mind. She doesn't leave a lot of room for me to tell little Tina about them, since she cast that 'don't start another story' look to me. Worst of all I really don't know what happened to Papa. She won't tell me, and people around town just shake their heads and walk away. That only leaves me in more confusion."

"'Berto, I can't believe she never told you. Then, again, she may have felt you shouldn't have had to hear it as child. Now you are near being a man, and I'm thinking it's all right you should know."

" Yes, Tió José. For my own sense of mourning, I really need to know. Plus, I feel as if there is some way in which I could help Mama." We sat leaning back under the sunshine, silent with our own thoughts.

It still really breaks my heart to see my mother crying. She holds in all the pain of the memories of Papa and never tells anyone. I was pretty sure she never had opened up to any of her friends. In fact, she shut out all the friends she had surrounded herself with. But even worse, it hurts my insides not knowing how my father left us. He left us emotionally much earlier, but now he is gone completely. He and I had such great times together, and now both he and Jesús are gone. My father, brother, and best friend Luis—they are all gone. My mother is not the same as she was, and Mama's parents' family lives in other cities too far for me to visit.

The time I've shared with Tió José is great, although it doesn't re-place what I had with my Jesús and Papa. His boys are cool enough, but we don't feel like real friends should. Man, do I miss Luis. When we hung out, we did everything together. He and I did it all and were ready to take on the world. Then it all fell apart. Now I could see my world back if Tió José would tell the story of my father's last moments. Maybe it could give me some sense of my papa, and a real connection, if only for a moment.

"Well, Paco, your father, was so distraught over your brother and the accident, he couldn't deal with it all, and his best answer was in the bottle. I'm sure you know he drank, but it was worse after dealing with the aching loss of your brother. Anyway, the short end of it was, from what I understand, he was fueling up that bus—you know that bus he had painted, the one your mother hated, saying it was a disgrace to the honor of God. Well, he was gassing up the tank, which was artfully surrounded with angelic clouds, and missed some of the tank with the hose. It had spilt on him, and the smell from the early booze already on his clothes didn't help much. He finished pouring the fuel and missed the hole for the cap. It spun around, and he tried to catch it with the

23

heels of his feet. The cap rolled down the highway ramp on the right, and he went after it. The hill he took in bounds, and because his senses were slowed from the alcohol, there was little to stop him. One last hop, and Paco landed in the middle of the lane of traffic going west. The first car going west was able to swerve and miss him but in doing so that car hit a fast bus going eastbound. There was a small fire from the bus' engine, and then your father's pants caught fire from the combination of the fuel and the spilt alcohol. Much of his body was burnt in first and second-degree burns, and a local from the gas station threw a blanket on him to stop the burning. But by then he was really gone. The local doctor said he made it to the clinic, and all the while Paco kept muttering, "So sorry, so sorry" and "Love my family, love my family."

"Dios mio. That's terrible. Why again, and why? First Jesús, and then Papa. Both in car accidents." I shook my head side to side as I looked at some cracks in the back porch floor.

"Yes, but were they accidents that could have been prevented? There's pain in the memory for both." Tió José stood up, stretched, and turned around to look through the door.

The sad story affected me, but I still wanted more information. Still no one has told me the rest of the story behind my brother's passing. There is a connection between the two, and I wasn't sure about it all. He left me to wonder what it all meant as I got up to take my empty glass into their kitchen. He patted me once on the back as I went by into the house.

~ 4 ~

MARIA'S HOME

When I returned home a few hours later, Mama walked out from the kitchen as she heard me come in.

"Roberto, you will never imagine who I ran into at the market. The mother of your friend for years, Luis, and she seemed to be good. In fact, after I asked about her family, I thought it would be nice for the two of you to see each other, so I invited the whole family to come to our party."

"Mama, that's interesting. I haven't seen him in years. It's been at least four to five years since we have hung out."

"Why is it that you stopped playing football with each other? I just never understood that."

"I know, Mama, I never much understood it either. One week we practiced together every other day, and the next week he was much too busy with other things. So I stopped pushing practice and left him to himself. So his mother said she would bring him to the party, huh? Was that with some motherly prodding or an actual conspiracy working out right there in the market? Which was it, Mama?"

I rubbed the scar in my hand for a second and then shook my head when I pushed my hair back.

"Now, Roberto, you know I would not force them to come. I just reminded her of the great friendship you two had as children, and that you had no real connection now like what you two once had. She agreed that it was in fact an interesting idea, as long as Luis' head could be level, for I assume his hot head has not cooled much. "

"Is that what it took with Papa also? Just a few simple reminders or nudge once in a while? I never knew how you two really first met. Why not tell me? It would do me good to hear of your beginnings."

25

"I do not wish to dredge old memories of that hurtful man who allowed our family to experience so much pain. It is too much for me to even think of," she said as her shoulder shivered.

"Come on, Mama. Think of his early years. What was that first moment like? What drew you two together, and then worked its magic into marriage?"

A slight smile began to appear at the side of Mama's mouth. "Well, okay. Paco, your father, began working with his father on one of those run around buses. His father somehow scraped up the money to invest in one and began running routes through a series of towns, and finally on into Huehue. Once Paco turned of age, he started working the door. There he navigated the people in the bus, routed other traffic stops and turns that his father had to make without the help of signs or lights. Back then there were even fewer traffic lights and signs than there are today. One Friday afternoon I was walking with your Tió Rosa, and Paco jumped from the bus as it was driving to the left of us. He commented something about the sun shining off my hair and asked if I'd like to ride for a while on his bus. I quickly told him, 'I don't ride with strangers from other towns, especially ones as young and bold as you.' He laughed and rambled away in a smoky muffler mess."

"I didn't see Papa as the caballero type; he always seemed quiet and withdrawn. Except when we played, of course."

"Oh, he could be that many a time. But when it came to his passions, he found a way to voice his thoughts." The small smile still remained.

"Go ahead, Mama, how did the next time you met go?"

"Well, the next time was a few weeks later and school was about out for the year. I was ready to be done with it and strolling along with Tiá Rosa again. We were joking and laughing about something some kids in school had done that day. Then, I suddenly stopped laughing as I heard a series of coughs and sputtering from a long bus turning the corner. Rosa and I both giggled and put on our best serious face like when it was test time in Mr. Rodriquez's math class. With our faces staring straight ahead, arm in arm with Rosa, I saw a flurry of frantic waving from my left side. There was your father, a fiery red rose stuck in his teeth and a bouquet of freshly picked flowers in his right hand. He had his father driving slowly up the street as we walked home, and Paco was swinging from out of the front door of the bus with his left hand gripping the bar and the other hand waving the rainbow of colors. Those colors were bursting with color. For a moment I thought, out of the corner of my eye, I was looking at one of those colorful magazines from the hair salon. Then he jumped from the bus in front of Rosa and me and asked if he could walk with us for a while. We nodded politely, but all I could do was smirk at his walking with us, and on we walked.

"He asked about my classes and which I liked best. He said he really liked my smile and could only wonder at ways to make me laugh. So he kept trying to joke to just see if I would smile at all. Rosa, she giggled at this game when she walked with us. We stopped after a while, and he bought us a soda. He had thought to even bring money for that. After that it was picnics along the river outside of town, walks around the town, and then drives with them on the bus into the city. We laughed and had such fun together. We went to football games and cried when our team lost again and again. The only time it was okay to cry for your father was when his team looked really bad and lost. And they lost because they played poorly and not because the other team played that much better."

"Wow, that's how you two got together? And here Papa always told me that you were a gift from the gods."

"Oh, that. He claims that he went once a week with a gift of a bottle of whisky, candles, and incense for the Shaman at the place where the old gods are still worshipped. There on the altar, he waited weekly for his wish for me to spend time with him. So he said I'm an answer to prayer. I just wish he would have eventually turned his prayers away from the old gods. I always prayed for him and spoke to him about God, the God that Father Angelo explained about—God who is great and powerful.

"Later, when we were able to get into our small home, I placed a statue of St. Joséph behind the backyard porch to watch over our home. Your father, he just snorted and then strode to the church with booze and candle in hand. Later, I placed another statue of Michael here for safety for our family, and your father again just prayed to the old Mayan gods."

I loved the joy in Mama's voice as she retold for me her times with Papa. It didn't happen often that she would share her memories with me. I was also excited that she had finally mended her lost friendship with Tiá Rosa. That meant more fun time with our family friends of old for Tina and me. Now a party for us, and Mama and Tiá Rosa were good together in planning the details of a party. Tina started to talk more about it, and the air in our house got more lively. It was almost like old times, and I started to count the days until the party.

~ 5 ~

MARIA'S HOME

I remember when I was a boy, my mother constantly reminded us how great friendship is and that one should never take one for granted. Years ago, my mother and her friend Rosa, blended their families together as if they were a single, large extended family. Every Sunday after Mass, there was a great luncheon where the childhood friends would each bring their favorite dishes. Food for our family brought us together, and each Sunday was a special time to share among close friends and family.

Worry about everyday problems fell away as bowls, baskets, and platters were passed around. Each person brought not only their close family, but also any parents who were still alive and even assorted aunts and cousins. The cousins were the most fun, since it seemed there were so many to play with. The party transformed a small house with a large yard into a living and breathing unit. People who tended to be shy and quiet livened right up like one of the tomatoes that ripen overnight in our garden. The assortment of food, laughter, and music among friends that hang together like blue skies with funny clouds mixing in, brought real happy times that were true. I knew it was true because of the non-stop smiles and chattering.

At least once a month the luncheons would turn into a party. Celebrations came up so easily, from birthdays and anniversaries to Easter and Christmas. There would be more food, more fun, and lots more music. Music began with one of the uncles picking a guitar after lunch, and soon everyone was singing along. We would sing the old songs that are never played on the radio any more, and are remembered only as they are sung among friends. Then we'd sing songs we knew from the radio, and the voices got much louder as the kids recognized the words and music. After what seemed like hours, it was time to cele-brate. The cake came out and firecrackers exploded loudly.

As we fought for the best piece of the cake while it was being cut, the tallest uncle hung a piñata. When we each got a chance to attack it was my favorite part of the day. It spun around so quickly, and I thought so many times it would fall for sure. It stayed up in the air for a long time. Even as the candy began to spit out over our heads, it still hung by a few small strands. Then, the last boy with the stick would come and knock one final great swing. Then we all laughed until we fell on the ground and landed with our arms flung around each other. Those times were full of fun and glee. Now they are like lost dreams, times I can barely remember as I wake up.

My family had such a strong bond, and I felt even more kinship while with Mama's friends on Sundays. Those Sundays are long gone, since we stopped celebrating years ago. Once in a while I asked Mama about the luncheons after Mass and why now we only eat with just three of us. She responded with a silent smile and moved on with her work about the house. So I just dreamed of the memories and that one day perhaps our family might have the joy it once had.

Yesterday, Mama and Tiá Rosa spent the day making homemade tortilla dough. So this morning they must have used Mama's outdoor flat grill to create their family honored tortillas. I woke up that morning to the rhythmic hand smacking, side to side, as the shells grew in size. As I rolled over and out of my bed, I danced lightly to the beaten sounds and thought about how good they would taste. Of course I've eaten them for years, but Mama's are so good that she's been told to sell them at the market. Early this morning they made the masa, the cornmeal blend, and then spent three hours cooking them. While making the tortillas, they put the beans on to simmer and stacked the shells in a large wicker basket lined with a large cloth.

While Tiá Rosa finished the last of the tortillas, Mama insisted I get dressed and go with her to the market. She claimed she needed my arms to hold all the ingredients for her next dish. I wondered what this could be since many of our meals consisted of beans, rice and well . . . more beans and rice. She mumbled something about beef and vegetables under her breath as I ran through the back door to catch up with that fast walk of hers. I guessed she was planning a meal she hadn't done in a while, and I was to be her worker. Where was Christina to help, especially when going to the market is women's work? I could be sleeping in and she should suffer just as well. As I followed behind Mama, I blurted out the question on my mind.

"Mama, what are you making today? It sounds different. And where is little Tina?"

She simply nodded and said what was obvious to her, "Your sister spent the night at her friend's house and will be home by this afternoon to help in planning. Carne Asada over our tortillas and my salsa is what I'm making"

I just loved it the last time she made the Carne Asada. Mama made great salsa with tomatoes, vinegar, oil, fresh cilantro, and some chili peppers from our garden. We spent what seemed like hours shopping at the market, and finally we made it back home. By then Tiá Rosa had left to go to her own house, and I was sent after her. Mama shoved me out the back door, yelling, "Hurry and take these to Tiá Rosa, for she needs them fast now." I hopped out with a shrug and ran down the block.

I carried three bags full of vegetables, and I thought I'd drop one of them for sure. Tiá Rosa was going to make her famous soup with all these vegetables. Once I arrived at her home, I knocked with a twisted kick from my left foot and almost fell backwards over her porch. I saw Tió José start laughing, but I didn't think it was funny at all. Tiá Rosa held the door and told me to walk carefully up the steps, and to pay no mind to José. I asked her how she made her soup that Mama spoke of so much.

She said, "I take these good looking carrots, yellow squash, yucca, tomatoes, and potatoes you picked for me and chop them into big chunks. Then I simmer them in a beef broth, and sometimes I add some beef pieces to it, if I have some around." She sorted through the remaining bags and looked over to me. She asked, "Roberto, what about fruit for our party? Melons or plantains? How will I make the sweet fried plantains? Dios mio, I'll have to send Carlos or Cesar up to

31

the market before they leave for the day. Maria, God forgive her, I know she is planning much and forgot to tell you."

As Tiá Rosa was placing the vegetables on the counter to arrange them into sectións, Tió José walked into the kitchen and wrapped his arms around Tiá Rosa. He laughed and said, "I hope you don't care much, but I invited my sister to your party tomorrow. She is bringing sopa also."

I love to meet new people and try foods from new cooks. I wanted to ask lots of questions. I started with just one.

"Tió José, what kind of sopa is your sister making? I love sopa. What kind is she making?"

"Well, Roberto, aren't you full of questions? Are you planning to be a chef one day or what? Or are you like me and just love to eat what the women around me put in front of me? My hermana's sopa is from my mother's recipe and is the family specialty—chicken sopa. The chicken is simmered to just tender and it's so tasty, while the vegetables are pretty close to what you brought us today, depending on how my sister feels as she shops today."

I walked back home at a much slower pace. I was thinking about all the food preparation and the different food choices. My thoughts made me feel like it was Christmas morning when I was a boy, with all the different images jumping in my mind. My stomach gurgled as I thought about the food, and I realized I hadn't any lunch yet. When I arrived home, I was surprised to see Tina sitting there.

"Tina, you're home already. Just in time for lunch, I see," I tried to say in a teasing way.

"Adelina had to go with her family early to the market. So I came home," she said a little defensively.

"Mama, what is it you and Tina are eating for lunch? Do we get to try some of the meal you have started for tomorrow? Boy, am I ready!"

"Roberto, come sit next to me today." Tina's face was full of smiles. "Move your chair closer, for I must tell you something. Adelina's sister, Angelina, she has been asking me about you. She wanted to know if you were talking to any girls or not. I said I would ask you and let her know next week."

Tina set her tortilla on the plate and laughed while drawing a heart with her right forefinger. She pointed where it would be and smiled up at me, expectantly.

"Oh, Tina. I'm not interested in Angelina. Although she's pretty enough, she never wants to talk about books that she has read. She only wants to talk about her hair and how nice her nails look. What are you eating? Oh no—not rice, tortillas, and beans, with some little cheese. Mama, where is the love of your children?"

I looked behind Mama's back for a plate she was hiding. She set the plate down with the same lunch in front of me, and smoothed her clean apron. Touching her hair in the bun she had up, she deeply sighed,

"Oh, my son. Quiet now. Eat and eat more. I need you strong and full of energy to move chairs and then carry them to Rosa's house."

"Mama, I don't want to carry all our chairs there. Call Tiá Rosa, and ask her to send the boys here, and they can pick them up."

Mama sighed again. "Roberto, just do as I ask. Eat your fill now!"

After the light supper we traditionally eat, lunch is always a bit more. I read some in my room. I tried to separate my thoughts into areas of importance and had a hard time doing so as Mama was banging away at the pila. It sounded like she finished the dishes in those big sinks and was beginning to scrub some clothes. She uses that sink for it seems like so much. I remember her giving Tina a bath in the larger one of the two without the drain, and I suppose I was cleaned in it too. Now she's humming one of her tunes and doesn't know she's doing it out loud.

I wished our house was bigger, and if Papa were still alive, perhaps we could have been able to have a nicer one. This small adobe house is something I'm not too proud to live in. I know Mama felt she stepped down in living like this. She came from more, and though she told us we are all Chapines, her side of the family was Ladinos. Ladinos were more willing to accept Western culture, while Indians still embraced the old ways. Papa's family, she reminded us children again and again, could not seem to leave the past where it belonged. We know she loved Papa but could sometimes feel bitterness and shame in her voice.

33

Finally, I just hunched over with a pillow to block the melody from Mama and tried to sleep. I was done dreaming about food. Now I really started to worry about tomorrow. The fiesta will be lots of fun with the family. It was fun to watch television at Tió José's house, especially because we don't have one. Tiá Rosa is going to bug me again about a girlfriend and what I'm doing with school. It's been years since I've had an actual conversation with her since she and Mama were not talking much. But now she's helping Mama to figure out my life for me. She and Mama both have told me I ought to go to San Carlos, where they had heard tuition was free. They both whisper how smart I am, and how I need to attend the main university in Guatemala. I know it's been there for years and years, but I don't know if I want to go there. This Chapine needs to travel and get educated in and about the rest of the world. I'm not sure how and where, but it won't be here. Perhaps it will be in the United States. Felipe, one of my father's cousins, has family who work there, and he's told me how they send money back to their family. But then he also cautioned about the corruption along the border. At the party tomorrow there'll be family who have traveled, and I'll listen to them and see. Yes, and my old friend and his family will be at the party.

Luis . . . we haven't spoken in five years, and I don't know why. We had been friends for four years, and then when we were both eleven years old it was done and over. I went to his house for a few days in a row and tried to meet up with him after school. Each time we actually met, he would simply say, "Go Away!" Finally, after days of pushing him to talk to me, he stepped up to and put his finger in my face, yelling, "I'm not your friend any more, just leave me alone!:" I was blown apart, like a fire cracker at my last birthday, torn in pieces on the ground to be stepped on. We had been buddies and companeros who were inseparable. Now my partner had left me alone. We had been in the same classes and same football teams, and we just hung out naturally. Looking back, it was tough. My brother died when I was eleven, and then my father died when I was twelve. God seemed to leave me without any real friends in my family or age group. Mama would say there had to be a reason, but I saw no reason then.

What would it be like the next day as we spoke again for the first time in seven years? We had seen each other over the years, but had always avoided speaking. Once in a while, a glare was occasionally sent my way, and it sent shivers through my spine. But I moved on, and eventually made a few friends, but we never got close again like brothers. I missed Luis terribly.

~ 6 ~

THE DAY OF THE PARTY

Today I still have mixed feelings about the party. Mama and Christina insisted on going over to Tiá Rosa's house early to help her with final preparations. I agreed to carry some food items with them to her house. Once there, I smiled when they asked about my helping them. Although sometimes I like to help cook in the kitchen, this morning I really feel like reading more of Lewis and Clark when they explored the Americas. It was a book my last teacher had spoken of and I found an old paperback copy of it. Those two guys explored early America, paving new paths with adventure. I waved the book in my hand and headed out the other door to read on the back porch.

No one mentioned where the other guys were. I thought they must have been working down the street on a car. Me, the only man around, I felt better alone with a book away from the ladies. I still could hear the conversations among the women in the house. They gossiped for a while about relationships around the neighborhood while they unpacked and sorted the food. They shared how men behave as the pots started to heat up on Tiá Rosa's old stove, and Christina giggled loudly. The great smell of the vegetables cooking together made it out to the porch, and I wondered how the sopa would taste when done.

"Maria, I hear somebody tapping at the front door. Can you see who it is while I stir in more beef broth to my sopa?"

"Rosa, this is your home. Are you sure you should not go to the door?"

"Maria, years ago my house was the same as your house. Your family became part of mine. Today, you act as though we are not even friends. Our friendship has not died but has remained like embers in a fire. It's a fire that's not blazing hot but still smoldering a bit. So,

36

please stir the fire today, and let's have some fun like we did years ago." I sighed some and tried not listen. I didn't want to hear more emotions spill out within my hearing.

"Fine, Rosa. I'll go to the door if that's what it takes to quiet down your incessant talking," Mama giggled like she was a teenager again. I smiled since I hadn't heard much of that lately.

"Isabella, how are you doing? Come in, come in. Bring in your boys too." Who is that at the door? Luis' mother is talking to my mother? What's this going to be like? She's coming to the party, but I wonder if she was ever as upset with me as Luis? Was it a family issue?

"Thank you, Maria. Luis, take your brother with you. Find a spot to sit and watch people come and go here at the party. Maria, I hope it's all right I came with both the boys. My husband, he is no longer with us, so I cannot leave the younger one home alone. But we did bring fresh cut vegetables. Luis picked them, and I made a bowl of them." Luis carried the bowl filled with chopped tomatoes, squash, and peppers.

"Oh, thank you, Isabella. It was very thoughtful of you. These look delicious. So bright and colorful," Mama exclaimed.

"Maria," Rosa interrupted, " is this the friend you mentioned this morning? The one with whom you were acquainted years ago and have just lately been united? This is a small miracle that God is working out for all of us. One never knows what the angels are doing around us on our behalf. Perhaps Michael, the Archangel himself, is taking direction from God in our lives."

"Oh Rosa, I give God his graceful mercy. But let's not look for the work of angels and demons under every rock or work of my mouth, for that matter. But I would like to thank God in Him allowing me to see you and your sons again. Welcome to the party, Señora Isabella. Christina, speak to Señora Isabella."

"Yes, Mama. Hello, Señora Isabella. I'm Cristina, but most just call me Tina."

"Well, Christina, you can look right up in my eyes and don't have to kiss each cheek for me. Though it is nice to see one with such nice

37

manners. Meet my boys here. This is Luis, who is just about to finish school in a year, just like your brother. My other son, Eduardo, who has a crutch and thinks it is a sword, spear, and some days just a cane. He's about your age," Señora Isabella introduced them to her.

"Yes, Tina. Sit with these young men, and tell them about our meal coming up while I take Señora Isabella with us in the kitchen." Tina started to talk with them, asking more questions of Eduardo about his classes in school. I could hear very little from him and wondered if he could talk much at all. She also told them about all the food items for the party.

I looked up from my book and out beyond the porch. Carlos and Cesar returned and were walking up toward the back of the house. They cleaned up in the back pila with their father and begin to put the field together. Others ran up from the neighborhood, and I set the book down. I peaked inside and then turned around again toward the beginnings of a crowd.

Tiá Rosa's house is nice, but behind the house is even better. The area works great for football, and the boys and Tió José take every chance to play and practice. They construct makeshift nets using pails for the pila and the nearby rope from drying laundry to line the backside of the net. There are boys playing in the field that I haven't seen in years, and others I see every day that began playing. I hopped off the porch and walked up, and four and five yell my name, telling me what position to play and on which side I'm needed most. Since my brother was such a hot shot player, it's expected that I can play well. I hoped I could play as well as they think and debated which side to go to.

I took off my favorite long sleeved bright blue sweatshirt and ran out on the field in my worn t-shirt and tennis shoes. Carlos and Cesar motioned for me to their side, but I laughed and ran to the opposing side. A few friends slapped me on the back, and Tió José gave me a big bear hug in greeting. I nodded my head in the direction of a few unknown faces as the ball was thrown in, and Tió José passed it to me. I dribbled down half the field just past the back door of the house and give a wave to little Tina who was watching in the doorway. I quickly stopped as Cesar rushed for me, and I cleared him with a sprint to the left side of the field. I ran and struck the ball and aimed for the goal. I slowed down to catch my breath and waited to see if it sped into the goal. While I held my breath for a second, Carlos left his feet and cleared it with a volley.

One of the guys from the house down the street took the ball back down field. Carlos pointed my way with a huge smile and then shrugged. If he was thinking I've got to do better than that, he could join the other voices in my head. I knew I should have practiced with them the other day when they were out here after the last day of school. The last Stephen King novel I picked up at the library could have waited in my backpack for a while longer so I could have had more time working with the ball on aim and timing. Still, I just stole the ball back from Carlos. He can't move as fast as he used to, with the little potbelly he carries like the extra bag of chips he often has in hands.

I moved the ball between two twins, Rudy and Ramon. I knew they're both fast, since I often saw them run past my house in the morning when they're late to school. Each moved in for me from opposite sides, and I quickly thrust my right foot up to flick the ball. It seems like there are only a few people down by the goal, and Tió José jumped to stop the ball in place with his chest. He did a half turn and kicked the ball into the goal. Just as the ball rolled in, the whistle blew. Everyone on the field wondered if it was a foul called or a good goal. Then most of us remembered we hadn't asked for a coach or referee, so who had blown the whistle? Just then, my Mama she raised her hand and blew again. Many of us laugh, for some knew of Mama. An angry look came over her face, as she slapped her hands and yelled it was time for prayer from Father Angelo. I didn't know some of the people here today, but almost all seemed to know Mama. Though they had heard of her sternness, but even more were aware of her love and laughter. Will my face and voice ever bring people to think, as my mother's does?

We all rushed in line to the pila to wash up. The smell of food was already making its way through the hall and into this back part of the house. Ramon and Rudy didn't even stop to dry their hands as they hurried down the hall toward the dining area. I walked in and Carlos and Cesar had their plates full already and were convincing Tiá Rosa to let them eat outside on the porch just to the side of the pila. I made my way to the line forming in front of the two tables of food and drink. Just as I reach for my plate, another hand was grabbing from the opposite side. Startled, I look up a little mad. The guy had one plate in his hand already and was reaching for a second from my hand. I quickly made a joke about him getting two plates his first time through, when I realized it was Luis who looked up at me from the food he was looking over.

"Hey, Roberto," he said coolly, not meeting my eyes.

I became excited. "Luis, how are you doing? It's been a long time. I didn't mean nothing about two plates," I stumbled through my words awkwardly.

"Yeah, this second one's for my brother, Eduardo," his voice still cold.

"Oh, well. Where's he? I don't see him walking around. Is he helping your mother somewhere? Or are you just doing the food for the whole family?" I attempted to joke.

Luis suddenly got angry, "What you say, Roberto? Stupid…are you crazy, loco? He walks but barely. He cannot stand in one place too long before he starts to fall." He stood pointing across the room with his beverage hand, to where his brother sat, silent for a second. And then without much more time, he started again. "So, are you supposed to be joking again? Or are you drunk with too much booze like your drunken father? You should have been born an orphan and life would have been better for both of us. Your killer drunk of a father, he made my family a mess, and . . ." Stunned at Luis' attack, none of the food held my attention.

I stepped back and turned to face him while he was still talking, and I angrily grabbed his collar. When I went for him, my food fell to the floor, and I moved two steps closer. The plate hit the floor and cracked, and suddenly everyone in the room was listening to our confrontation. I heard some feet move about and from the corner of my eye saw Tina run to the kitchen.

Full of rage and confusion, I yelled, "What is it you're talking about? You're the one talking crazy. My father was a lot of stuff, but he was not a killer."

I pushed him back as I tried to think of what he was talking about. Luis swung with his right arm down at my arms with enough force that I lost my grip a bit, and he dropped both of the plates that he was balancing on his left arm. He pushed back hard, and the table fell forward onto me and we both fell down. Carlos, who was behind me, stepped up in time and caught the platter of chicken. He muttered, "Not Mama's chicken," and set it on the other table.

I scrambled to get up from under the mess of fruit rolling around me. Luis jumped up and stood right on the downed table, while my ankles were still under it and looked down at me. I looked up to my left and Tió José was shaking his head. He should have told me more than what he did before today. With people in a circle around us, Luis yelled again, "Your father ruined my whole family! I've got no father and barely a brother. Your drunk Papa did it all!" Some people around us seemed to know what he was talking about while I have no clue. But it's crazy talk.

I pulled my feet up and rushed for him with all I had in me. I didn't know what he was talking about, but I wasn't going to listen to more of this. He moved under my arms and then swung his foot to get me down. As he started to kick me, I hurled myself at him again. We flew into the wall together, and my favorite picture fell down and the glass cracked. He pushed me off him, and I saw Jesús' face in the frame. I felt a tear begin and pushed it away quickly. I swung my right fist into his stomach, and he just smiled. That smile made me real mad, and I punched his side, then his face, and then his side again. He doubled over and stepped back down the hall two or three steps. I jump over the old picture and moved toward him and kicked him a couple times in his shins. Luis braced himself against the hallway wall and threw his head at mine. I shook my head, trying to clear it some, and he grabbed me in a bear hug and twirled me around. He threw me down the hall toward the pila. As I staggered back some, he came lunging at me and threw his extra fifty pounds at me. The front of the sink caught us, and my back fell like a teeter-totter. He reached over and pushed me deeper into the dirty water. I wished by now we had been less muddy when playing football. My head was deep in the water, my ears were popping, and my nose was sputtering, as I was trying to breathe.

Hands began pulling me up by my arm. As my head broke the surface of the water, I heard the shrill whistle, people talking over each other, and Luis screaming something about, "Let me go! I'm not done! Let me go!" I stood up with some help from Carlos and Cesar' and shook my long hair till it splashed all those around me. A towel landed on my head, and I rubbed my face so I could see. As I tried to clear my eyes of the scummy water, Mama blew the whistle again and told us all to quiet down and settle into the living room.

She looked at us sternly as she pointed her finger in rapid-fire motion. "Now, boys, what is the fighting about? You two were friends for so long. Can't you try and be friends again?" She looked at Luis and then me, waiting.

~ 7 ~

THE BEGINNING OF THE STORY

"I think I can help with this problem, Maria. Some things have been left unsaid for so long between these boys. Perhaps it's time to bring them out." Luis' mother stepped in the direction of the three of us.

"Isabella, I'm not sure this is the time for you to talk about your family with the problems that it bears. We all sympathize for any situation you have dealt with in dealing with your husband, but I don't think it is appropriate for the party here. You, Rosa, and I can meet together for coffee tomorrow, or I'm sure Father Angelo has some time available in the church." Mama countered with a sympathizing smile.

"Maria, though I'm heartbroken about my husband and his choosing to leave the boys and me alone for so many years, he is not the topic I wish to speak of. This is about my family, but it involves yours just as much. For some reason, you have not chosen to openly deal with it and bring your son Roberto face to face with some of the demons hidden in our closets. If you would rather we not disrupt the party further, then I shall take the boys with you outside, if it is all right with Rosa that we sit on the back porch together." She finished with a smile herself but it still felt tense.

"But what of our boys, and the chance they'll fight more?" Mama asked Señora Isabella and looked around to the other adults.

"Well, I believe they both would like to hear my story as I tell my memories. But perhaps José would like to remember the old days on his porch with us, and he can stop the fighting if necessary." Her smile remained so slightly.

"Señora Isabella, you and I have not spoken in years, but I think it should be fine for us to listen to your telling while I tie each boy to a

43

chair with some rope I have out back. In fact, Roberto has just not long ago heard how his father passed, so maybe you might tell the rest of the story from the somewhere between the beginning and the middle." Tió José attempted to bring some laughter to the scene while giving permission to move the discussion on the porch.

"José and Isabella, I'm not sure this is a good idea at all," Mama protested still and I'm not sure why. Her and Rosa had those open heartfelt talks but now she wanted nothing of it. "It's not in the best interest of all that we dredge up old stories that are better left buried. And what of the food, and mess that must be tended to? We cannot just leave it." Mama pointed toward the sunken buffet tables in the other room.

"Maria, Carlos and Cesar will finish clearing the floor, and José's sister, Anna, she can tend to watching the food tables. It would be good for the hearts of these boys to know what is what, so they can go on with their lives. Let the dead remain, but let us help the living with their lives. I'll bring a pitcher of the Jamika out back for those boys, José will bring the cups, and Maria you will bring a handkerchief to stuff your mouth." Tiá Rosa summed it all for us and we all went to the porch.

It had been years since I had talked to Luis's mother, Isabella. She did not seem that much of a talker then. She was quiet but a hard worker. She was always busy, either taking care of the family by cooking, cleaning, shopping, and doing laundry or doing her side job. Her side work became very popular, and people all around town asked her to create clothing for them or their children. She created unique designs in the clothing and often imprinted the town's emblem imprinted in them. As a boy, Luis and I watched her go by on the bus as we walked to school. She would take armloads of clothing to the market and sell it to people walking by on the streets. She had a friend who shared a booth with her, and customers came to recognize her items when she was able to get to the market. When Eduardo was a baby, she would take him and he would sit propped in the cradle and watch the various shoppers walking by. Eduardo loved watching people, and I think Isabella used him to help sell items since he smiled and laughed with almost anyone who stopped to shake his hand. He picked up on the feelings of people, even as a child. It was incredible how his face would change based on the smiles and laughter or frowns and pouts from people who stopped at their booth. Now that I know something horrible had happened to Eduardo, I wondered how his moods were now when he talked to people in the family or the neighborhood. There was so much hope for him as a baby and now he has little life in his face.

"Roberto, stop looking off into space while you're tying your shoe laces. Sit up and listen, and act like the good boy I raised you to be!" Mama scolded.

"Yes, Mama. I was just daydreaming about things. But I'm not so sure I won't pick Luis up by his feet and toss him across the field if he comes at me again."

"Yeah, well, say something else smart about my brother and your head will be ear deep in the pila sink and . . ." Luis returned my stare from across the room, obviously still angry.

"Shush now, Luis. Stop all that noise about what you're going to do."

Even Señora Isabella was scolding us.

"Mama, I don't want to be here now anyway. I don't know why we came, and we should just go on with our lives, away from these people and their party."

"Luis, you sit there and be quiet. I know you heard much bitterness from your father and me about this story. You really only heard the hurtful parts and not the whole truth. Your father, he did not help much in his sullen anger, and it was probably better for us all that he chose to leave for the capital."

Tiá Rosa interjected, "Here I thought we were going to hear the story of truth, and from down the hall all I hear is more threats. I've got the pitcher of Jamika in my left hand, and it's ready to pour any moment if we have more threats. Then, José can tie you boys up in the road to see who gets hit first. The last time he did so with Cesar and Carlos, the small truck almost won the chicken game, but Cesar rolled them both over in time. José, he tells me he would have waved the truck in time, but I still wonder about it."

"Rosa, take these cups and stop sidetracking Isabella's story with my little prank." Tió José retorted.

"Rosa, is there water too, or must we all drink this cold purple drink that I have never learned to like? Maybe I should go and get coffee for some of us." Mama pleaded and pointed toward the kitchen through the doorway.

"Maria, just sit there and be as good as the boys should." Rosa had the last word on the subject. Luis sat on a stool next to a wooden chair where his mother sat. I sat in the swing next to Mama.

We all listened as Isabella, Luis's mother, began her story. Softly she spoke, and we all got caught up in the history. It was the same story for many around us and not new for them except for Luis and I, who were still trying piece together fragments of a story we had not fully understood. More so me, evidently.

"My husband, sons, and I looked to grow as a family. My husband, Rudolpho, and I agreed that with my sewing talents we could start making more money for the family. Rudolpho worked hard on our small farm, but we still struggled. At first we did well, where we worked together to plant and pick the fruit on our small farm and then sell it on market day. When our crop came in, Rudolpho would ride west out of the mountains with a truckload of others. There, hours away, he would work picking and harvesting larger crops for the owners who needed much help. He'd be gone for days at a time, and I always feared for his life. The rides west were not easy. The trucks were so full one barely had room to sit, and most of the people smelled as if they had not bathed in weeks. The road was terribly rough, with large holes and bumpy uneven spots along the way. The first two years we were married, I went with Rudolpho to make money on the other lands, and it was just unbearable. After hours of riding without rest or a break to eat or relieve ourselves, I could barely keep up my own spit as I tasted and smelled the dust filled rut called a road and the bodies thrown around the back bed. I remember when the truck finally rumbled to a stop, some of us fell off, gagging and stumbling for the closest water. Rudolpho and I had some fun working the fields that others owned, as we laughed and spoke about the future. We planned a family, and dreamed of what we might name our children one day. With the money we made, we saved some to make our home more enjoyable. Rudolpho bought a larger pila for me to wash and cook in and better equipment to cook with. The next year we bought supplies for me to sew with, as I often reminded him of the skill my mother had taught me. Soon after that I was pregnant with Luis." Señora Isabella paused and smiled at her eldest son sitting next to her.

"Well, Mama, I thought the only reason you had to sew was to make clothes for me. I guess not?" Luis wondered aloud.

"No, Luis. The gift of knowing how to sew had been a good gift passed on from the women of my family, and I wished only to get better at the skill at which I'd been trained. Rudolpho soon realized how good I actually was in creating all kinds of clothes and repairing torn items. Word spread around the neighborhood about my sewing, and I had people dropping items off and even requesting certain items for their children. One of my neighbors had a large family, and she had to work to keep her family in clothes. She introduced herself and explained how she sold some of her items at the market in a booth. The booth did not cost much at all to rent, and she was able to pay for it from a percentage of what she made in one day. Her name was Sophie, and she was very nice. She also had great business sense and helped me think about making money for my family."

"Mama, you must mean Aunt Sophie. She comes around all the time and is always telling me to wash and comb my hair back and even change my shirt. If she is not my aunt, why does she nag like one?" Luis inquired.

"It's no wonder she tells you about your hair, Luis." I snapped out before I could think what I was saying. Still confused about of all of this, my bitterness hadn't really been squashed. Pushing my shoe harder in the wooden floor, I couldn't stop. "It's long and stringy like the dog that hangs around my house for scraps. Have you never seen a comb?"

"Shut up, you little wolf. Your hair may be shorter, but it's more mangy than mine. You look like you belong in a pack with the animals

I used to hear late at night." Luis grinned at me, he face looking dev-
ilish to me.

"Enough, you two. Sit and listen to Isabella. Roberto, hold your
tongue or I'll wash it with some of Aunt Rosa's special soap." Mama
scolded me again.

"Sophie is my longtime friend," Isabella continued. "She came
alongside me and told me there were many who wished for space at the
market. Many wandered the streets trying to sell their goods, but she
had a good spot at the corner of the main area. The booth was part of
her family for years, and she was willing to share the space. She explained that she could only be there at the market three days a week
and asked if I wanted to use the space on the two days she did not.
There was no reason to leave the space empty with so many possible
customers there. I told her I could not create enough new clothes to put
out all at once, but she came up with a plan for me. She said I should
place a few samples out and take orders for what people wanted.

"So, after a year of the market business, I created a flow of business. Soon people told their friends and family about the items I made.
Also, word spread about my ability to repair torn and tattered clothes.
It became known what days I would be at the market, and people
would come just to see me. It was really nice to see men requesting
items for their wives, children buying for their parents, and wives for
their families. I loved being in the market, selling and talking to the
crowds. I did not have to yell loudly as some do on market day, since
many came looking for me. I would calmly watch people walk by and
sometimes point to something I had finished making lately. Other
times, when ladies stopped to look at my baby, they looked at the
blanket he was snuggled in. It worked nicely to show other items that
the customer might be interested in. This small business I got involved
in was a real blessing from God."

"Yes, God is good, Isabella."

"Yes, Maria. You're right. I'm grateful for any time God places His
hand in my life. I just wish He had kept on my life a bit more when I
needed it. After three or four years, my business and friendship with
Sophie had really grown. The two days a week I worked at the market

helped our family, and we were able to keep more food on the table, especially as the two boys grew bigger. I would take the bus on Tuesdays and Thursdays to Huehuetenango, where the larger market was located. I suppose I could have stopped in San Juan Ixcoy and worked their market, but Sophie had the booth in the larger, busier market in Huehuetenango. Paco, the bus driver, your father," she nodded in my direction, "was always very nice, and he would pick me up on my corner instead of making me walk all the way to the main stop. I suppose he was a good enough driver, and as best as I would expect, compared to some that race around these mountains. And we all knew *Jesús*, your older brother." Luis's mother smiled at me and looked sadly in my mother's direction. "Such a good boy with the ball but also a boy who took his job seriously with his father. He knew how to make the people welcome on the bus and make them laugh with just a twist of his face. But when it was time to direct and help his father on that bus, it was all about the business.

"The ride to the get to the market sometimes seemed so long. What with the bouncing in the seat on the roads full of holes, vast stretches of the highway, quick swerves around curves, and endless jams in the towns in between, the weekly journey became an adventure in itself. The traffic jams scared me most, when Jesús would calmly wave cars to stop or signal Paco to turn around the bus and then yell a direction. You could see sometimes that Paco got restless waiting for Jesús, and he would calm himself with a twist from his bottle hidden under the seat. Sometimes Jesús jumped forward or backward around the cars, even as they sped around his waving arm. I think he forgot at times that these intersections we sat in were more than just a football field, and full of much more than a guarded opponent. Oftentimes I had to bring Eduardo to the market for there was no one else to watch him. Sometimes Sophie could care for him, but most times she had too much to do to care for a young child. So I brought him with me, and we waited for the one break along the way to eat a bite and rest. Most of the time we would play children's games, and practice talking, or he would sleep in my lap against the windowsill. After a while, there was some regular rhythm to the ride that we could rest. Although when we stopped, I worried about any jerky motions, as sometimes happened when Paco tried to keep pace with directions and motions from Jesús. Paco would sometimes be too quick or slow on the gas or brake, which always brought some loud honking our way. I prayed that they would think of a better way to do these signals."

"I felt much the same way, Isabella. I told Paco he should find another chapino to ride his bus and business. But he spoke much of family business, and how he would have a team of buses for his boys. Now where is the team but laying amid a set of gravestones?" Mama looked out across the backfield as she said the last in almost a whisper.

~ 8 ~

THE STORY CONTINUES

"I know it's tough to think about Maria, but I must go on. This day I speak of, it was seven years ago and it must be laid out for all to hear. We had been driving for a while, and Eduardo was asleep on my lap, lulled by the engine and soft singing of the men at the front of the bus. They always sang the sad slow songs with that deep bass of theirs. The bus slowed to a stop just as another road intersected it. Our road was going to another town along the way to Huehuetenango called San Juan Ixcoy, but we stopped at a small shack where another road met it. This road came up from a town called Soloma, and the bus would stop for some that might walk and wait for a ride to either San Juan Ixcoy or on into Huehuetenango.

"That day we were almost to the intersection where the road from Soloma meets and joins the road traveling to Huehuetenango, and suddenly we noticed a van at the stop with a family there and the van's hood was up. Jesús saw it too from where he stood hanging in the open doorway, and although he already told his father there was no one at the stop, he motioned to him to slow down so that maybe they could help. The van had the parents in the front, and I could see they were yelling with the man's hands speaking for him as some men do. One child was in the back, while the other was wandering about the shack that served as the rest and bus stop. As I was trying to see them on the side of the road, an inflatable ball hit the back of my head on our bus. I turned and realized these two boys had been hitting it back and forth to each other before it had hit me, so I gave them a stern look that mamas give. The younger boy laughed and hit it to his brother. They continued to play, and I was ready to turn and scold them since their father, who was himself trying to see about the van, would not. But then the ball

51

bounced two rows up. I turned around to follow its path and saw a child up there trying to hit it back this way. Instead, he hit the ball forward and it hit Paco on the back of his head. Paco quickly snapped his head to scold the children. He set his bottle down and angrily waved his finger toward the boys with the ball. All of sudden there was a crash, and I was out for a minute." All of us in the room seemed to move silently forward in our seats.

"I shook my head to clear it and saw a complete mess. I heard screaming from all over the bus, but worst of all my Eduardo was silent. I felt him breathing shallowly but steady still. He was still and quiet. I yelled for help, but no one heard me as everyone else was running about scared and restless too. With blood dripping on my legs, and spots of my blood from my head sprinkled on the seat in front of me, I looked out the window on my left and saw a large truck. The truck had been carrying tires that had spilled over the road, and people in the back of the bus were still sitting, rubbing their heads, and shaking them. Other people were walking about, helping those who had fallen over the side of the bed of the truck by wrapping them with pieces of torn clothing. I got up and yelled to those in the street for help with my baby, and a few came over to the back of the bus as I opened the back door with a shove. They looked in at my poor baby and me and just shook their heads. One turned and saw knitted clothes spilling from my bag and asked if they could use some of them to stop some bleeding. I just nodded my head as they took away my week's work.

"What about my child and me? I looked for Paco, the nice driver. I was sure he could help me, and so I got up with Eduardo and walked to the front of the bus. I searched for Paco and found him nowhere. Although Paco had seemed so nice, perhaps he was like so many other bus drivers in these accidents and left his passengers to fend for themselves. I went down the steps outside and was relieved to see Paco right there. He was bent over the van with his arms wrapped around the lower half of Jesús. Jesús had his legs dangling over the van's hood, while his head was buried partially in the windshield. The windshield had not broken open, but it was shattered in a spider-web fashion all around his head. The van had somehow rolled a few feet back, and Paco had to run forward to hold his son. The one child who had run from the van had come back from relieving himself and was whimpering for his mother. The rest of the family lay in the van, and I was not sure if they were alive or not. I walked over to the crying child, patting and stroking his head with my bloody hand. He shrunk away from me, and I yelled for help from the group around the truck. Somebody should have cared less about getting out of San Miguel Acatán and more about helping the rest of us. I hoped that another car would come and we could call the police and an ambulance."

As Isabella told the story, it unfolded into more details like one of the mystery novels I love to read, and they started to make past events clearer. I remembered the times with my brother and father and thought about this accident. I saw why no one wanted to talk about it. Family, friends, and the entire town all thought Jesús was something greater than he probably was. He was a football hero for some, with his passion for life that all could see. It hurt to hear Isabella speak of the small things about my father and brother, for there were things about them I wanted to be like. Never did they give a second thought in helping others, making time to give kind words in small moments, and so the pain in the loss of family were all part of who they were. Still, Isabella spoke the story as if it were just yesterday, and we all just sat and listened.

"Isabella, here take a breath for a moment. Drink some Jamaica from the pitcher José brought us. This is not easy, and it hard for us too, as we have never heard it from one who was there." Tiá Rosa interrupted her with a sniffle and dabbed her eye with a napkin.

"Rosa is right, much of what we know is only bits and pieces. My husband, Paco, was well known on his route, but still it was not a well-kept schedule. So, it took a long time to hear of the accident." Mama said forcefully but ever so softly. She lifted her cup and sipped longer than usual for her. Señora Isabella began again and my eyes turned to her.

"Finally, after an hour of waiting and wondering what was to happen, the police came with an ambulance not far behind. Almost all of those on the bus and the back of the truck had left and started down the highway toward San Juan Ixcoy, while those who had come from Soloma were walking toward San Miguel Acatán. I could not see them in either direction, so I was not sure if some had been picked up by a passing car or were still walking. For them it was just another delay in their day and on they should go. It seemed most felt they had done what little they would do for us lagging or left behind, and they had to continue with their plans for the day.

"The police officer walked my way, and I asked him about the van, and what had caused the accident. He explained that the van had been in neutral and rolled forward. Paco, or Jesús, who was just stepping out to check out the van, must not have realized the van was rolling forward until Paco swerved the bus left to avoid it. Just as it swerved, a truck was coming from the opposite direction and collided into the back right side of the van while the bus hit the front left side. Jesús was the caught in the middle of the collision, as he was the one who insisted we stop to check on the family and their van. The policeman asked me if I knew what happened, and I asked why he did not care more about my baby and less about who was at fault. He just mumbled an apology and waved me over to the waiting ambulance parked beside the empty shack.

As I walked over to the back of the ambulance, the truck driver was stepping away with his bandaged arm and head. He was rambling on about more help with his auto shop. I asked him what was the matter, and he explained his cousin was in the passenger seat and had died when they had hit the van. He had just given a ride to the people in the back of the truck while transporting tires and parts, and though some were hurt, they had all left together. But not so with his cousin, whose head had shattered the glass of the windshield and then hung back limply into the seat. As one man looked at Eduardo, and the other bandaged my head, I wondered why the driver cared more for finding a new helper and the cost of the windshield, and less about his cousin. His cousin was gone now, away from this world. I turned to look at Eduardo, and cried again as I asked the Holy Father if my baby would make it past today."

"Thank God that Eduardo is alive today in this house," Mama interrupted with a smile.

"Yes, he is Maria, and I have much to be thankful for in that. But in that moment, I did not know at all what was to be. The man who was trying to give medical attention to him said he was breathing but could not tell about his other injuries. The bruises were obvious, but the rest we could not see or understand. As I asked him why my baby was not crying, I heard the policeman yell for some help, and the one who was working on my arm turned and ran over to the front of the van. It took the two of them to pull Paco from his son, as he was clinging to him. They finally just swung Paco off Jesús and set him against the side front wheel of the bus. The other man gave me back my Eduardo and ran over to see about Jesús' head.

"First they checked for a pulse, and I could not believe they said there was a slight one. I tried to look away but could not. It was Jesús they were trying to work on, and he had been so graceful in directing traffic just this morning when we left San Miguel Acatán. He had shown the same grace as when he scored at the game I had taken Luis to see the previous year at the center of the city. The three of them worked to get Jesús loose of the bloody glass from the driver's side windshield and finally pulled him away with pieces still stuck in the side of his head by his ears and eyes. I could see as they set him on the ground carefully that he was breathing with slight movements. His ribs seemed caved in and crushed from where he hit the hood hard when he was thrown from the bus.

"One of the men ran back to the ambulance and asked me to move aside as he pulled out the cart. They loaded Jesús on the cart and moved us and Jesús into the back. All the way to San Juan Ixcoy, I thought and prayed that both these lives would be more than still hearts tomorrow, especially when I saw that Eduardo did not move at all, and Jesús eyes just blinked randomly. Then he would stare at me, and I could do nothing but cry more and hold his hand."

"Señora Isabella, I do not like to interrupt. But what of my papa, Paco? He did not ride with you. What happened to him? And the family that was in the van, what about them?" She had said so much and I didn't know where to begin with my questions. So many thoughts had rushed my mind while she spoke, but I wanted to be polite. Now I couldn't hold back my questions anymore. Why hadn't Tió José told me more, or even Mama given me some idea of this tragedy?

"Well, the family . . . all but the boy who was wandering lost their lives. The crying boy was taken to the police car and left to be in his own sorrow. Your father, he did not ride with us in the ambulance. The police did not let him. They found his bottle rolled between the gas pedal and brake, and they wanted to question him more. I had asked the driver the same question, and he joked with the other worker that some drunks are hard to sober up. I snapped at them and told them he was not drunk, and this whole tragic accident was not his fault. But they nodded their heads silently and kept driving."

"Isabella, that seemed to be a very tough day for you and your family," Rosa remarked with a voice seeping with sympathy.

"Yes, Rosa. It was very rough for me. It was painful for me to see and more painful to deal with on the inside. The fear of the unknown as I rode into the city to the hospital had me very worried. Once we reached the clinic, the doctor said my baby was in a type of catatonic state, and they were concerned not only that he was not responding but also about any possible internal injuries. The doctor also worked on Jesús for hours it seemed, but he had internal bleeding that they could not deal with very well. He died after a few hours at the clinic.

"They transported Eduardo to the larger hospital in Huehuetanango, where he went through much treatment to find out he had received brain damage. He would never be the same boy again. He soon regained most of consciousness, but he lost much of his mobility. It was challenging to tell my family the details of my child's disability. Once we were able to come home, Rudolpho blamed it all on Paco. He was very bitter about the accident, and the loss of constant joy in his youngest son. At mealtimes he would often complain and threaten what he should do to Paco. We worked as a family to care for the needs of Eduardo as he grew older, but it was not easy. Luis often times helped in feeding, bathing, and caring for his brother. But young Luis also picked up on the bitterness from his father and not long after ended his friendship with Roberto. Our family plodded on and did the best we could with what God had allowed to happen."

"But, you still can thank the Holy Father that your family remains whole. You had each other to depend on." Tiá Rosa commented with some compassion while Mama remained silent. I studied her face and it seemed almost stoic.

"You are right," Señora Isabella hesitated, "to a point, Rosa. After a few years of the bitterness eating away at him and the stressful day-to-day care for Eduardo, Rudolpho could not take it any longer. He left us without warning or good-bye. I heard from his cousin, who said he lives in Guatemala City. There he works two jobs and tries not to think of us. He did write a letter saying once he had saved enough money that he would bring us some for the family. He promised the money for ease in Eduardo's care and maybe even a new home. The money never came in the mail or in person, and what was left of our family had to make decisions. We moved into a smaller home that my friend Sophie rented out to me, and I worked hard from home and still, at times, at the market when I could find care for Eduardo."

"I always thought Paco was at fault," Mama angrily began. "The police said it was an accident, but everyone from his route said he was to blame, that he was not alert because of his drinking on the road and not at home as most men do. I have hated him since then for his poor choices, and now this? How could you be so cruel to me and not tell me all of these details that exonerate my husband? Didn't you think our family was in pain too? Have you no heart, Isabella?"

"I'm sorry, Maria. I never thought about your family and its pain. The reality is that I was very bitter and had not come to see it in myself. I blamed my husband and then Luis for their bitterness and hatred for Paco. But I never admitted what I have felt until now."

"Now, now? Your tears have always known what is real, but my tears have been mixed with undeserved bitterness for a man who was killing himself with the bottle. And I felt no remorse for his dying until now. I can not believe this is happening now. To think I thought you were a friend of mine, especially with what our boys shared. You are no friend to hide the truth so easily from me!"

"Maria! Stop, for we are all very emotional right now. Curb your tongue and think of the stress that Isabella has been under all these years." Tiá Rosa stood up and put her hand gently on Mama's shoulder. "Think about it before you want to send her away in empty threats."

"Please, Mama. They deserve the forgiveness of God. It hurts me too, and I now understand the looks people gave me as they saw me walk and the whispers about my papa. Mama, Isabella has helped us see Papa as a man who loved and maybe drank some, but that tragic day was not his fault." I stood up and hugged Mama's shoulders.

"Isabella, why have you held this in your heart so long? It would have been so helpful to Maria if you would have told this story sooner," Tiá Rosa wondered as she wiped a tear with her other hand.

Señora Isabella bowed her head and shook her head. "Rosa, I do not know. What I know, though, is that I was really hurt and angry for what had happened to my son. I had to blame Paco, for there had to be a reason, if only the carelessness of a drunken driver. Now I think back and remember the tossing of a toy ball making the difference in a single moment for so many lives." She looked up and glanced at Luis and then me.

"So, my young Chapines who began a great friendship in your childhood. Your quarrel started with events you could not control, and people around you doomed it. But now you should think about bringing your friendship back to life. True friends are always in high demand, and you two had such a true bond." She smiled at both of us.

"I couldn't agree more, Isabella. They seemed good for each other, and Roberto does miss Luis so much. Even though he thinks of himself as quite the thinker, he still misses his friends." Mama said with a large smile herself.

"Mama, it's true that Luis and I were great friends. I'm not sure where we go from here. I've always been in the dark about this," I said and looked around for some reassuring.

"Well, Roberto, I'm still hungry." Luis stood up and laughed deeply. "You can start by getting us new plates since you did knock over all the food. We can only pray that José's boys have not eaten all of the favorites and left none for us to eat. This emotional female talking has left me wanting to be manly, and eating some meat and beef soup can only make me feel better. How about I follow you in to the kitchen and dining room and make sure you do not trip into the pila water?"

The rest of the day all the families at Rosa's house ate more, laughed more, sang some, and beat the piñata more than what had been done in a long time. It seemed to me two hours of healing had happened, and we did not need to speak of it any more that day. After the singing and laughter had died down, the boys and men all ended up again playing soccer. We played tough, pushing, shoving, kicking, and running with all the energy we had left. We cheered everyone on with the good plays, and though it was a passionate game, we did not hold any grudges. This was the best part of the day, and I felt it in my bones. Luis was on the other team, and I guarded him heavy, grunting and stealing from him. But still we did laugh with each other, so intense was the competition among us.

After the sun went down two hours later, we tired of the game and sat down around the back porch on the steps and worn out grass. There Tió José told us stories of his cousins and their times in Mexico and America. We had heard some of these stories, but now he told them in more detail as we were older and understood more of the danger. He had family that had hid in trucks, trains, and towns throughout Mexico. They somehow made it to America, and for years they sent money back to Guatemala. Some were deported home, and yet they found ways to return to America. He said the money they sent helped his aunt and uncle buy a bigger home, and extras for it. Soon, the family came to count on the money that was sent, and when they were deported back to Guatemala, the family quickly found money to send them back to America somehow.

I left Tiá Rosa's house that night wondering about the money I could earn one day. I knew I wanted to be better educated and someday be someone people would look up to. Also, I could be someone who could help with my mother's home and provide less worry for her and Tina. I felt that America, the land for opportunity, might give me the chance to be that man.

~ 9 ~

SAN MIGUEL ACATÁN, GUATEMALA, AUGUST 1998

Luis and I spent our last year in school building an even stronger friendship. We both felt the strength in bonding, given that our fathers were both gone. We realized that year how the American dream could one day be ours. Somehow we would both see it become reality. There were still bridges for us to cross in order to make that dream.

I had grown up in high school as one of the top in my class. Mama was very proud and pointed to all who would listen. She planned my college time for me and initially I had agreed with her. But when Tió José had told Luis and I story after story of his cousins in America and how their influence had drastically changed the lifestyle of his family, I wondered about the plans Mama had for me. Tió José's cousins had even helped set up his shop. Full of faraway dreams, I went away for higher education. But after a year of mediocre grades, I knew it was not for me. I could not fully focus when the seeds had been planted for my future two years ago. I came home in the summer with news for my family and Luis. Now sitting at the dining room table, I had to couch my word carefully.

"Roberto tell us about life at San Carlos, the university you attended. We only heard some stories from there, and now you are to stay for a while, and we should get to hear all about it." Although my sister had gotten older, she was still filled with questions.

"Christina, my little Quetzel, just like our national bird, so beautiful and bright for all to see. But there is more to life than stories and gossip; we must share in what we can learn in and around us, my little Tina." I waved my arms around the room, pointing to world outside.

"Roberto, you act like a teacher, and I just wanted to hear about your life. You can share that with us, you know." She sighed with frustration in her voice.

"Well, Christina, Roberto does have a point in that life is more than a series of stories and little pieces of gossip that we should hang on. I know that Father Angelo just two weeks ago mentioned that in his service, and I looked at Rosa and nodded. She always wanted to get me in trouble during Mass when we were girls, and now I see her tempting again sometimes. The Holy Father have mercy on her and then me, from this sin of gossip." Not more of this sharing and bonding with my mother and Tiá Rosa. Must I hear how they are learning and growing each time they spend time together.

"Mama, I did not want you to start up now. I just want to enjoy this dinner you have made," I mumbled as I scooped up beans with a wedge of tortilla.

"Yes, eat up. But know that your sister and I have waited. We have waited a long time to hear about school and what things you are learning while away from us." Mama started to cut a cake she had made just for my return. "So, do not brush this off so easily. We are your family, not some girls from school that you can walk away from. These weekends that you came home on the bus, you barely spent any time with us. Maybe one meal time, and the rest of the time you spent with Luis." She pushed the cake in my direction with a smile, though it seemed forced.

"You were the one who wished we were friends again. So why is it you complain now? I do not understand women. Girls, I could deal with not knowing, but my own mother. I would hope to understand her better." I slid my fork under a piece of cake and pulled it onto my plate. I smiled with anticipation as I took my first bite.

"Stop this conversation with yourself, as if I am not here. I am here and not happy to hear you speak this way. At home, you act as if you are a great intellectual, but I hear you talk with Luis like a couple of street boys. It is you who are hard to understand for I wanted more for you. Luis was and is not so bad, except for that temper of his, but you are meant for greater things and people. Move onto better friends and bring home some of the people with whom you attend classes. Rosa and I were speaking the other day of this, and we are sure that there must be smart people with whom you socialize. There may be even a few girls at this school who may appreciate your thinking."

"Mama, I don't know want to say to you. I wanted to become more educated so I could learn more, not to become better than other people. I need to go for a walk! I'm sorry, I'll see you later." I took one last bite of the cake, frowned at both Tina and Mama, and backed up my chair loudly. Standing, I quickly walked out the front door.

I can't believe my mother and her ways. I don't understand at all what she is thinking. I let the door slam on my way, and it has some effect for me. A Vespa drives by, and I wish I could be on that scooter. Fast and free from being someone I'm not. Here comes the sun as it begins to set over the highest part of the San Miguel, and my heart is happy in its sight. I begin to walk, because walking does make feel better. But I can't help but wonder what is beyond San Miguel. If only I had a ball to dribble while I was walking.

"Roberto, do not leave our home now! Stay here, finish your meal, and talk with us . . . me. Talk with me!!" I heard Mama yell out the doorway and I hunched my shoulders forward more into the rays of the sun. The door banged shut when she let it go, and I could almost feel her glaring after me.

~ 10 ~

ON THE BACK PORCH

Tió José sat in his chair on the back porch drinking some Jamaica and pretended to read yesterday's paper while watching us play football. Carlos and Cesar were playing against Luis and me. There was not a lot of skill in our play, but there was a lot of love for the game among us. I don't know how Carlos and Cesar could run so long, when I know that they were always eating. They must have practiced a lot out here to keep up the pace. I ran quite a bit, and so my stamina was all right. Still, I was having trouble keeping up with them. Luis was a natural athlete and had no problems at all with endurance. I thought that with my brother being a star player, it would have been passed on to me. Instead he left me with the love of the game but only little natural skill. The rest I should have worked hard to improve on, but sometimes I just didn't have the time.

With school out, I've been able to play almost every day here at Tió José's house. I caught up with them some on the weekends that I came home but nothing like what we have done lately. After José closes the shop, we meet behind their house and start to dribble until any and all who want to play show up. Tió José plays for a while, until he snorts and runs out of breath, and then he heads for the house. Today, it took him just ten minutes, and now look at him with the paper. He looked as if he is really reading it, but he actually had not stopped watching us.

"Hey, you boys, enough for an hour of football. Come to the porch and drink some Jamaica with me. It's my treat for a good game. Not a lot of good playing but a good game."

"Tió José, you talk as if you're a professional. You're out of the game with us in no time at all. Who makes you the referee and judge?"

"Look, Roberto, I'm old and can barely walk now. If you keep up with these questions, I'll look for my cane and use it on you. Why, I can be judge and referee! I was in many games when I was young, although not like your brother. And I'm really good at correcting the referee on television."

"Papa, I think I saw a cane we can use for you. The storm blew a few branches down, and I'll grab one."

"Cesar, you think it's funny to make fun of your father. How about I have Luis hold you over the pila and give you a quick shampoo? If I give him extra days at the shop working on cars, he may do it with a smile."

"Señor José, I'd have no problem at all drowning your son for extra hours, as long you don't ask me to wet Carlos. He'd probably pull me in with him, and then we'd both break the whole water system. You all smell enough when you sweat, and I couldn't stand another day's worth of it from dirty laundry."

"Carlos, how is it you have found a bag of chips to eat with sweat still coming off your head and hands?"

"Papa, this is the last bag. Just because I like to eat snacks I don't understand why people must bring up my weight. You know Mama says I'm just a bit bigger than her father, and he was known to eat much at meals."

"Carlos, don't be so defensive. You are big and strong like a bull. But snacks are to be eaten to hold you over till dinner and not right after football. When I was young, there were no stores just down the street to buy chips. You should really appreciate them."

"I know I do, Carlos. My mother and Christina make tortillas all of the time for us to eat, and I get tired of them as my snack." I looked at the almost empty bag in his hand. Then I looked out across the field, thinking about America. I turned back to José.

"Tió José, tell us more of your cousins in Mexico and in America. Luis and I have talked about them and are curious about what they do."

"Roberto, I'm thinking I shouldn't have begun to tell you of my side of the family. I know your mother already does not approve of them, for some of them live outside of what is thought to be the law. Although all of these men have good hearts, and the money they make in Mexico, and more so in America, is worth so much more here at home. They often think of the families they have left behind and miss them dearly. All of them send money back to us here, where we who are left make good use of it. They especially take care of their parents and siblings with less income. Why, even my auto shop is half owned by one of my first cousins. Without him I would not have been able to open, and I would not have made the improvements that I have done. I could not employ my sons now, nor give Luis work. In my family we appreciate what these men have done and the sacrifice they made in leaving to create more money for us who are left behind. But these guys are not angels or cowboys to be admired, and I don't think we should speak of them anymore."

"Tió José, in school we have discussed the economic problems that we face in Guatemala. I have thought much of this and even debated the issues with some of my fellow students. As far as knowing the grey area these people walk in when they are in Mexico and America, I know it is wrong. They are usually there illegally, and my mother raised me to know all too well the difference between right and wrong. But even though being there illegally is legally wrong, I'm not sure it is ethically wrong. I've thought of sin that Father Angelo has spoken of, and God from above condemns it. Some sins are very easy to see, especially when they are talked about in the Ten Commandments. Some sin is not easy to confess to Father Angelo when I seem to fall into it so well. But I'm stuck on this other issue in how God sees people who feel the only way to survive is to do these illegal things. Is it so much sinning when there's no other way to feed one's family or even just live a bit better than one is doing? How is it so wrong to want life to be easier for one's self and family? When I studied about America and how it first began, they spoke often of this certain spirit that they carried among themselves."

Cesar rolled his eyes, tipped his head back and said, "Papa, how is it we get lessons in our own local philosophy and American history? I thought we were going to hear more endless lies of how you used to run around when you were with your cousins. I'm not used to thinking this hard, and I know Carlos is still thinking of how to get away to buy more chips without anyone noticing." Cesar looked as bored as he sounded, and though I felt bad, I wondered why he didn't challenge himself to think more.

"Cesar, it's good to think outside of natural moves on the football field and even out from under the hood of a car. It's okay to let Roberto push you to think, for I would like you boys to question what you think about such issues."

"I think about deep things sometimes. I just don't bring them up," Cesar said defensively.

Tió José, continued, "Well, what about questions like who is God? Is there a Catholic God or many gods as our native Mayan religion would have us believe? What is our purpose here, and why is living so tough? What do we do with love among the women, love for football with friends, and even more, the love we have for our family? In fact, the love of family is something all people share. But we in Central America carry the love and responsibility of family like a heavy weight on our shoulders in life."

He stopped to look from his sons to me, a somber look on his face. "What is right and wrong in our minds compared to what others think? It is difficult to think of these things, and I have hardly any answers. But I think it is important when we at least think on them."

Carlos added, "I know that if we were a family with more money, it would mean a lot more to me. I hear about how well families in America eat, and some even eat three full meals a day. That, Papa, would be real living." Carlos shook his empty bag of chips.

"Luis, you are real quiet over there. What do you think about things like this? Or would you rather not think about them?"

"No, Señor José. I've thought about this often. It makes me angry that my father has left my family with little means to care for ourselves. We work hard as a family just to survive, and I wish mother had it easier. I don't understand why we're not born in better places so that we can be happier. Life would be so much better, and I'd probably have my father with us still. I appreciate the help with the job you've given me, but I'm not so sure it's enough for me. This American spirit we learned of in school years ago, I think Roberto and I both have it."

I had to agree with Luis. "Yes, it's a sense of wanting more. I'm sure some of it's in wanting to be more like the explorers of old, with a new trail to see around every corner. What is over that next mountain and across the next river, to speak of some American images? I don't think it wrong to think this way, especially when I want more for my sister and mother. The people I've debated with speak of loyalty to our country and promoting our people within. This is more important for some of our people, especially those who are born without a Spanish heritage. They have native Indian heritage, which I love and appreciate, but our society still looks down on our people. I know the friends I hang with at college and my mother would like me to take this road. The road of native heritage here is our country. We can all help make local and even national cultural, social, and perhaps political change.

"At the college we talked often about being part of the change Guatemala needs at the local and national levels. But, down deep inside, even though I'm known for passion in writing and sometimes speaking at school, I'm not so sure about such ideals as that. I spent some time writing a few articles for the school newspaper and liked it some. But it's not really for me; I want to be more focused in my learning and I need to move about. So, if you could share about your side of the family, Luis and I would not tire of your stories."

"Well," responded Tió José, "Roberto, Carlos, and Cesar will have to sit through more then. I have family spread all over the border of Mexico and into America. They have made their way in the last ten years or more. Some of Paco's family, Felipe, he wanted to go to America by working first in Mexico. Yet his grandson died brutally at the hands of a gunman. So not all of the dreamers for America have a happy ending. But I will speak of those who claim the American dream and are easily sending much money back home here to Guatemala. So, let me tell you . . ."

We sat for a hour or more, listening about these men in José's family. I did not idolize them. I knew they were men making choices, and many were the wrong choices. But they were choices they made on their own to better their lives and those of their families. I thought this could be something for me, and my brother of old, Luis.

67

~ 11 ~

THE ROAD HOME FROM SAN MIGUEL

"**R**oberto, I'm not sure about this. Your cooking for your family, and especially your mother, I'm pretty sure is not going to go well for you, my friend. Tina, she loves everything about you, so you could cook burnt tortillas and she'd eat them. But your mother, I'm sure she'd be wondering why you even want to cook for her when she wants to always do so for you. And why is it I have more food in my arms, but you are able to carry one armload and still dribble the ball?"

"Luis, you should not worry. They'll like my food for I have practiced following a recipe at school. I made a few meals for my friends, but they were not critics as I know Mama can be. I know also she might think it beneath me, but I love to be creative in the kitchen. It becomes another way to free my mind, almost like when I am dribbling the ball. You only wish you could be as skilled as I am!"

"Yeah, well, tomorrow we will see when we split the teams, and I play with Cesar on my team." He moved to steal the ball, and I slipped from him easily. " You'll lose terribly and then be forced to take back these bragging words."

"Let tomorrow come: I need to think about what I must chop first, cook, and simmer on our fire. They will both be so pleased with the food that they will be speechless when I tell them our plan."

"Roberto, they will be speechless, not because of your food. It will be you leaving school. It will disappoint them to see the golden one let them down with your own ideas." My pride in the menu a little deflated, I wondered if Luis was right.

"Well, what about *your* mother, Luis? Does she mind the idea of us packing and moving to Mexico in order to get to America?"

"No, she doesn't mind. Or she won't mind when she reads the note

I leave her," he said, strumming his air guitar absently. His eyes seemed to frown as he whispered, "I will not face her tone or look in her eyes, but I will wonder about the look when she sees the money I leave her. I've saved up money to make it easier while I am gone."

"What about money that Tió José said people use when traveling through Mexico for food and payment to the right people—the coyotes who help us cross the river and the guys on the train to slow down for us," I asked him in frustration. "All of this will cost money along the way, and we must be ready for them." I felt the worry creep from my stomach to the back of my throat.

"I have some money set aside for that also. José has been able to pay me well for helping around the shop in the last year. Roberto, what about money for you? Do you have any at all, or are we going to rely on my cash alone?"

"No, I saved some at school from little jobs I did. But Tió José has told me there might be a way to ease some of the worry."

"Well, what is this way of his?" Luis stopped suddenly and looked at me curiously.

"He said if we're actually thinking of this plan, he might be able to help. One of his cousins in Mexico can set us up with a route and contacts along the way. Once we reach the border city in Mexico, he will plan a route to America with us." The fear subsided as I realized the help we'd get. This could be done.

"We're almost to your house, and how will you cook in front of your mother? If it is to be a surprise, how will you work it out?"

"I have thought about it. Tina is walking with my mother to get her out and about for girl time. I threw out hints for her, and she picked up on them for me. I have a plan. Now if the food comes out well, then I can break the news to them about our plan." Luis held the door for me as I nodded a good-bye. I walked in and began to set about preparing my meal. It took me less time than I had planned for.

I heard the slight knock as the door swung shut and began to hear voices. I was glad that the food was ready, and I already had some portions on the plates. I didn't dare try to make tortillas to match the ones mama makes, so I bought those and warmed them up. I made a nice chicken stew that seemed to have a good flavor broth. One of my roommates at the university helped me practice this recipe from his family, and it looks good now. I hope it will meet Mama's standards.

"Tina, I smell something from our house. Did I leave the oven on from earlier today? I pray that I didn't!" Mama said as she was walking up to the house

"Mama, don't worry. You had everything put away as you always do. I think you'll be surprised when we walk in."

"Roberto, is that you walking about my kitchen as if you are a king in his castle?" Mama said when she entered the house. "And is that my apron you have on? You don't look the man that you should be with that thing on." She glared at the stained apron. "Your papa is going to roll over and spin in his grave. Just wait until I see him next, he will not forgive me for this, especially with his remaining son."

"Mama, would you please relax? I've made you and Tina dinner this evening, and I want you to try and enjoy it. Let go of the fact that I cooked, for you know that for centuries men have been great chefs." I had already pulled Tina's chair out and hurried to pull Mama's chair too. "Try to sit back in your chair, relax, and taste it."

"All right, Roberto. If you insist on this game of yours, your sister and I will sit and taste this meal of yours. I still do not understand the reason you would have for doing this."

Tina exclaimed, "Oh . . . um . . . it just smells so good, 'Berto. We could smell it as we walked up to the house. It was like following a trail you left, except it was in the air for our noses to catch up to."

"Well, Tina. I hope the mouth likes it as much as the nose. Mama, I'll explain why you get a meal made by me. But for now, just eat. Taste and try to enjoy." I looked at them and then their plates expectantly.

"Yes, Roberto, we will eat it and certainly enjoy the food you have made. But first a prayer to the Holy Father." Mama looked at Tina and bowed her head. "For we should not forget whom it was that really provided it for us."

As they sat and began to eat, I could see that I'd picked a recipe that met their standards. Of course, Mama's standards were what I was most worried about, since it usually did not take much to please Tina. But, it seemed as they ate, and started to point some more questions about this past year's school time at me, that they really liked the food. By the time I answered more of the questions and they had finished the stew, I began to smile as they each broke a tortilla up and soaked up the last of the broth on their plates. Now for the hard part. I thought about which way to start the subject, since I had argued in my mind different words to say to them.

"Well, you two, I'm glad you liked the meal that I've made for you. Now that your stomachs are full with what I've set before you, I need to tell you something that's important to me. I need you to understand—"

"Understand? Understand? I understand now!" Mama interrupted with fire in her eyes and anger swelling up in her voice. "This whole meal was a plan on your part, a game on your part to reel me in like a fish in the river. This is why your sister insisted on walking with her mother with whom she rarely wants to spend time walking with. So you two have been talking behind my back and probably now have some devious plan. What is it you two could want?" She looked across the table to Tina and then up at me with a barely a breath taken. "What means now will you try to break a mother's heart? Your cousin from the capital has written you and now wants to take Christina away? Or you want to join a football team and become a star like your late brother? What nonsense have you two cooked up for a mother to chew on and then cry tears as she digests it?"

"Mama, please. You must listen and not go on so." I begged of her.

"Enough. I'll sit still and listen as you did for me years ago. Just don't begin your story then, since I have work to do before bed time."

"Yes, Mama. I've told you and Tina stories of my life at university, while attending school. I love to learn much and soak up new information like a sponge. But it's not business management I want to do with my life. No, I do not want to wear a business suit, but it is a chef's coat I want to wear instead. I want to be a chef. I've heard much about this, and I have dreams of running my own kitchen. Also, I see how hard you've worked for us children, and I wish to help. Luis and I have talked and found a way we could make life easier for both our families."

"I should have known this discussion was somehow attached to Luis. He's a nice boy, but you two should have gone your separate ways and—"

"Mama, please. You said you would sit still and listen. Now I must finish my thoughts. For me to help you as I want to, and do these other things with my life, I'm traveling with Luis to America. There we will travel, and I'll find a job and become a great chef one day. I'll learn many styles and types of cooking, for America is what some call a 'melting pot' of people. From this I think I'll see many new things and not just this world we live in. Also, the money in America is very good, and I can send some of the money I make to you and Tina so you two can have a better life also. This way—"

"NO!" Mama interrupted. "Roberto, you'll not leave me. I can not stand the thought of losing another man in my family. It's not right, and God has allowed enough bad in my life. You could die just as our Marco, my younger cousin, did years ago. I can see it happening on the border or in Mexico. So, no! I forbid it!"

"Mama, you must not say this. I have already planned it. I'm not returning to the university, and my spot to attend there is already taken by another applicant. This is what I am going to do." I pulled the chair I was leaning on back and pushed it down for emphasis. I had thought she might be quiet, but instead another outburst came.

"Enough! We will not speak any more of this! Christina, off you go to bed. Roberto, I'm going to bed also. You, you do as wish! You should go on and act as if you do not have a mother who loves you here in her home. Do not touch those dishes or another thing in my kitchen or pila. You, my son, have done enough damage in this house tonight, and I do not wish to have other things broken. Our hearts are in pain, and it's enough for one night."

I sulked as I wearily walked to my room. My heart was heavy. I could still hear her mumbling as she got ready to go to bed. I fell down on my bed with my clothes on and wondered if I should have done anything differently. I flipped over and buried my head in the pillow.

There was not a better way to prepare her for my plan to leave as there were not any good ways to say good-bye. Even the thought of it hurt me, and Mama bears the pain of loss in her other two men. I felt for her, but still I had to go. Tió José will plan the details for us. There is little chance we will lose our lives as Marco did years ago. As I drifted off to sleep, I began to dream of life in America. What will it be like there?

~ 12 ~

ROBERTO'S HOME

I woke to the smell of eggs cooking and Mama humming a tune of hers. I cannot believe that she would be in a pleasant mood after last night's emotional stress. And there I was sensing fresh eggs as if it were a holiday here in our town. Maybe this was her way to butter me up and ready me for the blow from her and Tiá Rosa to change my mind. I rolled out of bed and stumbled to the kitchen. Morning time in the bathroom could wait, for now I had to taste some of this breakfast while the moment lasted. Putting the smell together with the taste would be the beginning of a great day.

"Oh, Roberto, here you are. I didn't mean to wake you too early. Was it my noise that got you up?"

"No, Mama. I had to get up after my nose told me that something was different."

"Well, Roberto. I haven't cooked you a real breakfast since you left for school. Really, I planned this breakfast for you and thought I should do it today."

"Why, Mama? I hope it is not to change my mind from leaving. I have already decided and nothing will change it. I have a sense that perhaps you are planning to gang up on me with Tiá Rosa to convince me not to leave."

"No, my son. You're a young man now. I thought hard and prayed so long last night and actually did not sleep very much. The holy Virgin Mary spoke to me in a dream during the sleep I did get. In the dream, she walked with me down the street between Rosa's home and ours. She told me to trust in God, and that she would continue to intervene on our families' behalf. I told her of my fears of losing you as I had lost your father and brother. She explained that my faith was real enough, but I had to trust even more in the plan that was in place for your life. You were meant for great things, and I was not to hold you back." Her eyes and smile seemed to glow with love.

"Mama, I'm not so sure about how great things in my life will be," I hesitantly said. "I just know I want to reach for more and go places where I can be able to try to make things really happen for me." My voice was feeling stronger. "To do this, I think it's best for me to make my way to America. It was the place where dreams were meant to come true years ago, and now some people are still seeing some of their dreams fulfilled there. I want you to not only have faith in how God works in humans' lives but also some faith in what I can do with my life. I have this need to go out and do more."

"Roberto, I think I am beginning to understand. Some of this same feeling was in your father, and you're so much like him. I think that's why he loved to drive that bus of his. Even though the locals mocked him and his bus, calling it a "killer tomato" in one breath and "Jesus Bus" in the other, he never tired of life on the road. He was never content staying at home with me but instead was up early with coffee in his hand ready to go. The coffee in one hand, and waving crazily with the other hand, with that silly kiss he left early in the mornings before the sun even came up. I wished he had a different job. I stood in the doorway, wondering if he wanted to come home as eagerly as he left. Dios mio, I loved your father and miss him so much still. Yes, you're more than a bit like him." She dabbed the corner of her eye.

"Mama, I don't know what to say, but I love you." Suddenly I noticed an envelope sticking out. "What is this under my plate? A bag of money? Mama, what is this about?"

"Roberto, this is money I've set aside for you. I was planning to give it to for school. Instead, you should now take it with you."

"Mama, do not give this up. I will be fine with the money I have saved. I cannot take this." I looked up at her, holding the money. She pushed my arm down.

"Shush now, 'Berto! It's decided. You will be successful, and then you can repay my love and loan by sending some of these things you dream of to me and little Tina."

~ 13 ~
TIÓ JOSÉ AND TIÁ ROSA'S HOME

I was still unsure about Mama's gift and response. I didn't know how to feel about her comments. There was so much to think about as we planned this move. We needed to have faith in Tió José's resources; I hoped it all would work out. I walked the remaining steps to the back porch, tapped on it, and then sat down on one of the chairs. Luis had already arrived and sat strumming his guitar lightly across from me. Tió José came out smiling and handed Luis and I both a cup of ice-cold water. He waited for one of us to begin.

"Tió José, are you sure about all these details? You're able to set it all up with your cousin? Can Luis and I trust him with all our lives and money? Is the money we've saved even enough for what we wish to do?"

"Wait, wait, Roberto! You rush with the questions. I know you are happy to finally be decided on your plans, but you must leave time for details. You'll soon know all that there is to be ready for this great trip. Look at Luis quietly strumming. There's not a bit of worry on his face, and yet your eyes look as if they are crossed."

"I'm sorry, Tió José, but I'm one who likes to have everything ready. I don't want to worry about any problems that may come up. I want to be completely prepared for whatever comes in our path." I looked at my shoes—one lace was loose, and I retied it.

"Yes, yes. I've known this about you since you were a child. But, my friend, it's not that easy. Things will not be easy on this trip you are planning. It's full of potential danger, and sometimes anything can happen. You must be ready for anything that can happen. Your Tiá Rosa, she and I have talked much about this. We went together for a long drive to Chichicastenango, the big city with the largest market in the country. She had wanted to shop some and then move on to our main reason for traveling there. We went to Iglesia de Santo Tomas, the chapel some say is the heart and soul of Chichicastenagno—you know the one, where 450 years ago the Dominican priest built it right over holy ground of the 'old ones'? The Mayan worship site houses the chapel there that has both traditional Mayan ceremonies and the Catholic Mass. Rosa met with the priest there and made confession with him and then prayed for you. I don't know why Father Angelo is not enough; she has prayed with him so many times. I guess a big church means the priest is more powerful in his prayer to God. I don't really think so, but I walked on over to the side street while there.

"Rosa and I had both prayed and then quickly worked our way down the steps between the crowd of people lighting up and burning that copal incense. So, from where I'm looking, I think you're covered with your traveling. They're all watching you—some of the 'old gods' and the main new God that Father Angelo says is the only way to die and live. I'm fairly all right with living myself, so I just hope you'll still be around next year or so." He took a breath as he looked out past us with a distant look in his eyes.

"Tió José, I know you and Tiá Rosa have loved many years, but it seems you're getting more emotional as we talk about this trip." I broke his gazing with my question. "Will you miss me so much?"

"Look, Roberto. The boys will miss you more than I. Carlo will miss the chips you bring him, and Cesar will want to teach you to be more humble as you lose to him in football. But what I will miss most is the cash you'll owe me if you come up dead or maybe locked in some Mexican jail," Tió José laughed. "I'm investing in you, and then I can some day see your mother and sister better because of it."

"What? I don't understand. How have you put money into me? I thought you were just getting names of family for me?" I looked at Luis, who only smiled while he continued to strum lightly as if he known a great secret all along.

"Look, 'Berto, you cannot travel through Mexico and into America with the little you have saved up. There are many hands to grease, and though some are family to me, none are my brothers. They're all cousins who expect to get paid like all business men, and the few Quetzales you have saved will not get you farther than the river at the Mexican border."

"My mother has given some money also. Do you still need more to make this happen for me and Luis?" I felt frustration in my voice and tried to quiet it.

"No, my young friend. It's already done. This is what we want for you, as you have said it is want you want. Rosa and I have agreed, and I have sent the money by wire to those who require it. I've thought it through and then talked with them. Not only can you trust the men who will be your guides, since they are family, but they will wait on full payment once you reach America."

"I don't know how to thank you for this," I slowly said. "What can I say?"

"Don't say another word. Do this—don't get sent back, as some get deported, and don't get hurt or die along the way. It's enough money that I'd like to see it back in my account at the bank at San Miguel. Who knows the next emergency that the cash could carry me away from or through? I pray to the gods often that we are safe here, as years ago I saw a great earthquake and some bad hurricanes."

"Tió José, it's been years since we in Guatemala have had such bad things happen to our land. I'm sure all will be fine, as it has been for years. It's been so long since we have seen large catastrophes that the school textbooks speak of them as some long ago event."

"Well, Roberto, it becomes very close to you, and you get real acquainted with the problems these disasters carry fast. Just as I don't like the way the wind carries the ball after it is kicked high across the field, I know that all each player can do is wait until it drops. Only then can he react to where it falls and deal with it as best he can. So must we deal with things in life as they happen to us."

~ 14 ~

EN ROUTE FROM SAN MIGUEL TO HUEHUETENANGO · FALL OF 1998

Goodbyes are hard for me. In fact, both Luis and I felt the same way about leaving. It was something we decided to do without actually saying goodbye to the ones we loved. Both Tina and Mama had known I was leaving this morning, but none of us had spoken about it at all when we off to bed. Tina had the saddest eyes I'd ever seen from her as she sulked to her room. I had written her a short good-bye poem that ended with far away hope for us. Mama whispered she would have eggs as a treat, to kind of soften the blow for her in the morning. I wondered what treat I could have left Mama to soften the blow for her? I supposed the blow had already hurt her, and so she walked on in her mind without any to notice it but wearing a new smile to mask the pain she really felt. It was all because of me, and I couldn't change what was to be. Luis, he left a note for his mother and a box of sweet chocolates for his brother on the table. I thought to myself, *It's enough, and soon we'll send money to them. They will see this is best for our families.*

We caught the earliest bus available before the sun came up. We each had a bag under one arm and grim looks of determination on our faces as we waited at the corner. This was one of the same corners that my father and brother used to stop at two to three times a week. I know their route changed once a week or so, depending on when the market was open, but so many people counted on them. And now I know that many more, in fact, had looked forward to their smiles and waves and how they showed compassion. It's something I wish to do also, but sometimes I just don't really care to, or know that I must do what is best for me. Is that so bad?

"'Berto, look up! It's coming. Freedom on wheels is here to take us on our new trip." Luis smiled and sighed as we looked at the bus coming our way.

"Yes, there it is. My father used to be so proud of his. What do our chapines call it now? Oh, yeah, I remember it now, the 'killer tomatoes.'" I laughed at how silly it sounded to say and even look at. My father had his decorated his so much better.

"Why you laughing at it, 'Berto? You know these bright buses that some have even painted red. They are favorites for armed robbers to stop along the way. So the drivers must drive with courage and passion, sometimes even a crazy spirit to run from gunned thieves. I've heard of the accidents with some of them and how bad they have gotten along the great Panamanian Highway. There have been four- and five-car accidents with many people hurt or killed. It's no wonder they have nicknames like 'killer tomatoes,' the people probably 'splat' just like a ripe tomato and you know the juice pours out like—"

"Oh, can you just shut up now?" I interrupted. "I can get a real good picture without you being so descriptive. How about you just get your money ready so we can get on this leap of faith we're taking." I switched hands, as the bag got heavy, and wiped the sweat on my shirt. Opening my palm, I looked at the aged scar from years ago when Luis had saved me from drowning. I wondered if even now we could stay above the water.

"All right then. I don't know what's your problem. I'm just saying those drivers tend to be real aggressive types, 'cause they have to."

"Well, Luis, my dad knew how to drive one of those buses and he wasn't crazy. He took pride in his bus and the people; he cared for them like they were his family. Remember the story your mother told us, and how he took time for his customers?"

"Well, your papa, maybe he was special or different from the rest. All I know is that most of the drivers I see and hear about could earn medals from the Guatemaltecos Army with their moves on some of the roads, if they ever had to serve in the military."

"Whatever, chapino. Twist that old guitar better as you climb up on the bus, so it doesn't hit any babies as we walk to the back."

The bus stopped for us, and we both stepped up and paid the man. There were empty seats in the back, side to side. It worked out well for us, and we both leaned back to set our heads against the windows. The bags dropped to the floor, and we rested for a second, not saying anything as the bus started moving forward. I pulled out a couple of books from my bag on the floor and couldn't decide on which tattered paperback to start. The James Bond book was full of adventure, but I finally went with the American western novel by Louis L'Amour. It's about some Sacket family that came together in a time of trouble, as real families should. One cowboy got caught up in problems outside of himself, and his family were there to free him. I've lost my father and brother; they were my support when I was younger, and Tió José has helped me greatly. My mother, she loved me so much, but my new family was Luis, and it felt like we were the blood brothers of old. We didn't have to say it; it was just a bond we had.

What's he doing in his bag, anyway? I wondered. He hated to read, so what was he looking for?

"Hey, Luis. What you got? You aren't really reading something, are you? I can loan you one of my books, but there are no pictures to make a moving slide show like we used to do years ago. Besides they're in English!"

"Funny 'Berto. No book, just my headphones. I got the cassette tape of Alux Nahual, their album from 1987 called *Alto al fuego.* I've also got *Conquista* from '82, and they both really rock. I could listen to them all day long."

"Well, hopefully it won't be all day long. You know when the first stop is?"

"Why, you already have to let loose? We just got on a few minutes ago, and you want to stop?"

"No, I'm just wondering. I like to plan it all out in my head, you know."

"Remember what you're uncle said. You just can't know it all ahead of time. Just roll with it as it happens to us, and we'll be all right. Where did I put my guitar? That just sounded like a great line to a song I could start writing." He scratched his scar underneath his ear and strummed a quick air guitar stroke, while he smiled at his joke.

"Man, I wish I had a shotgun like this Sacket guy so I could shut you up already."

"What? I can't hear you good; the guitar solo is playing, and it's the best part of the song." Tapping his headphones, his head swiveled to a guitar riff solo that I could even hear.

I started reading the American western novel and lost myself in the scenery of the Americas. I've never traveled except in my mind to far away lands I've read about in different books. America must be very beautiful with its changing scenery. Here in my land, I know it can get different from the mountainous area where we've lived to the more flat lands in the central area where I went off to school. Of course my favorite area to visit as a child was Lake Atitlán, which some claim has the most beautiful lake in the whole world. It's more than ten miles wide, nearly a mile high, and it's surrounded by steep hills, large volcanoes with towering cones, and numerous Maya villages. I loved the few visits there as a child when the mornings would bring a serene calmness shimmering with the scenes of volcanoes and clouds in its wake, but the afternoon sun would bring the Xocomi, known as "the wind that takes away sin."

The more interesting beauty mostly unknown to me as a child could be seen in the coastal areas off the Atlantic area or to the other side on the Pacific coast. Friends I had made when I was away at school came from both of these regions, and often my eyes lit up as they talked of the differences between our areas.

Actually the Atlantic area had an entirely other culture that I had been barely even aware of until I met another student from the area. In our classroom history class we talked about the numerous diverse groups of natives across our country, but my friend, he spoke of stories of the Black Caribs as I had never thought of. In the 18th century, escaped and shipwrecked West African slaves mixed in with the native Caribbean population. Originally the new group's blend was known as Black Carib, but after a time they became known as Garifuna. After a series of skirmishes with British forces, groups were uprooted and exiled. From this exile many migrated to parts of Central America from

Honduras to Belize, including the Atlantic coastline of Guatemala that fronts the Caribbean Sea. The Garifuna are a unique race among our people with a language, culture, and cooking style that sets them apart from the rest us. My schoolmate coolly represented his coastal region with ease, and often carried a devil-may-care attitude.

It really struck me as I began the old west novel from America how the Americans prided themselves in being explorers who pushed their individual limits in settling their land, and yet so many other peoples have done much of the same. These Garifuna had adapted in their new environment and then drew upon their circumstances to find their own small joys in whatever lands they migrated to. Now they seem to be one of the happier groups in Central America, if ever there is any real happiness. Will I find such a deep sense of happiness farther in North America? I read on for a while as the bus sped along the highway, bumping and jerking at each curve as it swept its way though the mountains. Soon I drifted off to sleep like an American cowboy slumped over the saddle of his horse as it plodded along at the end of a day winding through a trail.

~ 15 ~

TRAVELING ON THE BUS

I awoke with a start as the bus slowed to a stop, and I saw Luis crack a smile when I shook myself up from the side of the window. He's always there to see me trip or bump my head, and although he'll help soon enough, there's usually some pointed laughter going on first. I glanced around and wondered aloud how long I'd been out.

"'Berto, I've played at least two cassettes, so it's been almost an hour. You look like that old hound dog in the house next door to ours, half asleep most of the day with hair matted over its face and tongue hanging out while it snored like a choo-choo train. I wish I had a camera, 'cause you looked funny."

"I'm glad to see you got your funny bone around, and life is good for you." I said while shaking my head slightly to wake up, frustrated with Luis.

"Oh it's funny, and I hope you keep making stupid faces all the way to the USA for me to keep making jokes at you." He was grinning even more.

"Jokes? I thought this friendship was bigger and better than just jokes along the way?" I sighed, pushed his arm off my seat and turned to look out the window at the last of the people walking up the bus steps. "I don't know about dealing with that bag of tricks so much," I mumbled under my breath.

"Look, hombre, jokes are what they are and they're what you get.."

"Excuse me, señor. Is anyone sitting there in the seat behind you?"

"What, señorita? Oh, that seat with my guitar? I forgot about it there." Luis tried to reach for it quickly but got tangled with hands and headphones.

"Look, Luis, just move that old beat up thing. Hurry up, will you!

She's got two bags in her hand, and someone is with her. We don't want them to drop any of their bags, and the only seat open back here is your guitar."

"All right, all right. Here you go, señorita. I've got room for the guitar in my seat, and I'll just sit up straight instead of lying back. I'm sorry about that." Luis had taken off his headphones, moved the guitar up a seat next to him, and smoothed out his wrinkled shirt while his smile only got bigger with each movement.

"Muchas gracias. I'm very thankful for the help. My mother, she does not like to sit up front where everybody watches."

I smiled, and Luis laughed a little as he said, "We love to sit in the back and watch everybody too."

The girl tilted her head and smiled herself. "We're going to meet with my family, who must apparently help us decide which university will be best for me to attend. I'll be the first in our family to go to the university, and so it is a big decision." The Indian lady poked her daughter with her elbow, and, I'm sure, muttered a curse under her breath.

"My Mama wonders why you two aren't in school like my brothers are." The well-spoken girl with the darting eyes asked.

We looked at each other and I stuttered, "Even though we still look young, we're done with school. Now we're men, and we're ready to really live." I hoped my words didn't sound too proud.

"Well, one of us is a man." Luis interjected. "Roberto, he still needs to grow into one yet. He was away last year at the university, and now he thinks he's a man of the world. He's the one who still looks like a boy, while I'm sure you thought I was the older brother." Luis looked at me and winked. I glared at him, shrugged, and smiled.

"Luis? Older brother? All right. He's still trying to grow into that suit, and so far it's still too loose around the shoulders and arms. He thinks he's too big for that suit and it feels tight, but really he too has some growing to do to actually fit it properly."

"Oh, I see. We're not just talking about clothes here. You guys are thinkers, and I think maybe some type of dreamers too, huh?" The potential student turned to me and looked directly in my eyes. "And university for you. You must be the smart one. I like to talk to smart ones, but only if they are as they seem." Her eyes shot down to the book in my lap and back to Luis's voice.

"Oh, yeah. Roberto here, he's a smart one, but even more of a dreamer from way back. He has thought of all kinds of things he wants to be when he grows up. We're still waiting to see what he's good at, except the dreaming and thinking parts. Sometimes he's even good at talking band and maybe cooking, if you can believe what he says about it." The last he finished with a smug look my way.

"Hey, Luis. Cut it out! Now I told you both my mother and sister, they liked the food I made them. And my mother, she's no easy critic."

"All right, almighty chef, relax some. Take it easy, and maybe one day you can cook for a king or even the President."

"Luis, you don't know. Someday I might be that guy serving it up to the high and mighty in the courts of the rich and famous." I laughed aloud at the thought.

"Oh, Mama, who is it the gods have gotten us to sit with? This ride, it may be a headache and it may be fun." Her mother glared at her and shook her head, as the girl's eyes seemed to laugh while darting from us to her mama.

"I guess it may be fun to listen to, but it's tiring when we can't agree to disagree. A better friend would not mock so, but—"

"What is mock? Oh, you mean jokes? Señor Sensitive, he can't stand to be compared to the local dog and feels that it is a real smear on his face. Or should I say a lick on his face? You know like the mutt, when he's happy to see you feed him?"

"Oh shut up, now. Give the bus a break from your talking," I said with a grin.

"Señors, my name is Margarita, and this is my mother Raquel Lopez, and we are from Soloma." The younger interrupted us with a sweet smile. "What are your names?"

"Señorita Margarita, this is Luis and my name is Roberto. We are from San Miguel Acatán. If you don't mind me asking, what of your jackets? They are very beautiful and must have taken a long time to make?" I motioned from mother to daughter.

Margarita smiled and her face seemed to light up like a candle in a dark room. "Roberto, my mama, she has been listening to you, and she and I wonder about you." She glanced from me to Luis. "We can hear chapines, for it's in your voice and even the manners. But you, Roberto, I'm not so sure about you," she says to me with a turn of her head. "It seems to us you try to talk as chapines but act and speak more as Ladinos. Now you ask about our clothes, and it's like you don't think much about our history."

Both seats were silent for a full minute, and the women exchanged a look and shrugged lightly. Señora Lopez quickly spoke a phrase or two in their native tongue and watched our faces.

"Well Margarita, my mother taught me much about my Spanish heritage, while my father tried to give me some of my Indian history." I looked out the window as we ran over a pothole, and the contents splashed the sides of the bus. I looked out the window for clouds and saw only sunshine. "The sad truth is that my father lost that battle in the telling, when I lost him at a young age from a tragic death."

"Roberto, you make a very sad joke, but I will not tell you the reason it is a bit of funny and a bit of sad. But Margarita, I try to help him see our Indian heritage, but Roberto has been pulled from two directions as to who he is, and so we traveling to help find him."

"Okay, Dr. Luis, enough of explaining me to the ladies." I pushed his elbow resting on my seat, glaring at him.

"It's all right, my new friend," Margarita tapped on my hand lightly as she started to begin a lesson. "Let me tell about some history here in the mountains. Each village, you can tell who they are by the design and colors of the weaving in our clothes. It is something the women pass on to their daughters with pride, and I am happy to have been given such an interesting gift from my family line. Some modern women, more the ladinos, don't wear the traditional clothes. But in our part of the village we do. This jacket you ask about is called *huipile*, and we like them long and flowing, with a bright white about in it. Soloma also is known for its pretty necklaces made of gold painted beads that we make ourselves."

"'Berto, you know my mother, she makes these same huipiles. You never pay enough attention as I try and tell you." Luis interrupted her with a smile. "Her colors and designs were different, as she made some details that spoke of our San Miguel. You know that I helped her to try and sell the ones she made at the market, and you even saw me carry some on the bus. Sometimes, you are so full of reading about other lands, you forget the details in our days here at home."

Margarita allowed him to finish and notes, as she continues our history lesson, "As far as history in this area goes, there's a village not far from this route called Todos Santo that is also famous for its huipiles and other textile products. You know even the men there are known for their crocheted handbags. But that village is even more known for the drunken horse race that's held each year on All Saint's Day. It goes back to the time of the conquistadors and involves mixed games of drinking, horse racing, and endurance. Villagers get an early start drinking, race and stop to drink after each portion, and continue until they fall off their horses. It is known all over for being a very crazy time, and I would have thought you had heard of it."

"No, we have often talked of crazy bus drivers señorita and funny tourists who go to Zaculeu every so often," Luis slyly said.

"Oh, yeah, Zaculeu, a good local Mayan ruin that was a center of power for our ancestors. It's a great area for defense, and those conquistadors had a tough time getting through, so they just starved that area into giving up," I added with some satisfaction.

"Oh, Roberto. You act like you are one of the descendants of the Indian, but you talk like the Spaniards of old who conquered them. I pray to the gods you would stop wishing you were an explorer. We must find out who you really are, my friend."

"You won't find me in a song, so I don't know how you'll figure me out Luis."

"Look, Roberto, I know much more of life than just chords and lines to songs, I—"

"I wonder why we're slowing down so much? I cannot see over this guitar in front of me. Is it an accident?" Margarita comments to her mother in Cakchiquel, her native language.

Her mother responded, "It's only a local policia stop checkpoint;

we will be through in no time. You complain you have no boys to talk to, and now you interrupt them as they talk."

"Margareta? I don't speak Cakchiquel very well," says Luis, "But I think you said my guitar is in your way even though I moved it. Let me switch places with it. Can you see better around my head versus the wide case of the guitar?"

"Well, your head is a bit bigger than it is," Margarita snickered, "but it moves about more as you talk. So I guess it's better than what it was. I can see the policia in the street ahead of us. They seem to be waving us, and so I guess it's okay for us."

"I'm sure it's all right. I used to ride this way to Huehue a lot, and this isn't that unusual. You shouldn't be worried. They're only checking these things for our safety from bandits along the way. You can never be too safe. I see much need for it as many men are just crazy."

"Luis, you seem to know much about the world. Have you traveled a lot?"

"No, I'm not a man who travels a lot, but I listen very well as others tell stories of their lives and the things they have seen. I know soon I will tell their stories in song and sometimes liven up some with a little less truth. But there's always some basic truth there that I can tell as people tell their history."

"Well, you can tell pieces of a good story, but I wonder if the guitar is just a prop piece to meet girls, or if you play it as well. If you do play, do words of a story come to life with the music, or is it just quiet strumming?" She leaned over and picked a string on one of the top frets. I looked away.

"Oh, no. The words I feel tumbling around my head come alive as soon as I start to strum the strings. It's like a magic spell, like the Shamans of old who speak to the gods above, and the words are there like a whiff of smoke from incense and a prayer." How poetic was that? Not bad for a guy who doesn't even read much.

On and on they talked, and me, I just sat in anger. I wish that it were I who could speak so well to girls. All I have are my books that I read, which is no real tool to impress any of the girls. I thought Margarita and I had a special moment when she spoke of Ladinos versus Chapines within my character, but it must have been her way of teasing. I looked again in her eyes and saw little interest in me. When I look into the eyes of a pretty girl, I lose all thoughts of my own and can't think of where to take the conversation. Tina's older friends tried to speak to me, but they cared little for anything I was interested in. I could not see talking to them, when I would have to sit and listen about their hair or the need for shoes. It is not easy for me to get past "hello" with the ones who care about real things, and here Luis was so working the talk like a Guatemaltecos Don Juan. It's not fair at all how he does it, and me, I'm stuck again with the Sackett character. That family is interesting, but not nearly as much fun as it would be talking to a pretty girl. Luis has the best of the moments riding today, as he has interest and beauty to captivate him, and I have only a slow moving interest in a badly worn fiction novel that will never come alive as real as the two people in the seats behind me.

~ 16 ~

HUEHUETENANGO

"I don't know why you're moving so fast. You know that the next bus is not for an hour and half. We have plenty of time to get something to eat and be back before we must take the other bus on the Panamanian Highway. Let's stop at the one restaurant on the corner by the market—the one we used to go to all the time. Slow down. It's right around the next street." I pointed to the right, hoping he would stop so I could catch my breath.

"Hurry up, slow one!" Luis growled under his breath to me, keeping his pace. "Can't you move any faster? I have to do something, and we have to go now."

"I don't understand, 'cause it's still early. The restaurants are just opening, but many people are not even in their shops yet." Where is it he wanted to eat?

"Yes, I know. That's why we have to run." Luis glanced up to the skies as he started to slow down. "Oh, thanks be to the gods of old. There's one there."

"What? Someone is already in the market. Oh, I see. You want to get a gift for the girl we have spent some time on the bus. Aren't you just so, Romeo?"

"I don't know this Romeo, but go sit down while I bargain with her." Luis snapped at me. Luis was not only good at talking to the girls, but he was also very skilled in working the buy at the market. I think it was probably because he watched his mother use a whole different set of plans to convince locals and tourists to buy her product. She was a natural at convincing someone they needed something, and yet many people found a way to still say no to her. So, he had heard all the ways to say yes, no, maybe, and all the tone or nonverbal communications in between. I usually just paid whatever they asked for the first time and moved on. My mother never spent time working in a conversation over an item to buy. She knew that most times they weren't that well off, and it was best just to give the price they asked. Luis' mother tried to explain to me once that it was fun for many people to do this type of bartering. She went on to tell me that those in the market planned that most would not pay the suggested price, and it was actually part of the market scene. I accepted this with a shrug, and thought how Mama told me that for many years ladinos had chapina buy for them anyway. Now it's different, and it's more even I guess.

After ten minutes, Luis walked over to where I was leaning against the walls of the Hotel Zaculea in town. He had a beautiful chain swing in his hand, and I smiled, knowing his thoughts. I turned as he jogged into the central courtyard behind me in the hotel, and wondered what he was going to do. He ran with his arms pumping, head forward, and feet working to keep up his upper body as he made it to the middle of a garden with colorful tropical flowers scattered all around. He swung around, and then suddenly stood from his crouching. He turned with a big grin on his face as he had one huge flower growing from his hand. I stomped in a bit of anger as I walked out of the hotel doorway. He ran by me, waving me on to catch him. All this effort for a girl he's going to say good-bye to tomorrow anyway. What is it with him and impressing the girls?

"Hey, compadré. Slow it down some," I yelled in frustration, as he even seemed to pick up speed. Then he finally started to walk as he passed the fountain and then the Catholic Church. I could not understand why we had not just come in the way we were going before, when he bought the chain. Then, soon after we ran through the square we came to where the city came alive on certain days for the market, with its string of booths full of different items to sell. I stood back again as he stepped into a familiar booth to both of us. He quickly looked around to be sure no one was watching. Then I shook my head, thinking how he's so good at hiding what is really going on. For then he hung the chain on a nail with a hanger that held a newly sown vest. He took the flower and slid it down the right side pocket so that the stem pointed four inches past the side of the ruffled curtain hanging off the wall. It brushed the side of the table and the buds pushed inward on the vest. He stepped back and dug in the pocket of his jeans and pulled out a locket. The locket opened with a snap, and I skipped two steps to see the picture. Luis, he jerked his head as I leaned lightly on the old, rickety table where the ladies laid out the latest fashion.

"Shush, quiet down you mutt of a dog. She'll be here soon, and they know me all around here. Come around fast and hold the vest in place while I put the locket on the chain."

I held the vest with the flower barely in place and the chain swaying a little as I nervously looked around the market, and then it hit me. Luis wasn't buying these things for the girl but for his mother. Even for as long as I've known Luis, there are times he surprises me.

His mother was known to be about fifteen minutes late after the market opened when she came, since the bus schedule was not set on the time the market opened. Just as he got the clasp shut, I stole a quick glance inside the locket and saw the picture. It was Eduarda and him, sitting in their living room with the guitar on their laps from three years ago. Eduarda had his fingers over the third fret, reaching to push in the strings as Luis strummed with his favorite pick. They were laughing, and I pictured their mother too in the background smiling. Eduarda was really too big to sit on his lap, but that's probably while they were laughing so. Luis smoothed out the material of the vest and left the locket ajar.

Then he turned with a grim look, and we jogged between the booths across the way. After a minute of jogging, he started to sprint. I wondered about the time and thought he was worried about the bus. I caught up with him behind the hotel, and saw him pulling backing the underbrush. It hit me then, he was most worried about his guitar we had stashed next to our bags before we started walking through the market. I looked at my watch and noticed we still had an hour before the bus.

"Can we go eat now? Or are there other errands we must do while my stomach grinds away a new song for you try to play?" I asked him while strumming the air with my imaginary pic.

"You sound like your cousin, Carlos. We'll eat now, for we really have few meals left here in our own country, eh?" he said with a hint of sadness.

"Let's hurry and go to Jardin Café for a late Chapin breakfast. Remember we ate together there before I went off to university?" I tried to lighten the moment.

"All right, Roberto. But you were the one that said we should try and save Quetzals."

"Yes, Luis. But soon enough our Quetzals will not be worth anything, and we must use them all up. Plus, it's a good reason to spend, after saying good-bye."

~ 17 ~

EN ROUTE TO THE MEXICAN/GUATEMALAN BORDER · OCTOBER 1998

We made the bus in time leaving Huehuetenango, and it was only an hour's drive to the border. Fifteen minutes into the ride and already Luis had begun again. I'm not sure if it was my luck or just fate having fun with me, but Margarita and her mother were back on the bus with us. Luis told her that the god of travel and the god of friendship met over a bottle he left with the local shamen so that they could continue their time. She ate up his lies with a shy grin from the corner of her mouth and knew he was only trying to impress. I wondered still why she didn't protest, and she just smiled as Luis kept on rambling on. I could read the look in her mother's eyes. She was not happy with this conversation, but I quickly looked away. All I wanted was to make the border and meet up the guy Tió José had set us up to meet. The border had a town call La Mesilla, where many crossed over into Mexico legally.

I could hear Margarita as she finally opened up more and told Luis that she and her mother would meet her cousin, uncle, and aunt to discuss education. They traveled in Mexico and Guatemala, and would help her decide where she should go to school. She told him that she would probably visit the university in Mexico and perhaps she and Luis might meet up again. Of course, Luis laughed and just said, "Maybe." This isn't fair at all; I must find a way into this.

"Excuse me, Margarita, but university life is not, not uh, uh easy. I was, uh, uh there for a while, and it was very hard at times."

"Roberto, where is the university, and did you like it there?"

"Yes, Margarita, very much. San Carlos is where I attended."

"Why not complete your education there?" She had turned completely around when she asked and looked right in my eyes. I straightened my head and back from the window and looked up to the ceiling for a second before answering.

"Why? I'm not completely sure, but I feel I want to get a different education elsewhere," I muttered slowly, finding strength in last few words.

"And where might that be? San Carlos is known to be a good school." I looked at her face and she was still looking at me. I glanced at my shoes. The laces were untied again.

"Roberto wants to learn in America and not just here in our native land. He is going to be a great master chef in the land of dreams coming true."

"Oh, again, the fun at my expense, Luis." It was easier to glare at him angrily than hold her stare.

"You should relax, my friend. Don't be so sensitive; you act like your sister when she used to pout."

"Roberto, you have a sister? What is her name? How old is she? Does she—"

"Margarita, you ask so much for this thinker," Luis leaned his head further across the seat when he interrupted her. "He needs more time to know what he should say to you. He's just not—"

Margarita interrupted him with a smile spreading. "Luis, I have to agree with Roberto. You are a little mean sometimes, and I wonder how you two have had stayed friends for so long."

"Yes, señorita. I wonder the same about us," I smiled back and lifted my head up to catch her smile still. "Luis is a good friend most of the time, although at times he pushes the jokes farther than some. My sister is still young. I think she is thirteen or fourteen. She acts like she is already twenty-two and speaks like a mother hen. Her name is Christina, and I know I will miss her and our mother both as we leave this country." I shook my head and looked back down at my book in my lap.

"Family is really important, and that is why we're traveling so that I can make a decision that is based on information we hear from those we can trust. We have some family that live in Chiapas, a state in Mexico; there's a college there, and we must decide if I should study there or stay here in Guatemala." I looked up again at her face.

"We too spoke to family about our decision to move, but it was not a complete agreement all the way around. Somehow some in our family have had to come to accept our decision and hope it's the right way." Luis tapped fingers impatiently on my seat. Couldn't I have even a few minutes of conversation?

"Si, Roberto. We all sometimes wait and find out later if it were such a good decision to do what we have done. It is far easier to look over our shoulder at what we did yesterday than it is to walk with head high and feet skipping forward with a real plan for the path ahead of us. So, wise ones try to make decisions a gift to themselves where they accept advice from others who have unwrapped their own gifts and now can share some of the unknown reality with them. The crazy passionate ones, they run on to what they think is best, not listening to the pain and joy of others' past experiences so that real life can be taught to them. No, they will learn some day too, but not in this moment."

She brushed some hair back from her eye, gazing past me through the window over my head. What other thoughts lay hidden behind those words?

"Señorita, you are very wise in what you say for such a young lady. Sometimes I think I know enough to take on the whole world out there, and they will see and hear me. I guess I need to remember I have still much to learn and—"

"'Berto, you have learned much at school and think a lot," Luis stopped tapping as he interrupted me. "But you still do not see, and so I think I will show you how to see. I will help you open your eyes to the life that you have been blind to. Wait, and I will show—"

Margarita's mother interrupted our conversation by whispering to her daughter, "Margarita, I don't like you talking to these young men so much. They will think you're flirting with them and that is not proper."

"Yes, Mama. But we're just talking and it's interesting to me," she said just loud enough that I could hear it.

Her mother shrugged and shook her head. Then Margarita looked at Luis and said, "What were you saying, Luis?"

"What I was trying to say is that life should be lived in the moment. It is like playing a guitar spontaneously." His fingers magically found the pic and played lightly in the air.

"Yes, living for the moment is nice, but you must plan ahead as I am for my university studies," she responded while watching his fingers playing his air guitar.

I added, "I like to plan too by listing in the morning all the things I need to accomplish that day." I tugged on my bookmark in the novel resting on my leg. One side had my packing list while the other side noted this year's goals.

"Si, my friend. You are sick with a very dangerous illness. I must cure you of it. I will help you as a friend, even if you say I should be a better friend."

"Luis, why would you want to fix him? You can try and show him the way you think, but you must let him grow on his own. We all must find our path that gods of old have paved for us with their machete in the bush. You should not try to steer him down your path, but let Roberto follow the one that is meant for him. These are not easy paths we walk along, but ones that have ground that is full of rocks, holes, and sharp branches that stick in our way. You have to walk in the center of the path, not look back too often, listen to those whom you meet that have walked that way before, and then keep walking even as it gets a little dark."

"But señorita, you know Roberto, he's afraid of the dark. He sees more spirits after dark and then doesn't know who he should listen to."

"Dark! You'll see dark after I black out both eyes. Then when the gods want to open your eyes, you will try and not be able to do so. They will be stuck shut from my right hook, and then who will laugh?" I started to laugh at my words even as I spoke them.

~ 18 ~

LA MESILLA, THE BORDER CITY BETWEEN GUATEMALA AND MEXICO

I had fallen asleep again to the small talk of Luis and Margarita and was content when she asked continually about his music choices. My thoughts were spinning after her well-spoken words carried the weight of the world around us. Most of the girls I met thought more of their friends than trying to carry such a conversation. Talk of music from Luis lulled me to sleep, and the routine talk from the bus driver and his worker helped comfort my soul.

I shook my head groggily when I heard the driver swear under his breath when he had to suddenly gear down to brake. Comfort turned to frustration. My family had done that same job, and I did not like to think of them as I rode this "killer tomato" or "chicken bus" as I heard some tourist call it. I used to find lots of fun in watching for my father and brother, and today I wish there was another way that we could find to get out of the country.

The bus rolled to a stop, and I shook the hair out of my eyes a couple times and pinched my eyes with my finger and thumb. I wet my hands and run them through my hair and sat up to untuck some strands stuck from the back collar and the bus window. Luis and I both jump up from our seats to walk up front. Margarita touched each of our hands as we slowly walk past her seat. I see Luis over my shoulder run his fingertips under her wrist, smiling while balancing his guitar with his left hand over his left shoulder. I shivered and shook my head, glad to be at the steps. The driver nodded a good-bye to each of us while his worker stood with one hand on the door and his right hand ready to steady anyone stepping down.

After stretching my arms high in the air while standing among other passengers in the street, I looked up for my bag. Our bags had to be thrown on top of the bus for space, and the worker helping at the door was now handing bags down to the driver for the ladies. I guess men's bags rated less care, and I waited for him to throw our bags down with all the other men's bags. I was glad I only had books and clothes in my bag, and I guess that's why Luis insisted on paying the extra to have his guitar in the seat next to him. I stood there looking around and noticed the huge banner that stretched across the street two to three blocks away. I could barely make out the words, and supposed it said something about "This way to Mexico." I looked around and shrugged, and Luis looked at me with a question. We both stood there just waiting. Tió José said there would be a guy that would meet us here, but didn't tell us much more.

After a few minutes, the bus was emptied and all the baggage was in the street in front of a produce market. The market had melons, red onion, plantains, tomatoes, and huge squash all laid out along the walkway. I set my bags next to a barrel of yellow onions while Luis set his guitar against a tower of baskets with zucchini sticking out at it like a set of dueling banjos. The girl just inside the doorway saw us and smiled a bit in the corners of her mouth. I smiled back and turned around to nudge Luis. He thought he was such a Romeo, and he didn't even know who Romeo was. He tried to smile her way then but a customer needed her attention.

Our bus rolled away to gas up to go on to its next stop further in Guatemala and still there was no sign of this guy. We stood there for another moment and then decided to walk down the street to the corner. We looked up and down the street at all the traffic. Some of the guys driving those red three-wheeled cabs pulled out from a parking spot and then gunned the gas pedal like they were racing in some American track. People didn't jump back, and it was like they knew the driver would be coming at them. Although my family drove much of the roads with real passion, I never get tired of how common the indifference to pedestrians is. While I was watching the one red cab speed away, another one pulled up right in front of us. Luis and I both jumped back as it screeched to a stop, and the driver beeped two times. He jumped out of the three-wheeled cab and smiled.

"Roberto and Luis? I'm Custódio. Your Uncle José sent me. Let's throw your bags on top here, and I'll tie them down."

We both grab our bags and watch him jump around the taxi like a circus monkey. He wasn't tall but seemed bigger than us. Maybe it was that his arms were longer and stronger, and the tattooed fish on his arm swam some when he pulled the ropes tighter. I noticed some dried blood on his forehead when his face scrunched with a final tug on the passenger side, and he grunted. "Finito! Get in boys."

"Do you need some money right now, Custódio? We're not sure about things and—"

"Look, Roberto, your uncle took care of everything. He sent ahead all the monies. You have no worry, and I'll take care of it all. I'll see you are set up to get on your way into Mexico without any problem," Custódio explained as he reversed the cab and gunned it into gear.

"Are you sure? Cause we can do our share. It is no problem," Luis sputters his words out in surprise while Custódio blows a stop sign.

"Luis, is it? I do this all the time, and of the expenses and planning have been taken care of. You just sit back and let me run this situation."

"Why the red cab? I thought you would have something else, and do you know you maybe shoulda stopped back there?" I hoped he didn't detect worry in my voice.

Custódio turned back and widely grinned, "I do have my four-wheeling old Chevy Blazer for the back roads and riding by the river. But here in La Mesilla I have this to make some extra money around town, and people don't wonder about me. And you know I have a few friends, so I don't even really worry about the signs."

"But what about the traffic? What if one bus or taxi comes speeding around that last corner?"

"Oh, Roberto, you are a worrier I see." The cab lurched a little as he tapped the brake to slow slightly when a Vespa scooter cut in front of us to turn left at the last intersection.

"Well, maybe. Do people wonder about the blazer, or do you hide that?" I breathed out a deep sigh.

"No, my friend. Most of the time I tell them it's for driving longer distances, like if I have to run out to Huehue. You know I couldn't trust going any real distance with this baby-wheeled cab."

"Custódio, what is it with your name? Not many here in Guatemala have a name like that."

"You are right, Roberto. But my family has lived here a long time on the border and knew I would probably stay. It seems like most of my family feel as if we are guarding the river between the two countries, and my first name means guardian in Spanish."

"So where are you taking us, Custódio? Tió José did not give us many details and I'm just wondering."

"Well, since you are practically family, we're going back to my house for the evening and then we'll eat some of my leftovers."

"Hey, Custódio! What is the ringing?" Luis interrupted him while he was looking around. " Sounds like a bad cow."

Custódio sped up and jerked his head around to the left with a grim look on his face.

Then he started ranting, "Alejanro, stupid police. What is it you want? Didn't I pay you last week for the money I owed? Or did Maryanna, did she call you already? Her and her mouth, she probably called her sister, who then stopped in with coffee to tell you. Can I have no peace and privacy here in this place? What is it about me and—"

Luis looked at me and winked and laughed some. Me, I wasn't smiling, and I asked him, "Custódio, what's going on? You think you should slow down? Perhaps even stop for the police? Besides, what will you tell them about us?"

He grunted under his breath, continued to mumble as he pressed the gas even more.

The little red demon couldn't seem to go much faster, and this really old, dented, and bondo'd Crown Vic wailed alongside of us. The policeman, Alejandro, I guess is waving at us to pull over, and I blinked as he swerved right for us. This was crazy, and I opened my eyes to see him dart around behind us, and that's when I heard the diesel bus fly past us. Now, I see why he swerved and nearly sideswiped us. After that we all may have needed some bondo.

Grass and stones were flying all around, and finally Custódio had to slow down. We're all coughing and choking away the dust while the right back wheel fishtailed some from the stop. Luis poked his head out the left side, while I looked around the back for the beat up Vic. It slammed on its brakes, and I was blinded this time only to hear some local Indian dialect I didn't recognize. From the tone and speed of his voice, I was thinking he was not happy. The door was banged shut so hard that it swung back open and hit him. I hear Luis snort, and I finally could see after I rubbed my eyes to clear them. Custódio got out and yelled back retorts in the same dialect. I catch pieces of what they're saying, especially when they mix in Spanish. Alejandro stomped his foot and yelled something and then we heard, "Shut up, Custódio. You idiot! I didn't drive away from my coffee just to get into it about some fight you had with my wife's sister. I can see she got her shots in; the cut is still on your face. I warn you to duck faster when she's upset. You don't listen, and I try to tell you. Karen, the produce girl, sent me out here to find you and these boys. Now take this guitar out of my back seat before I swing it like a bat at you."

"Guitar? What Alejandro? Your wife didn't send you after me nor her sister?"

"No they didn't. Although, Maryanna, she told me today was not a good day when I saw her in the morning. Me, I thought she was talking about the clouds moving darkly in the sky, not flying saucers! I see chips from the coffee cup stuck in your hair and front pocket of your shirt from my sister-in-law's throw."

"Oh, Alejandro, you funny man. Long time funny! Haha!"

Luis and I broke out laughing, and when Luis started to cough from his laughing, he got out on his side of the cab.

"Hey, Custódio! Is he talking about my guitar? 'Cause I just remembered I left it in the street. I can't leave home without it," and he looked at me to help explain. Shrugging, Luis muttered, "It's a music thing you know."

I jabbed at Luis, "Maybe if you were less worried about saying your goodbyes to Margarita, you wouldn't have forgotten your guitar!"

"Here you go, young compadre." Alejandro took the guitar out of the back seat and gently handed it to Luis. While handing it off, he shouldered Custódio in the chest and stomped on his foot.

"Hey, stupid! What's that for? I didn't know you were helping me."

"That is for two reasons. One, for not letting me just help you and your fares. Two, it is for my sister-in-law. My wife, she would not let me eat dinner if I did not show you some of their love, even here!" I heard him blow out a hearty laugh.

"Well, thanks, you idiot. You still almost blew my tires out on this cab. Next coffee is on me tomorrow."

"Oh, you will have more than coffee for me, for we have to talk about quetzales you owe me still. But drive on now with those boys and tie down that guitar on that baby diablo."

We made our way back on Highway CA1 for two or three more kilometers. Custódio turned off on a small back road, and we puttered between potholes at a much slower speed. After a few minutes, I saw a burnt orange brick house on the right with a lean-to on the side. We got closer, and I saw the lean-to was missing a few back straps for the corner pole, and the wind took it up and down, like it seemed to be waving "hello" to us. The slant of the unsecured roof held a pool of water that dripped over the dirty white Chevy Blazer parked underneath it. The scratched and scraped front end of the Blazer was missing pieces of headlight. I wondered if it still could shine bright out here in the fields and trees along the back roads. The front end pointed downward, and I could see the back of the car, almost all the way up under it. Luis pointed at it, as we pulled in front of the house and up the drive.

"Hey, Custódio, you've jacked up the back end and gave it some nice suspensions back there. My boss, he did that before for some guy on his Ranger. I saw that Ranger later that week taking some fields by the river like it was nothing."

"Well, Luis, that's what gets me around the back fields along the Suchate River. Sometimes I just drive around the trails, trees, fields, and chipped stony roads that follow this creek that the maps call a river. I feel like an old Indian scout, who was checking out the land so he could better lead a party of explorers, just like in those American cowboy movies, except the scout never ended with the lady. I'd have to change that scene some."

Custódio laughed and said, "It's too bad there are no doors, 'cause sometimes an animal will find a way in. I left a package of donuts in the seat, and I came in the next day with a rat swinging it like a dog on a knotted rope. He and I were friends some until I had a tourist fare that afternoon. Then we parted ways quickly, and I shooed him out the back with my Angels' cap."

"Custódio, you have dinner on for us? I smell beans cooking. I'm getting memories of my mama's cooking."

"Roberto, I'm sure it's not going to be as good, but I think ChiChi is simmering some beans for us. I told him we were having company, and he could get 'em ready for us."

"ChiChi, is that your son?"

"No, Roberto. He's my nephew. He likes to stay with me some days. His father, Bolívar, lives just on the other side of the Suchate. We will talk of him in a little while. Let's go eat."

We helped him untie our things and then stumbled in the house. Luis and I both missed the extra steps and almost fell. Custódio put out his arm and caught us with a wink. I looked around to both sides of the porch, which extended out past the house. It had a couple chairs and a small, torn card table on one side, and an off-green rusty picnic swing on the other. There was a cup Jamika sitting on the card table, with a game of solitaire waiting to be finished.

"ChiChi, I hope you warmed up some rice and tortillas to go with them beans I'm smelling. You had better turn the fire down some, 'cause it smells like they're beginning to burn, Custódio directed his nephew.

We walked in the house, and centered in the middle of the room was a large table about eight feet long, with cut melons inside of a bowl on top of the table and fried plantains on a platter on the other side. A boy of about twelve was bringing rice in a pot from another room. I could see fresh chopped cilantro mixed in, and I wondered if this boy was planning on cheffing also.

He smiled easily and suggested, "You guys come here and go wash from the dust. Mama always says, 'God didn't make dirt to be part of the meal.' Tió Custódio, I was worried for you: Maryanna, she stopped by and she was not very happy with you. Her message was you don't need to come by for cake and coffee later. She said her birthday will come again next year, and then maybe you will remember. It was chocolate and very good."

"ChiChi, did she say anything about seeing me tomorrow? I gotta know if I should plan on when to find her. There are some flowers out back, and I can take them to her. That will help some."

ChiChi interrupted, "Hey, is that a guitar? I'd love to play, if I only had one to practice on. You've got longer hair, so it must be yours. All the rock stars got long hair," he looked right at me while pointing at my hair. I pushed some out of my eyes.

"ChiChi, this is Roberto and Luis. I believe the guitar is Luis's, and I'm not sure about his rock star status. Maybe we see in some years."

"I like to keep my hair a little shorter so the ladies can see in my eyes when I sing a song just for them," Luis chuckles. "Roberto has longer hair since he's always wanted to be a wild woodsman. The wildest he gets tho' is when he growls in his sleep at night."

"My growls are barely heard compared to the grunts we hear when you can't find your guitar. Sometimes you act as if that thing has a life of its own," I snapped back at him.

"'Berto, you know it takes on a life when I play from my heart with a song."

"If only you had a heart that went beyond superficial feelings in single moments." I pointed at his heart with a smile.

"Sometimes 'Berto, moments are all we got! And you sit stuck in dreams that may never come true." A smile barely hung on Luis's face but ChiChi and Custódio were almost laughing.

"I'm here in this moment, waiting to make our way to another country and create a new home. That's more than dreaming. It's reality with you, compadre!"

"All right boys, that's enough entertainment for ChiChi and me. Wash up back in the pila, and sit down for some dinner."

~ 19 ~

CUSTÓDIO'S HOME

"Luis, we're in the nineties now. You should play songs from these times. Those Eagles songs are mostly from the seventies, and I'd think you'd know some other groups. Don't you have some music from Central America?"

"Custódio, after a good meal I relax with some good classic rock. It's only natural for me to play 'em that way. I know some good groups from our home country, and you know I have some cuts on my head phones. They're good, but I like to be in tune with some of the best. 'Stairway to Heaven' is next, and it will put you near tears if I'm not careful."

"I wish that I can play so well one day, Luis."

"ChiChi, it's only a matter of love for music. Many have the dream of being a star, but only few make it big. It must be deep in your core to ground you like the roots of the tree out that window. The tree has a real sense of what it is and what it wants to be as it still grows. That's the same with me and my music."

"That's beautiful, Luis, almost like poetry." I pointed to one of my books sticking out of my bag. Shaking my head, I said "It's very sad to me that you can't seem to treat people with the same caring you have for your love of music. You could not say good-bye to your mother, even some parting words for your brother, and the girls they never get anything more serious than phrases in an old love song. The songs you sing for them are just means to a kiss, and nothing more."

"What, nothing more? They see my feelings as I strum my chords and know what I feel as look in their eyes." Luis picked up the guitar by its neck and pointed the headstock right at me.

I smiled and responded, "I don't think so. You hide much behind those eyes, and the girls think they see all the way into your soul. You give them a small stone, and they think they've found Mayan treasure in a few moments with you. Yet you have hidden that treasure deep below the ruins of old, where even the gods could not divine."

"Okay, Doctor Roberto!" Luis retorted, "I choose not to lie on your couch any longer, and this session is over! So, leave me be, you rangy, curly-haired mutt. I'm not sparring any more with you and your university words." Luis spat as he flung his favorite pick over at me. He gently set the guitar against the chair, walked out, and I heard him slam the outhouse door.

ChiChi shrugged his shoulders and smirked. Then he fumbled around on the floor and found the pick. With a disapproving look from both Custódio and me, ChiChi gingerly wrapped his hands around the guitar like it was a gift from the gods of old. He sat down on the old wooden chair, wrapped his feet between the legs, his left arm around the body, and his right hand on the top fret. I heard the pila water running in the other room, and then the spoon scratching the side of the bean pot. ChiChi looked at me expectantly as if I'd give him some kind of permission. I shook my head frantically, and Custódio was gesturing to him to quickly put it back down.

"No! Put it down!"

Luis angrily flung his plate down on the floor, and his second helping of beans scattered at Custódio's feet. He stomped the three steps to ChiChi and glared at him.

"You couldn't think to ask? You just pick up my guitar?" Luis demanded and then he woke ChiChi from his wordless trance with a quick kick to the chair's leg. Custódio jumped up with a start and strode over between them. "Look, Luis, I told him he could hold it for a moment and then maybe you would give him a lesson when you got back. No harm done to it, so relax, boy!"

Luis's voice had risen even more than usual. "I just finished saying it is my life, and he has it in his hands. I just got it tuned back up after being thrown around on the bus ride. This one," Luis gestured to ChiChi, "he needs to understand others' property. The guitar is not his to touch and—"

"Cool down your temper, Luis. I explained to you he was only curious about it. He has some childhood dreams, also, just as you have." Custódio held his stance next to him.

"Yes, Luis. He meant no harm. You always let that temper get the better of you. Find your way to let it go."

"Enough from you, Roberto!"

"I'm sorry, Luis. I shouldn't have picked up the guitar. I just wanted to see what it is felt like to hold in my hands. You made it look so easy as you played," ChiChi said.

"Fine, ChiChi. Just give it to me, please. Custódio, you said we could sleep in old bunkbeds in the other room. I'm going back there and practice some."

"Yeah, Luis, it's down the hall on the left." I watched Luis walk away and Custódio turned to me. "Roberto, you two don't hold much back, do you?"

"I don't know, Custódio. Although we're friends, it's as if we're more brothers and so must say whatever we think. I don't know if it is right or wrong, but it's what we do. You said earlier we must leave after some breakfast."

"We won't be eating a full meal, Roberto. Just some cheese that ChiChi likes with some leftover tortillas. We're to meet my brother, Bolívar, at a spot along the river. He'll pick you up and take you to the bus station in Comitán. Comitán is not far from the Panamanian Highway, and I know you've taken it some from Huehue."

"But what about tickets for the bus ride at Comitán? Will they not ask? And what then? Where do we go from this bus trip?"

"All right, all right. The bus fare will be settled up with no questions from the authorities. You'll not worry, for it's all taken care of. The people who need to be paid will get the money. You'll ride the bus to México City with Bolívar, for he knows the route well. He's good in these ways. From there you'll travel by train through Mexico. Bolívar will tell you more. You wait, he'll tell you."

I didn't like waiting on details. It didn't sit well in the pit of my stomach. It reminded me of the feeling I had when I decided how to tell Mama and Tina of my plans to leave for America. I worry over reactions and the unknown. I like it better when I know enough to see it in my head and then can plan for the unknown as carefully as possible.

I nodded to them both good night and found my bunkbed. Luis had laid his guitar to rest in its case underneath the beds and was seemingly asleep already above it. I pulled a string to turn off the light and grabbed the side to hop up. My back right leg easily made it, but the left slammed into the post with a thud.

"Hey Mutt, shut it up. I can't sleep with you breaking the wood in here."

"Shut up yourself, rockstar." I smiled to myself because I knew Luis and I would be okay.

~ 20 ~

THE RIVER CROSSING

It was good to eat the next morning, but I felt a little sad to think it was maybe our last meal in Guatemala for who knew how long. ChiChi spoke very little this morning. Most of what he said was in response to his uncle's answer as to what to do after we left. He would meet many travelers between this home and his father's place. It probably made for some interesting talk at his school. What would his friends think when he told them of his near battle with a houseguest over a guitar? Would he exaggerate the telling of it and would others prod him until they picture him strumming a chord in delight and slamming the guitar into Luis's toes? With a nod, he would have gotten up and slipped the pick into Luis's front shirt pocket, let the guitar fall to the floor, and strolled into the kitchen. I'm sure after days of retelling, the story would get better to every houseguest he met here in La Mesilla.

"Don't know if you heard it, but it rained last night for hours at a time. The skies were sparkling some, and it was probably messages from the gods. I hope that it was some omens of good and not evil. The sky is really dark still, and the sun never really came up, as far as I can tell. In fact it's still raining now, it's just slowed down some from early this morning. Get your stuff, and be ready to get wet and muddy this morning."

"Tió Custódio, my father called while you were checking the Chevy. He said people say the river has gotten high. He will still meet you, but it will not be easy crossing today."

"I thought you said, Custódio, the river was not much of a river. More like a big creek and was easy to walk across most days."

"Yeah, Roberto. That's what I said yesterday. Today, it is a different

111

story. The American westerns you read, do they never have bad weather with high waters to cross? Don't worry, we have ways. ChiChi, you grab my heavy rope and throw it in the back of the Blazer."

"If it was a creek yesterday, then we shouldn't we still walk through it easy enough today?"

"Yes, yes. The rope is just a safety measure for insurance. No problem for us."

"Roberto, he lives here along the river. You should not be worried."

"I know it, Luis. Just like to be sure."

We piled in the Blazer and rode away in the pouring rain. I don't see how it could have let up any, for it still was coming down—much worse than any rainy season I have ever seen. Custódio narrowed his eyes and leaned forward to see past the wipers that weren't keeping up with the heavy splattering. Luis sat with his head turned back some, gazing at ChiChi waving in the window. Maybe he felt some satisfaction since he left one of his picks behind with a note, "Remember the song in your heart."

The road wasn't much of a road at all, and we hit our heads every few minutes on the torn cloth of a ceiling. I couldn't see where we were heading, between the rush of rain in front of us and the constant waves milking the side window each time we hit a rock or hole in the road.

But after an hour of slow going, Custódio pulled the old Chevy to a stop near a string of tall, hanging trees whose branches wailed in the wind. Custódio said they usually would drive the kilometers to the river in twenty minutes or so, but the storm said otherwise.

Luis and I struggled to find the ponchos from behind the seat, and pulled the hood over our heads. Custódio had thought of everything, from the poncho to the tied garbage bags over our bags and guitar. He even stowed tortillas in some foil in our bags with a canteen for each of us. We had both nodded in unison and wrapped the canteens around our heads, old style. We all stepped out in water that reached up beyond our ankles, and it didn't take any time for us to be thankful for the ponchos.

Custódio had the rope in one hand and a flare gun in the other. We followed him into the tree line and came to the ridge looking down at the river. The picture I had in my mind of a flowing river as a streaming creek from home completely disappeared. The water was at least three to four meters deep.

Whoof and I stumbled back, falling over a protruding root in the muddy ground. I looked around to see Luis smile some as he pointed to the flare crossing over in an arc across another tree line. Custódio and Luis each grabbed an arm and hauled me up. My pants were muddy and wet, and I wished I had thought to get boots like Custódio wore. While I shook my old tennis shoes, hoping some water would drip off, high beam lights flashed on my poncho. I looked up and saw another vehicle, maybe a Blazer. What did they get a two-for-one deal? I could barely make out Bolívar in the window; he was mostly just a shadow with the glow of a cigarette with smoke winding out the crack of his window. Maybe I imagined the smoke, but I know I could see him holding the cigarette.

Custódio yelled, "Start walking toward the shore line." His head was turning frantically, looking for I couldn't see what. Then he hunched down after about ten steps and unraveled the rope. Custódio knelt over a trunk larger than me that had swung out over the water some and securely tied the rope. He tied the other end to his hips and motioned across. He got in my ear and yelled, "Wait till I cross and secure the line and then pull yourselves to the other side." He reached in the inside pocket of his jacket and pulled out two pairs of gloves with two knotted strips of rope. The gloves were crop workers', and each rope was less than a meter long. He looked in my eyes as he placed ropes and gloves in my hands and yelled above the rolling thunder that had just begun, "Pulley yourselves by tying the rope to your gloved wrists and wade or swim across."

Bolívar got out of his Blazer and slid down on his haunches to watch his brother. Custódio did a small rappel down and then stepped right into the water. The water came up to his waist, and the current swirled round him into larger waves. Even the smaller pool of eddies looked like whirlpools that wanted to climb higher. Custódio pushed his way through the heavy current. It wanted to tug him away from the focused imaginary line at the tree where Bolívar had stationed himself to prod Custódio on. Luis looked at me and shook his head. Where was my mama now that I could use her prayers? He just had to make it to the other side.

Bolívar pulled him up from the water and both nearly fell as they scrambled up the shore. Custódio untied the rope from his waist, and Bolívar went around the tree that was only a few feet from the water's edge. They wrapped the rope around hand over hand until it started to tighten and then looped it in and out for a couple of double sailor knots. They both checked the tautness of the line and nodded to each other and then in our direction, just as another thunder crack sounded and streaks of lightning lit up the darkening sky. This was beginning to look like fireworks in Antigua at holiday time.

By then we had placed our arms over the line and tied the rope to our wrists, just where the glove began to cover it. We both had our canteens strapped in one direction, and our bags in the other, so that they made it an X along our backs. Luis slithered along first, straight down the embankment, all the while carrying his guitar by its case handle facing up, like a soldier keeping his rifle dry. I followed a few steps behind and then missed my footing and slid all the way down to the river, burning my arms as they wrapped around the rope trying to slow the pace. Luis was just entering the water, and he broke my speed with a jolt.

"Ah, ha….on the gods of old that are holy! Don't push me, Mutt!"

"Sorry, Luis. It was an accident. Keep going now. We're all right."

Custódio and Bolívar were waving, and we heard Custódio yell, "Hurry up, you two! The current is getting faster. The storm is getting worse!"

We both wrapped our arms tightly around the rope and pushed our lower body as quick as possible going hand over hand. It was tough to find the best move. I tried to kick out and swim with my feet and felt my upper body would sink in. Then I tried to take long strides, but my feet would lose their footing on the slick rocks. Each time I felt some success, the current pulled me back one step. The waves and current were pulling us both down and back. So I struggled and kept my eyes on Luis, even as his guitar case wavered in the wind. I could see he was working to keep it steady above his head and not go under himself. We were over halfway across when the water seemed to get higher, and I struggled to keep my head above the water. I gulped a few mouthfuls of water as the whole shoreline lit up again, and I noticed Bolívar's Blazer was jacked up in the back.

Crack! I stopped and looked up and a whole tree was falling on the shore line in front of us.

"Look out!" I screamed to the men on the shore. They were scrambling underneath the rope bound to the tree five meters from the struck one. Bolívar was up under it and moving to the left and toward the banked up shore. As Custódio made it out from under the tied rope, the damaged tree came down like it had just received the final cut from an axeman. All in one glance, I saw it crush Custódio's shoulder, seemingly bounce once on the rope and then break it with a snap, and finally its branches came right at us.

I ducked one way in the water, and Luis went the other side of the rope. The guitar broke right in half, and the lower half banged into my shoulder while I was under water. After a few seconds, I felt a sudden rush of waves and it dawned on me that the rope must have snapped away; the struck tree freed the secured rope and the stress of it broke even our pulley ropes apart. We were both flung down the river like shots from a sling!

I broke the surface and saw Luis swimming in the direction of the top of the guitar case. It was caught in between two boulders in the river. I dove again and swam his way until I felt my hands bump something while stroking forward. I came up for air and watched, horrified, as the log that had just passed over me slammed Luis's back. His head bobbed in the water and then knocked into one of the boulders. Hand over hand, I was almost on him when a whirl of windy eddies took him and swirled him about deeper in and away down the river. I dove again, stroking hand over hand, until I saw him pop up again. Finally, I came upon him and grabbed his head in a half nelson. Kicking on my back now, I pushed the waves with my left hand and struggled to keep both our heads above the waves.

~ 21 ~

INSIDE THE MEXICAN BORDER
OCTOBER 1998

It was still raining. I wondered if it would ever stop. Another tree had fallen in the river ahead of us, and we were lucky enough to have it catch us after being taken for at least a kilometer or so downstream. I used the trunk as a brace and held onto a set of branches that stuck out into the water. The left side of the river was pulling at us to come back and over, but my grip was firm. I leaned back against the log and breathed deeply to catch myself. The sky was still lighting up, and thunder clapped again. What Mayan stories did Tió José have again about the gods when the thunder spoke out? Was that good or bad? Were the gods showing power and strength or punishment to man? I couldn't remember and didn't think it would matter much right now. So I waited in the water and prayed. I prayed to any god that would listen. And then I prayed harder to my mama's God, for perhaps he would listen, tho' He and I hadn't talked in a long while. Tired and wet with water still whirling about Luis and me up to our shoulders, I lay prone in the water and cried. Between sobbing tears of frustration, I prayed again and again for deliverance from this storm.

Finally, after what seemed like hours, the water calmed enough for me to walk us ashore. It hadn't stopped raining. I pulled Luis over some stony gravel, and we both lay there as the water pelted our faces. The poncho was sticky and seemed like it was sewn to my shirt. I had checked to see if Luis had a pulse but he was still unconscious from the blow to the head. I hoped he'd be okay. I didn't think there was much I could do right now. I had no strength left to even get up, let alone pull or carry Luis uphill. I sat up and undid my bag and canteen from around my neck. Luis had lost both his canteen and bag in the river, and I wasn't going to spend much time looking for them. With one hand I brushed wet hair from my face, and with the other I brought the canteen to my mouth. Licking my dry lips, I used my teeth to pull the cap and leaned my head back, swallowing a whole liter of water while the rainwater stuck inside my poncho sloshed down my chest. Bowing my head in frustration, I pulled off my poncho over my head and yanked it off. Then I reached for my bag from behind me with my left arm stretched out. The arm ached from swimming and holding Luis, and with another try and a grunt, I got it. I set it behind my head. I turned with a sigh, lying back down on my side with my head resting on the bag. Luis didn't have much of a pillow, but he wasn't going to know the difference. Soon after I fell soundly asleep.

I woke with two separate feelings on my face: wet kisses and more pelting rain. I pushed some hair out of my eyes, hoping my prayers had been answered. Praise be! Was it my mother happy to see me, or was I delirious? No, it wasn't my mother's dark strands of hair or her kisses smothering me in glee.

"Jonah, come here boy! Is that you down there? What have you found us? Jeremiah here would not stop his whining until we came out and looked for you. Now you have for us a gift? Come here, boy! Come here, now."

"Ruff, ruff!" He was talking back to his master, and he ran about Luis and me like we were two big bones he had just dug up. His tail wagged back and forth in my face, as I tried to push myself up from the slippery mud and grime. My arms had fallen asleep resting over each other, and when I started to pull them forward water came with them. The ground seemed to suck my arms back, until finally it loosed them with a loud splat, and mud splattered my face and poncho. At the top of the embankment in a clearing stood a man of the cloth smiling down at me. He towered on the ridge with his smock blowing in the wind, and his short-cropped, speckled gray hair was standing wet in the rainfall. He was a bigger man who was taller than most Mexicans I had met, with wide shoulders and large hands.

"Well, boy, you sit there while Jonah guards you," he pointed as he undid his belt. "I'll climb down and look at you guys." "Umm," Jeremiah whined to him, as if to tell him he wasn't scrambling down there with him. The priest struggled to tie one end of his long, heavy belt to a thick branch, with wet rope and bear-type claws trying to wrap it about. Finally he took the other end to help guide him down the slippery bank. I didn't think it would be long enough to rappel down like we had done, but by now the river's water had come back down some. And with only rain to deal with, the waves and crazy current didn't make it as tough to traverse.

"My name is Father Marcel, and what names do you boys go by?"

I had made my way to a crouch, and was easing into a stand when I grumbled back, "I'm Roberto, and he's Luis."

"You didn't kill him, did you? I wasn't planning on giving last rites today and—"

I looked up in surprise and sputtered, "No, he's my friend! Why would I kill him?"

"Don't know, but I've seen many friendships die over time. Sometimes even the people go with 'em," he said with a wink, as he seemed to dry out his beard in the steady rain. The beard wasn't heavy, so why he had to wring it out, I couldn't see.

"So did you get caught in the hurricane yesterday? The radio guys, they named this one Mitch. They say it has moved out to sea again. This one was bad, but you know I've seen some worse . . .", he rambled on as he leaned to check out Luis. Although I told him he wasn't dead, I could see he wanted to check him out anyway. I started to pet Jonah and said, "We thought it was only a storm."

"Well, Roberto. You don't have to tell all the details to me in one breath or even much at all. But we need to get you guys some help, especially your friend Luis. It looks like he might have a concussion, and I'm praying he'll come to soon. My old Suburban is a good fifty or so meters away," he looked up from the river shore as he scratched his beard.

"You can help us?" I asked him. Things had looked so bad, I didn't see a reason to hope.

He stepped over Luis's leg, "I plan to help you two, but the 'devil is in the details' as my old bishop used to say. He thought it best to pick only appropriate times to use that one." I heard him chuckle to himself.

"I can make it up the side and get some branches to make a stretcher. Like I've seen it in a western once, and we can haul him to your truck."

"That sounds like it would be fun and all," he commented as he started to take Luis hand over hand onto his back, "but I think we'll try the fireman procedure I learned a while back volunteering." With that thought, he held Luis' two arms with his left arm crossed over and used his right to help in the climb up. He seemed to know right where to step with only a second's glance and was already at the top while Jonah was still barking at him "good-bye" or "wait for me," I wasn't really sure which.

It took me a few minutes to make it up. I made my eyes follow his steps, but some of the markings were dripping quickly away from the rocks he stepped on. So I missed on the second rock and fell, with my arms catching me enough that my mouth just missed tasting mud pie. Jonah barked some at my heel, and I scrambled up the rest of the way.

At the top, I noticed he was dragging Luis across the clearing. Jeremiah was barking and snapping at Luis's mud caked feet, and it seemed like they were only a few steps from Father Marcel's car. I looked around and remembered my canteen and bag. I could leave the water, but not the bag. I used his rope he left and slid down to get both of my things. I needed my things from home; between money, clothes, books, and memories I couldn't do without them.

~ 22 ~

THE CHAPEL IN MEXICO

I turned the crank on the faucet off, after the hot water had run completely out. Father Marcel had said something about witch's head and to be careful with the hot water, as some had gotten zapped. I wasn't sure if that meant bug spray or electrical shock, but either way I wasn't planning on getting it. I was drying off on the right side of the dorms for the men, and he said there was another side for women. While walking out and drying myself, I noticed a dozen beds set up in three rows. Each bed had a thin blanket, a pillow slightly puffed up at the end, and a small lunch bag, folded at the top and sitting at end of the bed. I saw a single bulb shining in the center of the room, but my attention turned to the impassioned off key melodies of Father Marcel and the harmonies of whining Jeremiah and howling Jonah.

At the end of the beds I saw a large, spacious kitchen area through the open doorway and the three of them all looking down at a round, ceramic dish overflowing with dry dogfood. I could hear a DJ identify the last tune, and so the trio must have been singing along with that oldie from the sixties. Now they all just stared at the dish, and I wondered what each was thinking. Maybe they usually got better food and were refusing to eat this brand. Or perhaps they liked people food, and this was some type of training session. Whatever it was, I went to the doorway and knocked on the side jam.

"Excuse me, Father. But could I ask about my clothes, and where they might be?"

"Well, Roberto, I took those mud-drenched clothes and have asked one of the ladies from my parish to kindly launder them for you in the back pila," he answered with a smile as he grunted and tapped the floor with his foot between Jonah and Jeremiah.

"I heard you singing with the radio. You guys are good."

"Yes, well at first thought they were singing with me. Until I noticed they both refused to eat the new bag of food I got them, and now it seems they were both complaining about the new brand. I must say, some are too particular with their eating habits that they should think to break free from some mundane routines and try new adventures. Of course, with dogs they probably don't want to think so much, but I do see the playful side in them as they insist on running fields away from me and—"

"Yes, Father Marcel, I hate to interrupt, but what should I wear while waiting, and where is Luis?" I asked. Boy could he talk without missing a beat, and sometimes I just wanted to get to the point.

"Oh, there is a closet in the back corner that you probably did not see. It has some slacks and shirts you may borrow. Also, you may have noticed a bag on each bed, and one of these beds is for you to sleep in later tonight. Anyway, the bag has some basic toiletries in it that you may find useful. So take a look at the bag. Your friend, Luis, he is still out, so to speak. Another of the ladies in my parish, she saw to his bruises and cuts. We think he should waken soon, but we'll watch him still. He is in the room across the hall from mine so that we may listen and watch him. After you get dressed, come sit down and have a cup of coffee while I heat some soup for you."

When I returned the coffee was hot enough that it warmed me to my very heart and core, and I was glad to be here in this place, though I wasn't really sure what this place was exactly. I knew it had parts of the church here but had never seen beds and a kitchen available at home in Father Angelo's church at San Miguel Acatán. On the way in, I had seen some women, with their children sitting in a dining area. So, Luis and I weren't the only guests here.

I sat on a three-legged stool in front of a long prep counter that held the coffee pot with its warmer and cups of sugar and milk. Although my family wanted me to drink it black, I preferred sweeter flavors in it when I could. The kitchen was bigger than most I had seen, except for the one at the university. That was even bigger than this, with all the students it had to serve.

When Father Marcel had finished warming up soup for me, he set a steaming bowl in front of me with a spoon poking out of it and a cup of water. This was almost too good to be happening, but I had curiosity pushing me more than hunger.

I finally came out and just asked him. "Father, what is this place you have going on here? As we pulled up yesterday, the building outside had a steeple and towers with a bell, just like Mama's church at home. Last night I fell sound asleep, but this morning I got up to see beds all around with extra shower space. And then there are strangers walking around and children running up and down the halls. I just don't understand."

Father Marcel, he shook his head and chuckled some. "Roberto, I have a church I run here. I have my parish I care for in the area, but we do much more than only care for the local community. We are a sanctuary for the many travelers who come through this area. So many people are in need of help that we in this church try to assist them."

I set my spoon down to cool my mouth from the burning broth and asked, "Why do you need to help these people? Most of them, I would think, are traveling to America. They should be planning on not stopping but getting there as soon as possible."

"Yes, well, things happen in life. And sometimes life just happens to you. So many travel along this border, and it has become known as a popular route. Because of this, there are problems with bandits or gangs, police, and poor weather conditions. People prey on other people, especially when they are unprepared for it and are weak, hungry, or distressed. The bandits take the money that the travelers had saved up to cover the cost for guides and food, and then push them to work to earn back a way to continue on. The people are left without money and must find work or stoop to prostitution to survive. The police charge bribes sometimes and look the other way in order for the people to travel. Then the heat, rain, and even hurricanes take a heavy toll on people. So, here we are to be a sanctuary for people, a place of rest, and sometimes help them in better choices they make."

"But how did you get here to do this that you do?" I wondered aloud.

"Well, Roberto. I was raised here in Mexico but was influenced heavily by a local priest. He helped both me and my family and really showed God's love to our community. From this I chose to go to the US and studied to be a priest myself. Once I was close to completing my studies, the bishop and I planned a way to raise funds for this mission, a mission for people in real need. The project turned out to cost much more than I had planned, and I feared that it would fail. But God intervened and a great donation was made by someone who remained anonymous, and here we are today. It has grown to house more as the need has also increased."

"Father Marcoel, you must have a lot of love in your heart for the people to leave Mexico and then come back here to do all this. I still don't understand why you'd want to come back to this area. In America, things are so much better off, and you would be happier." I sipped some of my water and thought about what Tió José had said. "In fact, if you felt so much love, you could still send money back here to people. My Uncle José and his family have done that for each other and made great differences in their lives. It would still be—"

"Stop, now Roberto. You need to understand that sending money is all right for some needs, but others really must have something tangible in their lives. The Holy Father made it clear to me while I was attending seminary that I should be His hands and feet to work for Him. I initially saw so many problems here in Mexico while helping on a farm not far from here before I went to America. So many Latinos with dreams just like yours have corrupt and evil people take advantage of them. With nothing left in their lives, some people are left without any hope at all, and often times they will make worse decisions. Boys and men to turn to robbery, and some join local gangs, and all intention of moving to America and then helping their family back home is forgotten. Women and girls are left vulnerable as they may lose the men they're with through beatings and death, and vulnerability leaves little choice but to turn to prostitution or robbery. This mission is here to show God's love in a real sense to people who need outside help as they sometimes have no other place to turn. I thank God that He allowed the bishop I worked under to make it known this mission of my heart. Somehow it convicted others, and the funds came in to enable me to come and refurbish this chapel into the larger mission it is now."

"I hadn't realize the evil side of people was so bad, Father. I mean I knew about sin and the poor choices you speak of that people can make. But I never thought our own people would steal and work so hard against each other. It makes me so sad that you have to be here and yet happy that you are."

"Well, Roberto, you should know I have heard of a similar mission that is being planned near the Oceano Pacifico. I hear another priest is building one in Ciudad Tecun Uman, and his is supposed to be much bigger for the needs are certainly more in that area since it is a larger border crossing near the port."

I took a spoonful of soup that had cooled enough for me to taste it without burning. Then I swirled my cup of coffee around and tossed a gulp back. I dipped two fingers in what was left in the cup and ran my right hand through my hair in frustration. Tió José never told about this much danger in his stories. I remember the adventure he spoke about so many times—the way his cousins made it past police checks and slipped under or around border patrols. Evil that is so common was not something we really talked about much, or I thought about. The corruption we spoke about was more in local and national politics and not among the poor people. Poor people make up the majority of the people in my country and even Mexico.

Father Marcel picked up the pot of coffee, and then my cup. Boy, was he quiet. I didn't even hear him walk over to get the coffee.

"Roberto, have some more coffee and stop that worrying. You can't fix all of your problems in one breath."

I picked up the cup with both hands. I shivered as I thought about the different dangers that might come ahead for us that I had never thought about, and then the coffee warmed me enough to stop the shaking. I looked down at the floor, and Jonah was staring up at me while wagging his tail so fast it looked like it was swatting bugs during the rainy season.

~ 23 ~

AT THE MISSION

After a few days of rain, it finally cleared up and the sun came out. Father Marcel suggested a walk outside for a while with the boys, and he showed me the large field where guest children would play without worry. He had put in two small poles on each side of the field for games of football, and most of the grass had been trampled away. I asked how the children and the dogs liked his playing field, and he had just laughed as he pointed at where more men ran and knocked over the poles for the net.

I told him about my family and how much they meant to me. I sighed some and wondered aloud if Luis and I should go back home to our mothers. They might need us more, and now Luis could need his mother's care. Father Marcel patted my shoulder and nodded toward the outside of the mission, and I noticed a mother with her son walking by hand in hand. He asked about my father and where my brothers were. He assumed that I must have at least a few brothers. Not wanting to correct him harshly, I only shook my head and kicked a taller weed growing too close to the goal.

Although he seemed to love to talk, I didn't feel like it much. Father Marcel tried to make me feel better in telling me how many boys are without fathers due to drugs, alcohol, or bad accidents. I didn't know whether he was a prophet, or just practicing, or if he was trying to be a doctor and fix me. I didn't need fixing, just answers as to whether to go on further in Mexico or to go back home.

I thanked him for showing me around and left him to go check on Luis. Jonah and Jeremiah both ran alongside me while I ran back toward the back of the chapel. Jonah barked twice as I shut the door behind me, and I left him outside with his brother and master.

Father Marcel had set up Luis in a private room down the hall from the room that worked as a dormitory for men. I saw an older woman close his door, and she walked down the hall to the open kitchen and dining area with a tray in her hands. Maybe she was hoping he had come to and was going to feed him some soup. I picked up my pace, thinking it could be true. It seemed like the dishes and spoon rang some, like empty cups and silverware do sometimes. I grabbed the door and rushed in.

"Luis, are you up and awake? Come on you, you ugly dog! You must be faking it to fool me some?" I stepped over and shook him a bit, but he didn't budge or move at all. His chest lightly moved some as he slowly breathed, but there was no other stirring in him.

I sat there in the late morning light in a beaten up wooden chair with a stringed wicker-type back. I would have preferred an all-wooden back so the strings wouldn't poke in my back. I leaned my head back some as the sun shone through the window from the other side of the bed and laid my arm on a small table next to me. I felt something scratch my arm and noticed a rosary there next to a book. I picked up the book, and read the title. A book of prayers and rosary. How fitting for me while waiting for Luis to waken. I stretched out my legs and pulled out one of the picks that Luis had brought from my front pants pocket. I leaned backed again, and lightly strummed the prayer book with the pick. Could I play a song and pray? To whom would I pray? The God that my mama spoke of so often and now Father Marcoel is so faithful to, or what about the gods of my father and Tió José, and the work the shaman can do in gifts on wooden altars? Maybe I should have found a Mayan shaman near here? I just didn't know what to think or feel. Luis was my friend, and the one who understood me most. My mama, she tried to see deep inside me. Luis and I were more than friends—we had become brothers. There was history we shared, and nothing could take that away. I just hoped he was not hurt so badly that I would have to leave him behind.

"'Berto, is that a guitar you're strumming there or a book you're trying to read through some Mayan magic 'cause I could use magical food for my stomach."

I jumped as he started laughing at me, and the book fell forward and onto the floor. The rosary beads slipped from my left fingertips when I settled back up in the chair, and he just laughed all the more. Finally, I jumped up and ran over to the bed and bent over to hug him. I tried to hug him, and it turned into a crazy bear arm hug. And I guess that was all right. I stepped back away from the bed and shakily sat back down in the wooden chair.

"Luis, man, I'm so glad to see you awake! I didn't want to think what would happen if you would have never woken up. This is great, and I better go the priest to get you some—"

"Wait a minute, you happy mutt! I got to know why you were playing some book with my pick. Where's my guitar?" Luis frantically turned his head side to side in the room. Searching for it. "I don't see it in here. Roberto, where is it? Where is it?" His voice raised quickly from his quiet, sarcastic, and calm tone to one with a much higher pitch.

"Luis, hey, calm down. You've been out for days and don't know what's happened to us." My thoughts were awash with confusion, and I felt like the water of the stormy hurricane cover my thoughts. What should I say? "Do you remember anything at all? What of the river, and—"

"Look, I remember the river and crossing it and carrying my guitar." His hands went high in the air over the bed, as he played back the crossing. "So where is it now? Did you put it somewhere safe? Or are you getting new strings for me?" He looked deep in my eyes with those questions.

"Luis, you just woke up and got to be hungry. Stop worrying about that guitar, and I'll get you some."

"Shut up about food, Roberto!" Luis screamed at me as he jumped up and grabbed a water bowl on a side bedstand to his left and threw it at me. I ducked to the right as it flew into the door just to the left of me. The sponge and water fell to the floor with the cracked pitcher. I pushed the hair out of my eyes and pushed away a tear. I didn't know what to say or do. I just stared at him. Luis sat down on the edge of the bed and shook his head and arms violently.

"'Berto, that guitar. My papa gave it to me. It was the last thing he did with me, and he played some simple chords for me. Now you can't tell me where it is. Please just go get it, and let me play it some." Again he looked in my eyes.

"Luis', I can't go get it. I'm so sorry, but it was lost at the river. I almost lost you, and Custódio, he's gone now too. And I am so sorry about—"

"Hey, what's that noise in here?" Father Marcel knocked and pushed the door open at the same time. Then he almost slipped and fell over the china, but he caught the handle of the door to steady himself.

He looked around at the mess and smiled as Luis looked up at him from the edge of the bed. "Well, well! Luis is awake now! Thanks be to the Holy Father from above. It is good to meet you finally, young sir! But I see from the broken bathing china you aren't a happy patient. It's fine, as we have more in our kitchen cupboard. My name is Father Marcel, and I'm very pleased to see you sitting up!"

"Luis, this is the priest that was kind enough to take us in after the hurricane and shelter us with—"

Luis looked up as he started to stop shaking and asked, "What hurricane?"

Father Marcel chuckled that heavy laugh of his and said, "Why Mitch, of course. He came through with a real vengeance but didn't stay too long, just long enough to shake us up around here more than usual. You see that we in this area—" Here he goes again. His kindness is great but how much must we hear?

"I'm sorry, Father, but Luis just woke up and I was going to ask you for some food, and he'll be sure to hear your stories later. Can we get him some soup or something?"

Father Marcel seemed to love to educate everyone about almost anything he could. But I thought Luis needed to eat. He left the room mumbling about youth and their lack of zeal for learning, where the broom was, and if he had any soup left.

When I heard Father Marcel's voice down the hall still mumbling, I turned back to Luis. He had stopped shaking, and now he just stared at the floor. He didn't speak or look up. He only seemed to focus on his

128

blistered feet, still sore from the jagged rocks in the river. I fingered the pick between my thumb and fingers.

"Luis, I'm sorry. I didn't realize where your love of music came from so much. I would have tried to understand more, and—"

"Look 'Berto. Don't try and read too much into this. It was a gift that really meant something to me, but it's not like he gave me a passion for music. That passion is in me and not something he handed to me as a boy." I was silent for a second.

"Well, anyway, I'm still sorry about everything. Now that you're awake, we have to figure out what to do. When you are up to moving, do we stay here, continue on into Mexico, or head back home?" I hoped this wasn't too much for him already.

"Hold on a minute, Roberto! Back home? Stay here? Why are you talking like this? What about that American dream you spoke about?" His hands waved around, pointing off to America.

"Well, you know Custódio is dead. You may not be completely well enough to travel, and we can't stay here in this mission much longer. We have to think about what is best under the circumstances. Plus, there are more dangers on the way to America than we have been told about. It might be best if we think about turning back to our families where they can care for us. And we can help care for them in person."

~ 24 ~

ON A GREYHOUND BUS

The bus, a large Greyhound that sounded like a train pulling out of town, with its loud engine that wheezed heavily when it started and stopped, rode really smooth. I picked up my jacket that slipped under my shoulders and fixed it under my head so I could fall back asleep. That coat made it through Hurricane Mitch and helped lull me to dreamlessness without the deep potholes, crazy traffic, or loud passengers I was used to in my home country's buses. This ride, though loud too, is still so much nicer than in Guatemala or even Mexico. I'm not sure if it was maybe less the bus and more the quietness of the people and the quality of the roads.

I gazed out the window and saw little of anything except the beauty of valleys, mountains, plains, and all kinds of other terrain I'd only read about until then. The other people seemed to take in the greatness of this land without a second thought, and every time I wake up I see more to appreciate. The land and roads are all empty, but the vastness we drive through seems to change almost every hour. I feel torn between the tiredness of this trip where I just want to get where we are going, and yet somehow pulled ahead and beyond with this American storybook land I saw unfolded before me.

I've had long daydreams about this land, and the variety of wrinkled and worn paperbacks have only fueled the embers that have stirred my random flickering thoughts. Maybe I should have never picked up those books that tourists randomly left in the Guatemalan city where I attended the university. I had read in high school about explorers and the Western movement in American. But the contemporary novels they left behind, like King, Grisham, and Crichton, showed me a new world of the culture in America. If I had read more of the required reading at the university, there might be less of this moving in my insides on the bus ride. Tiá Rosa's, she used to ask, "How is your stomach today?" It was a mixed answer for me, but her Cesar would always answer with a grin while licking his lips in hopes of a snack. I soon came to see what she was actually asking. It was our native Guatemaltecos way of asking about one's heart, and how it was feeling. The pit of one's stomach holds the feelings that are most important. Love, fear, courage, depression, and adventure have all been more than just hunger pains deep in my stomach.

A knee jabbed into the back of my seat, and I mumbled, "Luis, I'm still trying to sleep."

"Wake up, Roberto," Luis laughed with a snort as he shoved his feet into the back of my seat. "You sleep too long, you'll miss this America you've boasted so much of as we drive through it."

I sat up and looked out my window. Luis knocked me on the back of the head with his new guitar as he moved it into his lap to strum a few chords. I turned around and slapped his head with my paperback novel, and he just smiled that old grin of his. He strummed the chorus of our favorite local tunes we used to sing as boys, and I started to laugh. It's good for us to laugh again. We haven't had fun on this trip, and it was supposed to be an adventure full of fun. Reality hit us hard when we saw our dreams ready to fall through our fingertips. Luis had lost his guitar in the river, and what little money he had brought in his bag was lost. Our guide, Custódio, was gone from us and we were really partly at fault for his passing from this life. But mostly we lost our spirit for life, and I wasn't sure what to do next.

Father Marcel was so kind in moving us forward and on with our lives. It took Luis another week before he could walk more than a few feet without falling. After we went through all of the food the father had in his cupboard, he had had to send one of the ladies to the market for more food. Luis refused to talk to anyone or even look my way when I stepped in his room. Father Marcel finally made dinner that he personally cooked, and he required us to have time with him at his kitchen counter. He sat us next to each other with hot coffee and empty plates. Of course, there were plates of tortillas and fried plantains, but

131

when we smelled the pollo stew on the stovetop we both tried to get a view of it. The aroma of the simmering chicken broth with pieces of meat floating on top of the zucchini and carrots took my breath away. We had been eating beans and leftover tortillas but not homemade stew.

"Boys, these are just like your mamas make and one of my parishioners cooked it all this morning. Coffee will be all you will have unless I see you two start to talk like the friends you are. Jonah and Jeremiah are licking their lips, and they can share the stew with me. I can easily heat up beans for you two again. So Luis, you my young friend must forgive the things that have happened with you, for Roberto did not control them."

The smell of the stew and sweetness of the plantains couldn't move Luis. He sat there with a grim look on his face. Jonah was wagging his tail in the kitchen, and he barked at Father Marcel who just smiled. Father Marcel raised a ladleful of stew to his nose, breathed deeply, and sighed. He shook his head and looked over to us. He winked at me, stabbed a piece of chicken meat with a fork, and waved it lightly in the air as he pulled it from the fork with his left hand. Jonah barked, jumped up, and snapped it from the fingertips of Father Marcel. Jeremiah ran in, barked three or four times, and looked up between Father Marcel and us.

"Luis, hug and forgive so all will be well again," Father Marcel chuckled.

Luis slapped my head with the palm of his hand and yanked my hair in the back. I jumped up and gave him a half hug and then hit him with a light undercut from my left hand. He grunted and laughed at me.

"At least you didn't kick me when I was lying down in bed!" Luis said with smirk.

We ate our stew and the rest of our lunch, and Father Marcel said we should take the boys for a walk. Jonah and Jeremiah barked loudly in excitement when they heard their names spoken, and Luis and I grabbed a ball that sat in the corner begging to be dribbled. Luis snatched the ball up, and I ran out calling the boys' names. The dogs ran ahead quickly, and we passed the ball between us. I took the ball, yelling, "Goaaaalllll!" and shot it between two uprooted trees a few meters in front of us. The ball rolled to a stop just between my imagined goal, and Jonah picked it up with his teeth and twirled it around in the air with Jeremiah nipping at the ball at every swing of Jonah's head. Luis caught up with me, a little out of breath, laughing at the game the dogs played.

"Luis, should we give up and go back? Mama would be happy to see me, and I know your family already misses you. And you can't say you don't miss them."

Luis stopped and looked at me. He shook his head for a second.

"Roberto, what about those dreams of yours? My dreams haven't died either, you know! America is still waiting for the next Latin rocker, and they haven't even met me yet. Would your father, or even brother, give up now? What would they say about going back? Your family took dreams and made them moments to live for while awake!"

I licked my fingertips, and pushed them through the inside of my eyes and then up my forehead. Shaking my hair out of my eyes, I nodded in agreement but didn't know hat else to say. He was finally awake and ready for life again. Me, I felt like I was the one who was out cold and he was splashing water to bring me out of it. Luis, he was really a good friend for me and knew what I needed.

"Roberto, you awake now? What do you say? Let's go to America, and make money and meet new people!" Luis looked out past the trees and beyond.

I smiled, and said "Yeah, Luis, let's go find our dreams in America and make 'em real!' I grabbed the ball away from the dogs and threw it with a wild toss across the trail from which we came and sighed deeply.

We finished out that day preparing for our journey. We got together our few items that made it through the river and added to them the clothes donated from the mission. The father was kind in thinking of underclothes and socks, new ponchos, some hats to keep the sun out, and even a paperback book for me. He called it a classic, *Dante's Inferno*, that he had read while in America, but I wasn't sure I was up for diving deep into that much thought. Custódio's brother Bolívar, though he was still grieving the loss of his brother, made ready for the next part of our route through Mexico. When Father Marcel called Bolívar on his cell, he asked him to bring a few items from the market while coming out to the mission.

Bolívar greeted us when he got to the mission and then spent a few hours walking with Father Marcel and the twins in the garden and fields behind the mission. Luis and I could tell from their hand gestures and half hugs that Bolívar was thinking hard about Custódio. They must have been really close. We knew they were partners in business along the border, but Luis and I could tell little more in the time we had spent with Custódio. There was a feeling of comfort with his nephew, especially in the way he seemed at home that night we were there. Bolívar and Father Marcel shook forearms, and the father patted him on his shoulder.

Bolívar nodded a greeting our way while we were finishing our last breakfast there, and then he stooped to pick up our bags to load into his Blazer. I jumped down from the stool in the kitchen and reached out to tug at his sleeve. He jerked his head back with a start and smiled as I tried to apologize for his brother's death. Bolívar set down the bags and turned around the rest of the way, ruffling my long curly hair just like Jesús used to do years ago.

"Chico, you boys have no guilt to bear from that night. This was an act of God, and we just bear the fruit of it. If any shame is to be carried, it would be on my shoulders." He checked the straps on our bags to be sure they were tightly shut.

"But Bolívar," I asked, "What do you mean? You could have never known about the storm."

"Yeah, Bolívar!" Luis exclaimed as he jumped from his stool and nearly fell. He waved his guitar pick, downstroking his words with small rhythmic strokes of the right hand while he tried to phrase his questions and regain his balance. I thought then he hadn't quite recovered and shouldn't have been trying to move both body and mind together so quickly. "That's just crazy! Bolívar, how can you even be thinking to carry any blame at all? The fallen tree, the high winds, the shifting currents—none of it could be controlled. I don't see how this is your fault!"

"Well, Luis," Bolívar slowly shrugged his slumped shoulders and stuttered on, "our . . . our cable news. It . . . it spoke some the night before about the storm getting worse, and we didn't take it into account. You boys were scheduled through José to come in and over, and we wanted to keep you moving."

I looked at him and pointed out, "High chance of storm is no hurricane."

"We have the technology to know daily how the storms are progressing, but that morning I just failed to check." Bolívar smiled sadly and gave a smart tug on his jacket. "I usually check every morning, and I don't know why I didn't that time."

He shook his head again and boosted both bags over his back. He mumbled under his breath something about a bus schedule. He strode toward the door with some purpose, and I caught a look from Luis and stared after Bolívar. Luis followed him out, while I stopped at the kitchen counter near the coffee maker and dropped a note of thanks I had written. I was almost glad Father Marcel had been called away from the mission to help a family nearby. It wasn't much of a note, and I couldn't adequately say in words all Father Marcel had done for us. I wrote of the choice he made in acting to help us so much, but what I appreciated most were his words of wisdom for us. He shared them with me at just the right times, like Mama weeding with one hand and straightening the base of the plant with the other as she tended her garden. It must be a gift from his God, that he knows how and when to say what needs to be said. I left the note and started to walk. Then I turned back to the counter and doodled smiley faces next to a set of paw prints. His twins were real heroes for us.

~ 25 ~

RIDE TO VERACRUZ

That day we piled in the back of Bolivar's Chevy Blazer and drove for four or five hours, although it seemed like all day. Bolívar decided to take us to Veracruz himself, and although it was a quiet ride, it was much better than the bus ride we could have been on. Bolívar explained he had family in the city to visit, and that he didn't mind saving the money. We both thought of different ways to find out more details as to why he actually came with us and did not just put us on a local bus with a few parting words. It's not like he had to work something out with us about the death of Custódio on the drive, since he barely spoke during the whole drive. Why not just do what he had been paid to do from Tió José and move on with his life? After a few hours we stopped at a local cantina for beans and tortillas. While waiting for us to finish eating, Bolívar pulled a pad of paper from his jacket pocket and made some notes around a list of names. Luis and I exchanged looks and asked, "What's with the list? Are you a hitman now?"

Bolívar snorted, "Nope, not me!" He pulled out his beeper from his belt to check for messages and checked his watch and jiggled the phone plugged in. "Come on, boys, time to go." I had heard about those newer mobile phones but had never seen one up close.

We slid in the back, and I noticed Bolívar flick his cigarette out the door as he slammed it shut. I thought he'd light up again to keep his stress level down, but he didn't. Luis and I used our new jackets as pillows and fell asleep. While I was still half asleep, I heard Bolívar talking in hushed tones. I nudged Luis with my foot from the far side of the back seat and nodded toward the front. Luis opened one eye and rolled over deeper into the corner of the seat. I caught pieces of phrases about Custódio being gone, money, and ChiChi. I leaned my head away from the windy passenger seat and tried to hear more. I kept one eye shut, and still saw Bolívar looking in the rearview mirror as I heard something drop on his console. There was a curse mumbled, and I saw him reaching for the phone. He struggled some to get a grip on it. He must still be getting used to having a phone there in his truck. Then he sighed some as he sat up and seemed to push it in the cigarette lighter. Ten minutes later, while Luis was still sleeping, I heard Bolívar answer the mobile phone on the first ring. He told the caller something about family and that money was still to be made. The conversation went on for a little longer, and I just turned back to the wind to worry about tomorrow.

Bolivar told us about the train ride at the stopover while eating, and that it was not an easy one. The ride on the train was long, sometimes even weeks. This ride I was worried about, especially with so many things that could go wrong. What about policia catching us, bandits robbing us, or even getting our food if we were going for so long?

I hadn't heard much of the train, except its nickname: El Norté. The officials watch out for illegals trying to cross, and locals are told not to help them. There are some charitable ones who apparently throw produce at the train as it passes by. Now I wish I hadn't heard these rumors, or instead, maybe Bolívar could take us all the way to the U.S./Mexican border.

I shook my head some as I felt the wind against the window, and it echoed from the one side to the other ear. I poked one finger from each hand in my ears to clear some air, but nothing popped or opened up. We weren't high up in the mountains, so I didn't know what was wrong. I shivered some and rubbed my arms underneath my new long-sleeved shirt. I looked over at Luis breathing to some off beat song in his dreams and couldn't believe how easily he slept. Wasn't he even thinking about tomorrow at all? I kicked his feet that were practically pushing my legs and woke him up with a little start.

"Luis, are you cold? It seems, like, kinda cold in here. Should we turn on the heat?"

"Roberto, you have the jacket and shirt the priest gave you, and I'm feeling like it's the hot season back here." Luis smiled. "I don't think you're getting sick. You worry like an old Mayan lady who has no money for the shaman. Now you worry and think you're getting sick. Just—"

"But Luis, maybe we should ask Bolívar to take us all the way to the border. We can give him some of the money I had left stashed in my bag. You know it'd be better if he got it than some policia or bandits. It's partly our fault about Custódio, and we should do something." I shook my head and pushed both hands through my hair and tugged on back along my neck.

"Roberto, I knew you were listening in too much to the locals talking about the train and illegals on it. We will be one of them, but we'll be ready for it. Stop trying to reason a way not to ride that train."

I looked up as Bolívar grunted in agreement. He smiled in the rear mirror, and I could see some of the yellow at the edge of his teeth from his smoking. I hadn't see him smile much and wondered about it now. "Yeah, Roberto, you are worrying way too much for a boy who's becoming a man. Where is your sense of adventure I heard you boys were searching for? And stop thinking I might take you the rest of the way through Mexico. Its not happening! And I—"

"I'm sorry, Bolívar," I interrupted and I felt my voice drop, "I meant no disrespect."

"I know, Roberto," Bolívar answered, "but I have meetings with my family that can't wait. And I have to explain some details of Custódio's passing to people who asked to hear of it in person. Really, the drive isn't but an extra day or so, but I have committed to others and even my family back home."

"I understand, Bolívar. I got to thinking and my mind carried me away."

"Well, look Roberto, I am still setting you guys up. Your uncle José and I have talked to be sure your remaining details are settled. Calm yourself down, all right?"

"You spoke to José?" Luis asked. "Did he say anything about our families? Are they doing well?" His voice had risen some and I smiled in agreement.

"Watch it now," Bolívar laughed some, "you might show some love. We can't be letting people past lyrics and strums of an air guitar."

Luis's questioning look turned to a scowl, and I snorted. He just turned to me and then rolled back to the window to sleep. I asked myself how Bolívar picked up on who Luis was so quickly. He caught me looking at him as he started to light a cigarette after pulling out the phone charger. While he took the first slow pull from it and blew a couple smoke rings, I saw him wink at me with that smile of his.

~ 26 ~

HOPPING THE TRAIN

True to his word, Bolívar set us up well. He spent time with the locals and got us familiar with the schedule for the train. We discussed at length the best time to get on it. Then he planned with us the exact day to prepare to board the train, although it wasn't much more than a couple of days after we arrived in Veracruz. The night before, I realized why we needed the exact time, day, and place, as he explained that he had paid a change of hands to pay the conductor in slowing the train at a certain spot outside of the city. He even ran with us to show us how to jump and reach for the train, using one of his cousins to drive the Blazer for us to practice. He kept repeating the importance of timing and balance so we learned to jump at just the right time. Many chose other spots to hop on the train, but his source had said this was a good one that fewer people knew about and that was actually safer. The policia didn't watch this spot, and there wasn't as much gravel. At other spots outside of the city, people had legs and arms broken or sprained when they lost their footing or their grip reaching for the boxcars.

Bolívar suggested we ride on top of the cars, as the officials checked the cars more often, and the payment he gave covered the workers not looking for us on this train. After more talk about our journey, Bolívar finally wrote down our next contact at the border. He apologized that it would be a little longer trip, and it might even be a week longer than some might take. But his family lived in Ciudad Juarez, which was farther north and east than some routes that stopped toward Nuevo Laredo. One of his cousins would watch for us at the first stop and put us up in his home. Finally, when we parted ways, he gave us each bear hugs with bags of tortillas and fruit to keep us fresh.

140

His lasting words to us were, "Remember Custódio, and go with the gods in the winds."

I've been riding a bus for most of my life. I rode with my father, and then my brother and father both. After they were gone, I rode with Mama to the market and helped her with shopping once a week. The bus was an animal I had grown used to from my youth, but the train became a whole new pet to learn to love. Traveling on the bus gave me fond memories like a puppy that cuddled in the house with you, but a snapping, slobbering hungry wolf was more the picture of riding the train.

Bolívar had explained to us that the train would slow to a crawl, and we could easily hop aboard. He had paid through a number of hands and guaranteed we would have no problem getting on the train. So we waited outside of town until we both heard the humming of the wheels as they ground against the rails. Luis shushed me quickly, and we searched through the scattered trees for the cross-country train. The air smelled of bad exhaust, cattle cars, and the braking system as it held back the speed coming out of town. We turned to each other and laughed, as we knew it was slowing down just for us. We could see the tops of the train through the branches blowing around our heads across the bend. We stood and stretched our knees, readying ourselves for the moment. It came into view and seemed to be gaining speed and not slowing.

"'Berto, run now," yelled Luis as he jumped up and sprinted forward. I hurled after him and breathed deeply as I pushed my feet into a run. "Faster, faster!" Luis turned his head as he got closer to the side of an open boxcar. I was already out of breath when I heard others yelling, "Run, run . . . you can make it!" I looked up slightly and noticed a bunch of guys waving us on. I heard a heavy grunt and saw Luis reach for the train and then pull himself into the side of the car. I took another hard breath and ran even harder. When I reached for the sidebar of the car with both hands, I missed it with my right hand and just caught it with my left. Hanging for what seemed like minutes, I grabbed for the inside door with my right hand.

"'Berto, I got you," Luis said as he pulled roughly on my hand.

141

"Don't let go!" I yelled as I grabbed for his arm and tried to get footing on the side of the car. I missed with my feet and jammed my knees into the floor of the car. Luis stepped back into the car and pulled with all his weight. I felt a huge strain on my wrist and up my arm and then fell face forward into hay that smelled of manure.

I pulled my head up in disgust and wondered aloud to Luis, "So much for the train slowing for an exchange of hands.

~ 27 ~

EN ROUTE TO THE MEXICAN/AMERICAN BORDER

The time we spent on the train seemed to last for months, but it was actually about three weeks. At each stop we observed the habit of others hidden on the train and found ways to adjust to life on the move. We jumped down and scrounged around with others for some type of food, especially after the first week when our supplies that Bolívar gave us ran out. It was especially a blessing from above when the local people in some towns saw us coming and threw fresh fruit our way. It was like the surprise favorite meals Mama used to make, and we tasted the juiciness of the citrus fruits for hours after as it dripped down our cheeks, and we had to wipe it with our sleeves. Luis and I both sniffed our shirts later and just laughed at how enjoyable those small moments had been.

The worst part of adjusting to that life was watching out for the trainman. In the first week, we were almost caught hiding among some hay, but then some boys stomped on the roof to distract him. Since then we had asked the others what and when to watch out for him. The other boys spoke of stories where boys who were caught were thrown off at high speed and broke limbs. The girls who were caught, well those stories were left to hang unspoken. A lump caught in my throat as I thought about how often people wanting a better life were so easily abused in this life of traveling. Where were the ones who really cared about others in life? Weren't there more like Father Marcel here in Mexico?

After weeks on the train, our ride was finally over. We were with some other boys about half our age, but it was their second time coming this way. They had been deported to Mexico, and they were going back to America to the jobs that were waiting for them. They walked with us as we tried to find food among some restaurant's scraps, and then someone called my name. I looked about to see where it had come from.

"Hey, boys! Roberto and Luis, wait up!" A man yelled as he trotted up to us. He had long straight hair that hung over his ears and even into his eyes when he stopped suddenly in front of us. He wiped some sweat off his neatly trimmed beard, put out his hand, and introduced himself.

"I'm Salvador, boys. I've been waiting and watching for you." After shaking our hands, he waved his hand forward and pointed. "Let's get you some beans and tortillas to eat. You guys have got to be hungry."

He took us to a small diner and ordered up some fresh lunch for us, where we sat at a table with six chairs by a back wall. It was great to finally eat real food again. The diner even had chicken stew like Tiá Rosa used to make, and we were in heaven, except this heaven had a Mexican mural painted on the wall behind us. It depicted rebels fighting for their freedom with long swords sitting on wild horses. I stared at it with questions for Salvador, but he had stepped out the back alley to his Blazer. Now I wondered if the family had invested in a fleet. He came back with an armload of stuff that he set on the table and something that tapped on the floor. Luis and I put down our forks and leaned in as Salvador spread out bags of stuff.

"Wow, what is all this?" I asked as we began to open bags full of new clothes.

"Clothes! Jeans, shirts, underwear, and you name it, you got it. I was named with purpose by my mother, Dios mio, because she knew I would save lives."

"So, Salvador means 'savior'? I'm not sure how you have saved our lives yet," I told him. Salvador smiled and then broke into laughter.

"Just you wait and see. In America, you will fit in with Levi jeans, Stetson cowboy hats, and Journey t-shirts. All the police, they will think you are some Texan boys coming back through El Paso from

California. But getting you on that American bus, that's still the fun part." Luis kicked me and smirked as we heard him mention fun be-cause we hadn't really had too much lately. I went to kick him back when I knocked the table leg some, and something banged to the floor. All three of us poked our heads down under the wooden table, and Luis took a huge breath in.

"What's this?" Luis reached in and asked as he pulled up a guitar case. Salvador's beard showed just the beginnings of a smile.

"Bolívar told your Uncle José about your accident. Not only did he send money for new clothes but also a little extra for this guitar. He said life would be a whole lot easier with it." Luis open the case and stared in wonder. He strummed the strings and held the fret with his fa-vorite chords. He closed his eyes and gently strummed. Salvador slapped me on my shoulder, sipped from his beer, and leaned back to tell us our next steps.

Salvador explained how we would ride in a truck across the border. He had a cousin who was delivering fresh coffee this week across the border, and we all would hide behind cases of them in the back of the truck. The coffee company had a good reputation and required little checking at the border. Sometimes people floated on tubes, waded, and swam to America with him, which involved more risk and more money. The riverbed was sharp with rough stones and waves that we were glad to miss, and the patrol around the river was unpredictable. Salvador's face became strained as he told of times when he and his le-galized American cousin spun off on a juiced up dirt bike in a dust of wind when the patrol suddenly went by. You could see the sadness he felt in leaving behind the people who paid him to safely reach a new land of money for family back home.

"I'm sure they'd find me the next time around," he grinned.

~ 28 ~

FINAL STAGE INTO AMERICA

The certainty in Salvador's voice reassured me that our final leg in this part of the journey was to be less worrisome. But fate must not have been listening to the tone in his voice. I coughed from the fumes of the diesel as the bus pulled away from our latest stop. My shoulder shivered when I thought of the fear I felt while we rode into America.

Luis and I jumped up behind Salvador at the coffee storehouse on the outskirts of the city. We nestled easily behind four cases stacked high and full of packed coffee bags. Salvador sighed. "This will be no problem at all. You boys are practically family and this coffee is trusted along the border. No worries at all." He leaned his head back on the truck wall and fell right asleep.

We rode for an hour or so at a steady pace. The truck finally slowed and then stopped suddenly. Moments went by and I stopped breathing for a second. As soon as we heard two knocks on the outside panel of the truck, the truck sputtered up and sped up. After about five minutes or so, the truck slowed down again. It stopped with a jerk, but we were prepared for it that time. Salvador had thumbs up, waiting.

Suddenly there was loud and continuous pounding on the back door. Luis nudged me and whispered, "You going to answer the door?" I shook my head with a weak smile. We heard the driver slam his door and mumble a curse under his breath about a schedule to be kept.

"Let's see your coffee from Mexico, senor!" We heard the border guard yell out as he still pounded.

"Sure, sure, señor. I open the door for you." The driver unlatched it loudly. "You guys hardly ever stop me. Our company has the best coffee on the coast of America sold. You know we are good company." He swung both doors wide open.

146

I heard somebody hop on the back step and into the back. Then a second body scrambled up.

"Jimmy, check those boxes on the left while I move around these on the right." The top two layers were moved about three rows in front of us and I started to sweat more. I felt the sweat on my neck and I wanted to shake it away. I heard two boxes moved on our left with little effort.

"Charlie, there's nothing here but coffee. This truck is fine. I need to get back to my thermos of coffee Mary Ellen brewed for me." The voice pushed his top box back in its corner.

"All right, Jimmy. You're right." I heard a large sniff. "I smell only coffee and no body odor."

"Well, Charlie, I'd love to crack open a case and take home a few bags of this quality coffee. I bet the beans are better than what Mary Ellen buys and brews." I heard them walk to the door and jump down.

"Jimmy, you'd better watch it. Mary Ellen may hear of you complaining about her cooking and coffee." I heard the door slam shut and I sighed deeply.

"Charlie, it best you stop talking!" I felt a body slam against the panel side of the truck. Salvador smiled and crunched further toward us.

"Jimmy, ease up now. It was nothing but a joke!" Then I heard the door latch shut and soon the driver's door opened and shut. The truck sputtered to life and we made our way into America. I looked at Salvador and whispered, "No worries?"

He shrugged, leaned back his head, and fell back asleep for the remaining hour to his cousin's stop.

BOOK II

Few things are more beautiful to me than a bunch of thuggish, heavily tattooed line cooks moving around each other like ballerinas on a busy Saturday night. Seeing two guys who'd just as soon cut each other's throats in their off hours moving in unison with grace and ease can be as uplifting as any chemical stimulant or organized religion. —*Anthony Bourdain*

I think the most wonderful thing in the world is another chef. I'm always excited about learning new things about food.
—*Paul Prudhomme*

I wanted to learn everything I could about what it takes to be a great chef. It was a turning point for me.
—*Thomas Keller*

So who the hell, exactly, are these guys, the boys and girls in the trenches? You might get the impression from the specifics of my less than stellar career that all line cooks are whacked-out moral degenerates, dope fiends, refugees, a thuggish assortment of drunks, sneak thieves, sluts, and psychopaths. You wouldn't be too far off base. The business, as respected three-star chef Scott Bryan explains it, attracts 'fringe elements,' people for whom something in their lives has gone terribly wrong. Maybe they didn't make it through high school, maybe they're running away from something-be it an ex-wife, a rotten family history, trouble with the law, a squalid Third World backwater with no opportunity for advancement. Or maybe, like me, they just like it here.
—*Anthony Bourdain (Kitchen Confidential: Adventures in the Culinary Underbelly)*

The grill station is hell. You stand at it for five minutes and you think: So this is what Dante had in mind. —*Anthony Bourdain as a line cook*

~ 29 ~

PORTER'S HOUSEBOAT RESTAURANT
JUNE 2004 — FIVE YEARS LATER

We were getting a second push late after the lunch rush, and I needed just a little more pop afterward. Caitlin and I had just gotten the line all stocked and cleaned, and then the tickets started rolling in again. I enjoyed sipping my cola at the machine in the waithall, soaking in the whole sense of the restaurant business.

The variety of kitchen noises could be heard in a portion of the non-smoking section of the dining room. Voices snapping orders from the kitchen, plates dropped at the server stand, sportscasters naming scores overhead on the hanging televisions, and the bartender calling back drink orders all could be heard in various tones around the dining area. The restaurant dining area was beginning to fill up, and I could see those people sitting at tables 21, 23, and 25. These tables were larger booths that tended to fill up more quickly, since they seated larger parties, had ample arm and elbowroom, and provided a clear view through the window of passing boats gliding out on the lake. The downside to these tables lay in their closeness to the kitchen, which sometimes, as in the case of this evening, gave off a blend of sounds not unlike a song that just can't get in key. It's almost like when Luis tries to write his own songs.

Some guests, full of what the *Food Network* has made of the culinary world, request to sit near the kitchen while most tolerate the nuisances to get the payoff in not waiting for other coveted seats. Of course, if it were an open kitchen completely visible for all the guests to see their food being prepared, perhaps the order of the cook's line may be different as eyes watch their professional work ethic, demeanor, and attitude. But at Porter's Houseboat, an independent, family owned, casual dining steak and seafood restaurant, our management insists on creating and maintaining a sense of professionalism among all the staff. But many of us miss the mark by a wide margin. I feel a bit guilty when I hear the interview of the two top across the aisle.

"I appreciate you meeting me for this interview, Chef Curtis. This restaurant certainly is nice, and the décor is really different. It seems to be a mixture of a fishery off the Great Lakes and a local steakhouse. The waitstaff are dressed a bit differently from other places where I've eaten. It's interesting to see a shirt with a knitted *P* inside a fish staring at a steer's head and then a house resting on the river on the back of their shirts."

I waited for Chef Curtis to give his answer. Sometimes he wisely speaks like a father you wished you had, and other days he screams like Father Time searching for his watch. But he circles his head around his rather large shoulders and it cracks. He smiles, fingering some loose strands in the cropped hair back of his receding hairline, and sighs. "Well, Thomas Wilson, it seems you are rather observant for a boy just out of high school. I gather in this high school VocEd class, hospitality management/culinary arts made some kind of impression on you."

Chef Curtis looked down at the boy's resume and back up to the student's expectant eyes. Chef had told me how he had obtained his education from various chefs in the school of hard knocks, spending time on both coasts, and Chicago, New York City, and ended up back near family. His family raised him in Dearborn, and now some lived in Livonia, Bloomfield, and even Auburn Hills, not far from the restaurant. Curtis had taken some management classes at Oakland University a few years back, and had been certified through the local *American Chefs Federation* chapter as a CEC. It lapsed a year or so ago without his renewal.

"For your piqued interest, Mr. Porter, this restaurant's owner and founder is a meat and potatoes man who loves to fish and hunt, and thereby also loves to eat fish and steak. He is a down-to-earth man who blended his love of the outdoor life, the importance of family in the home, and great food prepared well as a mission statement in this business. So take care with any mocking notion I think I might hear."

I peaked over the rim of the booth a little and smiled. Chef couldn't help but put young men in their place. I know he has let me know my spot easily enough.

"Well, umm, Chef Curtis, I've just graduated from high school, but I am enrolled at Oakland Community College in their Culinary Art's Program. The career and technical program was not just a class but also a two-year program in the Hospitality Management field of study. That CTE program gave me a pretty good idea of what the careers are like in Hospitality, and I believe I want to be a part of that. I certainly meant no disrespect with my comments on the décor of the restaurant here."

"Well, Mr. Wilson, I can appreciate your intentions to be part of the culinary world, but I'm not sure I'm inclined to be the potter who moulds you to be the chef you hope to be. There are chefs in the area that hire young aspiring guys like you who pay as little as possible and run them ragged till they drop, laughing in the name of ACF altruism. I smile some while training some culinarians but still attempt to give them a little respect along the way as they consider this profession. Nevertheless, my kitchen is currently fairly well staffed, although I—" Suddenly I stepped back when Frieda, a veteran server stopped at the edge of the booth where they sat, her eyes darting to the waithall with its noise from the kitchen window.

"Pardon me, Chef Curtis, but there's some drama in the kitchen, and my table 25's been waiting twenty-five minutes for broiled whitefish and rib eye medium rare."

"Why thank you, Frieda. Listen, Thomas, we can finish this interview tomorrow afternoon, if you'd like. Why don't we meet at 2:30 again and see where this conversation ends?"

"Thanks, Chef. I will be here on time, promptly at 2:30," the young man promised.

Frieda, her right foot tapping on and on, rolled her shoulders a few times and waited anxiously for the chef to react to her comments. Chef

Curtis ambled his stocky frame out of the booth, and grunted a gravelly snort, and lamely smiled as Frieda quickly strolled over to greet her newest table. Frieda Schultz tells me often that she was one of Mr. Porter's opening hires. She has a fast gait in her walk on those stubby legs, and it takes some effort for her swinging arms to maintain pace with them. I hear her with that high-pitched voice greet the table while I hurry back into the kitchen. Taking the back way around to my station, I checked my tickets on the sauté printer and turned my pans back up from low heat. I noticed Chef Terrance had taken over the board.

"'Berto, you've got five seafood fredos all day, three pan fried whitey, and how long on that baked cod. It's holdin' a party of five." Chef Terrance, is a twenty-four-year-old African American, who was recently promoted to Sous Chef. He and I talked about how he had graduated from Oakland Community College in their culinary program and had worked at Outback and then at the Rattlesnake Club.

"Chef Terry, three of the five alfies are up, with two more in two minutes. I'm platin' all the whitefish now, and the cod just went in," I yelled down the line.

"Roberto, I need that cod on the fly, stop everything and get it moving ASAP!" Terrance's voice got a lot higher on ASAP, almost yelling.

"'kay, 'kay, Chef, but I've got two broiled lunch catfish up, and I need an all-day on my steaks, with their temps," I stammered back.

"Chef Terrance, all the entrée salads are up, and I'm runnin' to the bathroom." Caitlin, the only female line cook on the schedule, curled her apron up and laid it on the edge of the dish area counter.

"Chef Terr, I've got those steak tips portioned like you asked, here you go." Henry the prep cook had a wrapped third pan in his hands, red-gloved hands dripping blood.

"Whoa, whoa, all right Caitlin hit the jon quick, and Henry drop the steak tips to Roberto down the line and take off those gloves. 'Berto get me a steak tip Stroganoff on the fly—you're going down! Get it together now!"

Chef Curtis stopped at the corner of the line, one direction of hot food and the other corner of the cold food line.

"Terrance, where's Caitlin and why isn't she on the line with six tickets hanging on the board?"

"Oh hello, Chef Curtis. We got a little late afternoon push, and I'm helping get through it." Terrance stopped and looked over at our executive chef.

"Terrance, you're not helping the people on the line for their sake, it's part of your job. What do I pay you for, except to make sure this line does not go down? How about table 25 for Frieda? It's a rib eye and broiled whitefish?" Curtis asked and stepped toward the ticket minder.

"Chef, I don't have a ticket on the board for Frieda. She's been asking and I've been trying to tell her." Terrance began to exclaim while pointed to the board of hanging tickets with his left hand while his right hand held the last ticket that had come in.

"Excuse me, Chef Curtis, but we have three tables that are looking at 15 minute ticket times, and table 25 is now at 25 minutes," Charlene, our female floor manager asked through the window.

"Char, give me a second to get it together back here," Curtis replied.

"Look, Chef, my guests don't care about you collecting your thoughts or moments with your staff, they're hungry and have to get back to work!" Charlene slapped the steel counter and pushed her blonde head into the window.

"Charlene, I'm not in the mood for your sarcastic mouth or little mannerism. Now give me one minute, and then I'll deal with the table issues."

I watched Curtis check the ticket times quickly to the second hand clock on the wall above the line expo to the first ticket.

He mumbled, "Thirteen minutes: not good, but not fifteen minutes. The guests always seem to add a few minutes." He shook his head and smiled a little.

"Terrance, hang that ticket back up and step down and drop a rib-eye MR and broiled whitefish. Mark the rib eye quickly and get it on high. Be sure the sides are in for both. Then go find Henry and get Caitlin out of the bathroom."

"All right, Chef, I'll make sure the food is down. But Chef, we never got a ticket for Frieda's table," Terrance sighed and pulled the broiler out.

"Terrance, just go find Caitlin and Henry and get back up on the line. Ticket times are behind, and the best way to recover is to get everyone moving together. Roberto, look at me and get your foot off'n that crate. This is no time to be retying shoelaces. When you start to go down and you know you're missing calls, let the chef in charge know. Get an all day, and get help if it's available. Now here's an all-day: first off, five seafood alfredos, three pan-fried whitefish, baked cod, three prime rib sandwiches—all MW and on the fly. For the missing table, I need the rib eye MR and broiled whitefish. Don't care where everything else is, get that rib eye and broiled whitefish going right now and give me a realistic time!"

"All right, Chef, all right, Chef, I gotcha. But I still need five minutes on that table on the fly." Chef Curtis nodded once toward me and looked back at the tickets hanging on his board to wait and see. The printer started to spit out orders for two new tables, and Terrance walked up and pulled them off. He handed them to the chef and smiled.

"Chef, Caitlin and Henry are back up here with me. Who do you want where?"

"Terrance, you and Henry go swing down and work with Roberto on that end of the line, Caitlin can assist me in putting up these couple of griddled sandwiches. Have Henry check sides and set-ups for you and Roberto. You help Roberto plate up all his food as it comes up."

"Yes, Chef," the three said in unison. He smiled and orders for three more tables printed.

"Now Chef Curtis, it's been five more minutes, and Frieda's table is really antsy out there. Do you have a time frame I can give them?" Charlene stood in the window asking.

"Yes, Charlene, I do. Let them know it will be fewer than five minutes and the food will be at their table. I wish you had notified me that we were seating more tables earlier. It might have been helpful for us all around," Curtis smiled with that last comment. She started to move around the corner.

"Well, your back of the house staff should be able to handle a little heat when it gets busy!" She stood glaring at him and moved a few steps more down the line. He backed away from the board, turned and looked at her.

"Don't think of crossing the line here and now, Char. Let's just take good care of our guests." He turned his back to her and looked directly down the line to his staff.

"Chef Curt, all the alfredos are up, the prime rib sand specials are getting their fries and then they're up, the broiled whitefish has one minute, and the baked cod is up." Terrance rattled off to the chef while cleaning a rim of a plate of meat juice, winking at Roberto.

"One more time, Terrance and Roberto, the fish is up but about the rib eye—can I get that before day shift ends or must we go into dinner hours behind the eight ball?"

"Thirty seconds—it's still a little rare." I grimly turned the steak for its last mark and slammed the broiler. I gritted my teeth. I didn't mean to slam it so hard. Chef snapped a sharp look at me.

"Roberto, don't give me that half minute crap. I need real times! If it's still rare, and it will take at least a half minute to plate and put in the window, then it's more like three minutes!"

"Weeze, I need plates all up and down the line! Hey, Luis, plates, now! Chef Curtis, the rib eye will be up in one minute now, and the whitefish is up. If you want to sell her ticket, I can guarantee the steak will be up by the time she gets to the window." I yelled loudly down the line to Luis, hoping my confidence showed some now.

"Luis, stop leaning over the tank area trying to talk to the girls, and bring plates up to this line. I want more entrée plates in this hot window right now, and then stock the glass salad plates in the fridge. Terrance, don't you and Roberto start that 'it'll be up by the time she gets back to the window smack,' cause the table has already been waiting. I'll run the food myself to the table once it's all up together, hot, sauced, and sharply presented. Even tho' we're busy, there's still no reason for all the plates not to be perfectly presented."

"All righty, Chef, I gotcha." Terrance smiled and patted Roberto on the back as he pulled a pan of sautéed asparagus for the rib-eye.

"Terrance, finish plating and have Henry help Roberto clean up the line. You take over the board, and I'm going to speak to a few guests, perhaps smooth over any wrinkles they're feeling. Frieda, stop stocking the lemon wedges and run your food. It just came up! I'll be along shortly to see them in."

"Certainly, Chef Curtis. Don't you worry about a thing with them folks. I've sweet-talked them and they're fine. They're having two glasses of Merlot on you, Chef. Perhaps you may want to stop and check on the vintage I picked."

"I'm sure whatever bottle you cracked from downstairs is fine. Just go check the rest of your section, and keep your staff in the dining room pre-busing."

I took a deep breath. Some rushes really wear you down, especially when they come unexpected. Lunch was over and I was ready to cool down to start my afternoon prep and restock.

~ 30 ~

EN ROUTE HOME

Luis laughed loudly as he popped the clutch and tried to get the car into gear. The light turned green, and the cars behind us were honking, one after another. I padded my ears with my palms and stared at Luis.

"First gear, you crazy chapin! Put it into first, push lightly on the gas, and ease off the brake," I tried to calmly remind him. I should have never told him he could start driving the car I bought from our landlord. I would have thought with his experience working at Tió José's garage that he knew all about driving stick shifts. I guess fixing them is a lot different than driving them.

Luis finally got the Mustang into motion. "See compadré, it is not so hard. You must be patient with it, and with a gentle touch treat it like a woman. Me, I know much of this and have still to teach you all of what I know. So watch and listen as I—"

"All right, Luis, just get us home without any more honking horns. I've had enough of the stares," I leaned my head back into the passenger seat and looked to the passing cars on my right. He thinks he knows so much about women and now cars. This wasn't the only time he had gotten stuck in gear and not moved at all. I've smiled many times from my spot in the kitchen as he has tried to talk to some of the hostesses, and they barely crack a smile his way. I still give him his due, though, since he doesn't give up on any of them. I'm not sure if that's because of his high sense of self-esteem or that patience he brags of. American cars and American girls, Luis has grown to love both of them with a passion—almost more so than the guys born and raised here.

"'Berto and Weese, come on over here! We could use two more on the courts, and we just started," Octavio yelled from across the street as Luis turned into the lot of our building. I waved at him through my open window.

"Well 'Berto, should we go pick up a basketball game with Octavio?" Luis asked me with a grin as our heads snapped with a jerk. His foot stomped on the brake, let off the clutch, and the car jerked to a stop in the carport. Grateful to be home, I looked over at him. "I think we can change and run over and work on our game."

I just laughed when I lifted my head up and rolled up my window. I checked my watch and the sky.

"Yeah, let's go try shooting in the rim this time and not just at the backboard. We'll change into some shorts and tennis shoes and play some before I leave for work at McDonald's in an hour. The sun is out, and it's a good day to run," I said as I pulled out the keys. After I got the general key to our building out, I started looking for the apartment key as we walked to our apartment.

"Hurry up, Roberto! I've got to go the bathroom," Luis yelled as he pushed on the door handle as I was trying to push in the key. Finally it turned, and he knocked me into the dining table, running down the hall. Why couldn't Octavio just leave the door unlocked for us? He knew we always came home about this time, and he's just across the street. I looked at the table and tried to center it a little after I pushed it from the center of the room. As I fixed it to its dented spot in the carpet, I grabbed the mail scattered around under the table. It seemed like a small deck of cards I was picking up, and I began to sort them. The bills get tossed to the center of the table, and a couple of letters to the left and right. Luis doesn't care about which side of the table the mail was set, but I like to have my stuff always on the left. I prefer a neat pile on the corner of the table, away from darting eyes as friends walk in. Octavio doesn't get any mail and doesn't send any out to anyone. Luis and I have sent most of the money we make home, usually by Wells Fargo or a money order to the city bank in San Miguel Acatán. Octavio is a distant cousin of a Tió José, and though he has been in America for over fifteen years, he doesn't speak to anyone in Mexico or Guatemala, unless it's business related. I still haven't figured out why he seemed to leave his homelife completely behind and doesn't dwell in the past with even a picture.

Here in America, he speaks to everyone we meet. Everyone in the neighborhood knows him, and the guys can always get him in a game of hoops. He runs up and down the court like he's still in his twenties but hardly ever makes any shots. He laughs when some say he needs to grow taller, maybe watch less soccer, or even practice the basics like dribbling and shooting. I'd agree with the last, but I've got less room than he has to talk about the game. I do talk some, though, especially when we watch American soccer and wish it could be our players we were watching in the Latin countries. Although he had lived for years in Mexico, he still has the heart of a native Guatemalan Indian. I've tried for years to get him to tell about his family. He told me he'd worked with Tió José years ago, but he wouldn't give any other details. So my mind just wanders about the trouble they probably got in crossing borders and running from the police. Now they're both settled down in their own way. Octavio takes in new guys every so many years and helps them get settled here in America. He has the connections and set Luis and I up with new identification. Even the bank tellers never questioned it or gave a second glance at us. When I checked about the money he needed, I heard one last time that it was settled up. I asked him later how the identification worked so well, and he smiled with, "Some people happily give parts of their body in death, while others give up the name they proudly wore."

"Traveling, traveling! Little man, you got to dribble some! You always mark me and look at you," Octavio yelled at my partner.

"'Berto!" Little Man swiftly passed the ball underhand to me, and I tried to fast break past Luis. Luis sprinted to catch up and jumped just as the ball left my hands. Little Man was already at the rim and rebounding easily to shoot again with a quick dunk. Between his wide shoulders that kept Luis from reaching for the net and his long legs and arms, we all fight to play on his team in the pick up games. He's humble enough, and takes anybody that asks first. I learn from him every time I play, and today I think I could practice his rebounds more. We played for about forty minutes, with our shirts dripping with sweat.

My shirt could have been a bath towel hanging on my back. Squinting through wet eyes, I saw the time on my five-dollar watch. We were taking a breather. Little Man and Octavio were sharing a few beers from a cooler nearby, and Luis was quick to take the one offered.

"McDonald's is calling me, guys, and beer on my breath won't make the supervisor happy," I yelled to the wind as I jogged back to our apartment to shower, change, and get some air back in my lungs. I would have to clean up in two minutes, just enough to soap and rinse, to make it on time. Sometimes, I wish I could feel all right working one job like Luis. Luis laughs and says his other job is in the gigs he keeps trying out for with new local Latin bands.

I paid back Tió José the money it cost to get me to America two years ago— the last of his investment, and I paid my mother back last year. Now, I send money every month to Mama, and she plans for Tina's university time. Tina will need money for food and her room. American money goes a lot further in Guatemala. Soon, I will be planning on classes for me here in America. I've talked to the chefs, and they told me about CIA and Johnson and Wales. Those are like a far away land for me, and I can't even dream of going there. I listen to the other cooks talk about the schools they attend for culinary arts locally, like O.C.C. and Schoolcraft. They don't seem to struggle. If I can plan it well enough, I'll work for Chef Curtis and attend culinary college. In the planning, I'll save my money and cut my hours at McDonalds enough to keep up my classes at school.

~ 31 ~

WORKING AT THE RESTAURANT

"Hot behind! Behind! Hey look, move it now, or I'm going to burn your behind!" Chef John is moving fast and must be behind in preparing the night shift's sauces and sides.

"Look, compadré, move when somebody says behind!" I yelled with a laugh while pushing the new guy against the stand-up.

"I told you, my name is Thomas, or Tom to my friends, or Tommy to people I don't talk to. And what about this fridge I'm leaning against?" The new guy started to explain.

"All right, Tommy," I had to interrupt and assumed he soon wouldn't be talking to me much, so I called him Tommy. "We won't be talking much when you're wet, burnt, and swimming on the floor waiting to go to the clinic. Let's just get on with this tour that Chef Terrance told me to walk you around. He's leaving early today, since he worked long yesterday on Chef Curtis' day off. I want to be done before he walks out."

I looked at him, and wondered how long he might last here. He didn't laugh when I tried to lighten him up some, and people around here sometimes really joke around. He was taller than both Luis and me, thin, a little pale, with not much beef on the bones. Mama used to look at butchered pieces that way, turning with a chuckle to leave it for a much poorer soul to buy for their weekly treat at our local market. At least he walked like he had somewhere to go, a little like Samuel does when the dining room is filled. Tommy stopped my thoughts short with his next question.

"Roberto, right? Who was that guy with the huge pot? What was his deal anyway?" He was pointing at our empty cook's line.

"Tommy, I guess I'm calling you that? That guy was night chef John, and the pot was a stockpot with cooked reds in them. He has to finish his whipped potatoes, and so he has to throw them in the oven to dry out." I looked him in the eyes and asked, "Didn't you go to some class or cooking school, or something? You can't recognize your pots?"

He looked around at the pots and pans hanging on one side and the utensils hanging above the back sinks. He took a breath and pointed.

"I know all this stuff, but I just had a bad moment. Give me a break and—"

"Forget it, Tommy." I sighed and tapped his shoulder. "Just listen to me and I'll tell you about all the stuff in this whole kitchen. Chef Terrance will come after me, and then Chef Curtis will have a talk with me. They know I follow directions well, and that's not changing today."

I frowned at him as he tried to see it all when we walked. I showed him the difference between the saucepans and sauté pans, noticing Luis had put the colander on the wrong side again. It was used often, and the chefs liked it hung on the outside. I wished Luis would care about the small things in the kitchen more. The management here notice the smallest things about how you work.

Tommy stopped near the prep table and turned. "Roberto, how long you been working here? You seem to know your way about the kitchen pretty good."

I shrugged my left shoulder and pushed some hair out of my eyes. "I been here for while. I think it's been about five years now I've worked here. But I have another job I work too." I checked my watch then and glanced at my shoes. I had to work later tonight and my shoelaces were still tight. It seemed like I had to retie them every shift.

"You really got two jobs? I went to school and worked at Mickey D's, and it was tough on me. I barely kept my grades above a 3.0," Tommy rambled on with a grin.

"Mickey D's and 3.0, I've never heard these before."

"Roberto, you know Ds don't stand for Detroit with a Mickey in front of it. McDonald's, home of the Big Mac. Like me on the soccer field and still carrying a good grade in high school." Tommy seemed to enjoy bragging some more.

"Hey, compadré, Roberto knows mucho about good grades, soccer, and McDonald's. He used to live for the first two, and McDonald's, he's lived there for five years," Luis pulled on my long hair, lightly slapped Tommy, and laughed while stepping between us with a handful of plates to put on the line.

"Wow, you've been at McDonald's for five years? You should be a crew leader by now!" Tommy looked at me with wide eyes.

"Luis, the dish machine is making that noise like its backing up again, so you need to hustle more. Roberto, don't make showing the new guy around the back of the house a project," Chef Curtis slapped me on the back of my head with a clipboard while his office door shut with a bang. He stopped, looked to the left past the waithall and into the dining room, nodding as two tables just got sat. He turned back to us and smiled right at the edge of his mouth. You could barely notice it, and Tommy looked scared. I kept my face while he looked down at the clipboard for effect. "Let's start doing some cooking soon, boys, all right?

I looked to my right at Tommy and said, "Yes, Chef!"

Waiting for a second or two, Chef Curtis tapped his left knuckle with the clipboard and looked right at Tommy.

Tommy stuttered, "Yes, Chef."

Chef Curtis chuckled with a sigh. "Boy, I'm glad you spoke up here. I thought I was going to have to change the schedule I'm holding and rethink hiring you, Thomas."

Tommy spoke up real fast, "No, Chef, I'm usually a better learner. I'll do better and listen for what you're saying or looking for."

Chef smiled quietly, "Well, good, since your teacher at that Oakland Technical Center spoke highly of you. I'd thought most teachers would speak the truth, or at least I'd hope so."

"Tommy, the walk-in, it's this way. You'll find all the produce up front on the right, with labels on the bins. The meats and chicken are in the back here, with chicken on the bottom." I held the door wide enough for him to see inside and nodded.

Tommy interrupted again, "I know about that. Raw chicken always goes on the bottom. You know you don't want cross contamination."

I smiled. 'Yeah, you got it, amigo." This chiquito doesn't have to prove anything to me, and Chef Curtis has already passed us to check on the printer at the salad station. I laughed to myself as he started yelling for JT, who was off the cook's line and in the bathroom and poked my head out of the doorway and to the right. Chef John came by me, grabbing a glass plate from the small freezer, and started making a house salad. I glanced back at him when I heard him mutter under his breath about JT while the printer spat out two more tickets. A second later there was banging on the back bathroom door. The kitchen was silent for a second as we all waited. Then I heard the chair from the backroom drag on the floor, and then it scraped on metal. I laughed.

"What's funny, Roberto?" Tommy asked with a weak smile, uncertain if it was all right.

I turned back into the walk-in. "Oh well, JT is taking a smoke break and not telling anyone. Now a guest could've waited too long for their salad, and Chef, well he's going to make a point to JT. He's locked him in to make a point about leaving the cook's line without telling anyone." I heard my name yelled from across the kitchen and motioned for Tommy to drop the walk-in plastic strip curtain and follow me out.

"Roberto, you and your shadow take over for Chef John on Garmo so he can finish setting up for tonight." Chef Curtis was walking down the line toward the walk-in. "Oh, and ignore any knocking you hear from the bathroom."

"Yes, Chef Curtis," I replied with a smile.

"JT will take over for you two in five or ten minutes and then you can finish your orientation with Thomas." He tapped me on the shoulder while turning the corner and I saw him stop at the employee bathroom. "JT, have another cigarette while you're in there." Chef Curtis dropped his clipboard on the chair propped against the bathroom door and turned back to the walk-in.

I could barely hear, "Yes, Chef" through the door.

I liked working with JT, but it seems like he has to have a cigarette almost every hour. Sometimes I think about adding up his smoke breaks in one day, but then I think maybe that's what keeps his energy going in the rush. He sure can handle a rush well.

~ 32 ~

THE BACK BAR DINING AREA

I had closed the kitchen last night with the new guy. Then I had turned around and opened the line to set up this morning. Chef Curtis knew I could handle the hours in back-to-back shifts without wearing down when he made the schedule. Tommy is the third guy I've trained, and so I guess he trusts me enough with that also. But I was still surprised when he told me I could sit down for my lunch today instead of trying to eat on the run. He explained to me that I should be aware of how the restaurant's management comes together. Mr. Porter approved my presence in today's meeting.

Chef Curtis told me to go ahead and make myself a burger while he went to gather notes from his office. After plating my mid-well bacon-cheeseburger I walk to the back of the bar area and noticed Mr. Porter sipping coffee. He invited me to sit for a minute. After a second sip and a snap of his timepiece, he seemed to look around without actually looking. He winked at me and began to explain, "When the floor is cut, two servers rotate tables sporadically. With the bar section of the restaurant empty and only a few tables in the remaining portions of the dining room, the restaurant feels like a ghost town. In any restaurant, the lunch rush usually comes in like a tidal wave, and sometimes returns with smaller bursts of current when the staff thinks it has receded for the day. Then the staff has to clean their area and restock it in order to be ready for the next shift to take over."

He picked up our table's saltshaker that was almost empty and shook his head. His comments reminded me of the small rush earlier this week, when I went to get a pop in the waithall after the main lunch rush. Then we got hit again with a number of tables, and Chef Curtis wasn't happy with our shift. We had a quick meeting on the end of the

166

line about being ready at all times for business, especially when its un-expected. Mr. Porter continued his thoughts for me.

"If there is a midshift or a double shift that one must face in the next shift, then no doubt each would be certain everyone is prepared to encounter another wave. Nobody likes to feel the sense of foreboding as one flails about in deep water, close to drowning because they are not as prepared as they could have been." He set down his cup and got up. He stepped to the side stand and placed a ketchup bottle in front of me.

"Enjoy the burger. Our meeting will start soon," Mr. Porter patted me on the shoulder.

I glanced up to the clock behind the bar. It's a quarter past three, and Mr. Porter began pulling tables together and moving chairs in the back corner of the dining room where the management usually has their meeting. That corner has a view of both doors leading into the restaurant, a view of the non-smoking dining area, and a long view of the bar that overlooks the water. The doorway by the bar leads to the walkway by the water, which goes into the shopping area, while the other doorway by the front of the restaurant leads to the parking area. He checked the timepiece chained to his vest underneath his suit to the sailboat clock above the bar. Mr. Porter proceeded to set collated packets in front of each chair when he heard the phone ring. He took a step in the dining room direction, stopped, and then looked back about the barroom.

"Frieda, have one of the servers get the phone please," he called across the room.

It rang two more times and he took long, quick strides to the phone. Looking around the dining room, seeing no one about, he picked it up.

"Thank you for calling Porter's Houseboat Restaurant. This is Frank Porter. How may I direct your call?" I looked up from cutting my burger in quarters to see a frustrated look on his face behind the bar.

"Yes, Duncan, I do. I need your incompetent behind back here to be part of this meeting. We hold the same management meeting every

167

week at three-thirty, and you need to be here for it. How do you expect to grow in my business if you are not actively participating in it? I need you be aware of our schedule and use the palm pilot for something other than planning outings with your social schedule."

Mr. Porter held the phone in one hand, checked the time with the other, and rolled his eyes just enough for me to notice. I look away quickly in case he glanced across the bar.

"Quick quips and comebacks don't make up for the fact that you're still not here. Not only should you be here to begin the meeting, but you should be prepared with notes and comments to contribute. Next time you leave, can you just let me know what's going on?"

He set the phone back down in its cradle on the wall, near the bar and shook his head. Now it was 3:20 and Mr. Porter set the remaining packets around the empty spots at the two tables placed together. With ten minutes to spare before the meeting was set to start, Mr. Porter nodded his head in my direction. I joined him with my lunch as he took time to review the outline he had typed up. I sit at a seat without a packet, thinking I wouldn't need one as I was not actually in management. While flipping to the second page, he smiled and slid a packet my way and nodded at me. I started to read his Roman numeral outline.

A chair that was scraped on the wooden floor as it was pulled out from the table startled me and I turned to see Terrance with a fruit juice in one hand and cigarette in the other, apron flipped over his left shoulder. Mr. Porter looked up from his outline.

"Terrance, we're sitting in the smoking area, but I would appreciate you not smoking. Also, feel free to change, leave the apron in the kitchen, or even just put it in the laundry bin and get a new one later."

"Sure thing, Mr. Porter, and Chef Curtis said to tell you he'll be right out."

The front door opened and three people filed in. Sandy, the evening lead server, strolled in first with a step that was light and lively, as if she didn't have a care in the world. Samuel strode in next, with a sense of a quick march in his step, always businesslike in his dining room management walk. There was a sense of purpose in his gait, like he was late for something that must be attended to. Last in this trio, Chef John walks in. He didn't look happy to be there on his day off, especially after working two back-to-back twelve's closing the kitchen. I like to know which chef is working what shifts, especially when I'm working back-to-backs or doubles.

Charlene, another dining room manger, was checking how much liquor was behind the bar. She looked our way and sighed with a shrug. She went to get Frieda from a table in the corner of non-smoking and pulled her away from doing the server schedule. Mrs. Porter, Marge, sat on the outside of the circle and readied herself with a notepad.

So as the management arrived, everyone fumbled to find a chair in which to sit. Chef Curtis walked purposefully into the dining room with a fast and long stride to his step. His long strides with a stocky, shorter frame made an interesting picture for the executive chef. Mr. Porter pulled his own chair out, searched all the chairs for those present, set his coffee down to the right of his own folder, and began.

"Good afternoon, everyone. I hope your day is going well. I'd like to get this meeting started. I've created a simple outline of our notes for today and have attached some articles from a few business dailies. I'd appreciate it if you would hold your comments until I ask for them so that we can maintain some order and move quickly through the material. First, on top of the page, you see the term *integrity*. Integrity is not something I can necessarily teach but can really only come from within one's character. All of us need to decide by ourselves how we will behave and have a willful sense of what is right in our choices—the way you dress, walk, talk to guests and coworkers. These and various other tasks convey the type of professional you are and really define for me the amount of integrity in you. I preface the meeting with this concept because it really has been burdensome to me as I watch the people in this restaurant, and in a sense the attitudes of all my staff reflect on my business and me. The concept, food, and location don't make my business, but my staff and their attitudes make it."

Mr. Porter took a minute to look into each person's face for a few seconds to reinforce his point. He sighed as Sandy was fixing her hair in a better ponytail and John was fixing his watch after pulling it from his ear. John tapped the watch, put it back on, and held up a small, opened notepad. Mr. Porter nodded his head while the chef and dining room manager were jotting notes, and Charlene was making check marks on the handout. He even smiled at me.

He sipped his coffee and began again, "Therefore, integrity in one's attitude transitions to my next point of teamwork throughout the day. Realizing the amount of stress one can encounter in the day, let's react at any given moment with an appropriate tone and professionalism in our voice and manner. People see your actions, and I would like you as management to model the proper ways in which to deal with problems. Take a second before you speak when there's a problem, and be sure it will resolve the issue efficiently to meet the needs of the business. "

Frieda raised her head and right hand together, "Mr. Porter, I think we do a pretty good job in our professional attitude around here. We all really try hard."

Mr. Porter smiled in his eyes at her, but the serious look remained on his face.

"I know most of us do behave professionally, but we as a team need to do a much better job of it. This team isn't consistent as a whole, and many times we are as fragmented pieces of abstract art rather than a picture blended easily together."

Samuel nodded slowly and looked at Chef Curtis. "I know that Curtis and I have been trying to work in the window to create more harmony and less tension during the rushes."

Chef Curtis turned from Samuel to Mr. Porter and agreed, "Yes, Sam and I have discussed the dynamics of the staff as they work the window, and my back of the house staff are working as a whole to do better in maintaining a stress free zone with the servers at the expedited window. John and I spent some time in the cook's meeting going over this." Chef Curtis pointed with a pen to his night chef. "Our night shift struggles a bit more in the kitchen since the cooks aren't as seasoned in their experience."

"Well, I'm glad you Samuel and Curtis have put thought into this issue. The window seems to always leave an opportunity to demonstrate either moments of chaos or peace in peak times of the restaurant." I nodded in agreement but he didn't catch my actions.

"And Frieda, Sandy, and I have talked many times about how that window is handled. We've tried to brainstorm ideas to minimize problems," Charlene interrupted and jotted it down on her notes. Sandy smiled for her part.

"Yes sir, Mr. Porter. We've been talkin'," Frieda added.

"Oh I'm sure you ladies have," Chef Curtis searched for a cigar in his pocket.

"Oh no, not to cause any problems. No, no. The Good Book keeps me in mind about proper ways to deal with people. St Paul, he spoke about it in—"

"Nevertheless, I appreciate the efforts spoken of." Mr. Porter interrupted her with a nod. "It is great I'm not the only one looking at the best interests of my business. But we still must do more in those issues. Moving on, my third point, as you may know, the labor environment in the restaurant field is becoming much more diverse. This diversity indicates a mix of cultures where employees may speak and act differently from what you are used to. America was built on this melting pot concept, but sometime people get isolated from different cultures and don't realize the appropriate way to manage them."

Frieda interjected, "But Mr. Porter, we've been different here for years and we all have learned to adjust to each other. There's Polish, German, Irish, Greek, English, and some blacks all working here. There isn't much new to that idea. My family came over to Ellis Island, you know."

Mr. Porter looked directly at Frieda for the third time and slowly smiled for some emphasis. "Frieda, I appreciate all our history here in America and even in this part of lower Michigan. But in fact just as people have dreamed of coming to America years ago through Ellis Island, so too others today dream of making America their home. Thus, we need to keep up with our culture as it still changes. Which is why I'd appreciate you'd say African-American for that particular ethnicity." He nodded at her with one short nod, while Terrance looked from her to Mr. Porter and smiled as his chair hit the tile floor. Terrance's elbow hit the edge of the large table when he slipped forward from leaning back on two legs, jarring the whole table some.

"Excuse me, guys," he mumbled while picking up his fruit punch for a quick sip.

"In addition, understand the Hispanic population is still becoming a larger part of our labor market, more often in the back-of-the house. All should be aware of any cultural or language differences and utilize those who are bilingual fully. We appreciate the strong work ethic that is clearly evident in some of our current staff." Chef Curtis pointed his pen again, this time at me, and Mr. Porter nodded his agreement.

"Well anyway," Mr. Porter continued, "in your days you may encounter certain situations that throw you off your plan, but remember to step back and think through the best possible strategy in dealing with each employee. If you are unsure, then please come to me or call me on my cell phone for some suggestions. I would much rather you call than step in the wrong direction when managing my staff. Now I've provided you with articles on diversity in the work force and the importance of teamwork in hospitality industries. You may copy them and discuss them in your separate staff meetings. Please reiterate these issues of integrity, teamwork, and diversity there also. I'm not leaving much time for discussion, so let's hear it."

Mr. Porter looked around from one distracted face to another. He kept a grim look as the only questions posed were about checking the number for his new cell phone versus the pager he had always carried. As the leadership began to disperse, Duncan, Mr. Porter's son, sat down behind his mother and reviewed her handwritten notes. He had come in noiselessly.

~ 33 ~

THE LAUNDRY ROOM ENCOUNTER

"Hey, 'Berto! What, are you crazy? It's nine in the morning; you closed McDonald's last night and we're both off today," Luis yelled from across the room. He must have me heard poking through our basket that works for dirty clothes. I'm the only one with cook's clothes, and it's easy to find mine. Through the door on the other side I could hear Octavio pacing his snoring like the border train going up a mountainside. He stayed out like that when he goes out for drinks after a pick up game, and last night wasn't any different. I walked by with my whites in our grey worn out basket, holding my stained chef coats by just strands of hanging plastic from the basket. I looked in our doorway, and Luis had his eyes barely open. They were still clear through the slits, and so I guess he didn't drink much with Octavio.

"You want any clothes cleaned for tomorrow? You know we're going into the weekend," I nodded at his small pile from yesterday in the middle of the room.

"Naw, I got some left," he muttered with a blink and turned his back to me.

I softly shut the door and shuffled down the hall. I was still tired from fourteen hours of work the day before. I hoped nobody was in the laundry room. I could throw in two loads and read my latest novel. I picked up a new author for me, John Grisham. I couldn't put it down, reading about justice for the everyday people. I walked down two floors to the basement and backed up into the door to open it into the hallway. I lifted my right foot automatically to back kick the door open. My foot held against the door for a moment before I swung it in a kick as I read the back jacket again about the story and wondered if the next chapter would pick up some. Turning to the first page of the next chapter, I started to read it and kicked the door in as I turned the page. Somebody was yelling, and I laughed at how real this author got. Then the door slammed back into my basket, and it dropped. Dirty coats and checkered pants spilled all over my novel like a gloppy sauce.

"You're only worried about your dirty clothes, and my clean laundry is now dirty!" A tall Hispanic young woman in a long, loose fitting flowery dress caught her falling basket, just as all her items slipped to the floor. "When will boys in this building become gentlemen? My Mama, she was right—"

"Uh, excuse me!" Stunned and confused, I stared into her deep, almond shaped eyes, noticing also the black flowing hair that was a bit tousled. She continued to complain about me, and I quickly stuffed my dirties back in the basket, burying the book underneath.

"I'm sorry, so sorry," I tried to smile while waiting for the next part of the stern scolding from the lifting voice and fiery eyes that dazzled me. "My name is Roberto, and I live upstairs. You must be new in the building, since I haven't seen you around—"

"I don't care to know your name, and I wish you haven't seen me." She looked right in my eyes as she gathered up her crumpled jeans from the floor. I picked up my basket, allowing the door to shut. "You're probably some kind of stalker they talk about on those TV shows. Just two months here and already somebody is watching for me in doorways." She snapped up her basket and her long hair flipped back from the heavy sigh. I wanted to look once more in her eyes but dared not.

I had set down my basket when it started to tear on one side. Then I helped finish picking up the last of her jeans and jerked my head up when she took a last, deep breath. I decided I needed to put her straight.

"Wait a minute! I don't stand and wait in doorways watching for you."

I stood up slowly, laying the last pair of jeans on top of the pile with my right hand and pushed back my unkempt hair with my left. This wasn't going well but I didn't care at the moment. I was no peeping Tom and I wanted her to know that!

She paused to consider my response. "Well, maybe I misspoke, but you looked like a shadow from my stairway. Thanks for picking up my clothes, but I'm still watching you," she went on some without taking much of a breath. "Why didn't you watch what you were doing? Do you always kick in doors with your eyes shut, or just when girls are trying to come out?"

I laughed at that and sarcastically responded, "Really I saw the Americano cop show taking down doors of the bad guys, and I thought why not me? And so I—"

"So, you mock me now, and this accident where I could have been seriously hurt." Her arched eyebrows seemed to question me and I couldn't answer yet. "Again, I wish I could see real gentlemen here in this country." I wasn't sure if she were talking to her mother, her God, or me. But I thought it best to say something.

"I'm sorry, again, but actually I was reading a novel. It was just starting to get more interesting. I should have picked a better place to read it," I mumbled at the end.

"Well! A Latino that not only reads but also comes with an apology. How nice to meet you. My name is Carmen. I've been here in America for a few months. I left the university in Mexico when my uncle asked me to come here and help in caring for my aunt. She has gotten quite ill." Gone was the edgy, defiant tone in her voice. It seemed to sing musically now, like notes on the scale.

"Carmen, I'm happy to meet you," I smiled at her, as the fire seemed to cool in her eyes somewhat. Maybe she was warming up to me. Whatever the reason, I didn't want to break her gaze. I set my basket down and nodded to hers. "Can I wash some of your jeans in my load since it was my fault that they have fallen dirty?"

"No, you silly boy! I can see yours are work clothes full of smears and dirt that I can smell," Carmen sniffed and smiled all in one breath. She seemed to be good at multitasking, as the chef would say. Even her sniffle sounded like a song.

"All right, then. How about I buy you a coffee? It will refresh you from the smell of bad laundry," pointing to the corner Tim Horton's with one hand and my checks with the other. Grinning some, I felt like a bad soccer official getting booed by the crowd.

~ 34 ~

KITCHEN WORK

She wouldn't let me clean her clothes with mine. Maybe I should have said I'd gladly clean them again alone while washing my work uniforms separately. Instead I asked her out for coffee and now what? I had stood still for another second, waiting and wondering. The image of me as an official making a bad call wouldn't leave my head and then her sniffing and smiling at me and my dirty checks. Well, they came clean enough and now I had to be ready for lunch service. But I couldn't stop thinking of yesterday's conversation and how it ended.

"I'm sorry, I don't have coffee with men I don't know well, let alone walk through the doorway," Carmen had smiled widely and shook all her hair behind her head. She moved the basket to her left hand, pushed the door open, and walked away. I had only just stood there and watched the door shut behind her and couldn't move for a minute. Finally, I pushed both hands through my hair, all the way down the back of my head and then picked up my ratty basket to start my laundry. The crowd still booed in my head, even as I pushed the coats into one machine. The other machine held the check pants, and it booed just as loud.

I jumped up to sit on one of the empty machines, opening my novel. I couldn't get past the first page of the next chapter. The lift and drop of her voice, the fire that cooled in her eyes, the quick rapid comments, and the smile that stopped my heart from beating—they all worked on my mind, making it hard to focus on another man's story. Can there be any sense of justice in his story, if I can't get coffee with Carmen? Thoughts of her kept taking over in my head, and I was not even sure if my station was set for the lunch rush. I hope so. I hate finding out I missed items once the rush has begun.

My sauté pans had gotten hot enough, and I added a couple of ounces of clarified butter to each pan. To the larger sloped side pan I added shrimp from the third pan and scallops from the bottom of the Randel reach-in with my gloved right hand, taking a quick sniff before tossing them in. Sous Chef Terrance was always saying how the seafood will turn faster than his girl's head at Great Lakes Crossing. Even though Chef Terrance graduated from Schoolcraft, one of the better culinary programs in this part of America, he was a laugh to work with when his jokes got the line to smile.

I quickly added a pinch of crushed garlic and lightly seasoned it with the salt and pepper mix. I heard the sizzle, turned to the other pan, and cut it off the heat for a second. I turned the seafood pan to lower heat, gave it a quick toss, and grabbed the other pan to set it up under my board. Sliding the back of my chef's blade along the board to push the mixed mushroom I sliced into the hot pan, I cut the heat back to medium.

I ran to the walk-in, grabbed a quart of heavy cream and half-and-half, and poured it into a six quart sauce pan on the back burner. After seasoning the mushrooms, I cut the heat down and checked the seafood. It looked good, the shrimp weren't pink, and the scallops had a little more brown on them, but I thought they were all right. So I turned off the seafood and saw my dairy was starting to come up to a boil, and I turned it down to simmer. I added a touch of red wine to deglaze the pan, just like Sous Chef Terrance had me do yesterday with them, and then I heard, "Roberto, what's going on with this seafood here? Don't tell me this is for our Manhattan chowder, or is it your lunch?"

"No, Chef Curtis. It's not my lunch. This pan is the garnish for the chowder, and I thought it was all right," I mumbled.

Stirring it some with a cook's spoon, he shook his head. "Roberto, the scallops aren't supposed to be that dark. I just want them lightly seared and then the heat should be turned down. Restart this entire garnish and hustle. We open in ten minutes."

I sautéed more seafood, starting with the seared scallops first. Then I added both sautéed garnishes to my bases staying warm on the flattop. I took a sampling of each to Chef Curtis.

"The house Manhattan chowder is fine, but the cream of steak and mushroom needs more seasoning. It also could be a touch thinner, add a bit more cream." He wiped his chin with his shoulder and handed me the plate. "Do we have more chanterelles and oysters that we can add to it?"

"No, Chef, the mushrooms were mixed, and I used them all from that five pound box," I answered.

"Well, adjust the soup of the day, and have Chef John taste it before you send it out. He just walked in the back door." He pointed with his boning knife from the corner he stood at. I ran to the walk-in for more half-and-half and started to worry when I thought about the list in my pocket of the four items I still had to prep before the lunch rush hit. Night Chef John approved both soups for me, and Chef Curtis watched me with a grin as I took each soup out to the waithall.

"Roberto, you have those soups good and hot for us? Is there a garnish topping for the soup of the day? And did you bring ladles, or should I send one of the girls to get them?" Frieda, the lead server who does the schedule, could never just ask or say one thing, and I had a hard time knowing what to say first when answering her.

"No, Ms. Frieda, I didn't grab any ladles, but they are hot enough, since Chef John temped them out with his thermometer. I know there is garnish inside but not sure about the topping. I think it's probably fresh parsley, but I'll ask the chef giving the meeting to mention it," I answered her with a fast grin.

I grabbed a half-cup of the Manhattan chowder to take off some of the hunger I was feeling, and this batch looked really good today. The kitchen has a house recipe to follow for it, with fresh seafood and homemade simmered stock, but it still tastes better when Chef Terrance or Chef Curtis make it. Chef Terrance was the Sous, but many times he was also the saucier, since the last full time saucier had not been replaced yet. So, he's second in command in the kitchen and tries to stay on top of all soups or sauces. But you could always tell when one of the preppers tried to make them.

"Karen, who opened with you this morning? I didn't bring up my copy of the schedule, and there are some things that aren't ready in this server hall," Ms. Frieda asked her as she brought back up condiments. Ms. Frieda moved me a few feet while searching underneath the bottom of the reach in, and I nearly spilled my soup.

"Frieda, Cindy opened with me. This is her first day shift since we trained her six months ago. You do the schedule and ought to remember she's only been on nights. The sidework rotation is different at night, and I'm showing her the ropes," Karen stopped after she set the mustards and A1 on the stainless shelf and looked right at Frieda.

"Karen, let's not start the day on the floor with any leftover attitude. I gave you your favorite station today, even though it wasn't part of the chart rotation." I swallowed the last spoonful, laughing at the moment as Ms. Frieda slammed the door some. "I know you didn't make a lot yesterday, especially showing the new hostess around the dining room. So put a smile on and see what Cindy is doing."

Ms. Frieda looked like she wanted to scold me too so I went back to the cook's line. I needed to stock lunch plates, soup crocks, and smaller plates for the French Onion in the hot window. I looked through the window and noticed the waithall had just enough for them. I made room in the hot window for more and went to the dish area. Luis had just run some through the machine, and I could see them still in the rack.

"Hey, Luis, stack those plates and crocks up! I need them for lunch, compadré," I yelled while I got some bleach for my sanitizer bucket.

I overheard Luis. "Hello, señorita, glad to meet you. I don't remember seeing you much here. What is your name?" He was busy meeting Cindy for the second time since she started here six months ago.

"Luis! I need those dishes ASAP. That's Cindy and let her be, she's a night shift server," I swung in their direction with my red bucket's handle. Cindy smiled a thank you to him while she walked away with the silverware basket.

"See 'Berto, it is my Latin charm in the air, and she smiled at me," he laughed as he handed me a stack of soup crocks.

"Hey, I can't take all those. I've got the bucket in this other hand," and I handed them back to him.

"Here I'll take them, if you tell me where they go," a new girl offered.

"Well, let me show you. Just walk this way." Luis had a stack in both hands and pointed with his head, directing her to follow him.

"Are you new here? I'm Luis, and you need anything at all around here, just ask me," he began talking and walking to the cook's line with her a few steps behind.

"My name is Julie, and I'm the new hostess here. I just started yesterday," she sighed after putting the cups in the window next to Luis's set. "Boy, it's really hot back here!" She tossed her head back to get a few strands of blond hair starting to stick to her forehead.

"The kitchen is a hot oven that cooks a lot of people in it, and that's why I stay cool in the dish tank. I'm the guy that carries people around here, so you just—"

"Luis, she's gone out in the dining room now," I laughed at him and pointed to Julie holding the rest of a paper towel she snagged while walking to the waithall. We both bent to peak through the hot window and could see her patting her arms on the way toward the host stand. He stared after her for an extra second, and then waved her away with the side towel he carried on his shoulder, tossing it back on his right shoulder as he walked back to the dish area.

~ 35 ~

CARMEN'S WITNESS

Luis and I had just let ourselves into the apartment building, and we were both ready to relax in the air-conditioned room, drinking some sweet tea. The tea is a close taste to our native Jamika drink, and the canned tea would feel good after working both jobs yesterday with non-stop lunch today. Luis took the stairs two at a time, while I pulled myself with the rail one at a time. I didn't look up when the door shut and thought it must be Luis going up to the next floor.

"Uh, Uh! My back!" she yelled when I looked up from bumping the bags she was carrying. Startled, I stopped and looked around the two large Glad bags and smiled to myself. Carmen tried to right herself as both bags tumbled to each side.

"Hey, are you okay? I didn't even see you coming down the stairs," I said as I reached for her left arm to help her up. "Did you hurt your back, Carmen?"

"Oh, it's Roberto again! Must you always be knocking me around or down with my stuff? My back does seem sore now," she said and looked at me while stroking her back with her right hand. "Thanks for helping me up, even though it was you who pushed my bags and set me falling on the stairs. And you can let go of my arm now. I know I'm a little shaky here in the stairwell, but I'm all right. Boys to men mistake gratitude for kindness as a signal of some kind. I have to ask my uncle about men and their ways."

"Look now, Carmen. You don't have to speak to your uncle about me yet. You can have some of the blame you're passing out, especially since you were walking like Santa Claus coming down here." I pushed her arm from my grasp and pointed with both my finger tips like the gunfighters I had read about. Her eyes blazed for a second.

181

"Yet you hope to meet my uncle? That's not likely if you continue to knock me down. And why is it my fault when you're the one trying to carry on a conversation with your feet? Why didn't you see me coming down, especially if you were walking like a normal person?"

"What about the bags sitting here? If you could see above or around them, maybe you would have seen me before I practically fell for you."

I tried to recover well but the comment had done more than slipped out. Thoughts of her had made it tough to focus at work and even sleep at night. "I mean when I collided into your bags." She shook her long hair back from her face, straightened it some, and smiled just a little in the corner, trying to mask her enjoyment at my discomfort.

"We've only just met, Roberto! So don't think you can go falling for me today. And as for these packages, I'm collecting in the building for others in need. Our church is having a clothing drive this Sunday, for the children mostly. Many people in the building have young ones that are growing out of their clothes," Carmen explained in one long breath. Picking up both bags for her, I started taking the stairs back down.

"Well, the least I can do is carry them out for you. Where should I take them? Out to your car?" I asked.

"No, just the main floor and across the way from the entrance door. You can set them by my door. That would be nice. I don't have a car, and so I usually ride with my family or take the bus," she motioned down the stairway to the right and I turned my head back around. Waiting, I stepped more to the left to let her lead the way. I heard her walk to the door and pull it open as I followed her slowly one step at a time. Already she strikes me as being different from the chicas I knew in Guatemala—so much more bold and confident in herself. Maybe the university life does that. The gods help me if I fall forward with her bags; the gods would never entertain the chance for Carmen to answer my questions with such bad luck.

"Set them down there." She pointed on the floor to the right of apartment 206. I put them down and looked at the door, up and down.

"Roberto, it might be nice for me to ask you in and we could share some Coca-Cola, but I don't think it would be good for me," Carmen smiled a little sadly.

"I don't understand it's only a Coke. It can't hurt at all, can it?" I asked her as I brushed my hair back and tried to give her my best smile.

"Look, Roberto, you seem very nice, tho' a little clumsy, and you have a sweet smile." She nodded just a little at my face. "The problem isn't yours but mine. I've made a commitment to myself and my God and that is not to go out with a man who is not a child of God."

"What is a child of God? I am my mother's child, for my father was good but is now gone. She and he both had gods they spoke of. But I'm no child of theirs, for they don't know me just as I know not of them. So we can get past this problem of yours, have a Coke today, and maybe coffee tomorrow morning." I went on looking for a way to a solution.

I thought we could meet more and spend time talking. She could see me for me, and I could finally feel like someone could understand me. These daydreams were fast turning to a nightmare, and I was still awake. I had to stop it.

"I am sorry, Roberto. That's the way it is for me." Carmen shook her head slowly while her eyebrows and cheeks narrowed into a frown.

"Well, tell me more of this God. My mother and Father Angelo both spoke of God often. But He was hard for me to understand, and I never saw much love from Him in our family," I explained with some frustration.

"Roberto, you come on Sunday with me to my church and hear the word of God. Maybe meet the pastor. Ask more questions after you have heard of God in his house with those who love Him," Carmen asked with a searching look in her narrowed eyes.

"I don't know, señorita. I would have to check my schedule at work and see. Sometimes I open on Sundays. Maybe, I will let you know."

I shrugged and looked up from the worn clogs that Chef Terrance had given me. They were good for the kitchen but they never felt tight enough. Tying laces in double knots gave my feet the security they needed. Life's path needed security.

"This is the apartment I stay at with my aunt and uncle." She looked again at her room. "If you want to come with us, be here at 9:00 in the morning and you can ride with us. When you search for a real friend, I can try to be one without us going out, but even a small friendship with us will not meet your needs."

"I know, I have thought of my heart that needs a deep sense of friendship and longing for a long time," I said with a bit of heaviness in my voice.

"Oh, my goodness, you think I can help meet that longing for you someday," she giggled and I started to frown. "Oh, I don't mean to hurt you, but the only way to find true fulfillment is through Jesus, the Son of God."

"He's this child of God you were talking about? Father Angelo spoke of Jesus, and Mama did also. I know he did great things for humans. Though I don't see how I can become him," I wondered.

"Oh, no. Jesus is the Son of God, but we humans can also be part of the family of God," Carmen exclaimed. "We too can become children of God and share in His glory. In fact Jesus came for all people groups in the world—even Hispanics from Guatemala." She smiled right at me and winked. "It is all due to God's mercy and grace when He sent Jesus to earth."

"All right, all right. Enough of the church lesson. You sound like those evangelicos my mother would talk about and warn me about. I can't listen to more of this; I'll try to be here in the hall on Sunday morning." I sighed deeply as I waved a silent good-bye.

Luis was probably thinking I fell out in the hall and was ready to come looking for me. I think it was really strange that she happened down the stairs after he had already gone up. Why wasn't he the first to meet her? Would the last half hour have been any different? I pushed myself some and jogged up the flight of stairs to our hallway. Turning the knob and feeling glad that Luis hadn't locked it, I rushed in to the refrigerator for a can of tea. I felt like I really needed one then.

"'Berto, where you been? I thought Octavio and I were going to have to start checking the halls for you."

Luis finished his Coke while Octavio sat with a bottle of beer in his hand and smiled at his comment.

"Roberto, I've been waiting around this afternoon to talk to both of you guys. You disappeared while we were here just wondering." Octavio was grinning at me. He motioned with the bottle, asking for an explanation. With a shrug I sighed.

"Yeah, I'm sorry. I actually ran down a girl in the stairway, since I was taking my time coming up. It took a few minutes to help her pick up her things and walk her to her door." I put the can of sweet tea to my cheek. It's beginning to feel like an interrogation, and I'm starting to sweat.

"See, Octavio. I told you it was more than him crawling up the stairs, tired from two jobs. He must have crawled right into her, spilling her stuff and her," Luis laughed. "I wish I was there to see them fall down." Then Luis stopped when he saw Octavio's face that was so serious.

"Boys, I know you know I do lots of different types of jobs in this area," Octavio began. "The American government knows that I am a landscaper in the summers and work with snow removal in the winters. My boss calls me when he needs me, and I tell him if I'm available. If I am, then I go work for him. Sometimes I help Little Man down the street with some of the small jobs he has around town. But what the government doesn't know is that my favorite job is to assist our brothers coming from Central America in finding the best spots for themselves in this part of the America."

"Just like you set us up, Octavio!" Luis interrupted.

"Yeah, but he doesn't put up everyone in his home, like he did us," I pointed to the living room we sat in.

"Well, no, I don't put up most of those I help. Roberto, you are part of the family, and so I've taken a bigger interest in you guys," Octavio waved to both of us with beer in hand. "But I'm trying to explain how important it is to me to be sure all our people that come here are well cared for. They are ready to work hard and understand what it takes to be a stable U.S. citizen."

"But Octavio, that should be easy enough for them. They should want to act right, with all the fruit of America they enjoy and often many send back to their native homes. Our families taught us the ways to live, and we try to act even better here," I tried to understand what Octavio meant.

"Roberto, you're right. Part of coming to America would be easier if only people chose to adapt to the new area and culture they were in. The problems come when people don't consider the differences between our cultures and often bring with them their own personal baggage."

I looked at Octavio and wondered why he had never before opened up to us before like this. Luis and I never really spoke of these issues, but they bore on my heart.

"Octavio, I know there are differences in our cultures, but I'm not sure about what baggage you're talking about," I asked him.

"Baggage isn't completely what I mean. It's more the things we do and say to be accepted here," Octavio explained. "Things like driving below the speed limit, full of caution, drinking at home and not in public, and acting less crazy than what we might have done in our home country. We each need to behave better than any stereotypes or assumptions that are made about us."

"All right, that's good to know—now that we've been here about five years. Why do you talk with us now about it?" Luis asked exactly what I'd been wondering.

"Well, we have another roommate moving in tomorrow. I'm picking him up and he'll share my room." Octavio cracked open his second beer from the fridge door. "Manuel is his name, and he's a friend of my family."

"Wait a minute," Luis spoke up. "We've lived with you all these years and have never had another guest or roommate. Why now? I mean, I'm not trying to be like we don't appreciate you, but we've been a good team and now you're gonna change it?"

"Calm down, Luis, and don't let this upset you." Octavio looked at him and then at me. I tried to glare at Luis, but I still wondered too. "He was sent back to Mexico when he was caught with a small amount of drugs. If it weren't for the fact he's Mexican, it would have been nothing. Now we're going to help him settle in a new city here in

America."

"You say, 'we're going to help him.' I don't quite understand when you are the one who is paid to do this," I commented and then immediately wished I could take it back.

"Maybe you have a point, but I thought you could give some back to this community I have helped you get used to. I want you two to get a job for him at the restaurant you work at. Your chef thinks you guys both do great. You guys I know are better workers than many people in that restaurant who take their job for granted. Didn't you tell me that young pregnant server said she was going to quit since she could make more money applying for government assistance than working in the restaurant? So tell me, what's another Mexican?" Octavio laughed at his own joke, since none of us were actually Mexican. "As long as Manuel can meet the standard of work ethic you maintain, he'll be fine." He shook his head and laughed.

"I don't know about that, since I don't know if he's a great worker in the kitchen. Does he cook at all, or even understand how to work a dishwasher?" I shook my head a little as I got up from my chair and tossed my empty sweet tea can.

~ 36 ~

LUIS' WALKOUT

The restaurant had pretty good business at lunch, and I went over for a minute to help catch up Luis in the dish tank. He had stacks of plateware piled on the server side of the dish area, and his stack racks got so backed up coming out of the machine that the machine stopped for a minute. I smiled that he didn't even hear the machine cut off, since he was trying to sing to the women as they dropped off their dirty plates and tossed the silver in the soapy tub.

"Hey, amigo, dishes can't get clean when the machine isn't on," I yelled over my shoulder while I pulled the rack over from the wall that stopped the dishwasher and started stacking the clean plates.

"Gracias, smart one. You done with your pop break at the machine and felt sorry for the dish dog sweating away over here. I'll get caught up, go on back to the other side of the line where the cooks stand around about now just talking through the window to the girls."

He grunted under his breath, his last words muttered about "cooks taking their after lunch break to regroup" with a dry laugh. All Luis sees is the line cooks planning ways to flirt with the female servers. I wasn't sure if he wasn't joking now, jealous, or some of both. All these years as friends and I still misread him sometimes.

"Relax, my friend. Just helping you out for a few minutes. I'm not sure if I should talk to Chef Curtis today or not," I said.

"What? Are you thinking of not talking to him about Manuel?" He stopped short after pushing his last rack in and looked at me. "You're not serious, Roberto? This is important stuff, and Octavio doesn't ask much of us."

"I know, but I don't want to push a reference when we haven't seen him work. It sounds like he was a little crazy before," I sighed some.

Pushing pieces of sweat under my matted hair back over my bangs with my shoulder, I wonder why I didn't ask to work the cold end on a humid day and not the broiler. "Chef Curtis respects me and you, and if we put this out there and Manuel doesn't work out, well, I'm not happy with the thought." I shook my head with uncertainty.

Luis stacked, sprayed, and pushed the next rack in with some force, and turned to me again. "Don't think too deeply about this and react stupidly for both us. You heard the speech Octavio gave. We need to look out for our brothers."

"He's not my brother. My brother and father are both dead. I have to look out for me and then you," I said as I glared at him. Images of my father and brother popped around in my head along with random pictures of my childhood when we ran down the field with the ball.

"Well, my brother is half-dead!" Luis swung his whole upper body in my direction while moving his feet two steps to the side. "'Berto we're alive today, fully. Let's act like it, and thank the people who got us here."

I stood silent looking at him.

"Get out of my area. I don't need any more of your slow moving help. You catch and pull like my old dog who wobbled blindly on three and half legs, near dying of old age."

I walked back to the line and started checking my set up for the night shift. His quick shots at me could make pieces of a song. When I get over being a little bitter, maybe I'll remind him. I checked the reach-in and saw I would need some onions sliced julienne and tomatoe concasse. I run to the back hall and grabbed a medium stockpot to blanch my tomatoes and stop up the sink for an ice bath. After I filled half of it with water and ice, I headed to the front of the walk-in cooler to the produce side. Pulling up my apron by its two bottom ends, I filled it up with twelve tomatoes. Heading out with a push on the small round handle sticking out from the long rod on the door, I stopped when I heard a loud giggle.

"Chef John, you say now. How come you're called night chef when we usually work together? Something's not right in Denmark, as my mother used to say," Cindy asked. Stepping back four or five steps, I tightened the grip on my apron and listen. Suddenly the door opened and Luis walked in with a broom. I hissed a "shush" to him and nodded toward the back of the walk-in.

"Well, Chef Curtis has stepped out for a while, and I'm left in charge," Chef John explained to her, "and Cindy, you need to check to be sure you're taking the oldest creamers to the right. We don't want to see any wasted."

She giggled again for a second, and asked, "Are you sure you were just checking the shelf I was pulling from? I think maybe you were checking me out when I walked in."

I rolled my eyes, and motioned with my elbow toward the door. Luis knocked the knob with his elbow. Luis seemed to stay back and chance more eavesdropping, but I wasn't listening to any more of this. Searching for my tomato shark on the shelf above the window, I started coring out the tomatoes. Luis walked past me with a growl under his breath, tossing the broom in my corner of the cook's line. He strode over to the backed up dish area. Chef John walked by to get a cup of pop, walked back by the line, and noticed my half pan of tomatoes. I had started scoring the bottom of them, and he nodded to them and walked to the back line. My third tomato was cut too deep, and I looked at it, wondering what Chef John was thinking when he nodded at me and my tomatoes. I run a sani towel on my area, cleaned my blade, and dropped the tomatoes in the boiling pot of water in a big basket. Knowing I've got just a few seconds, I pulled the half pan to take to the dish area and heard Luis still banging away. Setting it to the side, I stopped and looked over at the dish area window. Luis caught my look, nodded over to Cindy bending over to put creamers in the server fridge. He smirked, shook his head, and yanked a rack of glasses from the counter to then rotate them in the beverage station. He had talked to Cindy before, even asked her out, I think. But why was he so upset?

"Luis, why do have to make so much noise back here? The guests can almost hear you with all this racket," Frieda complained to him. He looked up at her and stared. "Really, Luis, I'm not trying to be mean. But you are rather loud. Our guests would like to dine with some more quiet," she scolded, I think trying to be nice still.

"Enough!" Luis yelled as he slammed another glass rack down on the counter a few feet from the dishwasher. A few water glasses shattered, and she stared at them with her mouth open wide.

"Leave me be, you hen-pecking waitress. Just go and gather some of your chicks around you for their own correcting." Pulling up the rack, he slid the broken glass onto a dirty half sheet pan and tossed it into the garbage. Looking up, he caught my gaze and winked. Just then, I remembered my tomatoes. I hurried back to my stove, pulled the basket from the hot pot and dropped it in the ice bath, and wondered again how to read my friend. Shaking my head, I could hear Frieda letting out all her anger on Samuel. Although her venting sounded like balloons slowly being squeezed free of air, Samuel listened. The dining room manager usually remained calm in the dining area, and I could see when she finished her rant that he had come to a decision. He found some dirt on his pant leg, wiped it clean with a two quick hand swats, and then turned around to walk to the dish area.

"Luis! Stop what you are doing now!" Samuel stopped Luis in his steps when he was picking up a stack of clean platters. "Give me your apron and punch out!"

I sprinted back toward the dish area, and watched them both. Luis didn't move at all, waiting to hear from someone to help him. I was thinking of the words to help defend him. Samuel usually left the kitchen to its own devices and the chefs handled any minor problems. I wasn't sure how and if to get involved at all.

"Young man, I'm not joking. Take off that apron, punch out, and please leave right this moment," Samuel commanded him with a little more force in his voice. Silently, Luis set the apron in his hand, punched out, and walked out the back door.

I hadn't seen this before and wasn't sure what it meant. Was Luis done for the day? Or did he no longer work here? Should I walk out behind him, like in a show of unity I had read about in American history? I looked around and then down, and noticed my shoelaces were loose. I backed against the wall and tied them in a double knot. Oddly I was glad I hadn't worn the clogs Chef Terrance had given me. The printer on the cooks' line spurted a ticket, and I worked my way up the wall as it squawked.

"Everybody back to work," Samuel yelled with a steady force still in his voice. "Food to prep, food to cook I hear, and food to be served. Let's make some guests happy, and make some money too."

~ 37 ~

ROBERTO AND CHEF CURTIS

A little confused about what I should be doing and thinking maybe I should go talk to one of the chefs, I turned slowly back to my position on the line. I looked over at my stove and remembered my second batch of tomatoes. I ran over and pulled the basket, getting them in the ice bath right away. Knowing they were overdone, I started handling them in the sink, hoping that maybe they were still usable. Picking one in each hand from the sink, I turned them over in the air.

"Roberto, you know that those won't fly now. I'll use them in a sauce or soup where the tomatoes are intended to break down while cooking. Now take that sour face off, my friend, or you'll spoil the food around you." Chef Curtis lightly tapped me on the shoulder. "Luis will be back in the building as scheduled tomorrow."

Chef Curtis swiftly strode down the line, and I followed him, thinking now might be a good time to ask about an opening for Manuel. Chef must have already overheard the servers talking about Luis, Frieda, and Samuel.

"Samuel, what are you doing changing the water on the machine? I just walked through the dining room, and it seems like some servers could be cleaning their sections better." Chef Curtis had stopped, taken off his hat and scratched the bald spot on the very back of his head. Replacing his hat, he helped shut the door and fill the machine back up.

"See here, Chef! I'm done checking the machine and this area is just fine." Samuel slid his head back from the dish machine, standing a foot taller over Chef. "I've had to send home our dishwasher for the day. His attitude was completely unacceptable for the last hour, and then he had a blow out with Frieda."

"Understood, Samuel. But my preference is that you would speak to me or one of my back of the house management prior to sending home one of our staff." Chef Curtis seemed to be looking right through Samuel while they talked. "The kitchen staff sometimes has a keener sense of their people, and I'd like—"

"Chef, if we're going to have a meeting about this, perhaps we should take this conversation to the office?" As Samuel interrupted him, he motioned toward the other side of the kitchen, and I felt someone come up behind me.

"Gentlemen, the office seems like a splendid place to go. I believe all three of us should regroup there," Mr. Porter smiled. "If memory serves me from one of our last meetings, this issue of a team management attitude requiring more growth in this building was mentioned. In fact, I recall you two upper management suggesting a plan of sorts that would expand on the team attitude. Yet here we are. Today is a good day to make an example to discuss at our next meeting." He slapped the backs of Samuel and Chef Curtis, pushed them forward, and winked at me behind their backs.

"Mr. Porter, there's really no need to create time for a meeting with us, sir. We only had a few words in passing," Chef tried to persuade him. "I have a schedule to cost, review, and post."

"Oh, my friends don't pass on a few minutes to share an Arnold Palmer. I'm quite sure this won't take more than ten or fifteen minutes," Mr. Porter's eyes sparkled as he still pushed them forward.

"Mr. Porter, I prefer my iced tea alone, not mixed with lemonade," Samuel tried. "And it is true we've pretty much resolved this slight."

"Nonsense, I like to discuss where these issues may surface again. Almost like my professor reminded of us in business class, 'practice till it's almost perfect.'" Mr. Porter seemed to bubble over in his walk. "That professor suggested businesses could never quite get things perfect and so near perfection was the goal."

I wasn't sure what to think about their management situation, but it was interesting. Not that I was timing them, but their meeting lasted about fifteen minutes, and Chef Curtis came past the line into the back prep area with a real purpose. It looked like he felt he was even more behind and needed to get moving. Now I had my doubts if this was a good time to talk about Manuel with him while I finished setting up the end of the line for the night shift. I noticed a couple of the night cooks come in the back door and were going to the locker room to change up.

"Roberto, you need to finish up those vegetables in the next five minutes. Run a broom and wipe down this area, then punch out," Night Chef John ordered me. Chef Curtis must be on his behind about kitchen labor.

"Yes, Chef," I answered. "I'm done with these onions in one minute. I always make sure my station is as good as when I came in. Tommy is coming in to take over tonight, and he won't have a thing to worry about."

"Roberto, I want your area to be cleaner than when you come in. Raise your standard better than others." Chef John stared right in my eyes. "Some of my closes when I used to dance with the bottle were not something I was proud of. I've worked hard to challenge myself to be better, and with support from my sponsor and more importantly, God, my life has really changed. The point is for you to work at pushing yourself to be a stronger cook for yourself and not what you walk into or wait for someone to demand of you. Besides that, Tommy is barely ready to master his station on slow nights. So I would appreciate you have more than set up but completely prepared for a successful shift."

"I understand, Chef," I replied and wondered about the details. I know many chefs worked long hours, and that'll often lead them to give in to some drugs or excessive drinking. I never thought Night Chef John had a problem like that, since he carried himself with real professionalism, although I did hear that little episode in the walk-in with him and Cindy, and I'm not sure what that was all about.

"Roberto, your apron is sitting on your shoulder and you're smiling. I hope that means you're not on my clock now and heading home." Chef Curtis turned to me, seeming to know I wanted to talk.

"Chef, I know you're busy right now, but I just wanted to ask you something and—" I started.

"I hope it's not private because there are twenty pounds of fish I have to trim for tonight, and I'm thinking you want to talk about Luis. Well, rest assured, he still has a job here," he explained. "I made sure of that, since he is one of the better dishwashers I've had here. I know you two are cousins or something."

"Well no, Chef," I stammered. I needed to get on with my real questions. "Luis and I grew up boyhood friends and came to America together to make life better for both our families and ourselves. But that's not my question."

"I see now, you want a raise. Well, you are one of the best cooks I've trained and hired. You seem to hunger for learning more and doing better each day. I appreciate that in you. But as I previously told you, private matters should be in the office. Wrap this trout up, and we'll take a walk outside. I could use a few minutes of fresh air," Chef Curtis complained with a smile.

Once the fish was wrapped and stored in the walk-in, I caught up with him gazing outside at the back parking lot.

"My outdoor office suits me better sometimes. You work two jobs and yet show passion and the beginnings of leadership. I have great hope for you, Roberto. That's why I asked to have you sit in on the meeting the other day."

Stunned, I stood silent for a moment. Then he started walking again along the back of the building and I kept pace.

"Chef, I wouldn't mind a raise at all and I really appreciate you telling me what you think of me. But actually, I have to ask about another friend of mine. His name is Manuel, and he would be a great worker in the dish area. He really needs a steady job right now, and he would do well here. You're a fair man, and I know you could give him a break. He won't let you or the kitchen down." My words ran out, spilling quickly like a mop bucket knocked over, and the squeegee wasn't going to push it fast enough.

"That's fine and true enough, you giving a reference for someone. The situation is that I'm not sure we need another full time dishwasher." Chef shook his head once. "And I know I just said how proud I am of Luis, but his temper isn't good for my kitchen. Especially when I have to go and deal with the aftermath with my boss. Your Manuel might carry some of this same hot-tempered blood in him. Why now does he need a steady job?" Stopping our slow walk side by side behind the restaurant, he leaned against the brick and waited for my reply. I could hear the waves under a couple of boats on the other side of the restaurant.

"Chef, he hasn't been in any huge problems. Just a few things that have brought him down, and he needs a break. I heard you were the guy for years who was all about second chances. I even heard you had a guy who cooked with a tether here."

That might have pushed him too far, and it was rumors I had heard. But he smiled, with a hint of pride. I just hoped he would not make me swear his papers were legal. I could never know with any certainty.

"Well, people sometimes need a second chance." Chef scratched the back of his head. "We need a couple of shifts picked up, but Luis might end up losing one day. After today, it's a reality he should face for a while. You'd better explain to Luis so he'll bear the news when my schedule goes up. I'll put Manuel on the schedule based on your word. Send him to see me tomorrow at two-thirty after the lunch rush."

~ 38 ~

EN ROUTE HOME

The drive was much better than I thought it would be that day. I had worried when I punched out that Luis would be still holding onto his anger, and I would have to deal with his venting all the way home. Instead I came out to see him strumming his acoustic guitar on the curb for Julie, the new hostess he had met the other day. She must have been coming in early for her shift, and he convinced her to sit for a few minutes. She saw me and hurriedly got up to go, glancing at her watch to see if she might be late. But Julie had a big smile as she ran into the back door of the restaurant, and Luis was still loudly strumming his favorite rock ballad. Bon Jovi, I think. I shook my head, started the car, and he hopped in the passenger side, grinning with no worries at all. I pulled onto the highway, keep my speed right at the posted limit, knowing the police wait for guys like me to punch it. They can ask me their questions because now my papers couldn't be any better. Luis was still humming that song of his, about some young couple trying to make it.

"Luis, you could have been suspended or even fired today," I put it out there and interrupted his tune. "Chef Curtis saved face for you and even some of your schedule."

"'Berto, you worry too much, my friend. That waitress, Frieda, gets in everybody's business and Samuel, well, he's got his shirt tucked in too tight." He leaned his head back, sighing some. "Everything will be fine; all of them in that kitchen know what a great worker I am."

"Luis, Chef had to go to some meeting on your behalf. He wasn't happy about that," I said while putting it into first too quickly and stopping short. I looked over at him with a smirk. His lesson was just a week or so ago, and he was much worse then.

"Roberto, I appreciate that from him. But he should do that anyway, 'cause he knows and sees what I do around there," he said with a wink and a half a shrug.

"Well, anyway, I spoke to him about Manuel. I asked him to think about a job for him, well I really kind of insisted he think about it." I grimly watched the traffic ahead of us slow down and began to brake the Mustang.

"I know you're worried, Roberto," Luis said. "But it needs to be said for our benefit. Manuel has got to be a great worker, so I wouldn't even worry. Stop staring at the cars around you; they're not the enemy. The kitchen will be fine, and so will Manuel." I shifted into fifth gear and passed an older lady on our left who was trying to peek above her steering wheel, not even looking at Luis. Frustrated with Luis, I pumped up the volume so I could listen to WRIF, "the home of Detroit Rock-n-Roll." Then I noticed Luis hummed along, tapping the dash with his palms. I glanced at his drumming hands, which frustrated me even more and switched to WNIC, "Detroit's nicest Rock." Luis stopped drumming when Elton John came on.

After getting in the building, we walked into our two-bedroom apartment. There was a guy sitting at the kitchen table with a cigarette in his mouth and his feet up on a second chair. He had a bit of a pudge stomach and legs that seemed longer as they hung extended across the room. He was dangling a beer between his fingers on the table over today's mail with his right hand; ashes from the smoke in his left hand fell on yesterday's mail. He was mindlessly watching a Latin soap opera on the cable station. Our mail and TV table—he was abusing it now as if it were his. I knew he had moved in at Octavio's insistence, but how about a little courtesy for other people's stuff?

"What's up, guys? You must be Roberto and Luis." Setting the beer down on my cell phone bill, he got up to shake our hands. "I'm Manuel. I hope you don't mind me watching your TV, but Octavio said I could make myself at home."

"Oh, it's no problem," Luis said as he put his hand out to shake Manuel's hand. "I'm Luis and this is Roberto." I half-heartedly put out my hand, and we shook.

"How was your trip here to Michigan?" Luis asked him.

"It was fine, except we had a long bus ride from out west." Manuel looked at both of us, waiting for a second. "You boys never lived at all in the western states? I spent time in Texas, Arizona, and California. They were all beautiful in their own way, and this Michigan doesn't seem to have as much natural beauty."

"We came right to the Midwest when we moved to the United States. Michigan is a lot prettier than you know. You just got here!" I thought about some of the fancy and colorful Lake Michigan plates I had seen. "There are over a hundred lakes in this Oakland County alone. Does Arizona even have a lake?" A little edge to that last comment. Oh well, you can see he doesn't care about our table.

"Don't get your head thinking too much about it, the sweat might start spraying out." Manuel smiled at the beginning of his own joke. "You don't have to defend Michigan; I'm here to stay for awhile."

"We like it here, and the area really accepts us. The people, they ask some questions but don't over do it," Luis tried to point out and then asked, "Tell us, Manuel, if Michigan wasn't your first choice, how did you end up here? Was your travel here to Michigan rough?"

"Well, I can tell you a bit of my story, but it goes like a lot of our people's stories." Manuel finished his beer and stood up. "Let me get another beer, and I'll tell you some of my history."

"We'd like to hear it," Luis added.

The chair legs slammed to the floor when Manuel got up. Walking to the kitchen, his legs told the truth. He looked over six feet tall with broad shoulders and long arms attached to them. The chair legs woke my thoughts and I raised my voice a little higher than planned. "We don't often hear of others' routes here, and we wonder about them. I'll be back in a minute, so don't start the details right away."

I took a moment to think about Manuel while I used the toilet with some relief. Waiting for the hot water to settle in, I wished myself happy birthday while washing my hands like Chef Curtis showed me. I walked by Octavio's room and stepped back when I saw it was partly open and he was on his bed. Bending over his side, I stirred up his left shoulder and picked up his headphones with my right hand.

"Octavio, can I talk to you for a second?" I asked him and wondered if he was napping.

"Roberto, why are you shaking George Clinton in my head? Good soothing doesn't come or stay long, you know?" He took off the headphones, and I could still hear the soulful mix of jazz and rock.

"Octavio, I spoke to my chef about Manuel, but I just don't think it's going to work out." I leaned against the windowsill that looked over the back lot. "The chef said he could come in to talk to him, but I can't let Manuel go in there. He's already stained my bills and had his feet on our furniture. If he can't care for our stuff, how will he function in a kitchen which needs much more detailed activity? I know he's your friend, or client, but he just can't be totally trusted! They trust me at the restaurant, and I won't jeopardize that trust." I felt the confidence rise in my choice of words, the more I said. I felt he would understand.

"Roberto, lower your voice some. Know this, my young friend. Manuel, he is more to me than just a client. So, if you can't help him and refuse to be near him, then Roberto, you and I will see less of each other because I will no longer help you!" Octavio pulled his feet over to the floor, and pointed at the door. "I hope you have made good credit, 'cause you'll need it when you try to find some place new to live! Think a little more about this reference at the restaurant and how quick you can be at finding a new home."

"Octavio, you wouldn't do that to us, would you? We are compadrés here, aren't we? We don't know the streets well, and I can't get a lease signed easily."

"I know what you can and can't do, Roberto. If you have to leave this building, what about the girl, Carmen, you told us about? What will you do about meeting her in the hall? And of course, the bigger problems are in finding a landlord willing to take in unknown renters and then appliances for a new place. My friend, it's not so much of a problem with Manuel. Is it really?"

Octavio turned his back to me, laid back down, and put his headphones on.

~ 39 ~

MANUEL'S STORY

"Manuel, we made it across the border in a coffee truck. They checked the crates of coffee in front of us but we were lucky. The coffee company had a good reputation, and the border patrol gave up looking for anyone in the truck. It was interesting for a minute or so."

Luis laughed loudly and even snorted some at the end. It scares me when something makes him laugh that much. I walked back in the dining room, turned a chair around to sit and listen to Manuel's story. I wondered if he were planning on a third beer while he blew two long, deep breaths that sounded like a freighter we'd seen on the Detroit River. Octavio took Luis and I fishing at a couple of different spots to show us around when we first came to Michigan, and those big boats were huge for that river.

"You two seemed to have it easier crossing over here. Between luck and a well-connected coyote, it's a good combination." Manuel began to outline his journey for us, lit another cigarette, and stared at it for a good few seconds. Maybe he wished for a better type of fix, and he finally took a deep pull on it. "I told you I've lived in different states here and gone back to see my family a few times. I had a wife in Mexico at one time, but she got tired of waiting for months to see me, and she didn't like the risk in coming here. Most times I chose to go back, except once I was deported. But that's another day with its own story behind it."

"We'd really like to hear about that too, Manuel," Luis stopped him, excitement in his voice, like a stallion begging to run. Any piece of adventure, Luis wanted some of that action.

"Tell us about the routes and how you dealt with them," I encouraged him. "We were in the dark, so to speak, in our trip here."

"A few spots in the river are narrow enough to cross by swimming and wading, but those rocks and stones are not easy on your feet." Manuel wiggled his bare toes, and we could see a few old scars. "Soon I learned to pay more for crossing in tubes or tires, with the coyotes checking for police who don't take the money on the Mexican side."

"But Manuel, what about the journey through Mexico itself?" I asked him. His eyes came up from his ragged feet and took a second drag on the cigarette. The puff rings floated to the light, and I hoped it wouldn't take on dark hues in the ceiling after two packs. He followed the first few rings and then looked over at us.

"My family doesn't live far from Mexico City, and my ex-wife, she's in the same city. One of my friends dropped me in the capital, and it cost me $120 from Mexico City to the border. Once I get to the border, I've got to wait for the coyote my friends set me up with. The hotel was about twenty dollars for a few days, and the food cost eight to ten dollars. The coyote showed up at my hotel after three days, and I paid him around $3,000. I was glad to leave that hotel this last time. This lady wouldn't stop bugging me till I paid her for some religious junk to keep me safe in my travels. She buried part of a statue behind the hotel, and after taking my few dollars, she put a chain of some kind around my neck. The chain hung long on me, and I was glad to have it when the coyote had to pull me from drifting too far in the river. He grabbed me with that long, curved hook and caught the chain from around my neck, keeping me within reach of his ferry as he manned us across the river. We were helped to the shore by another coyote, and they pushed up my tire. Two guys smiled when it also flipped on me. I paid $175, and we left the river far behind."

"You paid everyone in American dollars?" Luis asked him.

"Remember, I'd already worked in America for years and was returning from family visits. My first few times over were much more scary." Manuel looked up at the ceiling, seeming to remember. "The more money you pay, the safer it is. The people you pay, pay others. These others, they look like they don't see you in Mexico. In the U.S., it's not as easy. This last time I was riding with the American coyote, paying him his cash. I had put my damp head back in the passenger seat for a nap. I woke up all of sudden, the sirens flashing and blaring. I peeked in the rearview mirror, and they were waving us over. I opened the glove box, shoved my stack of twenties I had left in it. I pulled out my old Texas license and hoped it would pass their inspection. My American coyote checked all three mirrors and pulled over to the shoulder with gravel spitting up. We couldn't see outside, and I wasn't sure if he was scared or not when he got his wallet from his back pocket."

Luis was leaning forward in his chair, the back legs off the floor, and his hands holding his face with elbows resting on his knees. My chair had somehow moved up a foot or two, and I rested my head over the back of the chair, gripping the sides of the chair and reddening my knuckles. I glanced at Luis, and we both waited to hear how Manuel's coyote would deal with the American police. When we came across the border we were lucky enough to worry little about any authorities. Manuel lit another cigarette and moved to go the kitchen.

"Compadrés, you don't mind I get another beer?" Manuel smiled while his chair hurriedly scraped the tile floor.

"Manuel, come on now and hurry!" Luis laughed and stomped his foot. He almost fell forward and I caught him with my left arm to steady the chair. "How much drink do you need to finish the story?" Luis asked him.

"Settle back you two, so I can take a few slow drags on my cigarette and a few good swallows of cold Corona." Manuel sat back in his chair, taking a deep drag on his smoke, exhaled, and then leaned back his head to down at least half the bottle. His head dropped down some, and he looked directly at us. Seeming to relish in this moment, he began again. "Well, the dust and gravel settled and I heard 'tat...a tat..a tat' on my window side. I jumped some, scared. 'Roll down this window, you quiet Mexican! Do it now, or I'll put a bullet through it!' I looked to my driver, questions and some anger in my eyes. He raised his hands in frustration, and I had some choice words that I whispered to him. I turned my head to more knocking, this time harder and faster. Rolling down the window, I yelled, 'No comprendo, señor oficial?' The police, his left hand followed the window all the way till it was opened up and then slapped the back of my head with his right palm. 'Illegal! Show me your papers! Now! You know papers? Officers ask for those mucho times in Mexico at many stops, I know!' The policeman's voice raised even higher. I stole a look at my driver, and he was watching it all just happen. Thunk! The policeman, he grabbed my shirt and slammed my head to the seat! He patted my front pockets, looking for papers or money, I wasn't sure which.

"'All right, Deputy Randell, he's got no money or papers,' I heard my driver say as the policeman cocked a pistol in our direction. I leaned my head and shoulders back against the seat, not wanting any bullets to spot my shirt. 'Go ahead and take 'em if you got to, but I'm not wasting any more gas while you just harass him. Or if you're done, your take for this week is in the back. Lift up the back seat in the back of the cab, and you'll see it's in the usual paper bag.' The driver pointed the gun over his shoulder to make his point, smiling while he gunned the gas some.

"'Johnny, I've been waiting for you to come on through here this week. You're a day late and my wife wants to go shopping tonight. Revving your gas, that's not nice, since I watch your back speeding through this part of the country.' The policeman grunted at my driver and stared between us for a second. 'Speeding, Hump!' Pow! He shot right between us and took out the police radar sitting on the center of the dash. I swore under my breath and then said a fast prayer. Then I told Johnny, my driver, I figured—"

All of sudden we jumped as Octavio's voice interrupted Manuel's tale. "Hey, Manuel, you're scaring these guys about the American police. You need a fire to tell these stories by," Octavio grinned as he pushed his body away from the corner of the hall. I don't know how long he had been "holding that wall up" like Night Chef John says to the closers. Octavio took Manuel's beer from his hand and finished it. "American police, they mostly want safe neighborhoods. Many of our brothers come here to America, escaping from their bad activities and the Mexican government. They make a wrong impression for those of us who only want to make money to send back to our families in our home country."

"But Octavio, you tell us always to be careful around the police. Even here so far from the border?" Luis asked him. I nodded my head but didn't want to push the discussion too far right now.

"You are right, Luis. I say that too. But it is better not to push anyone to be suspicious of us in any way. Why not walk with your shoulders straight and heads high? Let everyone think we belong here, just like them."

I wanted to agree with that. But I wanted to walk proud for integrity in my work and name and not because I should belong here. I've never taken for granted where I've been and where I am today.

~ 40 ~

AT THE SPANISH-AMERICAN CHURCH

Carmen caught me at the back of the church when I came in. I couldn't get up in time to meet her in the hall, but when I went by her room, I found a note with directions for the church. She showed me a printed bulletin and explained the schedule of what she called Sunday worship. The bulletin was laid out nicely, with the name of the church on the cover like Spanish-American Church. I wondered about that name, until I realized they were switching from Spanish to English throughout the whole service. The bulletin laid out the order of songs and the page numbers they were on, but it seemed nobody used the book to sing from except me. Most of the people sang with expression in every word, like they really meant it.

Different people prayed over everyone on the stage, all the people around really paid attention to every word. It was like they really cared about what they were doing in this building. When I went with the family to listen to the priest, Father Angelo couldn't keep many awake when he spoke. Mama, she of course sat on the edge of the seat and pinched my ears if I started to nod off. She knew what was right to do.

The pastor at this Spanish-American Church just finished talking about what Jesus had spoken. He repeated again the same point he made earlier. I sat there listening as he summarized a segment from a sermon on some mountain. Others nodded around me, but I was interested as he brought up again seasoning with salt. This sounded just like Chef Curtis at work, and I thought about how many times he stressed seasoning evenly all the proteins that went on the grill. Even the vegetables that were sautéed for dinner entrées got seasoned, but what did salt have to do with church? It was confusing, and I glanced at the stage when he spoke of Christians influencing the people around them.

Although I still wasn't sure what the pastor meant, I did remember Chef explained often to me that the guest couldn't taste the real flavor of the meat without seasonings like salt and pepper. The pastor prayed when he was done talking, many mumbled "Amen," and I sat silently trying to think this whole seasoning thing through in church.

"Young man, is there something I can help you with?" I brought my eyes up from the floor I was staring at and quickly looked around for Carmen and her father. I saw them talking and hugging an older couple two rows ahead of me. The stranger continued talking, and I turned to look at him.

"Oh, are you friends with Carmen and her Uncle Oscar? They're a good family at this church; you must be a good man in spending time with them." He waited for me to say something, and finally I answered him.

"Carmen invited me to come today to visit with her and see what a 'child of God' is. That definition never came up, but instead more questions kind of came up as I listened to the guy talking," I said with some uncertainty. Should I even trust this man with my thoughts? He might mock me for not knowing what the rest here seem to.

"My name is Santos, and I appreciate your telling me what you were really thinking. Not everyone is comfortable saying what is on his or her mind when one has questions."

He put out his hand to shake mine, I told him my name, and we shook hands firmly. I didn't need to try to be cool because he just seemed to want to accept me. He pointed to the guy from the stage toward the door.

"That gentlemen talking to people on their way out. That is our pastor, Pastor Pedro. He'd be happy to answer your questions, though I can try to answer one or two myself."

"Pastor Pedro? You mean you don't have a priest here? In my home country, the priest spoke at the chapel and explained to us about how we should live. This seems quite different," I said while noticing my shoelaces were tied but not as tight as usual.

"Well, my friend, I know the Catholic Church is rather different than what you have seen here. In fact, I grew up here in America, in

Texas, and my mother raised me in the Catholic parish near our home. Although the two areas are of the same family, they are cousins of a sort. The Church here in America has a much different face than even you may have seen in Latin America," Santo said with a grin.

"I've known two different priests in Central America, but one was trained here in America, and both were very generous and kind to me. Isn't that what this God is about?" I asked him. "I mean, my family spent time with the Catholic God, but some family spoke of the old ancient gods we had. They acted like our gods of old could act on our behalf just as well as the Catholic God my mother wanted me to pray to," I went on, not letting him answer as my thoughts rolled out.

"My friend, God is generous and kind, as you have said. But He is also just, holy, and righteous. He doesn't allow for sin and men who continually walk in it. This is why we all need to find Jesus and accept Him as a gift from His father." He patted my shoulder, sat down and pulled out a black leather book. I bent over to tie my right shoe and tried to find Carmen.

"Santos, who is this you're sitting with hiding in the back rows of our pews?" the pastor guy came up and asked him. The pastor looked older, maybe in his forties, with an easy smile and eyes that shined. Santos seemed real nice, but this guy looked ready to break into laughter. Maybe those couple jokes I thought I heard on the stage didn't go well, and now he was going to try again till somebody at least smiled. He came around to the next row and leaned over to talk to us.

"I'm Pastor Pedro," he said as he reached out his hand to shake mine, and I gave him my name. "I'm glad to see a new face even though it's so far back in the church. Somehow, Santos, we must get rid of some pews to move people forward," he smiled at his own joke. "Anyway, it's nice to meet you, young man. And what are you two talking about, Santos?" The pastor looked down at the book in Santos' hand.

"I was just about to read what Paul said about man's sin and its consequences," Santos said while flipping thin pages in his book.

"Gentlemen, it was nice meeting you today. I have to go home and change." I pushed myself up and tried to find Carmen with a look to say good-bye. "I'm scheduled to work this afternoon, and I can't be late."

"Roberto, wait a minute." Santos urgently grabbed my arm, and I looked at him with a little frustration. "We are having a block party next Saturday. We could use some strength in moving supplies for the children from the semi-truck. The kids love it when we come in for these parties, but we never seem to have enough men around to assist with the heavy lifting. Could you spare some time for us?" The pastor asked me.

"I don't know. I'm on call at one job during the day and scheduled at four for the second job," I said with a shrug.

"Everyone would appreciate any help you could give, even for a few hours." The pastor started to smile and then grinned. "I know Carmen comes to every block party to lead the singing with the children. Oscar, he helps unload the truck and set up tables. I'm sure they'd both love to see you show up."

~ 41 ~

AFTER WORK

It had been a tough day in the kitchen, and I was tired. I was not looking forward to that evening when I had to work the later shift at McDonald's. At least I was not scheduled till six, so I had a little time to charge up before going back out. Lunch ended later than usual, and prep wasn't done yet. I finished my restock on my station after checking with Chef John, and then got a couple of the last few items to prep from Chef Terrance. Chef Curtis was off today, and Chef Terrance was running the kitchen. I liked working with him since he remained calm and never raised his voice, and I always seemed to learn something when working with him. I soaked up his expert culinary comments like the sponge I used to clean the Mustang on hot summer days. After icing the fish that were cut, wrapping and storing it, I cleaned the prep area and punched out. Looking around for Luis, I assumed he must be waiting at the car outside.

Walking through the restaurant, I wondered why Duncan and Charlene were bussing the same table together. I noticed their hands brush while wiping the tabletop. They each had their own way in letting the employees know they were management. Duncan supervised different parts of the business under Mr. Porter's watchful eye while Charlene split the dining room shifts with Samuel. Looking away from them with a frown, I heard pieces of their conversation about labor, cutting the floor too early, and lastly something like canceling dinner plans. I turned the corner to pass the table across the bar and saw Luis sitting drinking a Corona. He usually passes up on Octavio's Coronas in our fridge, but there he sat with some servers. I heard his full laugh while he finished telling a joke, and I slowed my steps some.

"Roberto, come sit with us for a few minutes," Karen suggested to me. She was a lead server who alternated with Frieda in supervising the servers for their daily duties, and I liked her. Not only was she pleasant, but she stayed on top of her job while watching others, yet she did it without snapping at people. I sat across from her with a smile, and Luis made room with a slight sigh on his side of the booth.

"Yeah, it was a rough lunch on that line," said Cindy as she smiled at me. "We could hear the tension in the voices back there today. Chef Terrance even snapped at me for a second, and he never does that." Cindy sighed, tousled her blond hair, and emptied her beer.

"I heard you talking in the kitchen, Cindy," Luis looked in her eyes. "You stayed calm and ran that tray quicker than my last load was brought out."

"Thank you, Luis. I'm so glad you agreed to sit with Karen and me." Cindy lightly touched his hand that held his beer and smiled. "I've felt a little down, working mostly night shifts for my first five or six weeks, and I wasn't used to lunch where it's a lot faster paced sometimes. I was afraid people didn't notice how hard I've been trying."

"Oh, I see a lot from my dish area. I know I've heard the way you're so polite when I pull the bus carts in for the hostess. Your customers must really love you," Luis pressed on. He was picking his words well.

"Oh, they really love you all right," Karen said with a roll of her eyes. "I mean you know how to work the people, especially the guys with that 'blonds sometimes make mistakes look,' but good servers need to do more than that. No offense, girl, but you ought to try to learn the menu better, focus on selling it clearly, and then get the right food to the table." Karen winked at me and I nodded slightly.

"Cindy, you've got a great personality," I said while pushing my hair back from out of my eyes. "But she's got a small point; Chef Terrance raised his voice because you took out the wrong plate and didn't ask him to check it when you did. You know if you're not sure, you should always ask."

"'Berto, you're not her boss, so stop trying to act like a supervisor," Luis glared at me and then kicked me under the table. He must really like this new girl.

"Oh, Luis, that's nice to take up for me, but I like to know so I can get better," Cindy said. "I'm really only still learning the lunch."

"Excuse me, you guys. Is everyone punched out here?" Duncan stood right over me and made me jump some. "And even more importantly, we're all over twenty-one with these beers in your hands?" He looked around the table. I felt some satisfaction that the owner's son didn't see me with even a Coke in front of me.

"Don't you worry none, Duncan. Charlene already checked with us ten minutes ago," Karen reassured him. She pointed to Charlene behind the bar with her Budweiser.

"All right, then," Duncan mumbled and stiffly walked around the bar, checking on guests sitting there. All four of us followed his back with our eyes, but no one said anything. Just as the silence seemed to need breaking, and Cindy started to finish complaining about lunch versus dinner, Duncan stopped midsentence with a guest and stared at Charlene talking in hushed tones with the well-spoken and curly haired wine vendor. She seemed to sneak a glance at the Duncan's end of the bar but leaned in a little closer to Mr. Tall and Handsome as he showed the difference in two white Zinfandels. I knew Duncan and Charlene were seriously dating or engaged, but were they arguing at work?

"Lover's tiff at work?" Karen smiled slyly. "That's not very professional, and let's hope that doesn't get back to Mr. Porter." I looked at Karen when she said that last part, and searched her face for truth or half- truths.

"You guys, I have to go home. It was interesting talking on the other side of the line for a few minutes," and I pointed to the back lot with my head. "Luis, if you're riding with me, let's go. Or you can find another way."

"We're having a few more beers, Luis, I can drop you if you need me to," Cindy said.

"If you don't mind? It's been real nice sitting here, just talking to you girls," and Luis practically pushed me out of the booth. I got up to leave and saw him sigh while they fell back into complaining about the kitchen and its supervisors. When I pushed the door to leave, I looked up at the sky. Would there be answers to any of my questions? I couldn't understand Luis, and it didn't feel right just hanging out after work for me. I felt like I should be busy doing something else. Though I know Luis has his own motives in the company he tries to keep, the more women who give him attention, the better he sees himself. As I was walking to my car, Chef John closed the cardboard dumpster, walked toward the back door of the kitchen and by my car, and nodded at me while I unbuttoned my chef coat. Tossing it over my back, I looked down at my t-shirt to see if there were any stains.

"Roberto, looks like you should have worked harder, there's not enough sweat on that white undershirt, Chef John pointed at my chest with his cigarette. "Are the day shift servers still in there whining into their drinks?"

"Yeah, some of them are still there. Luis and I sat with them for a while, talking about today's lunch," I answered with a little surprise. He probably didn't need to know we had sat with them.

"So, where's your roommate, Luis? He's not with you now, or is he in the bathroom?" He asked while repeatedly stomping out the last bit of fire in his cigarette with his Sear's Diehard work shoes. Chef Curtis tries to get all the cooks to get those Diehards, since there's some kind of guarantee for the sole. I think some salesman gives him a kickback.

"He can't hold his tongue much," Chef continued. "Mr. Loud Mouth. It's a good thing he's fast in the dish tank." The cigarette finally went out as it slid deeper in a cement crack.

"He's having one more Corona, and with somebody else buying it doesn't take much for him to say yes. I'm guessing he's catching a ride with somebody," I said trying to make little of Luis's absence. I looked over at my Mustang and wished I was in it.

"He's sitting with those day servers and somebody is buying his beer? Who was buying yours, Roberto?" Chef John stepped in front of the Mustang when he asked me. Looking at the back door of the restaurant, I stared for a second.

"My mama pushed me not to drink, and so I really never started the habit, Chef. I sat with Luis and the girls for a while, and we talked about the problems that went on during the lunch rush. Some people really like to go back over stuff in their mind." Chef John looked at his watch hanging on his chef's coat and moved his weight from one foot to the other. I wondered what was really on his mind.

"Roberto, who was buying the round at the table? Did Cindy buy Luis his Corona or what?" he asked me.

"Like I said, Chef. I don't really know who bought him a drink," and I pushed my hair back while fumbling for my keys in my pocket.

"Just tell Luis that Cindy has no real interest in him. She's not his type at all. She cares for a lot of people, and some guys take it as flirting. Tell him to move onto some other girl with his lyrics and guitar strumming. And I hope your set up is as good as you think, because if I have to send somebody back for stock in the walk-in, we'll talk tomorrow."

He slapped my shoulder while he laughed at his joke and headed for the kitchen door.

~ 42 ~

HELPING AT THE CHURCH

I waited in my car, half asleep as the neighborhood started to wake up. I was still tired from the day before and the shower was good enough for the ride over here. I should have bought a coffee from 7-11. Though McDonalds didn't have me on last night, the guys convinced me to go with them to a bar a few miles away in Waterford. I sat staring at my Bud Light, while all three of them just laughed more after each bottle of Corona hit the table with a thud. Manuel kept bugging the waitress to find the ESPN station that carried Mexican soccer until the bartender told us, "Cool out or you're cut off!" They laughed some more and bet on the Tiger's game instead.

"Roberto! Is that you in there?" Santos shook the driver's side with his fist banging on my window. Shaken, I quickly unrolled my window.

"Hello, Santos," I stammered. "I got here and didn't see anyone so I laid back to get a few seconds of sleep."

"Sleep, well that's good for us all. I hope you got more than a few minutes, 'cause we need you fresh this morning." Santos rattled my head like a bear and I was awake then. He opened the car door, and his smile was bigger than I had expected. I slowly pushed myself to stand up, grunting low in my throat. I made an effort to smile, though my body doesn't smile with only four hours sleep.

"You act surprised," I said as I shoved the door shut. "I guess you didn't think I'd show up today."

"Well, honestly, I'm a little surprised. Not much, though. I never put anything past what God does in the lives of people, especially ones He's drawing to Himself," Santos looked up at the sky. I looked up too, searching for some doves or something, maybe clouds parting. Shaking my head, I tried my wit on him.

"Santos, I'm searching in the sky and I don't see Him up there. He's supposed to be up there pulling a long tug rope, weaving me all around some symbolic river here on earth?" I asked him. He pointed to a semi-truck that was pulling into the parking lot of the parish and began to walk toward it.

"Roberto, God would have us all come to Him and accept His gift that He sent for us. The drawing He does for those whom He pulls and finds different ways to show His mercy in the world." Santos stopped mid-stride and turned to look at me. "Look careful around you today and tomorrow. Even think about years past. God shows His love in the smallest of moments and then sometimes in bigger times too."

"What, what . . . do you really mean?" I mumbled. I really wanted to know how he knew there were big and small times that have affected me in my life. But he didn't hear me.

Klunk! The chain banged from the back of the truck, and the driver unlocked it. Santos yanked with both hands on the small red ropes under the bed of the truck, and the end started to inch out.

"Dear Lord, where has my strength gone?" Santos muttered. "Roberto, come on over and help me pull." I jogged up the last few steps and grabbed one rope with both hands.

"On three," Santos sighed as he caught his breath. The driver pulled back the door, laughing loud enough for us to look over at him for a second. Santos glared at him for a few seconds, and a smile came up around the corners. He must know him, but our count didn't start until the driver mumbled an apology with his own little smile.

"One, two, and three!" Santos heaved on the right and I pulled hard with him. The ramp rumbled some as it came slowly, and we both gave it another good tug until it pushed us back with a jerk. The ramp got heavier when it finally came to its end. The driver was watching from the side of the truck.

"Watch it, you guys! Your feet and—"

"Drop it now, Roberto!" Santos interrupted as he yelled at me. We jumped backward and laughed. I looked up into the truck, and it was filled to the top with all kinds of stuff. There were rows of six-foot wooden tables, three stacks of wooden chairs, three or four boxes of large tents, and the machines carefully wedged on top of the tables: two popcorn machines brightly painted red, two snow cone machines with splashes of blue clouds floating on the side, a cotton candy machine with a clown painted on the side holding eye popping, colorful balloons, and a small, yellow nacho machine with a long beak for the cheese to come out. In front of the chairs rested two grills with charcoal stacked on them.

"Santos, you bring help just to stare at the load? Or we gonna start unpacking?" The driver drives the truck and brings jokes at no extra cost. I didn't see him climbing up the ramp with pep in his step. Chef Curtis often hits me with that after I work a couple of doubles in row. Fifteen hours a day, two days in a row. Well, it's hard to move fresh on the third day or so.

"Roberto, come on up and let's do it," Santos nudged with that smile that creeps up on me. He hands me the first propane grill with hardly a breath, and the weight is heavier than I thought.

"Don't drop it now. That one is the church's grill!" The driver snapped from behind me. I sighed and twirled around to hand it to him with a grunt of my own. He just laughed loudly as he trotted down the ramp with it, the propane tank noisily knocking against the stand. I grabbed two folding chairs under each arm and walked in the same direction.

After about twenty or thirty feet, I came to a corner of two street blocks. There stood a wooden sawhorse stopping local traffic, with a sign stating, "Street Closed for Block Party." On the other side a half dozen people stood around talking loudly in a mixture of Spanish and English. There was a tall, slim, American balding guy with gray hair helping the Hispanic driver adjust the propane tank to its stand. The group's discussion slowed when I walked up with the chairs, and the American stood up to come my way.

"Well, hola! My name is Matthew. I see you've been recruited to help us! We really appreciate any help given." He went to put his hand out to shake and instead laughed while he took two chairs from me.

"Here I'll take some and follow me. We'll set up along behind the sidewalk. That's good there. What's your name?"

"I'm Roberto," I answered and started to walk back toward the truck.

"Theresa, come say hi to Roberto." Matthew pulled a woman from the circle of laughter toward me. I put my hand out to shake it, and she shooed it away like a Mexican fly.

"I give hugs around here, sweetie," she said with a shine in her eyes that I hadn't seen since my mama smiled at me. Hugs were good, especially from a mama. This one, she seemed like a mama. Although she had medium height and hair shoulder length, her personality naturally captured those around her with simple gestures and movements. No sooner was she done greeting me when someone yelled her name.

Theresa responded, "What is it, Mary? Juan called to say he would be late. So trust him at his word today. I don't want to have to settle an argument with you two every other hour when we're trying to run a fun day for the children. Matt and I have our counseling sessions in the evening, and now isn't the time. And Matt, what about the long tables? Is Santos bringing them soon? We have to start setting up the games for the children."

Theresa seemed to talk all at once to each one around her without even taking a breath. I started jogging back toward the truck to join Santos. I cut across somebody's lawn instead of cutting the corner straight, wondering how long she could go on, and thought some mamas aren't so different. Hopefully that wasn't a mean one moving the shades of the house I just ran in front of.

In the truck, Santos sat shaking his head and rubbing it.

"What happened to you?" I asked him.

"The snow cone machine slipped when I moved the popcorn machine and it bumped my head. What took you so long? We'll be all morning to empty this thing if we don't get a move on." Santos pointed to more tables and chairs.

"Some American wanted to introduce me to his wife, and she hugged me."

Santos smiled. "You met Matthew, our Michigan missionary, who helps us grow our church in this community. We love him, but his wife—well Theresa we love even more!"

"But why?" I asked, leaning my back against a stack of tables, stretching out for the lifting sure to come.

"She's got a way we all love about her. She accepts people for who they are, and makes a person feel comfortable in talking about just anything," and Santos's smile came up around the edges again.

"Yeah, she seemed a lot like my mama to me," I said aloud without thinking as Santos pushed the first table I was leaning on. I stumbled awake to get on with our work.

After moving a half dozen tables that were long, heavy, and in various stages of falling apart, I started to wonder how many they would need for a "block party." Matthew got excited each time Santos and I came around the corner with another table, pointing to the spot where it should be placed. We'd turn to head for another table, and his wife nicely asked to have it moved again.

On our next walk back to the truck, the driver, I guess not much of an introduction for me from him, carried a single chair on one arm and a cola in his hand. Every few seconds he stopped to sip the cola, and he'd rest his upper body on the chair. Santos winked at me and accidentally tripped on the chair leg. The cola fell to the sidewalk, spilling into the cracks. I didn't want to laugh but couldn't help it as the driver ran after the trash can.

"What's funny coming from the sidewalk, Roberto? Our driver losing his drink or seeing him chase it down?" Pastor Pedro yelled to me. I hadn't even seen him, and he stood at the top of the ramp.

"Hello, Pastor. Nice to see you," I said while jogging up the ramp. It banged some from my speed and weight, and I slowed to an even walk. When I was almost at a complete stop to shake his hand, somebody tapped the back of my leg. It buckled some, and the pastor grabbed my arm to steady me.

"Carmen, that wasn't nice to scare Roberto! The ramp isn't the most secure of spots. You felt that when I handed some chairs to you and your uncle," Pastor Pedro scolded her. I turned around and looked down. She stood to my right with her left hand tucked behind her, trying not to giggle. It wasn't working and finally her face broke into a loud laugh from down inside the stomach. Her Uncle Oscar kind of glared on my behalf by bending his head to her side and pulled on her ear to stop the giggling.

"I'm sorry," she sputtered. "But he deserves it some. You know he ran into me twice in our building. After all, I think he needs work on his balance."

"Well, if it weren't for Pastor Pedro's quick reach, Roberto would be face down in the cement," Oscar shook his head while pulling himself up to the back of the truck. He handed Carmen a chair. "Another reason I can thank God for sending us a Peter. He's quick to pull others to safety, still remembering when Jesus did so for him."

"Oscar, sometimes I work hard to live to my name sake. Peter of the twelve was a great tool, a rock that God made to change much of the New Testament world. Like Paul and Peter, the more I draw closer to Jesus, the more work I see He needs to pull me toward Him," the pastor started, and I hoped this wasn't a sermon coming on. "He helps me see my sins better and I find more I need to repent of. His Holy Spirit speaks to me, assuring me of some progress I make—"

Just then a walkie talkie sputtered and interrupted him.

"Santos, I haven't seen much action from around the corner lately. We have much to do to be ready for the program that Theresa has planned." Matthew's voice came out strangely clear and loud. "If you don't mind, let's keep the pack mules going."

"No problem, John. You're the trail boss for this move," Santos smiled and pushed the right button on his walkie talkie. "We were interrupted by the on-site boss."

"Tell pastor, 'Work, walk, and talk at the same time.' Over and out, Matt here." And the line went dead, and we all just laughed for a good minute. Americans and Hispanics don't seem to always mix well, but this church group seem like they get along well enough.

~ 43 ~

EN ROUTE TO A PARTY

"Roberto, one night of hanging out won't kill you." Luis pushed my shoulder and I put the Mustang into gear when the light turned green on M59. "We all live together you know. And I remember you used to say I was a great brother to have."

"Yeah, well you were the only brother I had after I turned five or six years old. So the bar wasn't really set very high for you," I grimly said and tried to smile. I really didn't want to go to this party at Octavic friend's house. They all knew how I worried what Mama would think if I started to drink or smoke. Thousands of miles away, and she still held me close. It's been years since I've seen her, but she writes me every month. She emails Christina more often, and we keep up on each other. They both worry over me and Luis, but I tell them both that one day I will be the chef I promised to become.

"Roberto, make a right at that light. We're almost there." Octavio pointed past my ear from the back seat. I knew I should have told Luis to sit in the back. I hate getting directions from the back seat, but Manuel was telling Octavio about some adventure in Mexico.

"Look at all the cars, and listen to the music!" Manuel sighed. "These parties, they remind me so much of home. In my hometown we drank cheap beer, sang till long after the stars came out, and weaved away on the back roads on our used Vespas. The laughing, listening to live music, and dancing, this yard could be a home in my countries' town. Look there, an old motorcycle and a couple of scooters." I pulled along the curb behind a row of old cars, and set the emergency brake.

We walked up the driveway, and Octavio banged on the gate hatch. People milled around the backyard, dancing, singing, eating, and, of course, drinking. A smiling short Latino with a cigar lit in his mouth waved to us and motioned with his eyes to a guy sitting in a lawn chair in the garage. A plate of limes lay on a table to his left, and the Tequila was just being set down when he pushed himself up with a jump.

"Octavio, it's good to see you, my friend! It's been a few months, and nobody drinks Corona with a smile while he loses hand after hand."

"Max, you don't have to bring up your winnings every party. Though with you being the host, I guess I can forgive you." Octavio smiled broadly as he grabbed the Corona that Max handed him.

"You brought friends like I told you to. I remember these boys from a year or so ago." He looked at me and nodded. "You were the cook, right? Well, don't be too hard on my girl's enchiladas. She worried all day long about how authentic it would be."

"No worries, Max. I'm sure the flavor profiles will come shining through," I tried to reassure him.

"Well, the other one here, Luis? Where's the guitar? I thought you carried it with your beer everywhere," Max pointed to his empty arm. "And you got to be Manuel. Octavio said something about you coming in soon, and here you are."

Max didn't miss much at all. He acted cool, calm, and laid back with clothes to match that walk of his. He had new jeans and a button down shirt that opened to just reveal his cross that he randomly rubbed like a genie's jar. But his eyes seemed to always be darting about, and I could tell he knew where every guest was at the moment. And apparently he caught even the slightest of comments from everyone around him, even as the guy at the gate motioned our way when we came up. Max to his right at the gate stooped to the large bucket of iced beer and pulled out three for us. Octavio took a pull from his, Manuel and Luis both snapped their caps with sly smiles, and I slid my Corona back into a corner of the bucket.

"Hey, cook, you no drink my beer? It's a party tonight and drinking is part of the fun around here." Max laughed and pulled the beer out, pushing it against my cheek.

"No offense, Max, but I'm doing the driving home tonight so these guys can get lit up. A little favor for friends, no?" I said and gently pushed the Corona back into the bucket. He popped the cap himself, drinking half the bottle in one gulp.

"I think the last time you guys came over, you were that driver then. I'm starting to take it personal, and I'm thinking one beer might not hurt your senses too much," Max said and waited for me to answer. I wasn't sure what to say, and I backed up against the back of his house.

"He worries some for what his Catholic mother thinks, and he tells her much of what goes on in his life. You should see all the letters in his pile," Luis joked.

"Well, the Catholics here in the neighborhood don't mind if I drink or smoke some every week or so. As long as I make sure to do the confession with the priest, it's no problem at all." Max smoothed it over some. I wasn't sure why he brought up about his standing with religion. I didn't think he or Octavio thought about it much.

"We didn't think you thought much about God, Max. Especially when we see how much fun you have in your life." Luis sighed a deep breath.

"You guys think some of us aren't worried about things. We all sit and worry about if a car hits us or someone pulls a gun down the street," Max said as he looked across the yard. "We all have to think about life after death, and my priest told me to keep coming to Mass, bring my money, take Communion, and check in on confession. I do as he says enough, and I'm not worried. Not to say I don't wonder sometimes, but what are you going to do? Maybe have another Corona?" And he laughed loudly as he reached for another from the iced bucket next to the outside of the house. My roommates, or friends, depending on my mood, drank and smoked long into the night. I grew tired of listening to them argue over the best and worst Mexican soccer teams, but even more tiresome was the crazy conversations Max continued to try and carry on with me after every couple beers. I couldn't understand the way he felt the need to keep coming back to talk about God, mock the Catholics, and then tell us what to do with our lives. I thought he had it all figured out—all his ducks in a row, as Chef Curtis likes to say, the way he earlier joked about confession and giving money to the church. I guess I'm not the only one who has a hard time pegging God and what He's doing with us here on earth. The drive home wasn't much fun for me as I thought about who God is and what He does with us. Are we like puppets to Him, and He's up there creating a good story line with the angels kicking in some ideas? Life seems so full of questions. If we're God's children, why don't we all feel loved? How come God isn't here or there for all of us?

"Hey, Roberto! Wake up! You almost blew that light," Octavio yelled out with a long slur. "You need to be careful, we don't need any deputies or even Waterford Policia stopping us."

"Yeah, Roberto, it didn't look like you had much fun tonight." Luis said as he looked at me. "I can't understand why you can't have just one drink with us at a party." Just then I saw the lights flash, and I swore under my breath.

"That's why! The police will pull us over any time, and I have no idea why," and I heard Manuel grunt what could have been a laugh mixed in with a burp.

~ 44 ~

THE TRAFFIC STOP

I was glad nobody had brought any beer with them in my car. Although my Mustang smelled heavy from Manuel's cigarette smoke, and I thought fresh air would be nice. After finding my license and insurance, I waited for the tap on the window, and when it came Manuel jumped some. I smiled, and thought about the truth in his stories.

"Hello, officer," I said with extra calmness in my voice after I unrolled the driver's side window.

"Driver's license and insurance, young man. Do you know why I've pulled you over?" The Waterford Township officer asked. I thought it was a sheriff, but we were pulled over by a local. Maybe I'd get some mercy since we lived just a few miles away.

"No, sir, I'm not quite sure why you have. I noticed you at the corner back by the strip mall, and I didn't think anything was the matter," I said nonchalantly.

"Well, you stopped under the light on Telegraph—almost like it was an afterthought. It seemed a bit erratic to me. Have you and the boys been out at a party tonight? I think I might just smell some liquor, and that doesn't make for good driving in—"

"Look officer," I interrupted the cop. "My friends, they've had a few drinks tonight, but I've not had a single beer," I sighed, trying not to sound flustered.

He smiled a big grin and opened the door for me.

"All right, Mr. Designated Driver. Follow me to the sidewalk here and walk a straight line down the center. Don't stop till I say so," and he gently pushed me away from the sounds of the traffic on Telegraph Road toward an empty parking lot. I concentrated on my feet but didn't want to focus too hard and make myself nervous. I stared ahead at a

226

bright street light as the officer grunted, "Looking good so far." Then I heard a loud tapping and another voice yell.

"You boys in there have identification too? Unroll this passenger window and hand us your papers. All three of you—NOW!" I turned from the partner who pulled me over to see the action. The other officer seemed younger, less confident in his manner. I hope he didn't have something to prove to anyone, anything at all.

"Turn back around, amigo! Find and stay on that imaginary line you picked, or we'll be driving you all back in our cruiser for the night!" Mr. Big Grin tapped me with his night stick.

"Hey, señor! What are you laughing at back there? Something funny here? We can haul this whole car to the impound and just wait for somebody to pay the fee. You guys will all be stuck in our yard," Young and Loud shouted as he hammered my windows and then my trunk with his stick. I could hear the glass window try to crack and the car bounce, as he must have pushed the back down with a lunge. Manuel never knew when to keep his mouth shut. Luis at least figured out when to stop his play in time.

"Johnny, let that Mustang be! Get back to the cruiser and check the IDs." Big Grin didn't sound like he was grinning any more as I heard him swear under his breath and then I heard static. Behind me, his feet stopped keeping pace with mine, and I stopped and turned my head to look at him. He was taking a call from his shoulder piece, and then he picked up his shoulders with a deep breath. Leaving me standing there, he strode to the cruiser's passenger side.

"John, are these guys legal or what? I just got a call about a heavy pursuit off of Opdyke, by the Silverdome. They need back up, so let's let Mr. Designated Driver take home his drunken amigos." Big Grin waved me back to my car and laughed with a snort.

"Hey, Designated! You and your boys are clean for now! Take 'em home and keep them away from the bottle for a few days. Stop *at* the lights not *under* them," he yelled through his open window while he pushed the flashing light further back on the hood. Big Grin, Young and Loud, and me, Mr. Designated? Quick names for a few seconds in time, and I'm still shaken up. If it weren't for some guy running from the police, one of us might have cracked under the looks and tone they were giving us.

I really didn't know what kind of friends my roommates were. Do friends really act this way with no thoughts for what could happen to us? Octavio had taught us to really watch ourselves—"keeping ourselves under the radar," as he laughingly called it. A little too much Corona in him, and he couldn't rein in either Luis or Manuel.

~ 45 ~

AT THE SPANISH-AMERICAN CHURCH

"You boys, I really appreciate the fact you were able to stop by our church for a while. So many people are too busy, and I just needed some strong arms in organizing my rooms here in the basement. My husband, Matt, will be down shortly to help. He had two phone calls to take. One call is from our home office in Dallas, and another from one of the church members asking advice about the school system for her third grade son. Sometimes it's difficult to understand why the school and parents—"

Therese nodded her head in the direction of a storeroom and waved us to follow her. She had begun speaking in Spanish for us, even though we didn't really need her to do that. Five years in the States, along with my desire to learn English, have paid off. Luis rubbed his fingers and thumb on both hands and smiled at me. I shrugged and patted the wallet in my backpocket to remind him I would pay him the ten dollars we agreed on for his time. I shoved him in the shoulder after he blew me a kiss and hugged himself. He had bugged me all the way here, quizzing me on what more I would do to get time with Carmen. He stumbled a few steps, and I knew there was more to our help than her.

"You were talking about parents and school people, Señora Theresa?" I asked her while we all looked at the dozens of boxes on the floor. There wasn't much room to even walk.

"Oh don't worry about my stories. It's kind of you to try and get me to finish, but you boys should just get started. Sometimes I talk on so," she replied.

"Ms. Theresa, your talking doesn't bother us at all," Luis interrupted her. "Your Spanish is almost as good as some in my family, and

229

your voice is like my mama's songs in the late evening from the kitchen."

"Luis, you are so very nice to say that. But boys, though I would love to stand and talk with you both, I have to rearrange the boutique's shelves before you come downstairs with all these boxes," she said with that standing smile in her eyes. "I hope you didn't think it was just a few bags and a box. People around here want to be generous for those who have less, and who I am to say 'no' to God's servants as they work their charity for us here in our little church?"

"Well, it sure looks like hearts are bigger around here—these boxes are double stacked with clothes, toys, kitchen utensils, and bathroom linens. This one by my foot has shirts with K-Mart and WalMart tags still on them," I mumbled under my breath. Ms. Theresa just smiled while I felt the new material between my forefinger and thumb. She clucked with a chuckle, and I stood up with a light sigh. Most of my clothes I bought at the flea market on Dixie Highway, except for the whites and checks Chef Curtis found a way to get me every time I needed a new set. He barely said much, just a passing comment that my check would be a bit lighter that week and gave me instructions to leave the stained jacket at home when I punched in for that weekend's holiday brunch. Luis and I made what seemed like a dozen trips up and down that back hallway and the stairway. The last two boxes felt the heaviest, and we stood frustrated when we walked in the church store.

"I'm tired and ready to be done," Luis complained to me as he moved the weight of his box. "Where are we supposed to put these last two? There's no hand pointing to a corner, table, or shelf with her smile. I can't even hear the singing. The melody I liked earlier today but now I just want some rest." He stood up with his box and leaned back against the wall.

"I don't know if her voice is as beautiful as you say, but she's got a way to convince me to keep going." I tried to explain it.

"Say what you want, but she reminds me of home. I haven't felt at home like that in a while, even walking up the stairwell and listening to a different song fifty steps away," Luis said with a tone that kind of drifted. It wasn't like him to talk of home so much.

"Yeah, I guess it's like that old song you used to play on the guitar, "Stairway to Heaven," and we're even in a chapel to get us there." I laughed at my own joke. He set down his box and glared at me. I waited for him to say something, but he picked his box back up as I shifted my weight from the left to right leg. He turned around to look for Ms. Theresa and mumbled "stupid mutt." It was one of his favorites from years ago, but I didn't hear any affection in his voice. My hair wasn't as long, but he still saw me that way after time has passed. Sometimes I wondered if he missed his mother as much as I miss mine.

"Did I hear chapel? Elvis sang about crying in the chapel; you boys aren't upset now, are you?' Ms. Theresa laughed at her own joke. "Well it's an oldie but a goodie, and I guess you two haven't heard it or him?"

"He supposed to be some great fifties singer, wasn't he?" Luis asked with a smile and a light grunt. "My friends heard about him walking around the city at the old Motown area still alive. We tried to find the spots he walked in the Motown museum last summer when we ate down in Mexicantown off I-75."

"Oh, I just love the authentic food there. Some of the ladies here in our church, though, cook even better than the food down there. In fact, you two ought to come for some great food we're serving next week, when—" she rambled on until I had to interrupt her.

"Ms. Theresa, what's going on next week with food here? We haven't had home cooked food in a while," I asked, very interested.

"We're having a revival dinner next weekend and sort of a farmer's market. Friday and Saturday nights our church is worshipping with song and sermon about Jesus's work on the cross for each of us. The farmer's market will be during the day on Saturday. Both Friday and Saturday evening some of the ladies will get together for a dinner that brings memories back of home food from their native countries. The food brings memories of youth, and yet our main focus is in remembering what God's great gift to earth is. Each of us can receive that gift. Do you boys know of this gift I'm talking about?" She asked us above our boxes. We both stepped back some and set our boxes down in unison, happy for a rest before taking those stairs again.

231

"It looks like a gift from heaven for us in your hands?" I asked, pointing to her tray. It had a pitcher of lemonade with two glasses. "The lemonade looks refreshing and sweat just started to stain the back of my t-shirt."

"Oh, my goodness, I had forgotten about the drinks," a smile beamed on her face. "I thought you two could use some cold lemonade. Today is getting warm, and the AC only works in the sanctuary. You two will never know how much I appreciate your help today. It has been such a blessing for me, since I've been trying to get this boutique more organized for a month now. Matt collected names of a group of local families that are struggling in Pontiac, Auburn Hills, and Waterford. We've invited them to come and visit one time each for this store."

"Wow, that's great!" Luis said. "That's really nice for your church to do."

"Our church looks for things like that to do often. We work hard to serve God and reflect His plan in spreading the Gospel." She shook her head and pushed a few hairs behind her ear. "That's why our weekend revival won't be what it's meant to be without you guys attending." I looked over at Luis to answer her, and he was looking for a spot to move our boxes. He was the one that hung on her melodies, and now his mind wanted to wander.

"Roberto and Luis, you don't have to answer me right this moment, but please consider it some. Your lives aren't intended to be forever on this land, and some day you'll see eternity. I fear the day for both of you." Her look, voice, and eyes were very serious. She said Matt would finish the two remaining boxes for her and nodded a good-bye with a warm touch on our shoulders. We walked silently up the stairs and out to the back lot.

~ 46 ~

BACK AT THE APARTMENT

The smoke from the outdoor grill clouded the air heavily and began streaming in the sliding door from the balcony. Manuel and Octavio each had a Corona in one hand and a cigarette in the other, while moving their heads about to keep their eyes clear of the rotating smoke. I groaned under my breath when Manuel blew two ring of smoke, set the cigarette on the grill's ledge, and rolled the franks with his bony fingertips. One dog propelled forward onto the wooden floor, and Manuel snagged the charred meat and popped it on a plate. In my mind, I heard a mix of voices that would be commenting about it: from Chef Curtis to Chef Terrance each storming in their word choice, to Night Chef John's calmer tone joined by Mr. Porter's stare, and lastly frantic shrieks from Karen or Frieda.

The sun shone through our window with rays that almost blinded me, and I felt like I should be doing more than watching MTV.

"Hey, Roberto, this dog is yours. Don't worry, I got it with these tongs before it fell downstairs to Oscar's folding chair," Manuel laughed with Octavio.

"You don't worry, 'Berto. I know you're afraid of those germs. I'll eat that one with chili and onions on it," Octavio yelled after gulping more of his beer, "the chili I got left over from the other day when we went downtown to Coney Island."

"We should go back and try the other one, that Lafayette! I love to judge a good contest," Manuel slurred when I moved around him to lift the grill lid. I got my own dog and set it on a plastic plate. Octavio spooned the boiling chili onto my dog, I tasted a bit and turned it down. Octavio doesn't taste scorched chili, but my tongue does, and it doesn't like it much. I flipped the grill lid back up, got another dog

233

plain, and brought it back into the living room.

"Luis, we got yours here. We just pulled them all off now, 'cause the game will start soon," Manuel walked in with two plates full.

"I wish we would have taped the Argentina/Brazil game, 'cause Guatemala will lose again today anyway," Octavio moaned.

"How come you guys always mock the Guatemalan team?" I shook my head.

"Roberto, you can't just live in the past games of Guatemalan football. We've all heard your stories of your brother and his local heroic plays. You know it's hard in the States to keep up with soccer in Latin America or even world soccer for that matter." Octavio nodded at me with a smile. After a few years of living with me, Octavio and Luis think they both have figured me out.

"I'm not dreaming of Guatemalan or even Mexican soccer." I sighed as I sat up in my chair to take another bite of my dog. "Today's dream is rest and relax and make it through next week. Maybe even go to this luncheon meeting Luis and I heard about next Saturday."

"Don't you boys always work on Saturdays?" Octavio asked.

"Usually we do," Luis replied with a smile. "'Berto mentioned the hours and hard work we both have done lately, and the Chef gave it off to us."

"Anyway, we all were invited to come out for a free lunch, some time at this church, and even some special events outside under some tents," I spoke out tentatively.

"All of us?" Manuel asked. "I haven't been to a chapel or church in years and don't plan on walking in one any time soon." He said after gulping down half a hot dog and reaching for his beer.

"You'd be stumbling in the chapel, Manuel!" Octavio shot out. "And then the windows would break when the lightning struck you."

"You guys all got me close to being arrested last week. I didn't like being threatened by those cops and having my license checked that close. You owe me." I looked at all three of them.

"Those rookies, they had little reason to hold us," Manuel laughed.

"Look at you laughing; they could have taken us in just with your mouth," I said.

"You just want to go 'cause Carmen will be there. And we have to hold your hand while you sit and stare at her," Octavio sneered at me.

"No, Octavio! That's not it," Luis interrupted him. "The American missionary lady invited us." Thank God, I guess. A little support.

"Why do we want to go and hear some gringa lady talk to us?" Manuel asked. "I get talked to all the time by rude gringa women at the restaurant." Luis and I both stopped in mid-stride as we were about to put another bite in our mouths.

"She's no rude gringa lady!" Luis raised his voice a little.

"She and all the people I've met are not the Americanos you talk about. They work with all kind of Hispanics, and treat them all with real kind love," I explained to Octavio and Manuel.

"Ha, ha! Roberto, you only care about these people to get to Carmen. You really don't feel anything for them," Octavio pointed to one of my books. "You think you can act like some character in your books and win her over through these people."

"These Americanos you two talk about," Manuel slurred while waving his Corona at Luis and me, "They just want to get more bodies in their chapel and show people how they can change you." Luis jumped and grabbed his wrist as it swung out with the beer in his hand.

"That's enough about Ms. Theresa," Luis held Manuel's arm firmly and the beer spilt when Manuel tried to move it.

"Oh, Guitar Boy steps up to defend a lady he barely knows, Octavio? When did either of these boys become men?" Manuel looked at him and then us.

"You've pulled both our strings, and now you're done singing that song." Luis threw down his wrist, swung his left for an uppercut into Manuel's gut and followed it with a quick jab to Manuel's chin. Manuel fell back on the couch behind him, and Octavio started to frown.

"Luis, Manuel talks too much! But you were wrong to put him out like this." Octavio shoved him back in the chair. "Sit back at the table and cool down while I check him!"

"So, I guess Manuel and Octavio, you two probably won't come with me next weekend," I said with a weak smile, more to myself than anyone else.

~ 47 ~

CHEF JOHN AT THE CHURCH

The tall, slim Latino wearing an Ohio State hat and a blue University of Michigan shirt pointed with a flag to the next entrance at the back of the church. He smiled while spinning his right hand to back up the pointed flag. We didn't need that much direction from a conflicted football fan; it was just parking after all.

"That guy needs another hand to make his point in parking or reffing a football game," Luis laughed and finished my thought. "You should see all the booths back there! There must be a dozen or more with no room to even walk between them."

He turned back around as I pulled up into the back lot, looking for a spot to park. A large stocky Mexican with a tool belt hanging loosely from his waist stretched his back from sweeping fresh cut grass blown on the cement and motioned to an open spot on the far side of the garage.

"Hey, boys, your Mustang will be real safe back there," the handy looking man said after splattering another pile of dirt back behind the garage. "I'm all done sweeping that side and most people are either already here, parking across the street at the mini-mall, or walking in. So I got you covered with this spot, you see and—"

"You go to this chapel regular, or you just work the grounds around here?" Luis interrupted his rambling.

"This ain't no chapel with a priest but a real nice Baptist church, and I'm a member of it," he said defensively. "Most people call me by my last name, Soto, and I don't mind much. My name fits my moods mostly, 'cause it means something like rough patch. I love working outside, and that's why I don't mind doing the work the Pastors Jacob and Pedro ask."

"Look Soto," I stopped him with a breath, "it's nice to talk to you but which way to the church entrance from here?"

"Oh, I'm sorry, guys, but you don't want to just go in the church now. Some farmers from the northern parts of Oakland County have brought their goods for our people, and even the neighborhood to look over. In fact, they even hired a chef to cook some vegetable stew for us as a demonstration, and he's set up right up—"

"Soto, can we cut through the church here by the garage or do we walk up the street?" Luis asked him impatiently.

"All right then, you two," Soto sighed. "Most folks are walking along the shoulder of the street up to the other entrance, and that way they can see the full effect of our market today." And we walked on the shoulder of the street he pointed out. It took no more than a few minutes to walk the short distance up and into the main church parking lot. There were at least a half-dozen booths lined up on each side of the lot, with farmers yelling at people to step up and check out the finest grown products. It reminded me of the crazy markets in Central America, though not nearly as loud as the ones back home. I wondered about the crowd lined in people, all stepping over each other to see better. What could be going on?

"Come on, Roberto," Luis laughed as he picked up his pace and heard a booming voice. I looked up to see Pastor Pedro standing on a milk crate waving people toward the booth he was in.

"Our next cooking demonstration is about to begin," Pastor Pedro spoke loudly and used his hands as a megaphone. "Step on over and see foods you can buy cheap to cook with easy. One of our neighboring churches has lent a member chef to show us how it's done, just like in the fancy restaurants you could eat at."

Luis and I both tried to stand taller, but neither of us could see over the crowd. "Hey, there's a big rock with a tree next to it," Luis began to run over to it while grinning some.

"The chef, he's done the show earlier today, and our members loved it. We all got a copy of the recipe, and many home cooks are going to try it out next week," Pastor Pedro was working the crowd. "My friends, you don't want to walk away from this."

"What's the pastor saying? I can barely hear him," Luis sighed while working his way up the boulder. He slipped from its slick sides but finally got his footing to reach for the lowest branch above the boulder. I pushed my head back and wiped my sweaty hands on my shirt. I scrambled up the rock but fell back again and then again, shaking my head side to side, cursing under my breath.

Luis laughed, "Come around the back side of the tree, 'Berto. There's shorter branches to climb on."

I pulled myself up one branch at a time and mumbled, "Not sure why you have to see the cooking demo. You're not even going to be a chef one day! Me, I'm the cook for Chef Curtis, you know!"

"Ha ha, you monkey mutt! I cook some, you know. My brother loved the lunches I made for him," Luis talked down memory lane again as I got my left foot settled.

We heard a sudden loud crack as the tree branch broke beneath my weight.

"Roberto, you all right?" Luis held back a laugh.

"Yeah, I'm okay. But the branch my right foot was on is broken now. I guess it couldn't hold me." I breathed deeply and rubbed my lower back.

"Too many greasy burgers for you, my friend, and it will get you every time."

We both turned as the microphone picked up the sound of steel honing a knife. I have heard the sound in my dreams, so many guys around me used one.

"Quiet, everyone, now the chef is going to begin, and this is—"

"Chef John! I can't believe it! Not him! He's here and cooking," Luis wheezed out while straining to pull himself farther out and up the tree branch.

"What did you say, Luis?" I looked at him from propped elbows.

"I've got this skillet hot enough so that it's just starting to smoke, and after one ounce of olive oil, I add the breaded squash to the pan. In the other hot pan, I've sautéed diced onions, fresh garlic, and tri-colored bell peppers. Next we'll add some of these homegrown Romas." He sounded like he was being filmed with Emeril.

The branch Luis was holding made a loud crack and I heard, "Aii, I'm falling!"

Luis let go of the branch that was balancing him, slipped off the rock, and fell on me. "Luis, what are you doing? You just broke my leg!" I yelled at him, then swung my head back as the branch he was holding flung toward us. It continued back and forth, like the hand of clock, until it finally broke.

"Not my Adidas!" Luis yelled. He didn't seem to feel any pain while pushing his finger though the hole the falling branch had made in his tennis shoes.

"Hey boys, you all right over here? You two are sprawled out. Are you hurt at all, Roberto or Luis?" Ms. Theresa stooped down to check us out. How did she get here? We still hadn't seen the cooking demo. Though Luis wanted to take action and not just watch.

"Hello, Ms. Theresa. It's good to see you today! We were going to surprise you some, and now you surprised us," I said with my best smile while he and I lay sprawled on the ground.

"Yeah, we're real glad to see you," Luis said, rubbing his foot.

"It doesn't seem like you're too happy to see me, Luis," she questioned him with her look.

"The tree inflicted some pain on him, and now he's lost his laughter," I tried to explain.

"Well, now, that tells of the pain," she said, "but what about the frown that won't end?" Still silent, Luis didn't blink at all.

"I think it's either his favorite shoes are ruined or the choice of chefs your husband has picked," I said with a sly grin.

"What's wrong with John? He attends a local church in Troy, and he's helping out today on his own time," she asked after stomping her right foot and folding her arms.

"What kind of churchgoing man comes to help here and then smokes all the time?" Luis surprised us both from his silent treatment to a sudden outburst as he pushed up off the ground with his right hand. He kicked my leg that felt like it would start to swell up soon and got his footing to stand. Looking over at the crowd of people that still seemed to be watching John, Luis glared at Theresa. "That chef, he

239

doesn't just smoke, he acts like a wild gringo. I can't see how you say your God can be any part of him."

"Luis, don't be so quick to judge him, or any Christian, in fact. We walk with Jesus, and He's in us, but we do fail and fall like any other humans. The sad reality is that we still sin, but we repent and try to recover in being Christ-like with our lives. It's a learning process, you see, just like most other steps in life we have to take as we progress in our maturity," Theresa explained to Luis while holding his gaze.

Luis smiled quickly, stepped over and gave her a hug. Stepping back after the moment of affection, he looked down at me and turned back to her with a smile. "Ms. Theresa, I feel your love for us, and see you are different than most. You remind me so of my mother's love, but you barely know us." His feet moved a few steps back and Luis glanced over at the crowd clapping around the table of sautéed food. "But if Chef John is one of these Christians, he shows no kindness or mercy from your Bible. He is too strict in the kitchen, especially for me and the other Mexican dishwasher. He doesn't even let us finish our own meals. And I see the looks he has for some of the girls we work with. One of them named Cindy gets tired of his attention."

I couldn't hear more because he just turned his back completely around and started a light run. It was like the run he had before with an easy gait that seemed so natural for him as if he were dribbling down the field. He had carried that same stride while playing football with me, when he ran through the market crowd to leave the gift for his mama, and even the faster pace in catching the train through Mexico.

"Luis, don't go yet!" Theresa called out to Luis with deep disappointment in her face. "The Pastor, his message, it's unforgettable!!"

~ 48 ~

DINNER ON THE CHURCH GROUNDS

At around five, they served early dinner to all who were walking about the church grounds. Much of the food brought back memories of home, since it was a buffet with different foods made by church members. The food table had a line of bowls with coleslaw, potato salad, sliced cucumbers and tomatoes, beans and rice mixes, a platter of tortillas, and two chafers with grilled burgers and hot dogs. It seemed funny to see an American picnic-type table mixed with Hispanic foods. Fried plantains and other desserts lined the coffee table, and they made me smile when I popped a couple in my mouth. It was good to eat while sitting under one of the trees behind the church. I had tired of the salesman who tried to sell me all kinds of produce, from huge bright tomatoes to hot red peppers and even huge elephant-type carrots. We didn't stock a lot of fresh produce in our place at home; most of the fridge held Corona bottles, Coke, Gatorade, lemonade, and sliced bread with eggs. Today's food tasted good for home cooking and not restaurant style. The eye appeal was lost some, but the flavors came out. My burgers had a better flavor since we always added light seasoning to the meat just before it went on the griddle.

"I hope everyone likes the food. Our grill chef was out back sweating some so we could enjoy it. The best is yet to come," Matthew, the missionary guy woke me from my thoughts as he began to speak on the microphone. Some people even clapped loudly. I guess they wanted to thank him loudly for the free food. "You all finish up eating your food and find a seat in the church. If you listen just now, we can hear the guitar and drums playing with a little singing." He got some people interested with the passion and smile in his voice. His speaking Spanish so well seemed to help his cause.

"Roberto, will you be coming inside? I think it might be a time for you to step into the House of God," Pastor Pedro suggested with a wide wave of arms and a big smile. Everybody today couldn't stop smiling. What are they up to with all this happiness? "Theresa said she found you on the grounds, and I've been praying that the Holy Spirit would speak to you and you will listen to His stirrings."

"Pastor, I've had no spirits today," I explained quickly. "Agua, I swear that's all I've drank today." I smiled and shrugged my shoulders.

"Well, Roberto, I don't doubt it you have had your fill today. But will you drink and taste of the best that Jesus Himself has offered? Why the Pharisees, they—"

"Pastor, I told Ms. Theresa I'd stay for the service but keep the rest of the story for inside. I need to walk some before you say much more. It looks like there might be a crowd inside, and some air is what I need now," I smiled weakly at him while trying to escape. I walked across a clearing on the side of the church and looked out toward the intersection of the two cross streets. Cars and trucks were driving fast up and down, a few horns blaring, but mostly there were just people with time lost on them. Somebody darted across the middle lane, and a minivan screeched to a stop. Life is here with us, and then it can be gone so quickly. I think it's sad.

"Hey 'Berto, you dreamin' again up there?" a voice yelled from the street below. I turned from the traffic light with a start and looked down the small hill to the street that the church sits on. Parked on the other side sat Octavio's old Chevy Nova, the one he claimed was a classic. It needed a new muffler, quite clear to me from all the smoke it shot out every time he gave it some gas. It was rusted some and the bondo he tried wasn't holding, especially with Manuel's foot shoved back underneath the grill. He was laughing as both Octavio and Luis clinked their Coronas and smiled up at me. Luis leaned lazily against the right side while Octavio sat on the hood closest to him. I wanted to motion something unpleasant to make a point that could be seen. But I was in a church parking lot, and so I raised my bottled water to them with a smile.

"Hey, Roberto, come down off that lawn and drink from a real bottle," Manuel yelled at me after he slid off the front of the Nova. "Go for a drive with us and live the life you were meant to!"

"Church going, that isn't much of a life for a Latino who lives with us," Octavio yelled up to me. "Get in the car and be with your real family." Luis lifted his bottle and shrugged up at me. Maybe I should go with them. They are my family here. The only ones I know."

"Roberto, is that you over there? Pastor Pedro, he's about to begin the preaching." Soto waved at me as he started to walk my way. I looked back down at my friends and roommates and decided to keep my promise to Ms. Theresa.

~ 49 ~

GOING UP FRONT

This seat we were in, a pew Soto called it, had enough room for Soto on one side of me and on the other Carmen sat with her father. The back of the pew wasn't very comfortable. Ms. Theresa and her husband, Matthew, were sitting in the first pew, holding a packet of folders between them. The room was packed with people, and most were paying attention to the pastor as he started speaking on the stage at this podium in the front. A band had just finished a set on the stage, singing with guitars and keyboards in the back, with most of the audience clapping loudly when it finished.

They all looked at the cross behind them on the wall, with the guy named Jesus on it, and the band asked the congregation to sing with them as they slowed the tempo down to sing about a "rugged cross." Many around me knew the song, and some sang it in Spanish. I had second thoughts. Maybe I should have walked down to the Nova: the guys were my real family and this pew thing wasn't my thing. You could say this kind of stunk, although not as bad as cleaning out the grill greasetrap!

I saw Soto walking up the steps of the stage and stand next to Pastor Pedro. I wondered what he was doing up there.

"Good evening, everyone. I'd like to thank you all for coming today." Then I heard Soto repeat it in Spanish. I didn't think they would do that here. Pastor Pedro continued and took short breaks for Soto to repeat in Spanish. "We had farmers from all over Oakland County, and even farther away, bring their goods to us. We were able to buy fruit and vegetables at great prices from local Michigan growers, and even some had cooked their food for us. Our sister church in Troy was quite instrumental in helping us put this together, and we thank God for their assistance. We had some great help in creating a wonderful early dinner that we enjoyed a few hours ago, with our kitchen helpers using some of the produce from the farmers for the meal.

"We can see a direct benefit from the food grown to the tasty food on our plates. Think about the fact the farmers had to spend time planting, caring for the plants, harvesting them, and then getting the final product here with us. The farmer puts a lot of work into creating that final product just so we can enjoy that dinner we had. Don't we all just feel still satisfied with it now?"

Pastor Pedro looked at us with a silent pause and a wide smile. I wasn't sure why or what he was waiting on. As a boy I had gone with Luis and his family to help in a harvest, but it didn't seem that complicated to me. The property owner had pointed to his field and with the cart following alongside us, we just pulled the fruit and tossed it in the cart. The pastor began speaking and reading from his Bible in the section he called Matthew, and it must have been true since he called it the gospel. The girls at work talk about their friends and when one of them doubts it, they state it's "got to be gospel."

"I would like to begin in the middle," the pastor started again after his pause for effect. "Jesus, the great Teacher, makes a great statement in verse nine. 'He who has ears, let him hear.' He has just a told a story to make a point and is reminding everyone listening that God gave them ears to actually listen with. The hearing then becomes an active motion and not something that they forget easily. I explained to you how our kitchen used the fruit of the growers' labor to create nice salads and side dishes for us to eat today, but why? We tasted the fruit of their efforts, and somehow I think the farmers feel it was all worth it. God works with us in a very similar way. Jesus is working with His Father, and is constantly investing in us the fruit of his labor. We were created by Him, He draws us to Him, and we must respond to His efforts. In the classroom or even at home, you parents have to constantly remind your children to listen when what you are saying is important. Well, Jesus is doing that here, He wants our attention!" Just before that I caught a smile come across Oscar's face as he nudged Carmen's arm. Like she doesn't listen? That's funny, 'cause she's one of the best listeners I've ever talked to. I wonder if she will walk with me later tonight, after this meeting. Will her uncle mind now that he knows me better? We won't walk far, and I'm sure people will be hanging around in groups.

Pastor Pedro continued, "'Still other seed fell on good soil, where it produced a crop that was a hundred, sixty or thirty times what was sown. He who has ears, let him hear,'" Pastor Pedro had read most of that section and I'd just missed it. Are we done? I put my hands on the seat of the pew, ready to push my body up to leave.

"Sometimes we read the Bible, and we have to reread it or ask the Holy Spirit what is meant in a certain passage. But read in verse eighteen where Jesus explains what He has just told His audience. This is a wonderful blessing when God takes the time for us to give a commentary on His own words. It makes me feel less of an idiot to think that Jesus knew He needed to take the time to go in detail so people would understand. Sometimes I need extra help in seeing what He would have me see, and God always knows the best means to meet my need to help understand what He would have me come to know."

This pastor talks a lot about himself. I'm not sure a speaker should do that, letting us know that much about what he's afraid of. Any time I let the window open a bit to show what I feel, my roommates see quick enough. Why do they seem to find a way to stomp on it with a grim look or bring it up a week later with a wink and laugh? Pastor Pedro read more and explained what he read, but I felt lost and tried to catch up with him. I looked over at Carmen listening and glancing at her book in her lap.

I heard the pastor speak much louder, and I looked up from the book in Carmen's lap. Pastor Pedro stood gripping his holy book tightly with both hands. His knuckles were reddish in color, and a little sweat seemed to be dripping just around his sideburns. It was even hard for Soto to keep up translating.

"Are you people listening now? Did you hear what I just read? Were you listening and hearing? Verse nineteen states, 'The evil one comes and snatches away what was sown in his heart.' Satan is the evil one, you know, and is anyone here doing any active listening today? He wants you thinking about soccer, dinner, or even time with a friend, spouse, or girl or boyfriend. Satan isn't happy you're here, so even though you are, he's trying to pull you away from the things of God.

"In another passage Jesus refers to Himself as the Good Shepherd, who wants to care for each of the sheep and will hunt to find just the one of His hundred who is lost. We all fall somewhere in the four soils that Jesus talked about here. Which one are you? Have you heard the Word and allowed Satan to pull your heart away? Or have you heard the Word before but found no real strength in hard times and fell back on what you knew best? Your way, was it actually best? Or did you make a decision for Jesus in your life already, and now anxiety and worry has taken over? Do you see less fruit in your life and less time with Him in prayer or Bible reading? Or without pride, can you state that you've heard and understood the Word? Does your life show a higher yield than anyone would have thought possible? Can you state, like Paul, you've fought the good fight? Is God pleased with the fruit you have from your life today and tomorrow?

"How about you? How do you feel about what your life shows daily? Are you happy with what you think, say, and do? Jesus came as a substitute for our sin, yours and mine, so that we won't have to stand in front of God fearful of all our wrongdoing. Jesus died on the cross 2000 years ago and took the sin of the whole world on the cross, where His father sent Him, and then turned His face from Him because of our sin. So today, make a decision, will you ask Jesus to take over your life? He has left the shepherd's field to search for you. Will you answer His calling voice and come to Him? Listen to the words and if you are moved by God, come to the front altar. There we have some deacons, as well as Matthew and Theresa, and others waiting to talk just to you."

The band guy sang softly and low: "Just as I am, but that thy blood was shed for me. And that Thou bidst me come to Thee, O Lamb of God, I come, I come." He sang it sweetly and I shook my head to myself.

"Some of you may be feeling God speak to you, but you are not sure. Let someone in your pew walk with you," Pedro's voice was really getting to me. A part of me wanted to just run out the back of this stupid church. I felt a tap on my arm and looked to my left. Ms. Theresa motioned to the front with a quick-motioned hand and smiled. She looked at me and motioned to the front. I didn't even feel my feet moving, but before I knew it we were up front. We talked about sin in a book called Romans and how everyone should be sent to hell. Then we talked about Jesus again and John 3:16. Ms. Theresa explained to me what it means to have Jesus in your heart as Lord of your life and how I needed to commit my life to God and ask Jesus into my heart to take over, not as a crutch, as my friends might say, but as a Friend and Savior.

Ms. Theresa explained that as Savior, Jesus saves me from an eternal death in hell and provides true joy on earth. She told me not to just say words I wouldn't mean but mean the words as a promise that I would intend to keep, both to God who knows all and is in charge of all and myself. Before we got up, Ms. Theresa pointed out a verse to me where a guy named David explains how God knew him even at birth and had a plan for him. So then she pointed at me and said, "God has always had a plan for you!"

I smiled and looked up at the cross. I smiled again and felt part of a big plan. It gave me a sense of security I had never felt before, better even than any security I felt with Mama in our home when I was young.

~ 50 ~

AT THE BASKETBALL COURT

"Roberto, we've heard enough about this conversion of yours," Octavio commented as he looked up to the blue sky in the park. "By all the gods of Mexico, I swear it's enough! A week has gone by since you made that Anglo God yours, and you can't stop talking about him. Little Man rolled his eyes and told me you sounded like his grandmom."

"Yeah . . . we . . . know heard all about . . . being saved from hell," Manuel sputtered while trying to catch his breath. "But we'll feel just fine down there. I'm pretty sure they got me in charge of one of the floors, and Octavio is supposed to be just down the hall," he said with a deep breath and a big laugh.

"I'm really not trying to preach to you guys." I tried to smile while catching my breath. That Little Man, he was tough to guard and worse to keep up with on this court.

"After we stopped, I was only thanking God for my lemonade and the life to drink it."

"'Berto, I don't know how you think you can learn and change so fast. But asking Little Man if he wanted to stop and pray when he yelled out about God after missing the easy lay up? We know that's not funny, and it sure sounded a little sarcastic to us." Luis looked right at me. "Did that Wednesday night Bible study teach you godly sarcasm 'cause we're supposed to be the closest thing to family you have here, and you're not acting much different than some of those other Christians."

"What's that supposed to mean?" I asked him. Was he listening in on my calls or following me?

"Well, that waitress, Frieda, I heard her talking about Jesus to the other dishwasher. But she sure can gossip among the girls on the night shift about some of your boys on the line." Luis smiled bigger as he started again. "Or about Night Chef John, who is supposed to go to the church in Troy and be so spiritual. You told me how he said he used to drink a lot and he still smokes. I've seen him leaning in to talk to two different waitresses near the coffee machine and watching them a little too carefully. They don't need him to coach them when they bend to pick up that food tray from the tray jack."

What should I say to this onslaught of questions? It was like getting gunned down in an ambush, and I wasn't ready with any answers. "Jesus, give me something to say here, and not just silence." I prayed silently. Then it hit me—something Soto said to me after I asked a couple of questions Wednesday night. Matthew, Ms. Theresa's husband, was talking that night, and he said again how we are all sinners. Even after we choose Jesus and the Holy Spirit is working in us, we still deal with sin. He explained that whole good vs. bad dog pulling the Christian's thoughts and actions. Matthew made a good point. Soto and I talked about dealing with how I will still be tempted to do wrong and will sometimes choose to do wrong. He said that God loves to forgive us when we sin and ask Him for forgiveness. Then he read from a letter that he said John the apostle wrote. It says, "If we confess our sins, He is faithful and just to forgive us our sin and cleanse us from all unrighteousness." That's hard for me to understand. Why would God forgive me just because I ask for it? How can I explain that to Luis and Octavio when I don't even get it?

"This bumper sticker Soto has, it says, 'Christians aren't perfect, just forgiven.'" I tried to explain it to them but mostly Luis. I was really praying for him, and Ms. Theresa said she would continue to do so also. "God knows, and you guys see it too that I'm not going to stop doing things that are wrong. Some of them are normal for us, but as a child of God, I'm trying to live for Him. In fact, with Frieda and John, God is still working on them too. But I've talked to them both about Jesus, and what He means to them. I know that they love Him and are trying to live for Him as best as they can."

"Oh, man! Roberto, you had to figure out a way to do more

250

teaching with us," Octavio complained. He swirled some water around in his mouth and spit it out. "All we want you to do is shut up about any God issues around us. The three of us would appreciate it."

"Except you can pray that Octavio not take the last Corona any more without getting a second case," Manuel snapped back. "It's no joke when I reach in the fridge and all I see is a carton of empties."

~ 51 ~

THE RESTAURANT BACK KITCHEN

It was hot on the line tonight. I took a sip from the cola and stood off to the side of the line for a second. Glad there was no food ordered on my end for the moment, I breathed deeply and watched the flow of business around me. Luis was leaning over the glass rack talking to Cindy and Karen while they emptied their trays. He was smiling and trying to convince them to stay for a drink after work with him.

"Luis! Hey, Luis, the racks are backed up!" Chef John yelled over to him. "Pull them quick and keep the machine rolling. We're almost outta plates on the line here. I can't serve without plates."

"Yes, Chef," Luis barked as he pulled a rack from the machine and then emptied the ones that had already settled. "Plates, plates, and more plates!" Luis mumbled as he dropped stacks up and down the line. Chef John stepped around Caitlin, looking down at Luis, and beyond him to Chef Terrance.

"Terrance, can you let the radio station stay and come down here? I need you to expo for a minute and take over for me. Caitlin will keep an eye on your end." Chef John waved the way to the window with his head. He strode back to the prep area and caught Luis heading back to the dish area. From my end of the cook's line, I could just see Luis and Chef John standing between the back prep area and part of the dish area. I stepped over a little closer but still out of their vision.

"Luis, stop for a second. I don't know what your problem is with me, but some nights I'm in charge of this kitchen. I expect you not only to listen to me but to do so without any extra attitude." Chef John stood right in front of him with his hands on his hips.

"Chef, I got no problem with you or anybody here. I'm just doing my job here," Luis said as he stared back at him. "So let me get back to

252

work."

"Luis, I'll step aside as soon you understand. Once again, you are an employee who needs to answer to management with a better attitude." Chef John looked down at him and flicked his hand to make the point. "Your name has come up in management meetings, and the kitchen staff is tired of covering for you. Do us a favor and watch your step around here. Okay?"

Luis didn't answer or move. Chef John shrugged and stepped around Luis to head back on the line. I watched this from the corner, still sipping my cola. As Chef John started to walk past him, Luis shot out his right foot and tripped Chef John, and he slipped on the damp floor, catching himself with his right arm on the hand sink.

"Chef, I guess *you* better watch *your* step, too," Luis laughed. "It's still wet back here some from the day shift's cleaning."

"Luis, what's your deal? I could have really been hurt!" Chef John turned to Luis, still holding the side of the sink. Funny but sad, that *It Hurts So Good* just started playing on the kitchen radio down on sauté station.

"Aw, you're not hurt. You're just fine and I can see and hear it in your voice. It's the same voice you used to pick at Cindy just the other day." Luis pointed toward the waithall.

"What's Cindy have to do with this? I'm talking about you stupidly tripping me for a joke, and I don't see what she has to do with anything." Chef John limped toward Luis.

"Oh! I'm stupid now! Another stupid Latino who doesn't understand what's going on around here. Well I see and understand," Luis interrupted him. "You run this kitchen all right, and when the day chef leaves, you are the big man in charge who can do no wrong!" Chef John put both hands up and took two steps toward Luis.

"Hold on a minute, Luis! I never meant to come across as a bigger man to you, but I'm just trying to do a job as night chef here." Chef John took two more steps in Luis's direction. Luis' eyes lit up even more than usual, and he suddenly grabbed a French knife from the prep table. He flipped it in the air and held it out as if ready to cut.

"You told Roberto to have me back off from Cindy, and the reason you push me away is to make room for your turn at her. At night you in charge of the kitchen and even in charge of the girl!" Luis waved the eight-inch chef's knife at Chef John with a sly grin. "Well, you're not in charge now, are you?"

Rubbing his right elbow, Chef John looked right at Luis. "You've got this wrong, my friend. I don't have it out for you, and Cindy and I are just friends for now. I'm not looking right now to hook up with anyone, 'cause I'm trying to get my personal life together," Chef John tried to explain himself as *Love Stinks* began on the radio.

"Well, you must have had a good day at that church, cooking your heart out with a crowd staring you down. The very next day, you were training Cindy on better moves in your kitchen," Luis accused him.

"Wait a second, Luis. You don't know what you're talking about," Chef John stuttered while moving closer. "You're reading too much into me and my movements."

"Yeah, well, you just moved toward me again!" He pointed at the chef's feet with the knife. As he pointed, Chef John reached out and grabbed Luis's arm that was holding the knife with his right hand. Chef John pushed down his arm and pulled his whole body around to swing into his chest. Still holding Luis with his right arm, Chef John used his left arm in a half-nelson over Luis's head. Luis quickly threw his head back into Chef John's chin, loosening the grip.

With a little less tension around his neck, Luis pulled back his right hand and stabbed John's right thigh. Quickly yanking it out, he turned grimly around and pushed Chef John to the kitchen floor. While shoving him into the floor, the knife was thrust into John's stomach. Luis looked down at the blood starting to seep through the white chef coat, and his eyes darted to the red hue coming through the checkered pants of John's right leg.

"Luis, you are stupid now. What is this crap you've done?" I snapped at him from the hallway leading to the back kitchen.

"Roberto, you give this Christian chef a hand. The blood is starting to scare me," he tried to smile. "I think I've got to go. I'll treat her right, I swear!" I grabbed two terry cloth towels while wondering who *she* was. I tied them together and bound Chef John's knee up. Then I heard a jingle and realized Luis had snagged my Mustang keys from my casserole dish on the back prep counter. The back kitchen door slammed, and I yelled to the line. I had heard the printer shooting more tickets, and Chef Terrance and Caitlin must have wondered where Chef John and I were.

"Chef Terrance, call 911 now! Anybody, please call 911! Chef John needs medical help right away," I tried to yell with urgency and still be calm. I looked at the knife protruding from Chef John's stomach. It looked like it might be right in the center.

"Roberto, what happened here? Oh, my goodness, is that John on the floor?" Samuel, the manager, asked me. I looked up at him and just nodded. Then Chef Terrance tapped me on the shoulder while bending down, and I stepped out of the way. He and Samuel wrapped the knife carefully with more towels, trying carefully to hold it and blood from flowing. Chef Terrance propped Chef John's head with a prepackaged bag of napkins and looked at Samuel.

"Samuel, I already called 911 on the house phone. She said Waterford's EMTs were on their way. I think they'll probably take him to St. Joe's ER," Chef Terrance suggested. I slid my feet backward in slow motion and looked back toward the cook's line.

"I need a cook here." Frieda was waving her hand in the expo window frantically. "My table has been waiting for over fifteen minutes. Medium rib eye with the catch of the day shouldn't take that long, should it?" After no answer, she walked around to the cook's line.

"Is there a chef, even an able-bodied cook in the house? Please!" Frieda looked around, walked down to turn off the loud rock music with a quick twist, and gave the matted floor one good stomp with her left foot.

"Frieda, come here." Caitlin took her by the arm to get her attention, after she ran over from the back prep area. "We've had a bad accident in the back of the house here. Apologize to your table, and tell the other servers we have an emergency. We will work to get these few tables out as soon as possible."

I took a few steps in their direction.

"Roberto, were you in the bathroom? Come help on the line with these five tables while the chefs are in the back." I stood there silent and frozen until Caitlin pulled me right on the line. She began to expedite the tickets by checking ticket times and setting the plates in a line per table, ready to put food on them and push them out the window. Then the shelf was empty.

"Where is Luis? I need plates now!" Caitlin looked at the pop machine and then ran over to the dish area. She grabbed a handful of platters from a stack of clean plates, handed them to me, and went back for a second stack. She yelled at me to put up a string of plates on the other end of the line, and I somehow did it all mechanically. I felt like a robot in a Star Wars' movie, moving my arms in and out of the broiler, legs to the oven, sending food into my hot window, just as I was told to, keyed in only to Caitlin's voice as we finished out the small dinner rush.

~ 52 ~

WHERE WAS LUIS?

Without a way home, I asked Caitlin if she could drop me off after we shut down the kitchen. Samuel paid the busboy an extra twenty dollars to close the dish area, and neither Samuel nor Chef Terrance were satisfied with my unspoken words. Of course, the worst part for everyone there was dealing with the Sheriff's deputies. Two showed up right before the paramedics came for Chef John. They must have received notification at the same time. They said they had to process the crimes scene. The problem was Samuel had the busser already pre-close the back prep area where it happened. The county deputies interviewed all the employees about what they knew of what had happened, who Chef John and Luis were to them, and how the first aid was handled with Chef John. They spent the most time with me, since I had been close to the scene. But the only words I said to them were "He was just lying on the floor when I went back to the walk-in for more stock . . . blood pouring out . . ."

They dismissed me quickly when I stood silent, refusing to say anymore to them or even Samuel or Chef Terrance. Even on the line, I didn't call anything back or ask questions. Caitlin had asked about my Mustang, and I shrugged to mumble about car shop. After that I was content with silence. She drove with the radio cranked. AC/DC and then Zepplin, blared on WRIF, but the music couldn't drown out the image. I had hoped that Caitlin's choice of rock songs might help me lose the picture. I guess that was her answer to tonight's horror. Every light she stopped at, I shook my head to clear the image of the knife sitting in Chef John's stomach and the leg bleeding into the matted tiled floor. I had stood in a daze after Samuel and Chef Terrance moved me out of the way, and gazed down at the broken pieces of a scattered puzzle. The blood droplets from his leg had dropped randomly, when Chef John subconsciously rocked the stabbed leg back and forth. The mat had been folded and run through the dish machine too many times, and so it lay in three pieces that the opening dishwasher set up. Now the pieces had real color to them, and we would need new mats for sure. Samuel had thrown them in a garbage bag and set them in the back room. I wondered why not toss them in the dumpster and then numbly thought something about forensics.

Caitlin pulled into our lot, and I touched her shoulder in thanks with barely a smile. I stumbled from the car and fumbled for my key into the building while carefully making my way up the stairs. Finding the key, I tried two times to work it into the lock, and then they fell.

"Roberto, here let me open the door for you." Carmen was getting out of her car at the same time. She reached to the door with her right hand. Pushing in the door with her right hand, she held me steady and walked with me by our mailboxes. "Are you all right? Did you have a drink or two? Or is it just another eighteen hour day between two jobs?" My hands shook a little, shivered one last time.

"No, I'm all right. I guess," I stuttered some. "Tonight was just almost the worst day of my life."

"Well, some time you will have to tell me the story of the worse day of your life, since you look pretty bad right now. Do you want to talk about it with me? My uncle is watching Jay Leno, but we can talk in the kitchen," Carmen suggested. Most times I would have loved to have just a few minutes of conversation with her, but now? "You know you're part of a family now, the family of God. Not just me, but all of us in the church are there for you. But best of all, Jesus told us to lay any problem on His shoulders. They're more than big enough. But we could start with some lemonade and just a little chat about your day."

"That sounds real nice, Carmen. But I really have to go up and check in on Luis," I breathed out, wondering where he parked the Mustang. "He and I somehow missed each other tonight. I've got to do some catching up." I turned away from her and started to walk up the stairs.

"Roberto, I'll be praying for you," I heard her sweet voice whisper just loud enough. I sighed deeply and kept climbing the stairs to our floor. I came to our door, and it was unlocked and slightly ajar. I cocked my right toes and pushed the door in with my foot. It lightly knocked the doorstop, and Manuel and Octavio both jerked awake in their chairs. I scanned the living room and kitchen for any sign of Luis, and all I noticed was the Porter's House shirt crumpled in the hallway floor by the hamper. Empty bottles lay toppled on the end table next to their crossed feet, and they smiled groggily.

"Hey, Roberto, you finally home?" Octavio smiled up at me. "A great chef's life is full of sweat and long work hours. You should let me find you a job with less stress and heat."

"You had some people giving out jobs, why'd I have to get a job as dishwasher with him?" Manuel sneered his question to Octavio. "Less heat for me in the kitchen, I could have gone for that. We go way back in Mexico, and this is what I get from you?"

"Manuel, you relax, I wasn't going to bring too much attention to me and you. I had gotten you new papers and you live with me. Too much help from me, it doesn't look good," Octavio explained.

"Enough of this! Where is Luis?" I asked them, but looked right at Octavio. "Where did you send him? I've got to talk to him!"

"Roberto, you have to calm down some. I can hear the worry in your voice," Octavio held this look of concern on his face.

"Roberto, you are yelling at us? We're your friends," Manuel asked. "These Americanos don't really care for you, and those church people who act like they care about you."

"Yeah, friends who fill their lives with lost and found. Lost time in the morning and found beer each night," I shot back at him.

"Look at Roberto," Octavio reached for another Corona at the corner of the couch. "Always the guy picking words so easily. But I agree with Manuel. You're angry with me and Manuel. All I have done is look out for you and Luis. Now a piece of your American pie dream is missing, and you are mad at me. Manuel and I, we have just helped Luis get his thoughts and moves together."

"I'm grateful you were here to listen to Luis tonight," I looked for the best words. "But he's the only brother I have left. I need to talk to him. I need to see if he's all right. We need to make the right decision and fast before things get worse and out of hand."

"Oh, we listened and then talked to him," Manuel laughed at that. "We have real experience with these things." Nodding after a sip from the freshly opened bottle, Octavio added his point. "Cutting a gringo in America is no light thing, Roberto. The authorities will be acting quickly, and so we gave advice that was needed."

"But I saw it, and it was mostly in self-defense," I tried to explain to them. "The first cut was a defensive response to being held and locked in motion."

"The police might ask why he had the knife in the first place, waving it about like a wanna-be gangster," Octavio suggested.

"But that was a spur of the moment thing with the knife to get Chef John to back off, and it got out of hand. Then the second cut, Luis didn't even mean for it to go in. I could tell that, it was in his voice," I wanted to convince them both.

"Roberto, it don't matter what we believe," Octavio blew deeply into his half empty bottle.

"The police, they have a way they see it." Manuel scratched his two day's growth. "The knife was left in the chef, and the guilty guy has run. There's not much left for them to figure out. There was bad blood, flowing hot, between the Hispanic guy and the stabbed chef, and now the police can see real blood flowing." I listened to Manuel, and realized even with dulled senses he wasn't quite as ignorant as I assumed. Get him in his own environment, talking about things he knows, and the elusive poetry spills. Simple thoughts, made right to the point from Manuel. I guess he's got more up in his head than the low life criminal I thought he was.

"Octavio, just tell me where you sent Luis," I pleaded. "He and I need to sort things out better between us. He needs me now more than ever before."

"Roberto, sad to say, but it's not going to happen. It's actually a matter of trust," Octavio rubbed his bottle against the side of cheek. "Luis agreed with us when we suggested it. We all have seen a change in you since you started your God talking life."

"You have trusted your God and His people." Manuel smiled slightly. "But Luis needs to be able to trust in people he knows that will come through for him, ones he has seen."

"He can't see God, but he can see me," I looked at my cracked and stained work shoes. The laces had come undone, and I wanted to bend down and tie them. How silly, when I'd be taking them off for bed soon. These shoes have held up to lots of bending and moving, and lasted for months. My feet feel good in them. I thought that Luis felt good as my long time friend and brother. "He should know even though I have put faith in God as my Friend and Savior, our years of friendship aren't wasted."

"Maybe not wasted, Roberto," Octavio held the bottle toward me. "Friendship is never a waste. But you have made him less of a priority, and we can all tell that. That's all right. We don't hold it against you." He looked over at Manuel and jabbed him with his foot.

"That's right," Manuel added. "All three of us understand. We just can't tell you where he is. It's better for him and you. Plus, Octavio has him moving to another spot soon enough."

I shook my head in frustration and walked away to our room, leaving them to finish their last couple of beers. Looking over at Luis's empty bed, I undid my laces and kicked my shoes into the corner. With real heaviness I changed into a clean t-shirt and a pair of sweats. Falling into my bed, it took an hour to calm my thoughts enough to fall asleep. I finally found sleep when I thought of the verse the pastor had spoken last, where Jesus talked about caring for people more than birds and lilies.

Tap . . . tap . . . tap. What was that noise? It sounded like knocking at the door of our apartment. I looked at my watch on the nightstand. It was one-thirty in the morning, and I had hoped to sleep until eleven. Octavio and Manuel were sleeping right through the noise. The hangover they were feeling still must be there. Who would be knocking so late? The loud knocking didn't let up. Shaking my head, I pushed myself off the bed and stumbled out of our room to the living room.

"Stop knocking, already! I'm getting to the door!" I yelled across the living room.

~ 53 ~

THE WARRANT

"Oakland County Sheriff's Department, sir, and we have a warrant to search the premises. Please open the door and waken the other residents," a deep voice loudly spoke through our door. I stood on my toes and looked through the peephole. Standing in front of our door with an envelope in his hand was a very tall guy with a mix of gray and blond hair and a short crooked nose. A shorter black guy stood to his right, reviewing notes in a pocket book, just like on *Law and Order*. I looked from the note-taking guy to the white envelope with the warrant, and I couldn't help but glance again at the pinky nose on that guy.

"You guys look official through this hole, but how do I know you're not imposters?" I asked while unlocking the first lock. I held off before opening the second latch. "Maybe you're here to shake us down or something?"

"Look, kid, open this flimsy door before I put my shoulder to the latch you're breathing on," the black guy stepped up to the peephole. Looking for my eyes, he didn't need to step up on his heels. I guess he was not so short after all.

"This warrant in my hand is no joke! Also, if you take a walk and look out down under your patio, you can see the Waterford Township Police in the complex parking lot. They are as a matter of courtesy, in case one of your roommates happened to be down the hall and decided to run. We're investigating an assault in Waterford Township at the Porter's Houseboat Restaurant," the older white guy yelled loudly through the door.

"Roberto, unlock the door," I heard quietly behind me and I turned to see the hand on my shoulder. Then I moved my shoulder some to see Octavio shaking his head at me. "We can't hide from them, and they're just doing their jobs." I pushed back the latch and opened it wide. Octavio and I both stepped back to make room for them to walk in. Two plainclothes officers walked in with an officer right behind them.

"Good morning, I'm Detective Wright, this is Detective White and Officer Percy from the Waterford Township Police Department. We've just come from the Porter's Houseboat Restaurant, and prior to that we met the victim, John Folson, in the ER at St. Joe's Hospital. We need to ask some questions of you, as we understand you are all roommates of Luis Gonzales," the tall blond guy, with hints of gray in his sideburns, explained.

"Yes, it seems the four of you live together in this apartment. None of you are actually family, and yet you share housing arrangements? I don't see the other gentleman who resides here," Detective White asked. His small pad was flipped open in his hand but he didn't look down at it.

"One moment, and I'll go get him up and around if you need to speak to all of us," Octavio smiled and walked to the room they shared. We could hear Manuel muttering about being awakened from his slumber. I smiled a little, wondering about the names of these two partners. It seemed wrong that Mr. Wright wasn't named White, and that Mr. White already seemed like he had to show how right he was. I thought older guys had enough experience and maturity, that their attitude would be less arrogant.

"Young man, is this situation funny to you? We can show you how serious it is and take you to a less pleasant environment," Wright scratched his nose and pulled a long gray hair from his right sideburn.

"No officer, uh I mean detective. My mind thinks of weird things sometimes, and I have to stop myself," I stammered.

"Well 'Berto, I thought you got out of the last ticket when we was out a few weeks ago." Manuel poked me with a clumsy right arm while pulling down his crumpled t-shirt with the left. He checked two empties left on the end table and finished off a third with a gulp. Laughing, he picked up the three bottles and even reached to the floor where Octavio sat at the couch last night for a fourth one.

"Give us another few minutes, officers. I'll take care of these and put them in our recycle box." Manuel walked to the kitchen corner and opened the Corona box wider. They noisily toppled in, and he shook them some till it seemed neat. He walked back and sat down, waving toward empty chairs. "The room, it's clean now. We're all up and awake. Let's all sit down; there's lots of room," Manuel slurred with a half smile. Wright and White each pulled a chair from the outside of our dining table. I sat in the love seat, while Octavio sat a few feet from Manuel on the sofa. Sheriff White pulled out his notebook again from his breast pocket, set it on our table, and flipped through two to three pages. I missed him sliding it in his pocket like a holster in my cowboy books. Just like *Law and Order*. I held my smile in, since I didn't need to see even the outside of a cell from a sheriff's department desk.

"Detectives, we don't know much of anything at all about this situation. Luis, he stopped home a while ago, barely spoke to us, and then left." Octavio explained with some confidence. "So, we don't know anything about an assault at that restaurant the boys work at."

"Well, we just left there and took a number of statements from the employees. In fact, Roberto, you were one of the ones the officers questioned," Sheriff Wright looked right at me. "We have some notes from the officers on the scene, and they suggest you could have been more helpful." Where was the good cop between these two? Maybe that officer should speak up and not just walk around.

"Yes, sir, here it is," Sheriff White flipped two pages and then another one. Like a marine sergeant, this one. "Roberto stated, 'He was just lying on the floor when I went back to the walk-in for more stock, blood pouring out' and not much else. We wondered why you couldn't tell us much more, as you are friends with the suspect and were in close proximity. But we'll come back to that," he tapped his little book with his pen and sighed.

"The officers on the scene spoke to a few waitstaff who said there was a number of problems between the suspect and the victim. One especially, Cindy, implied there was a little conflict over her. When we asked John at the hospital, he didn't think it was as big a deal till now," Detective Wright started to explain with a slight smile and stroked the back of his bald head. Did he shave it every night, I wondered.

"The fact is, John ID'd Luis for us right before they wheeled him into surgery. The ER doctors said it wasn't looking real good for him," White shook his head. "If he doesn't make it out of surgery, it would mean homicide charges and not just felonious assault. Luckily we made it in time to find out for sure who exactly stabbed him. He wasn't able to give us the full account, but he did say they ended up in some type of scuffle that ended with Luis stabbing him in the leg and then the stomach."

"So, Octavio, you seem to be in charge around here. The management at the restaurant suggested the lease was probably in your name, and yet you keep a low profile. We checked your record, and it seems clean," Detective Wright looked down at him. "We think Luis had more to tell you than just a passing greeting."

"Look, detective, Luis is a hot-headed and loud boy who is trying to figure out how to be a man. He dreams of being a rock star with women all wanting his attention." Octavio pointed to the guitar case in the corner. "He comes and goes around here, and so we didn't ask much when left." He leaned back into the sofa and took a deep breath.

"Tell us where he goes then. Where is the guitar? How long is he gone? Is he ever gone overnight?" Detective White peppered Octavio like a fast firing gun. "Who are his friends? Where do they live? How does he get there, since he doesn't actually have a car?" Octavio leaned forward again before he answered.

"By the way, Roberto, did you mind that he borrowed your car?" Sheriff Wright looked over to me as an after thought. "You had to get a ride home tonight, and the other workers said they had seen your car earlier that evening when they were taking a smoke break."

"Luis sometimes borrows my car. He and I are like brothers, so it's never any big deal," I tried to explain. Actually I was worried, since he really didn't drive it much at all. When he drove cars, they were automatic. He never could find the right gear with my Mustang.

"Hey, you guys, this ain't no trial! Roberto is a good kid, and he's not done anything wrong," Manuel blurted out. "You guys should relax some." Manuel pushed down with both hands from the edge of the couch, belched, pushed again with effort and weaved to the fridge for another beer.

"Sir, I don't think anybody here needs more alcohol," Sheriff White turned in his chair to Manuel. "In fact, I think we're almost done with questions for you guys." He looked over at his partner and got up.

"Gentlemen, you can look over this paperwork if you like," Detective crooked nose and fuzzy burns set down the warrant on the table. "So before you head back to bed, we'll see if Officer Percy found anything around your place. We appreciate your full cooperation."

"Officers, I thought we were going to talk more? We're done, and I don't get it," Manuel looked at both of them and over to Octavio, who had stepped out to the kitchen.

"It's apparent to us, you three roommates here have little to offer us that's of any use right now. Like my partner said, we appreciate your help," Sergeant White snapped his little book shut and stuffed it in his breast pocket. .

"Detectives, come here and bring an evidence bag," Officer Percy yelled from our hallway. I turned to look down the hall as the detective swiftly walked that way. The officer held something high above the hamper with his gloved hand.

Detective gray burns held his nose above the laundry hamper next to the object. He put on his own gloves and pulled in his partner's direction. He laughed and tightened a glove with a snap of excitement. "Take a look at this."

"Well . . . hooray! A work shirt with evidence on it," Detective White smiled broadly. "Blood on the elbow that somebody didn't see. This isn't your shirt is it, Roberto?"

"Uh . . . no sir," I uttered.

"Oh, just asking . . . in case, you know since you were there and helped John some without telling us about it. Humbly the hero and all," Detective Wright asked me. The sly grin at the outside of his face didn't go well with the nose leaning in at the corner of his smile. I started to feel my stomach sink, and it twirled some, like a pot of boiling pasta about to overflow.

"Well, this wraps up our time here. You boys sure you can't give us any info about Luis's whereabouts? We could take your inaction tonight as a sign," Detective White suggested.

"A sign? What are you talking about detective?" Octavio glanced from one to the other detectives. "We've told all we can, and there's no other signs or clues for you."

"Oh, it's a clue all right," Crooked face scratched his left sideburn now. "Without further assistance from you gentlemen, it suggests to us we should dig further into your paperwork here in America." Octavio jumped up and stepped forward, knocking his shin on the table. Wincing from the pain, he rubbed it some.

"Our papers are all in correct order! Our employers, the DMV, and IRS have all approved them. And you're not ICE to check us out that way!" Octavio glared at both of them. Both detectives had little smiles and waited to speak to be sure he didn't say any more. The officer stood off to the side, seemingly unsure what to think.

"Oh, but we have friends," Sheriff White softly explained. "I served with one of them in Desert Storm. We go way back and cover each other now and again. Brothers who serve, you know. My friend cannot only look up you guys with some time, but he can reach out to the Mexican government." I looked up at that and watched Manuel open the freezer for ice and gulped some water. "Oh, and at the very least, we could take any of you to jail for a few days with sufficient evidence."

"Well, honestly any of those ideas sound like fun to me. I always like taking somebody behind bars to see if they are able to remember more relevant information. But why don't you guys make some calls, and even check with some of the assailant's friends outside of this building. We would more than appreciate it," Detective Wright picked up the warrant and tapped it on the chair for emphasis.

"Detective, I promise you that we will make some calls on your behalf. We don't want you to think us uncooperative," Octavio grimly looked at them.

"Excellent! I'm glad we're all on the same page and in agreement," Detective White clapped his hands and walked toward our door. "Remember, my friend is one who doesn't need me to make more than one call. So we'll be back in a few days to see what you guys have found out for us."

"Gentlemen, don't worry about the door. We can let ourselves out." Detective Wright wrinkled his nose and lips with that grin of his. Detective White rolled the bagged work shirt under his left arm, and shut the door with just enough pull to slam it shut.

~ 54 ~

ROBERTO ASKS FOR HELP AT CHURCH

The sermon that Sunday was even better than the past few Sundays, and I only slipped asleep for a few minutes. I suppose that's good, since I was holding myself on three or four hours sleep. It seems like God is talking to me each week, and I have to keep my ears and eyes open for more information. That morning, Pastor Pedro had us look in the book of James as a base, but we flipped back often to another book called Proverbs. Though I didn't flip too much, I kind of looked on at Carmen's Bible or over at her father's open Bible.

Wisdom is a sense of understanding what is right to do for each of us at any given time. Pastor explained how God gives us wisdom, but we should ask Him. He showed us how Jesus said to His disciples to ask anything in His name, and He would go to His Father on our behalf. I can't get a handle on how great a friend Jesus is to us, not just up in the skies, but here in my head and heart daily. The ending prayer was over, and Carmen went off to visit some friends while I just sat there thinking.

"Roberto, are you back in Mexico or praying to our great God?" Santo interrupted my thoughts with a big smile.

"Oh, I think he was thinking about wisdom that James reminded us to ask for." Ms. Theresa grinned down at me while messing up my hair. "We all need that reminder. I know I ask God almost daily in my life for wisdom. Sometimes moment to moment, with small issues in my family or how to speak to someone who cut in line at Walmart."

Ms. Theresa was so good at speaking truth in her own life and not making it seem like it was just me who had a problem. I looked up to both of them and smiled. I was glad they somehow knew to stop and talk to me. If I said that thought, I'm sure one of them would say, "It's not coincidence, but a God thing."

"Santos, you know I'm not from Mexico, but I did spend some time there. My home country is Guatemala." I laughed at the thought.

"Well, it's been the path of many of us, as part of our lives' histories. But here you are today with us, and I'm happy you're here Sunday after Sunday." Santos hit me with a light left hook to the right shoulder with a glint in his eyes.

"I praise God often for you, Roberto. Not just your salvation to God and away from eternal hell, but your commitment to attend and be part of our church here. We can see growth in you as you draw closer in your relationship to Jesus," Ms. Theresa spoke with real love in her voice. A lump came from my stomach to my throat, and I nodded in thanks while turning my head slightly away.

"But tell us, was it wisdom you were thinking of just now? We would like to really know what you're feeling," Santos asked. I looked around some to be sure there weren't people around to listen in. But it looked like most of the church had begun to empty out, at least to hallways near the front and back doors. Pastor Pedro was over by the piano listening to a lady complain loudly about her hip and throbbing lower back.

"Well, you see it is wisdom I need, and I have a hard time thinking things through right now," I began to explain. "My best friend, Luis, who has been more than a friend to me for years, he's like a brother. He is closest family, aside from Mama and Tina back in Guatemala." I put my head in my hands for a few seconds and then pushed my hands up past damp eyes to get my hair back off my face. Ms. Theresa stepped around the pew and sat down on my right while Santos leaned in closer to listen better.

"Luis is a little crazy and has a bad temper sometimes. Well at work in the kitchen he—"

"Work, you mean the restaurant the two of you both work at? That Porter's House place by the lake?" Ms. Theresa interrupted. "Which lake is it on? I always forget. Oh, I'm sorry. Please continue, Roberto," Santos winked at me and smiled to prod me on.

"Anyway, I love him for being there in my life for so many years. I

270

trust him with so much, and until I trusted Jesus, Luis was my confidant with everything I really thought. Sometimes he mocked me, but it was in good fun and even for my own good to be sure of myself," I looked to both of them. Unsure of how much to tell them, I stopped for a second.

"Go on, son, this is important and we're not going anywhere right now," Santos reassured me.

"At the restaurant, he and the night chef, John, have had words between them a lot lately. Then last night, it seemed Luis lost it completely and pushed the limits between the two of them. I saw the whole thing, and it seemed Luis just wanted to say what was on his mind about Chef John, after he tripped him to get his attention. But then, the conversation got louder and Luis snatched a knife. Chef John grabbed him to calm him, and then Luis stabbed his leg, pushed John down, and stabbed him again." I took a breath, deep and long, and looked from one to the other. They both seemed to let out a sigh. "I don't think Luis actually meant to stab him either time. The first time was probably a reaction to being held in a wrestling grip, and the second was really an accident when he pushed him to the floor. I'm sure he's sorry about the whole thing and actually only wanted to get Chef John off his case all the time."

"That's really rough, Roberto. You're a friend with a big burden on your shoulders," Santo looked at my shrunken shoulders.

"Well, Jesus said to bring everything to Him, 'cause He loves us more than the birds that He watches over. And Peter reminds us to 'Cast all of our cares upon Him.' So let's pray together," Ms. Theresa suggested and I couldn't say much but nod in agreement.

"Dear Jesus, we know you are aware of all things going on in Roberto's life and that of his friend Luis. We know you have a plan for Roberto's life. Give Roberto wisdom in the choices for what he should think, say, and do in this situation that has happened with Luis. Please give your peace and assurance that your Holy Spirit is with him as comforter in all things," she prayed sincerely for me. I started to feel the tears, overcome with a sense of God in this place with me.

"God in heaven," Santos started. "I would come to You this

morning. I pray you give Roberto the sense of wisdom in what you have him do. Provide for him Your will in these matters, as they are quite important to him. You make your will known to us, if we only ask, and we ask now that You, God, help Roberto today." Santos was so confident in God moving in my life, I felt assured I would get an answer. But even then questions popped in head. Where was Luis? If I knew where he was, should or would I go and help him? What should I tell the authorities? I looked down at the Bible next to me, the Spanish-American one Carmen had given me. I turned a page in the New Testament, somehow hoping Jesus's words would give me answers right now.

"Roberto, God doesn't give instant answers much as we would like for Him to do. You have to spend more time meditating in prayer and reading His Bible," Ms. Theresa smiled slightly. "We will pray for you. My husband, Matt, and I pray together nightly, and we will keep you in mind. If you would like to tell us more, call Matt later today or on Monday." She wrote down his number on a card from the pew in front of us.

"Thank you both for listening today," I said softly. "I appreciate it and I do feel like it has settled me down. I just wish He could talk to me like on the phone or something." Santos chuckled some.

"We all wish that sometimes. The Old Testament prophets got that line, and even some in the New Testament, but we wait on the Lord in prayer and scripture." Santos pointed to my Bible that Carmen had given me, and then turned back to the cross behind us.

~ 55 ~

SAMUEL AND ROBERTO

I picked up a clean rubber spatulas and cooks' spoons hanging in the back prep area. It was late in the shift after lunch, and I liked to clean my station by switching out my utensils and sanitizer bucket. Tommy had wiped down both our ends, and I got the floors today. We often switched when we worked together. A perforated spoon fell from my handful of spoons and ladles, and Manuel laughed loudly when he walked out of the management office. Setting the clean ones down on the table, I stooped to pick up the spoon and looked down the hall. Manuel punched out at the time clock and looked back at Samuel sitting in the rolling chair.

"Manuel, we're not done with this meeting," Samuel stopped the chair in mid-roll and stood glaring at him. "Though your shift is over, it's not time for you to leave!" he said with that stern voice he used when making a point for us to listen.

"My dish schedule had me off a while ago, and I stuck around to have the sinks cleaned and new silver water. I even did a few prep items for Chef Terrance like he asked me to do this morning. What else, boss?" Manuel opened his arms and looked around.

"Just a few more answers to help us find some things out," Samuel said. "We really need to help the authorities regarding Luis and Chef John."

"What makes you think I know much about the Latino boy? He lives with me, but he don't talk to me much at all," Manuel laughed. "Ask his lifelong friend, Roberto, if you want his history or birthday."

"Some of the other staff have asked about Luis a few times. Walking by, I happened to notice you kind of just snicker about it. Chef Curtis and I believe you have more to tell the authorities. You can start here, today, with us." Samuel tapped the schedule to make a point.

"I go home now, boss. You ask somebody else about those two guys who had their fighting words, somebody who knows more than how loud Luis snores." Manuel threw his apron in the company hamper and winked at me on the way out the back door.

"Roberto, you know more than those same words you repeated to the Sheriff's Department about some stock you got that night. Come on in here," Samuel motioned to me. I took off my chef toque and wiped my head with my arm while walking slowly toward the open door.

"Samuel, I really don't know anything at all," I said slowly. Samuel looked up from the get well card sitting on the desk. It was filled with little notes and signatures, and I wondered why nobody had asked me to sign it. "I can't say much more than what I've told you, Chef Curtis, and the police."

"Well, Roberto, we have had some signs of Luis' temper a few times here in the kitchen at Porter's House. But why would he attack our night chef, John? It just doesn't make any sense to any of us. Apparently you two have been long time friends," Samuel waited for me to say something. I looked down at my shoes until I felt a hand on my shoulder.

"Roberto, we aren't trying to pin anything on you," Chef Curtis explained sympathetically. "And we really don't want Luis in worse trouble. But this problem needs to resolved quickly."

"Chef, I don't know where he is today. In fact, I didn't even see him come home to our place," I tried to explain to him.

"Well, that's probably true, but you have to know something more. Where would he go under these circumstances? I mean, I know he's like some kind of brother to you. But I've hired, trained, promoted, and even seen great potential in you. Yet this is how I get repaid from you and your roomies? One of my best night chefs is out of commission indefinitely. The reality is that he may not even live, and he's part of our family here." Chef Curtis pounded his chest to make his point.

"A family doesn't let one another down like this," Mr. Porter said in a deep throaty whisper. How many more management will line up behind me in the doorway of the office? "Family looks to support each other, even when one member fails us." He looked from Chef Curtis to Samuel and finally to me in grim silence. This didn't feel like how family should treat one another.

"Roberto, take our spoons to the line and then punch out. Tommy can work till four alone on the line, and he can tell me or Chef Terrance if he needs help." I turned my head to Chef Curtis and shook my head.

"Chef, I can finish out the shift. It's not a problem for me at all," I said.

"Roberto, we want you to think about your family here in this restaurant. What does it mean to you to work here? I don't want to split loyalties with you, but I invest in my kitchen staff on a deeper level than many chefs, beginning with appropriate pay, educational support, training, and cross training to promoting and even professional references."

Chef wasn't making it easy for me. I really looked up to him, and now what should I do?

~ 56 ~

ST. JOSEPH MERCY HOSPITAL

The nurse led the four of us down the hall, mumbling while she walked. The OR nurse would have to wait for further details of the storied love triangle. I rolled my eyes a little, and Ms. Theresa smiled at my expression, just pieces of that soap opera were enough for me. I heard enough of that from the serving line from our cook's window back at work. But the nurse who gave us permission seemed very pleasant and helpful while giving us details of John's condition. She explained that the surgery had gone well, but he still would be kept on this floor for a week or two until the wound had healed enough for him to be moved home. I wasn't too comfortable here in the hospital, and I wished Santos had been able to come. Ms. Theresa insisted on bringing Pastor Pedro and Matthew with us, and if it weren't for all of them, I could have just stayed at home. But she wouldn't even let me finish the sentence and threatened to send Matthew to pick me up if I suggested backing out.

"Excuse me, John, you have visitors today." Gossip Queen could lay a sweet tone in her voice. "We know you haven't had many guests in a day or so, so may I open the door the rest of the way?"

"Whatever, Lavern. Sandy gave me medicine a while ago so I may be asleep soon." John said it loud enough for us to all hear with Ms. Theresa holding the outside of the door. "But go ahead and let them in, 'cause I can already see Theresa's smile peaking in."

"Dearest John, we have so worried for you. All of us at church have been praying for you, along with the staff at your home church. You've been so helpful in the last year or so with our local ministries, along with so many other members from your church. We praise God daily for the love and willingness to serve in so many ways from you folks,"

276

and on she could go while we filed in behind her.

"Yes, we praise God, and remind others at church and our national missionary supporters, of how much we appreciate the local surrounding church support." Matthew interrupted her with a smile and stepped closer to the end table by his bed. "A New English Study Bible and Oswald Chambers are excellent choices of literature, but I'm not sure how much Escoffier will keep you awake." He laughed while picking up the heavy book on sauces from the famous Frenchman.

"Oh, Chef Curtis told me there'd be a test on some small sauces when I got back to work." John pulled himself up some in the bed, and Lavern moved in silently to adjust the lever under the bed. "I've skimmed through it for a couple old ideas that we could rework with our base sauce. But it's tough even in English."

"Hello, Chef John," Pastor Pedro took two steps toward the end of the bed away from me. "I've come along, as I didn't personally thank you for your last visit at our church. As has been said, we specifically appreciate your efforts with the cooking demo on our Farmer's Market Revival Weekend and, of course, the previous times as well."

"Pastor, it's always been my little joy to come to your church when I could. But why, Roberto, are you here?" John turned his head a little to look right in my eyes.

"Why, John, I asked him, of course," Ms. Theresa said without a second's beat. "He's been most concerned about you and has prayed with us often for you."

"Yes, yes, Chef John. I've been worried about you. We at work have all been scared about you in here." I tried to pick my words carefully and slowly.

"Well, I got the card from work and the flowers. They were real nice," John breathed out heavily. "But I'm not sure I even want you visiting me here."

"Oh, John, please don't say that," Ms. Theresa sighed.

"Chef, I was there that night and I—"

"Yeah, I know you were there. I saw you from the start of the whole conflict, but you never moved or said a single thing to stop it." Chef John glared at me with green eyes glowing. "It was as if you were a stupid statue who couldn't think about anything but himself."

"Oh no, Chef! I was thinking things. Luis didn't mean to do most of what happened. You have to understand! Luis, he—"

"Luis! Luis!" Chef John yelled with surprising force, and I ducked to the right as the fat Escoffier flew fluttering between Pastor Pedro and me.

Startled by John's reaction, we all stood silent for a second.

"I think it'd be best if you all leave John alone for a while. He's going to really need some rest." Lavern tried to smile in a calming way.

"I could use a cup of coffee from that stand I saw on the first floor," Pastor Pedro said. "Roberto, how about you have a pop with me?" He walked from the room, and I began to follow a few steps behind to the door.

"Lavern, my wife and I would like just a few moments with John before we leave. If it's all right with you, of course," Matthew asked her while she bent to pick up the sauce book.

"Lavern, they can stick around another minute or so. I'll keep my temper under check," John said and let out a deep sigh.

Pastor Pedro tapped me lightly on my shoulder. "Roberto, come with me,'" he whispered. "You've ignited enough fire in him today. Let him cool down now."

"I'll be down right behind you," I whispered back with a quick nod as he held the door to the hallway. I had to hear this conversation, even though I knew it wasn't right, and I stopped short of exiting the room. Something pulled in my head: a voice telling me to go follow Pastor Pedro while a second voice said I really needed to hear what they were going to say.

"John, we've known you for a long time. Why, I remember in Costa Rica, on that short mission trip, you came with your church to see us when we served there in the mission field. You helped build classrooms for the pastor's theology school," Matthew said just loud enough for me to hear.

"Yeah, I remember that year. I felt God really working in my life."

"Do you also remember how you shared with Theresa and I that God had helped you with your struggle with addictive behaviors? We talked about some issues of alcohol and minor drug usage, and how constant prayer, time in the Bible, and accounting yourself with a godly brother brought you out with a clean bill of health. But you and I spent time in prayer regarding God forgiving you and the guilt you still carried months later."

"Yeah, the conversation is still back in my memories. You said if Jesus forgives all of the world's sins, big and small, He certainly would have forgiven mine." I could hear the bed creak from moving again, but I didn't dare turn to look in the window. "But the issue, we figured out, wasn't so much Jesus forgiving me, but more me letting myself go. I had to get past letting my family and myself down, and most of all letting God down."

"Oh, John, forgiveness isn't easy for any of us. Especially when it comes to ourselves," Ms. Theresa said. "But Jesus spoke about it as something we have to continually work on."

"Sure I know, our associate pastor dropped a copy of his sermon on forgiveness at my bedside. Peter's question to Jesus, where he asked how many times do we have to forgive our brother, and Jesus answered him with seven times seventy, like we can't stop forgiving. I don't see that I need to memorize his sermon," Chef John pulled something from a drawer with effort.

"Well, John, we asked Roberto to come with us today because he feels real pain over the whole situation. He's trying to balance his new faith in Jesus with a longstanding friendship with Luis. You must try to understand this from his perspective, John," Ms. Theresa said with a deep sigh.

"You said he feels pain. What about the pain I feel? I'm the one who was stabbed by someone I've only tried to help in the work place, and his friend shows up here to defend him to me. Am I to listen to his emotional problems, when he's bringing more frustration to me in just being here?"

"John, we all need to be forgiven at times for poor choices, especially newfound brothers in the Lord," Matthew tried to prod him.

"I hear you guys, and I appreciate it. But you stand there looking at my Bible, while I'm lying here still having trouble even moving in the bed without pain shooting from my gut." The bed creaked again. "God's love and forgiveness—well it's a lot bigger and better than mine is today." I heard both of them say a prayer for him in parting, and then the door hit my arm. I walked toward the nurse's station, where gossip was waiting to be shared.

~ 57 ~

THE HOUSE WHERE LUIS STAYED

Driving home from work today wasn't too bad for a Tuesday. I actually got cut early, since I was all set up and Chef Curtis was working to cut labor. My Mustang showed up in the apartment lot yesterday, and Octavio smiled when I happily walked in with jingling keys. They had been in an envelope with my name on it in our mailbox. It felt good driving my own car to and from work again, planning my day on my terms. I had sat watching the *Food Network*, paying only slight attention to an Emeril rerun, and wondered where Octavio was. Lying back on the sofa, I nodded off for a few minutes.

Then Octavio came home and startled me from dozing with a joke about a bed being for sleeping and end tables being for drinking. I didn't laugh at him but just grumbled when I tried to adjust my feet back off the end table. He told me then how we just missed each other when he dropped off Manuel at the restaurant.

Wright and White showed up soon after that, loud and proud, at our door again. They again threatened in the hall to call their friend from ICE unless we agreed to help them. I sat worried, but Octavio winked at me with his hands open and nodded at the door. They came in, sputtered the threats, and Octavio said we had heard from Luis' friends. They demanded we take them to the last known spot he had been. So while Octavio drove the speed limit to the mobile home park five miles away, I asked him questions about his plan. He only smiled at me. We pulled to a stop at the clubhouse and parked.

"Boys, you best not be yanking our chains," the tough black guy named White said with some force. "This isn't a joy ride for us; we don't have time to be wasting today."

"Yes, this newest warrant I have in my hand suggests we not waste our time," said Wright with the streaks of gray and crooked nose meeting that weird smile. "In fact, ninety-six hours have elapsed, and now there is a national warrant out for him. So the fun's just begun and there's no looking back," he said that last part with a sly grin that wrinkled his nose, and I couldn't help but stare at it.

"Roberto! Relax now!" Octavio caught my attention back. "We understand the importance of this and have already made contact with people to help."

"That's great. I'm glad we're all on the same page," Wright nodded his appreciation in our direction. But White had already turned to the homes ahead of us.

"So where are heading here?" White walked down the first street on the right. "Two to three houses filled with Latino cousins who barely know each other till they come to America? Or even worse, a drug house, that sells to this whole area?"

"Now detective, many of these people are acquaintances of mine— hard working people, who carry two or three jobs and send much of the money back to their family in their homeland. All of them have their proper papers, of course," Octavio said with a hint of satisfaction.

"We're not ICE, nor do we even have them on that phone right now. Just show us where our suspect was last," Wright said with some impatience.

"Follow me for a couple of minutes," Octavio said while he walked past them. "It's only down here a ways." We followed him for five minutes, and then he stopped, after turning on a second street at a house with two cars. Both cars were older but in good condition. Two tire ramps were stacked to the right of the Chevy Nova with a toolbox sitting next to them. On the other side of the door, away from the parked cars, a string of hostas and pink perennials flowered. Wright gazed at the cars from his height, and looked up and down at the flowers. Wright spoke into his radio and informed the local uniforms to stay parked on the other side. He must have spoke to them on the way over. Just then White brushed Octavio's shoulders with his broader shoulders, and stepped up to the door.

"Oakland Sheriff's Department, please open the door." He knocked with some force, not unlike he did at our apartment. "We have a warrant to search the premises." I wondered about that, since I thought the warrant from the other day only covered Luis's residence.

"Can I help you officer?" A middle aged Mexican woman answered, holding the door slightly open. "No one is home but me right now. My husband, Alejandro, is gone to work right now. He can help you maybe tomorrow." She tried to smile.

"It's all right, Señora Papan. These authorities will not harm you," Octavio tried to assure her while opening his arms wide. "They are only looking for Luis. They know he was here lately."

"Oh, Luis. Well, he's not here anymore," she explained to us while shutting the door. White tapped lighter this time on the door, and she opened it slightly.

"Ma'am, we know you aren't happy to see us right now, but we would ask just to look around the home for a few minutes." White seemed to have in compassion in his voice.

"Yes, Mrs. Papan. You see there is a bench warrant out for Luis and it is somewhat urgent we find him. We won't be more than ten minutes, and we'll take care not to disturb too many things." Wright tried even more to smooth it over.

"Okay, then, if Roberto and Octavio say it's all right. I guess so," she said while she opened the door to them. The detectives waved at both of us to stay outside, and we walked around to a couple of lawn chairs sitting across the flower bed. Waiting on them, wondering what was to happen next, I stared up at the clouds sifting in the sky. After five minutes they filed out, like a couple of soldiers. One of these soldiers seemed to be balancing his weapons over his shoulder.

"This guitar, it's just the ticket. Fingerprints, and I think there's a touch of dried blood under the fret bar." White let Luis's guitar swing a bit, and Wright stopped at the door.

"Mrs. Papan, I'm sorry but it looks we will have to return tomorrow. Please let your husband know we will be coming by." Wright's voice still sounded nice but firm. He handed her his card and smiled under the crooked nose.

"You boys did have something worthwhile. Don't think we're done with you," White said. "We'll be contacting you again to see if Luis tries to reach you or if you hear any more about him."

"Correct! We won't beat a dead horse, but our friend at ICE is waiting to see if we need his help." Wright looked from me to Octavio with that smile.

"All right, detectives, we'll keep that in mind. And we'll wait to hear from you," Octavio answered them with a confident tone. We walked back to Octavio's car and headed back home. Octavio winked again at me but would give me nothing further about Luis.

In fact, I waited, wondered, and prayed for Luis for weeks on end. I had a sense that Octavio was randomly moving Luis from place to place with some plan of his, but he still wouldn't allow me in the circle. My feelings about it were mixed, as I still felt I could help Luis somehow. Santos, Ms. Theresa, and even Carmen felt it was probably for the best that I not know any of their planning. That way I wouldn't carry any guilt for not telling the Porter's House management or worse, the Sheriff's Department. Although I'm sure the guilt of giving even a piece of information about Luis could kill my sense of real brotherly love.

I was still trying to figure out what Pastor Pedro meant about the greater golden rule when thinking about how to love. Love wasn't easy to think through. Carmen agreed to take a walk with me along Commerce or Union Lake. That's all right by me, but I can't see how I can live with the love that Jesus talks about—loving people who persecute you, who don't pay you back what's owed to you, and even talk about you badly. I mean those people don't deserve love back, do they? I guess sometimes I felt I didn't deserve love back, and Jesus said He died for even me. That was a gift I gladly received. So, I guess none of us deserve this gift from God. But His Word says He gives the gift of salvation for all sinners, those with small or large sins. They're all the same. They all deserve judgment and yet they all can receive this gift of Jesus.

~ 58 ~

THE VISITOR AFTER WORK

Chef has scheduled me nights three shifts a week for the past two schedules, and I've had to rearrange opposite shifts with the manager at McDonalds. He explained how he needed more experience on these shifts with Chef John out for another month or so. It was nice that he knew he could count on me, but it felt like he still held some bitterness toward me, as if I could have done more to help with the conflict that horrible night. Or did he wonder still that I knew more and was just not informing the authorities? Somehow, I would have to regain his respect.

Chef Terrance, though, has seemed to see something in me. The last few weekends, he put me on the hot end and I didn't go down but once. That one time, he came down and got me out of the weeds until I could match the tickets rolling out of my printer to the voice of the wheel man. Tonight, he even had me run the wheel for a while until we filled the board with more than ten tickets. Then we switched, and I stepped back to float down and help on the hot end. It was exciting but nerve-racking to run the board and talk to the servers and the other cooks on the line. Some of the servers snapped at me from the server line, but I kept my cool.

"Roberto, finish your cola! I'm done now, and you said you would walk out with me after I was done with my closing sidework." Cindy startled me. "What were you daydreaming about? The TV wasn't even on sports but some old movie."

"Just thinking about working the line, our voices through the window, and how we cross the line." I sighed as I struggled to tiredly get out of the booth.

"Some of you boys in the kitchen cross the line all the time with looks and comments at us. We have feelings too, you know?" Cindy stopped to look at me, and I wasn't sure if she wanted an answer.

"A lot of people step over the line with what they say. Some of the servers treat the kitchen like we should jump when they speak," I explained. "And our line, the cook's line, gets hot, busy with sweat, hot grease, and bodies in a closed space. So sometimes it would be great if the front of the house could understand a little." She didn't answer, and so I thought about crossing the line. There was tension between cooks and servers in the window. I thought about the line, the border crossing, we crossed years ago to come to America. Octavio still helped other Latinos cross that border. Would he help Luis get out of the U.S. with the national warrant out for Luis?

"Roberto, you can let the door go now," Cindy said with fake exasperation. "And we do try to understand some. We bring you boys fresh ice water and pop."

"Yes, you do, Cindy. And we appreciate that," I said with half a grin. I glanced over at the far side of the lot by the employee side. A beat up S10 truck sat on the dark side of the restaurant lot with its tailgate down, one guy sitting on the gate while another leaned his back against it. Neither looked like they were talking much, but the one standing stared up to the stars. I couldn't see their faces in the shadows, and I slowed my pace walking some.

"Is something wrong, Roberto?" Cindy asked me nervously, and she stopped for a second to keep pace with my slowing walk.

"Just curious about that old pick up truck," I whispered. "I have a funny feeling who it is." The hoarse laugh sounded from deep in my throat wasn't funny at all. She looked over at me and smiled anyway.

Someone yelled at me, "'Berto, you walk so slow across this parking lot. Cesar and Carlos, they'd laugh at your energy now. And who's walking right next to you in the shadows at closing time? Well, it's Cindy, the girl with a second look from a couple of guys. Things could have been so different," he chuckled with a just a hint of melody in his voice and laugh. I knew it had to be him. A stranger who seemed familiar to me sat smoking silently next to him. Like a line from a book, I tried to remember where we had met.

"Wish we had time to talk about your Jesus tonight, Roberto. I hear He's more to you than just somebody on a wooden cross in the church," and the stranger blew a series of rings up into the air. Then he pulled a bottle from behind Luis and lifted to me before taking a long drink.

"Hello, Luis. It's good to see you're all right." I breathed a quick sigh and looked over at Cindy, who was frowning but still silent. "Good to see you again, Max. A discussion about God is probably better kept for another time, although it's one conversation I'd be happy to have with you." Max was the party host who spoke easily of religion and his philosophy on life with a bottle of beer in his hand.

"Yeah, well, I'll check my calendar and call you some time. How about if Ms. Silent Treatment and I take a stroll for just a minute." Max smiled right at Cindy. She looked at me, and I nodded in approval.

"He looks more rough than he is. He'll be a gentleman, or at least out here he will," I tried to reassure her.

"Not sure how to take that, Roberto." Max grinned as he walked backwards away from the Chevy pick up and started to ask Cindy what really lit up her eyes.

"Roberto, I need you to know something. You've been a good friend all these years. Although, we've always been close and we trusted each other most times, this time," Luis shook his head, "I couldn't take the chance with you."

"I don't understand it all," I quietly answered. "I was worried about you and knew most of what happened was an accident. I wanted to tell you if you and I could just explain to the authorities that timing and movements got carried away."

"Look 'Berto, they wouldn't believe any stories from my side. Suspicion about any truth I might try to say would take over in their mind! This is exactly why we couldn't tell you details of where I've been, and where I moved around. This new religion of yours got you all confused about how to treat friends, and even friends meant to be brothers. It's a shame." Luis looked at my feet and up to my eyes. I looked at his favorite tennis shoes and back to my Die Hards, thinking how different we were.

"I've changed but not from religion. I've changed because I now have a relationship with Jesus. He's made me rethink all the things I look at in life. Even my friendships," I whispered forcefully.

"Well, now this friendship is over and done, and you ain't gotta think about it any more. I'm getting a new job in a new country, actually one we traveled through years ago and now I will be more at home than here. I'm all set up with a new life, and I'm sure I'll have a few new friends," he smiled with that self-satisfying grin he had when life just happened to work out for him. I'm sure somehow Octavio had a hand in this plan with his contacts in Central America.

"But how did it work out? What about the national warrant to arrest you? Aren't you even worried about the detectives from Oakland County? I mean you—"

Boom! And boom again. A loud muffler popped as its car hit the bump in the lot entrance. A mid-seventies black Monte Carlo with tinted windows pulled up between us and Cindy walking in small circles with Max.

"What is this, you Mutt? Did you call someone when you two were walking out?" Luis yanked on the back of my head of hair.

"No, Luis, I don't know anything about this. I've never seen this car before," I said with desperation. The car stopped abruptly and the passenger side window unrolled.

"John! Oh, it's so good to see you out of the hospital," Cindy threw her arms through the open window. He was smiling, and none of us were sure what to think.

"Get out and let me see you walk about," she giggled happily. A frown got bigger on Luis's face, and I looked from the car to Max and over at Luis. Chef John opened the door and shakily got up and out of the car with a large smile. I could see the knife wound still impacted his movements.

"I'm glad I caught you here too, Roberto. I tried to make it here when you guys would be finishing up. My younger brother, Henry, offered to bring me up here. Our last conversation didn't end the way I wanted to finish it, and I wanted to clarify a few things."

"Well, I'm glad you're up and around. We were all worried." I tried to smile. Luis switched his feet and folded his arms. Max fumbled in his pocket for the lighter and lit up another cigarette. "Even Luis told me he was worried about you," I pointed to Luis to my right. I knew a half-lie was wrong, but I hoped God wouldn't mind.

"Luis, you may not believe or understand it. But I'm glad you're here too," Chef John smiled while reaching for something silver. Max, Luis, and I all stepped back some, without thinking about it. Luis and I both ended up moving toward the back end of the truck. Knives and even guns, both shined from silver. We all knew John still could make a real point, one that he'd been waiting to make.

"I've been keeping this silver pocket New Testament for you Luis. It was my first Bible as a kid, and I kept it when the Christian camp counselor gave it to me. God reached out to me as a boy, but later in life I left Him to be up in heaven while I did my own thing. God took me from weakest times and moments and lifted me up. I've tried not looking back in these last four or five years. But when you and I went about in the kitchen, I didn't look to God for His wisdom. I actually only thought of my own bitterness, but now—"

"Now what, Chef? Back here to show me Roberto's Jesus in that child's book and take the waitress that should've been mine?" Luis interrupted.

"No, Luis. Cindy is awfully pretty. But I'm not sure where that's going to go," Chef John shook his head slowly. "But I do know I have to refer to God with every thought I have. Like Paul says, 'take captive every thought and make God part of it.' Part of that 'pray without ceasing' deal, where God is part of my thoughts. Anyway, I need you to know I have forgiven you for what has happened between us."

"Oh , that's just great," Luis said. "You make it sound like it was all my fault. You forgive me but don't take any of the blame. You rode me all the time in the kitchen, and then purposefully cut me away from spending time with Cindy every chance you could."

"Luis, I did my best to do my job as a night chef. I had a responsibility to management to keep you on task throughout the shifts. It was never a personal issue with you," Chef John tried to explain. "But I wanted you to know I carry no ill-will towards you for the knife. I believe you didn't mean to hurt me as badly as you did."

"You're right. I didn't mean to cut you so deep. But," Luis looked into Chef John's eyes. "But you don't seem to see things as they were. I wonder if you didn't deserve just a little pain."

I heard a gasp from Cindy and I pushed my hair back and shook it lightly. Luis finished his thoughts. "You claim to know God, but I think you ought to listen better when you're reading that Bible." Luis knocked it down from Chef John's outstretched hand to the white solid line in the pavement. "I think Jesus said something about judging not until you judge yourself. Forgive me, yeah go ahead, but look in the mirror when you do." Luis kicked the New Testament to Chef John's feet.

"Max, get me out of here. I'm ready to leave. Roberto, hugs but no kisses my friend!" With that last comment Luis got in the passenger side and flipped a peace sign out the window when they drove away. He left to try and find the American dream back in Mexico.

The bond of brotherhood he and I shared seemed to be severed forever now. And with that sense of finality, I rubbed the scar on my palm where Luis had helped save me as a child years ago. I wondered for a moment if I would still feel pain in that palm any longer. I glanced at Chef John and realized how God's family carried stronger bonds of brotherhood than I had realized. John sought me out, showed his forgiveness to me and especially for Luis. I have seen growth in John's life, and I hope people see the same in mine.

About the Author

WAYNE STOLT has more than thirty years experience working in the foodservice business, ranging from quick service, casual dining, fine dining, health care, catering, and teaching. Wayne has a bachelor's degree in Hospitality Management from Eastern Michigan, and a Master's degree in teaching from Wayne State University. He is certified in ServSafe and also teaches it. He is certified as a ProStart Educator, with the National Restaurant Association Education Foundation, and a Certified Hospitality Educator, through the American Hotel & Lodging Educational Institute.

He is currently working with the American Culinary Federation to earn the Secondary Culinary Educator Certification. Wayne currently teaches at Riverview Community High School in the Hospitality/Culinary Career Technically Program, which is part of the Down River Career and Technical Consortium. He also teaches adjunct at Henry Ford Community College, in their Hospitality Management/Culinary Studies Department.

Wayne enjoys bicycling outdoors and nonchalantly studying service and food while eating out. He also devours storytelling via movies or novels. Although this is his first novel, he hopes to carry on the story of Porter's House Boat Restaurant with new main characters.

Wayne resides in Old Village, Plymouth, Michigan. He was saved at a young age but rededicated his life ten years ago. He is a member of Praise Baptist Church in Plymouth, MI. His prayer is that this novel serves as a witness for the gospel and glorifies God.

Wayne may be contacted via his website or on his facebook page.
www.chefstoryteller.com.
www.facebook.com/chefstoryteller